RISKING *forever*

A. M. KUSI

Published by A. M. Kusi 2022

amkusinovels@gmail.com

Visit our website at www.amkusi.com

Editor: Lauren Clarke of CREATING ink

Sensitivity Edit: Renita McKinney of A Book A Day

Proofreader: Judy's Proofreading

Cover Design: Regina Wamba of ReginaWamba.com

OTHER BOOKS BY A. M. KUSI

__Stepping Into Tomorrow__

(Book 1 in The Emerson Family of Shattered Cove)

__Risking Forever__

(Book 2 in The Emerson Family of Shattered Cove)

__Wishing for Yesterday__

(Book 3 in The Emerson Family of Shattered Cove)

__Promising Today__

(Book 4 in The Emerson Family of Shattered Cove)

__A Fallen Star (eBook FREE on all retailers)__

(Book 1 in The Shattered Cove Series)

__Glass Secrets__

(Book 2 in The Shattered Cove Series)

__Defying Gravity__

(Book 3 in The Shattered Cove Series)

__The Lighthouse Inn__

(Book 4 in The Shattered Cove series)

__His True North__

(Book 5 in The Shattered Cove series)

__In The Grey__

(Book 6 in The Shattered Cove series)

Brave Love

(Book 7 in The Shattered Cove series)

Hope Between Us

(Book 8 in The Shattered Cove series)

Beautiful Collision

(A Shattered Cove Novel)

One Holiday Kiss (eBook FREE on all retailers)

(A Shattered Cove Short Story)

Under My Skin (eBook FREE on all retailers)

(A Shattered Cove Short Story)

The Orchard Inn Series

(Our first complete steamy romance series.)

Spicy Word Search Puzzles: An Activity Book for Romance Readers

(This activity book is perfect for when you want something fun to do in-between books or take a break from reading.)

Romance Reading Journal: Record, Track, and Organize Your Novels

(This journal is a simple way to track, record, and review 100 of the books you've read.)

For a complete list of all our books, visit:

WWW.AMKUSI.COM/BOOKS

This book is dedicated to me. Because after two and a half rewrites, several anxiety attacks, and a breakdown later, I finally finished it only two weeks late.

"Trauma comes back as a reaction, not a memory."
— Bessel Van Der Kolk

"Moving forward with our grief is not the same as moving on from our grief."
— Marie

GET A FREE SHORT NOVEL

Join our newsletter to get a FREE short novel that's not available on any retailer. Plus updates about new releases, giveaways, pre-orders, sneak peeks, and more.

Visit the website below to join now.

WWW.AMKUSI.COM/NEWSLETTER

TABLE OF CONTENTS

Playlist   xv

1. Elise   1
2. Roman   10
3. Elise   18
4. Elise   25
5. Elise   33
6. Roman   39
7. Elise   44
8. Elise   53
9. Roman   60
10. Elise   64
11. Elise   70
12. Roman   76
13. Elise   83
14. Roman   88
15. Elise   95
16. Elise   102
17. Roman   111
18. Roman   118
19. Elise   123
20. Elise   132
21. Elise   143
22. Roman   152
23. Elise   160
24. Roman   168
25. Elise   174
26. Elise   187
27. Roman   195
28. Elise   200
29. Elise   211
30. Elise   224
31. Roman   230

32. Elise	240
33. Elise	249
34. Roman	263
35. Elise	269
36. Roman	280
37. Elise	284
38. Roman	293
39. Elise	297
40. Roman	300
41. Elise	308
42. Elise	315
43. Roman	324
44. Roman	331
45. Elise	341
46. Elise	352
47. Roman	358
48. Elise	364
Epilogue - Roman	373
Sneak Peek of Wishing for Yesterday	387
Acknowledments	397
Join Our Newsletter	399
Thank You	401
About A. M. Kusi	403
Also by A. M. Kusi	405

PLAYLIST

"Keep On" by Sasha Alex Sloan
"Rain" by Grandson and Jessie Reyez
"Lost my Mind" by FINNEAS
"Stupid" by Ashnikko Ft. Yung Baby Tate
"Do It For Me" by Rosenfeld
"Show Off" by SoMo
"You Broke Me First" by Tate McRae
"Dirty Mind" by Boy Epic

1

ELISE

"You can do this," Elise said aloud to herself in the rearview mirror.

Ding!

She focused on the gauges in front of her. Shit! The tire-pressure icon lit up red. She had so many of those little colored lights, you'd think she was collecting them like Girl Scout badges.

"Just one more reason you need this job. So go in there and convince this family you're their best choice for a nanny."

It's ten times better than free babysitting for my slimy two-timing ex.

Elise blew out a breath and squeezed the back of her neck. A tension headache was pinching her nerves.

Before she could overthink it any more, she shut off the engine and climbed out of the piece of junk that needed more work than it was worth. It seemed so out of place here next to the neatly trimmed yard, rolling green hills, and tidy garage. The gravel driveway was huge and rounded, lined with trees on one side. A white van parked by the edge of the house had an *Emerson Farms* logo on the sliding door. Colorful flowers adorned the walkway up to a massive wraparound porch. Planters with purple, pink, and blue flowers hung from the edge of the porch roof above the railings. Floral notes melded with the scent of fresh-cut hay sweetening the fresh air.

The sound of a screen door shutting drew her focus to the older Black woman smiling from the entryway with a wave. The woman's brown, purple-tipped dreadlocks swayed with her motion. "You must be Elise Aki."

"Yes, ma'am. And you must be Mrs. Emerson."

"Oh, please call me Renita or Mama E." She waved her hand as if dismissing the formality.

Elise scanned the property once more. Lush green grass with wildflowers poking through it covered the fields to her right. There was a barn and pasture down the hill, and another larger barn complete with a gravel parking lot she'd passed on her way up the long tree-lined driveway. "You have a beautiful home."

"Thank you. Come on in. Ariel is excited to meet you, and I've got a cup of coffee with your name on it or tea if you prefer?"

"Tea would be lovely. Thank you." Elise followed the woman inside.

The home was spacious and bright. Colorful rugs were scattered over the pine floors. Pictures adorned the walls of the hall and the living room she passed, which contained a mishmash of furniture.

Renita led her past some smaller rooms and a shut door before they entered a large kitchen that chefs' dreams were made of.

"Have a seat." Mrs. Emerson motioned to a stool at the large kitchen island.

Elise did as she said. A little girl with puff buns in her hair peeked into the room. Elise smiled and waved to her, but the girl hid behind the wall once again.

"Ariel Daisy Emerson, you get your butt out here and greet our guest," Renita chided while setting a plate of cookies on the table between them.

Elise's stomach grumbled embarrassingly loudly. She'd skipped breakfast and lunch—again. Her savings were down to almost nothing and her credit card was maxed. If her best friends Sam and Jack knew she'd been skipping meals, they'd be furious with her, but she didn't want to be a drain on them any more than she had been these last few weeks.

Renita pushed the cookies towards her. "Help yourself. Your tea will be ready in a moment. I have peppermint or chamomile, and I think black mango."

"Black mango, please, but I'm more than happy to get it." Elise rose.

Renita shook her head as the little girl walked into the room. "No way. You sit right there and get started on those cookies."

Ariel climbed onto the stool across from her. Her head was bowed, but the girl's eyes were definitely aimed at Elise.

Elise gave the girl her most friendly smile and signed as she spoke. "Hello. You must be Ariel; I've heard so much about you. But I have one question. Are you a mermaid, like the Ariel in the movie?"

The little girl bit back a smile, her eyes lighting up as she signed back to Elise. *"No, I'm not. But I want to meet a mermaid."*

"Maybe we'll be lucky enough to spot one sometime." Elise winked.

Ariel reached across the counter and grabbed a cookie. She bit into it as Renita set a cup of tea and jar of honey in front of Elise before taking a seat beside them.

Elise stirred a spoonful of sweetener into her tea. "Thank you."

"You're welcome. I don't believe we should waste each other's time. Let's get down to brass tacks, shall we?" Renita asked.

Elise's stomach clenched. Had she messed this up already? "Of course."

"I went over your references, and you seem more than qualified to take care of my granddaughter this summer. But what I'd like to know is why a young woman like yourself, with your degree, wants to nanny?" Renita didn't pull any punches.

"I'm actually teaching this fall at Shattered Cove Grade School, so this was perfect as I needed something to do during the summer. I've double-checked the date, and I would need to report to school a week before my work officially ends for Ariel. Would that be a problem?"

Renita shook her head. "It shouldn't be. I'll be back by then, and we can make necessary arrangements for her care. Are you new to the area?"

"No, my family is from Dark Cove, so just the next city over."

Renita's eyes widened. "Oh, well then, that's great. You already know your way around."

"Yes."

"And you're okay with the live-in position? You'd be staying in my son Roman's house. You passed the turnoff on your way in. You'll have a bedroom to yourself but share a bathroom with this little one." Renita motioned to her granddaughter.

"Yeah, that's fine."

Ariel reached for another cookie, eyeing her grandma. Renita glanced at the little girl. "Don't tell your daddy I let you eat cookies so close to dinner."

Ariel smiled and shook her head, holding out her pinky finger. Renita looped her smallest digit with her granddaughter's in a promise.

"Your resume didn't list your employment for the last two years." Renita's attention was back on Elise.

"I, uh, well, I was . . ." Sweat dotted her forehead as the newly scabbed wounds over her heart opened wide again. "I had a family situation that needed my attention." That was vague but hopefully professional. Elise was pretty sure if she spilled the whole sordid tale of her shitty judgment in men, Renita would show her the door. But she needed this job. She'd searched and there was nothing else that would allow her to make enough money in the two months before school started to save for a down payment on an apartment, and this was a live-in position. She wouldn't have to force Sam and Jack to put up with her in their guest bedroom any longer than the three weeks she'd already commandeered it for.

Renita's eyes crinkled, her keen gaze studying Elise for a beat. "Well, I'm pretty satisfied with our phone interview, your background checks out, and you obviously know American Sign Language well." She turned to Ariel. "What do you think, pumpkin? Would you like to spend the summer playing with Elise?"

Ariel licked a few crumbs off her lips and signed, "*Will you take me to the beach to look for mermaids?*"

Elise laughed. "If your parents say it's okay."

"*And will you give me cookies like Gramma?*"

"Well, I do love to bake."

"*Okay.*" Ariel nodded.

"She drives a hard bargain," Renita joked. "Ariel, why don't you go clean up your toys? Your dad will be home soon."

Ariel hopped off the stool and gave Elise a wave before disappearing out of the room.

Renita got up and grabbed a framed photo from the kitchen wall, handing it over to Elise. "It's just my son. His wife—Ariel's mom—passed almost four years ago. Since then, Ariel hasn't said a word."

"I see." Elise's heart broke for the little girl. A smiling Ariel beamed at the camera, holding a line with a small fish out in front of her. The man next to her smiled down at her like the little girl was his whole world—and he was one of the sexiest men she'd ever laid eyes on. He could have been a model with his toned body and six-pack, the likes of which she'd only ever seen on magazine and book covers. Damn, he was fine. And that was the dad she would be living with? Her skin heated.

But the last thing I need is another single dad taking advantage of me —no matter how hot he is.

"Roman is really busy in the summers unless it's bad weather. He's up before the sun most days and home after it sometimes. You'd have to be able to make dinner too. Is that a problem?"

"No. I can cook. I enjoy it actually," Elise assured her. It would make things easier if she didn't have too many run-ins with the hottie from the picture.

Renita smiled. "Great. Ariel has therapy every other Monday. And she's been homeschooled up until now. She's going to school this fall, so if you don't mind working with her on the things she may need to know?"

"Absolutely."

"And the salary is alright with you?"

"Yes, ma'am," she quickly agreed, handing the photo back.

Renita stood again and walked over to the counter to grab a piece of paper and pen, and return the frame. She slid a legal-looking document over to Elise. "Then I'd like to officially offer you the job. This is a contract with everything we went over on the phone. You go ahead and read through it and make sure it's agreeable to you."

Elise skimmed the particulars. At this point, it didn't matter if Mrs. Emerson required a kidney; she needed this job. She'd nannied during college but she'd never been presented with a contract before.

As if sensing her question, Renita explained, "There's a part in there about not speaking to the press or anyone outside the family except the authorities about the open investigation regarding the murder of my son's ex. I hope you understand the sensitive manner of this request?"

Murder? Oh, God. How much had Ariel lost? Had she seen her mother be attacked? Was that why she didn't speak? How strange Elise hadn't heard about the case. She'd been gone a long time from Dark Cove, but this kind of news usually traveled.

"Of course. I understand." She signed her name on the line and dated it.

Renita did the same and produced another copy for Elise to keep.

"Great. Now, let's show you where you'll be staying this summer. Did you need a few days to move in?"

Elise shifted on her feet, tucking her hair behind her ear anxiously. "I actually have everything with me." *Because I'm kinda without an address at the moment.*

"I like a woman who comes prepared. Perfect. Ariel?"

The little girl came bounding around the corner.

"Let's go show Elise her room in your house."

Elise followed them outside. Renita didn't bother locking the door. Elise had forgotten what it was like living in a small town.

"Why don't you drive back down the driveway? Take a left at the first turnoff. Around the corner, you'll see Roman's house."

Elise stumbled over her feet, quickly catching herself as the pulsing in her head got worse. "Sure."

"My son Nash lives on the other side of the property with his fiancée, Isabella, her son, Eli, and my grandbaby, Alba." Renita pointed to the other side of the property. "Ricky lives on the south side. And Nova's up on the hill—you went to college with her, right?"

Elise nodded and smiled. "Yes, her freshman year. So, all your kids live on the farm property?"

"I'm lucky enough to have all my children so close." Renita's lips turned up, the mother's love evident in her warm expression.

Elise gave a polite smile and tried not to be envious of people she didn't even know. But the affection with which Renita spoke about her children, the way she wanted them near, drew attention to the ache inside Elise. She'd never had that—her parents had dumped her at a boarding school as soon as they'd found what they'd assumed was an imperfection in her. That was one reason she couldn't go to them with her problems. It would prove them right—that she was incapable and not good enough. *They never wanted me before. Now that I'm a grown woman, I don't see them taking me back in.* She blew out a long breath and climbed into her junker, praying that it started and didn't embarrass her in front of her new employer.

The engine cranked and then puttered. All those blinking icons flashed on.

She gritted her teeth, sending a fresh wave of pain slicing through her head. She wanted to tear off her cochlear implant and take a nap—but Elise didn't have that luxury. She needed this job and had nowhere else to go.

"Suck it up, buttercup. No one's got your back but you," Elise chastised herself in the mirror.

The fresh burn of tears had her blinking to clear them as she shifted the car in reverse. A pit formed in her stomach. Anxiety snaked up her limbs and constricted around her chest.

Elise pulled out of the driveway and headed toward the next beautiful family home. She would be the best nanny. She would get enough money to rent an apartment before school started. And she would survive the next two months under this hot stranger's roof. Then she could start over. And no one would take advantage of her again. She wouldn't fall for another handsome smile or empty words. No—she'd learned her lesson and had the scars to prove it.

She peeked at herself in the rearview mirror. "You've got this, Elise. Show them you're good enough. You can do anything."

No one would stop her from rising from the ashes—especially not another hot single dad.

2

ROMAN

Roman Emerson wiped the sweat from his forehead before he pulled onto the road leading to his parents' farm and his own portion of land. The truck bounced over a pothole as a light breeze blew in from the open windows. It was only the beginning of June, but already he was working up a sweat in the bee yards.

He switched the radio off and slowly turned into his driveway so as not to jostle the bee equipment in the truck bed too much. A little white Ford Focus sat in his usual parking spot. Roman frowned and parked the truck next to it. He grabbed his lunch box and empty water jug from the passenger seat before climbing out. A quick scan of the property showed nothing amiss. Maybe his mom and Ariel were inside with someone? He opened the front door and walked in.

"Hello? Anybody home?" Roman called as he walked through the house and set the bag and jug on the kitchen counter.

When no one answered he did a quick search of the first

floor, but no one was there. Roman pulled off his sweaty shirt. He headed towards the bathroom to go through his routine of checking for ticks and then showering the filth of his workday away. Then he could go and pick up his daughter from his parents' place.

Thump!

Roman whirled around, his senses perked up.

"Mom? Ariel? Is that you?"

No answer.

But he was sure that'd been the guest bathroom mirror shutting. He stepped as silently as possible towards the room. His heart raced. Had someone broken in? Maybe it was a petty thief? The hair on the back of his neck stood on end. Could it be related to the murder on their property? Was it the killer who'd sent Nash that note telling him where to find the body?

Roman pulled out the knife from his waist, a tool he kept on him in the bee yards for work. Something rattled as he rounded the corner.

A tall woman bent into the open cabinet, pulling out bottle after bottle of pills. *Fuck, it's a break-in. An addict looking for a fix? Is she alone?* He scanned the room, listening for any sign of another intruder. How dare she come in here and violate his sense of safety. *What if Ariel had been home?*

Roman's heart raced as his chest heaved, anger morphing to fury.

"What the hell are you doing in my house?" he barked.

She didn't even flinch as she picked up another bottle— just read the back of it like she had all the time in the world while muttering something under her breath.

With the knife still wielded in one hand, he reached out with the other, tugging on her shoulder.

"I said, what are you—"

The woman screeched. She whirled around. Fear flashed in her wide eyes. Pain bloomed across his left cheek. He was knocked onto his ass from the unexpected force behind the blow. The knife clattered to the ground beside him.

"Oh, shit!" the thief swore, drawing his attention back to her. Her voice sounded a little different, but maybe that was because of the blood pounding in his ears.

Her black hair fell in messy strips from a haphazard bun. She stood towering over him, her dark eyes glued to him, unmoving. A few colorful tattoos peeked out from her short-sleeve shirt. A small septum ring glinted in the light from her narrow nose, right above her pert lips, pulled down in a frown.

His eyes dropped down her curvy build. She was taller than his moderate five-eight by a good few inches. She looked like a real-life Amazon warrior, only she was Asian.

"I'm so sorry." Her voice drew him out of his trance.

Beautiful or not, she'd broken into his house.

She moved towards the doorway, but he reached towards her. She stumbled, tripping over her own feet. The woman fell down so hard he winced.

She hissed and rolled over to her back, sitting up. "Fuck!"

Roman scrambled forward, grabbing her hands and pinning her to the floor. "What are you doing in my house?"

"Let me go, you psycho!"

He might have laughed if he wasn't fuming with anger. "Thief! Thought you could break in here and get your fix? You picked the wrong fucking house."

Her eyes dropped to his mouth. "What?"

"What are you doing in my house?" Was she high already?

She struggled under him, but despite her height, he was stronger. "Get off me!"

Roman rolled off her, positioning his body between her

and the door so there was no escape. "Oh, no you don't. You're not going anywhere until the police get here."

Her cheeks flushed as she got to her feet. "I just need to get—"

"Why the fuck did you break into my house? What are you looking for? Pills?"

Her eyes narrowed on his mouth. She shook her head. "I didn't—"

"What the hell is going on here?" his mother's voice boomed from down the hall.

"Someone broke in. Keep Ariel out of here and call the cops."

"You dumbass! That's the new nanny."

He blinked.

The woman in front of him took advantage of his confusion and darted past him out into the hall.

"Are you okay, Elise?" his mom asked, walking towards them. The assumed thief disappeared into his guest room, coming out with a device in her hand. She attached it to her head, one piece magnetizing to her skull and the other slipping in her ear.

She's Deaf. That's why she was staring at my mouth.

"Are you okay, Elise?" his mom repeated, standing in front of the woman as Ariel peeked up at them from the stairs with wide eyes.

"I think so." She flexed her already swollen hand.

His mom walked up to him, arms crossed over her chest, eyes narrowed. "What the hell are you doing, attacking the new nanny?"

"I thought she broke in. I yelled but she didn't answer. I touched her shoulder and she punched me in the face." He touched his cheekbone and winced.

"Serves you right for scaring her half to death."

"What the hell is she doing in my house?"

"I told her to unpack and get situated."

Unpack? Was this a live-in position?

It didn't matter.

"Why were you in the bathroom, going through the medicine cabinet?" he asked Elise, but the fight had drained from his voice. He'd pinned her down against her will and probably scared the shit out of her with that knife. He was an asshole.

"I was looking for some pain medicine because I have a headache." She pointed to the bottle on the floor, a generic ibuprofen. "That's why I took my CI out too. So I didn't hear you. I just turned around when someone grabbed me, wielding a knife like a psycho."

He sighed and ran a hand through his hair. "I thought you were an intruder."

"Didn't you know I was coming?" she asked.

"No."

"I reminded you last Sunday at family dinner," Renita said.

He pinched between his eyes and shook his head. "But you said you were interviewing, not hiring. Not moving someone into my home."

"You listen 'bout as well as your thick-headed brother. I told you we were doing the final interview, meeting her, and if everything was a good fit, we could move forward. Now, I don't have time for this. I'll take Ariel out for a few minutes. You two work this out—and you'd better be on your best behavior. You can't afford to have this nice woman quitting on you. She's everything you wanted in a caretaker for Ariel and more. Don't fuck this up," Renita warned him before turning to Elise and offering her a genuine smile. "Please give him another shot. He may not deserve it, but Ariel does."

Elise nodded, her eyes still wide as if she were unsure of the situation. He couldn't blame her.

"Shit, I'm sorry." His gaze dropped to the angry red marks contrasting with the light skin on her knuckles. "Let's get some ice on that." He reached out, taking her hand in his.

She sucked in a breath.

"Can you bend your fingers?"

She flexed her hand in his, a slight wince marring her delicate features.

"Don't think anything's broken." He dropped her hand. "Come on. I've got some frozen peas that should help."

Roman led her downstairs to the kitchen and grabbed out two bags of frozen veggies, one for him and one for her. He handed her the peas.

"Thanks." She slid the bag over her swelling knuckles.

"So, your name is Elise? Where are you from?"

She swallowed, confusion swirling in her eyes a moment before it was gone. Her voice came out much quieter than before. "Dark Cove." A moment of awkward silence passed before she spoke again. "I know this isn't the best way of starting off as your employee, but at least you know I can defend myself and your daughter." Her light chuckle seemed more out of nerves than humor.

"Yeah, about that . . ."

Her smile dropped. "What?"

He scratched the back of his head. "I—"

"The ad said you needed someone who knew sign language to tutor your daughter and get her ready for school next term, as well as entertain her. I'm actually a teacher. I'm starting a job at Shattered Cove Grade School in the fall. I promise, I'm more than qualified." Her voice held a hint of desperation in it.

Let me handle it. I'll find someone who will be the perfect fit. His mother's words came back to him. They'd spoken about it for months on and off, but he hadn't realized she'd meant this early. He hadn't even prepared Ariel. She wasn't used to anyone watching her but family.

"She mentioned you work long hours in the summer months, and she had a lot on her plate with the farm and the wedding, and then she's leaving on a vacation, right?" Elise asked.

"Yes."

Roman studied the woman in front of him—his new nanny—from her dark brown eyes to the cupid's bow of her plump lips down to her neck. His cock twitched. He was tempted to look a little longer but that would be highly inappropriate. He gritted his teeth. For the whole summer, the beautiful stranger was supposed to be under his roof. When he'd agreed to hire someone, he'd always imagined someone far less attractive, and most definitely not as a live-in nanny.

What if Mom did this on purpose? She was always trying to set up Nova. Maybe she'd given up on her and was focused on him now?

He shook his head. Would she really try to . . . It didn't matter because his mother's message earlier had been clear. This was his new nanny whether he liked it or not. It didn't matter if he was twelve or almost thirty-seven. When his mom took that tone, she meant business. And he knew better than to piss her off. He needed someone to care for his daughter, and he trusted his mom's instincts. He'd just have to remain professional.

"I think we should start over." He held out his hand. "I'm Roman. Nice to meet you."

She hesitated, lines appearing on her forehead as if she were asking herself if he was crazy. He definitely was at this point.

Her smooth hand slipped into his. Electricity hummed up his arm before she quickly jerked her hand away. She tugged her bottom lip into her mouth, her white teeth peeking out as she nervously chewed. The impulse to tug it out had his fingers curling into fists. His blood heated.

Roman released a breath. This was the first time he'd felt the stirring of arousal for a woman since his wife had passed four years ago. And it was one more big reason why Elise shouldn't be his new nanny. But it was too late to turn back now.

Fuck my life.

3

ELISE

I can't believe I punched my new boss. Can this day get any worse? How about this year?

The pounding in Elise's head hadn't gotten any better in the twenty minutes since Roman had pinned her to the floor upstairs. Now, he leaned against the counter in the kitchen, bag of frozen kale pressed to his cheek as he studied her closely. His chest was bare except for the wisps of dark hair smattered over his pecs and peppered down his defined abs before disappearing in a straight line into his stained jeans. Damn, he had a nice body.

He cleared his throat. Shit, she'd been caught gawking at him. Embarrassment heated her cheeks.

"I'll be right back." He set the bag back in the freezer and went up the stairs.

Elise sighed. *I just need this job until school starts.*

This was the month from hell.

Roman returned with a shirt on, holding out his hand to her, palm up with two pain relievers. "For your headache."

"Thank you." She picked them up while he opened the fridge and handed her a bottle of water.

She drank it down, swallowing the pills. The cool water brought a sliver of relief to the pounding in her head.

"If you prefer, you can take the hearing aid off, and we can sign for this conversation."

She looked at him and blinked, a little stunned at the offer. None of her hearing ex-boyfriends—nor her family, for that matter—had ever offered to sign to make her feel more at ease. Everyone expected her to be the one to conform.

"That's alright." She didn't want to start off this job with him making an accommodation for her though. Too many people had found ways to hold that over her head.

He leaned against the counter and crossed his arms over his now clothed chest. The material of his shirt pulled taut against his broad shoulders with the movement. He ran a hand over the coarse five o'clock bristles shadowing his jaw. Sunlight streamed in through the kitchen window, highlighting Roman's strong nose and chiseled features. His expression was hard, with two serious brows pulled together at a sharp angle, and a slight frown tugged his full brown lips down. God, that picture hadn't done him justice.

The door burst open. Ariel ran through the door with Renita not too far behind her. The little girl clutched her dad's legs and Roman bent down to hug her.

"Hey, sweet pea. Did you have a good day with Grams?" Roman asked.

Ariel pulled away and nodded with a smile before wrinkling her nose and signing to her dad. *"You stink."*

Elise bit back her smile as Roman laughed.

He playfully tugged on one of her puff buns. "I know, I haven't had a chance to shower yet." Roman flicked his gaze between Elise and Renita before focusing back on his daughter. "Why don't you go watch something while I talk to Grams, okay?"

Ariel lifted her hands, confidently moving them into signs. *"Grams said Elise will be staying with us and spending time with me. I like her a lot. She said we could look for mermaids! Please say she can stay, Daddy."*

Roman sighed. "Alright. Go on."

Ariel smiled at Elise before disappearing into the living room.

"Now, tell me everything is all settled." Renita cut her son a glare. "We talked about this, Roman. You agreed. What's your hesitation?"

Elise felt like she was intruding on a private family moment and she should leave, except her livelihood was on the line.

"I never said I was okay for someone to live with us." He turned to Elise. "No offense."

She shrugged despite the panic thundering through her. What else could she do? She needed this job and a place to stay for a couple months, just until she could get on her feet.

"And we don't need someone full time."

Renita's hands dropped to her hips. "Excuse me? Do you not work very long hours from spring to fall?"

"Yes, but—"

"And do you not have a seven-year-old who needs someone to care for her while you're gone?"

His jaw twitched. "Of course."

"Well, it sounds like you need help, then. You know I'm more than happy to have my granddaughter, and so are your siblings—in between our own work schedules. Business on the farm is picking up. I have more orders coming in for our homemade goods every day. We've gotten into three more farmers' markets this year, not to mention I have a wedding to plan on top of the events the farm usually holds. Your dad and I will be gone for a month, taking our trip we've been putting off for years. You need help, Roman, and it's okay to get that outside of the family sometimes."

His shoulders dropped on a sigh.

Renita continued, "You agreed I could find someone qualified because you didn't have time. It makes more sense for her to board here since she'll be working so early in the morning and late most nights."

"I don't think she'll be a good fit."

"Excuse me?" Elise straightened. How would he know? He hadn't even gotten to know her. Was it because she was Deaf? "I have amazing references you can check. I'm a certified teacher, and I know CPR. Proficiency in American Sign Language was one of the requirements and I'm fluent—there is no better way for your daughter to learn than from someone who is in fact Deaf. So what you may see as a hindrance is actually a positive."

Roman pinched the bridge of his nose. "That wasn't what I meant."

"What did you mean? Why would I not be a fit?" She wanted him to man up and just come out and say it. Say he was prejudiced against her for her disability.

He grimaced, opening and closing his mouth as if struggling with what to say. He finally shook his head. "Nothing. It's nothing."

"Great, now that that's all settled, I'll leave you to it. I'm sure you need to finish settling in, Elise. Oh, and I'll see you all at dinner in two hours. Don't be late." Renita walked over and kissed Ariel on the cheek before waving to them and leaving out the front door.

The sound from Ariel's TV show was the only noise in the room for a few minutes. Elise shifted on her feet, extremely uncomfortable with the situation. Anger at her ex for putting her in this position burned her veins. Ariel was a wonderful little girl—but Elise wasn't so sure about Roman. She didn't want to stay in his house, but she didn't have much of a choice. This was the only solution to her problems, so for now, she'd have to grin and bear it.

Roman sighed and shook his head. "I guess you're hired."

Yippee. "I promise I'll take care of your daughter and keep her safe and happy while you're gone."

"I appreciate it."

"What's your work schedule like?"

"It just depends on what needs to be done in the yards. I'm always home to tuck her into bed by eight. I'm home for dinner as often as possible, but summer is the busiest time for my bee business."

Bee business? Yikes. She nodded. "Okay. And what are your expectations for me? Other than the obvious—take care of and entertain Ariel. I know she has some therapy appointments your mom mentioned."

"Yeah. You can have weekends off. And I'd like her to start practicing things she'll need to learn for school in the fall. She already knows quite a bit. We worked on a lot this winter together. She's actually already reading the *Moon Girl and the Devil Dinosaur* series for the second time."

"That's awesome. And the list of expectations is very doable," she agreed.

"You said you're a teacher?"

"I was. I . . . took a few years off, but as I mentioned, I'll be at the grade school in the fall. Is that where Ariel will be going?"

"Yeah."

"I'm sure I'll get to see her then."

He cleared his throat. "When you're with Ariel, can you please have your CI on?"

"Yes, sir."

Roman blinked as his jaw pulsed like he was grinding his teeth. "Did Mom tell you anything about . . . her situation?"

Elise tipped her head to the side. "Just that she's non-verbal and that her mom was . . . um, that's there's an investigation going on about her . . ."

He shook his head. "My brother Nash's ex-fiancée was murdered. My wife . . ." He cleared his throat and looked towards Ariel in the living room. "Passed of natural causes."

Way to stick my foot in my mouth. "Oh, I'm so sorry." This family had been through more than one tragedy it seemed.

"It's important that if she needs someone, you're right there. She can't be left alone again when she needs help—do you understand?" His voice left no room for misinterpretation. This was gravely important to him.

Curiosity bubbled inside her. This seemed like more than just helicopter parenting. "That's not a problem. I'll have my implant on and keep a close eye on her at all times. We'll have a fun summer. I brought some things for us to do together. I'm excited to get to know Ariel and explore her favorite spots."

He ground his jaw. His gaze flashed as he stepped forward, tilting his chin to look her directly in the eyes as he pointed towards the living room. His voice grew quieter and serious. "That little girl in there is everything to me, and I won't let anything bad happen to her . . . so if I feel like she's endangered in any way, you will be fired."

His protectiveness and love for his daughter were his redeeming qualities—even though his faith in her ability made her hackles rise. "Understood."

Roman's pink tongue darted out as he licked his lips. He ran a hand over his head, his muscles bunching with the movement, but her gaze caught on his veiny forearm. Good God, why did he have to be so good-looking?

"Elise?"

"Yeah?" Her voice came out far breathier than she'd intended.

"You're just here to watch my kid." His voice was cold, devoid of any emotion.

Yanked out of her lust-induced haze, she blinked up at his severe expression. Clearing her throat before she spoke, she gave him a curt nod. "Of course. I'll be sure to stay out of your way otherwise."

Elise was the help—she just needed to remember that.

4

ELISE

Elise tugged down the jade-green sundress as she followed Roman towards his parents' home. He hadn't said more than a few words to her since their showdown in the kitchen.

Ariel's small hand slipped into hers. Elise looked down and smiled at the little girl.

"You're really tall." Ariel signed.

Rather than answer out loud and draw Roman's attention as they walked up the driveway, Elise responded in sign. *"I am."*

"Daddy says I'll grow big and strong if I eat my veggies. Is that what you did?"

Elise chuckled, feeling Roman's gaze on her skin as she answered, *"Yes, I'm sure that's part of it."*

"Wonder Woman is tall too, and she's one of my favorite superheroes."

"She's pretty cool." Elise stepped onto the porch, ducking out of habit, though the roof was still plenty of inches higher than her head. Her height had always been a source of insecurity

for her growing up, especially since all the other women in her family were just over five feet. But anyone who worked with kids knew they had no filter. That was one thing that drew Elise to working with them. You always knew where you stood with a child. Unlike adults, who might smile to your face and then stab you in the back.

"Ready?" Roman asked, his hand on the knob.

Elise smoothed a hand down her dress. "Yes."

Ariel nodded.

Roman pushed open the door and stepped aside, allowing her and Ariel to walk through. Renita and James Emerson's home was spacious and warm. She took off her shoes and padded towards the animated voices in the kitchen.

"Oh, good, you're here just in time. Roman, your father needs your help out back with the grill," Renita directed. "And I believe Eli was looking for you, Ariel. He's in the living room with Aunt Nova."

Roman headed straight towards a door at the back of the house without hesitation, and Ariel scampered off.

"What can I do to help?" Elise offered, gesturing towards the various salads and casseroles on the counter.

"Oh, no, you're a guest today. You take this cup of lemonade and find yourself a comfortable spot and tell me if you're settling in okay? I know my son can be a bit rough around the edges." She opened the fridge and took out a covered bowl of what looked like potato salad, then set it on the counter. "But he's been through a lot. He just needs a little patience and time to adjust. He'll see this is for the best and you're the perfect fit."

Renita grabbed two pot holders and opened the oven before pulling out a dish that made Elise's mouth water. Mrs. Emerson set it on the marble counter and stuck a serving spoon inside.

"That smells so good."

Renita smiled. "My kids' favorite—mac and cheese."

"Are you sure I can't help?" She sipped her lemonade. It was perfectly tart with just the right amount of sweetener.

"Oh, yes. Everything is done; we're just waiting for them to bring in the meat. I hope you brought your appetite."

"Absolutely."

"And who do we have here?" a voice asked from behind her.

Elise turned. A handsome dark-haired man stood a few inches taller beside her. Damn, he was good-looking.

"This is Elise. She's Ariel's new nanny and tutor for the summer. Elise, this is my son Ricky."

She looked between mother and son, but they shared no physical likeness. Maybe he took after his dad? Or perhaps he was adopted like Nova?

Ricky's eyes sparkled with a mischievous look as he eyed her up and down. "I could always use a tutor. There are some things I'd definitely like to brush up on, and I have a feeling you might be just the person."

She smiled playfully. "Does that line really work?"

His gaze flared and then he grinned. "You'd be surprised."

"Leave her alone, Ricky. You'll scare her away, thinking my sons are a bunch of unmannered hooligans," Renita scolded.

Ricky laughed. "Don't worry, Ma. Just making sure she feels welcome."

"Ribs and the rest of the meat is ready." Roman walked past, setting a large platter on the long counter. His dad was right behind him with hot dogs and burgers.

Roman flicked his gaze between Ricky and her before his eyes narrowed.

"Great. Everyone grab a plate and dig in," Renita said.

James and Ricky hung back while Roman started filling a small plate, presumably for Ariel. Nova came in with a boy and a woman who looked somewhat familiar. Behind them was another man who Elise assumed was Renita's other son, Nash, holding a baby in a little lime-green bundle.

Nova smiled and walked over to her. "Elise. It's so good to see you again. Mom just told me you were going to be spending the summer on the farm with Ariel."

"Yes."

"You two know each other?" James asked.

"Yes, Nova and I had a few classes together freshman year of college," Elise answered.

"I knew I should have gone to your college," Ricky said.

"Oh, like going to Dartmouth was such a hardship," Nova teased.

"Forgive them. They're always like this with each other." The woman beside Nova offered her a friendly smile.

Elise's lips turned up in a grin.

"I don't think I introduced you to Bella when we ran into you at the café last year. She's my soon-to-be sister-in-law." Nova gestured to the familiar woman.

"Hi," Bella said.

"Nice to officially meet you," Elise greeted her.

"Chat later, Nova. Get your dinner so we can eat." Ricky pointed towards the food.

"Just go get yours and stop whining," Nova said.

Ricky peeked over his shoulder before he turned back to her. "You know the rules. Ladies first."

Nova shook her head. "More than thirty years old and still afraid of your mama."

"Pot, meet kettle," he retorted.

Nova sighed and grabbed a plate. Elise followed, adding a little of everything. It all looked so good. Everyone filtered into the large dining room with a long table that fit the whole Emerson family and left room for at least half a dozen more. She found a spot towards the end next to Ariel, not wanting to intrude. But Ricky took the seat next to her, a hint of his spicy cologne wrapping around her.

"So, tell me, what made you willing to come to this crazy house for the whole summer?" he asked as everyone finished sitting.

She dug her fork into the macaroni and cheese. "The timing worked out perfectly. I start teaching in the fall." *Not to mention my other options were zilch.*

"Maybe we can hang out sometime," Ricky suggested as she took a bite, and holy hell, talk about cheesy goodness.

"She's here to watch Ariel," Roman snapped from across the table, glaring at his brother.

Ricky smirked. "I'm sure she'll have some days off."

"Excuse my idiot brother. He was dropped as a baby and thinks he's God's gift to women," Nova remarked.

Fuck, the last thing she needed was the already skeptical Roman thinking she was looking to hook up with his brother instead of taking care of Ariel.

"I'll be pretty busy. I have a curriculum to work on when I'm not with Ariel." She loaded another bite of the pasta and stuffed it in her mouth. Those two would not ruin her dinner. Maybe Renita would show her how to make some of this for Roman and Ariel.

"The offer stands if you ever want to let loose and have fun."

She gave him a quick nod to acknowledge his statement and turned towards Ariel. "What do you want to do tomorrow? It's supposed to be a beautiful day. And I'd love to see what animals you have on the farm. Do you think you could give me a tour?"

Ariel nodded and signed, "*Okay.*"

"And maybe if your dad says it's okay, we can go get some ice cream in town after?"

The little girl's eyes lit up. "*Yes!*"

"Actually, I'd like you to stay close to home—at least the first week. Next week, she has appointments. They're all on the calendar in the kitchen."

Elise swallowed down her disappointment as Ariel's hands flew into an argument with her father as she pleaded for ice cream.

Roman cut her a look before responding to his daughter. "I'll bring you home ice cream, okay?"

"*Fine. But I want cookie dough and mint cookie-crumble.*"

Elise stifled her laugh. This little girl knew how to bargain.

Roman's expression softened before he signed back to her. "*Deal. But you have to eat all your veggies for dinner first.*"

Ariel rolled her eyes. "*Deal.*"

"It's okay. We'll have lots of fun on the farm. I'm sure there are plenty of places to explore here. And I have it on good authority you're the expert," Elise said.

The corner of Ariel's mouth turned up. "*I am. Can Eli come with us too?*"

"Sure, if his mom says it's okay."

Ariel spun around to Eli on the other side of her, signing to him. Elise focused back on her meal, tasting the ribs that fell apart in her mouth. "This is delicious. Thank you so much for having me."

"You're welcome any time. We have family dinners every Sunday, but sometimes we move it to Saturday if the weather is better. And we have activities," Renita said.

"What are we watching for the next movie night?" Nova asked.

"It's Eli's turn to pick," James answered.

"What's that in your ear?" Eli asked, drawing everyone's attention to her.

"Eli, it isn't polite to ask that," Bella corrected her son.

"No, it's really okay. We can't learn unless we ask questions, right?" Elise faced Eli and pointed towards her CI. "This is a sound processor. It works a lot like your ear does to process sound waves. When I was little, I had a surgery to get an implant. That processor communicates with the implant under my skin, which will send messages to my cochlea—which is inside everyone's ears."

"I have one?" Eli tugged on his earlobe.

"Yes. It helps you process sound waves by sending them to the brain, which translates them to the sound you hear. This device helps me hear when I'm wearing it."

"*So you can't hear without it?*" Ariel asked.

"No."

"Is it like a hearing aid?" Eli asked.

"A hearing aid amplifies sound like a speaker. And this cochlear implant takes the sound and sends it directly to my cochlea and then the brain," she explained.

"That's so cool. So with this you can hear like me?" Eli asked.

"No. Not really. I still have a hard time hearing certain frequencies and things like timbre and pitch, which is like the range of a voice."

"Oh. Well, that's still pretty awesome," Eli said.

She smiled and focused back on her meal as the family conversed. The siblings ribbed each other, but it all seemed loving. Nothing like the meals she'd sat for with her family. There was a sense of love and community here in this house, and in the way Renita and James had opened their home and arms to her.

Elise looked up, her gaze catching with Roman's all too

perceptive one. Lines formed between his brows as he studied her.

Her skin flushed. Tingles raced through her limbs. Elise's chest contracted, making it harder to draw in another breath. She was unable to break away from his stare. Her heart raced. Why did he have this effect on her?

"Earth to Roman," Ricky called.

Roman shook his head as if he, too, had forgotten there was anyone else in the room. "What?" he snapped.

She wiped her sweaty palms on her dress-covered thighs, then reached for the cool lemonade to settle her nerves. *Too bad there's no vodka in it.*

"Are we going to the Fates' fields tomorrow?" Ricky asked.

"Yeah, that's the first stop. I think we can fit five yards in by later afternoon," Roman answered.

Yards? Were they landscapers? Then how did the bees fit in? She peeked at Roman again as she gulped down her lemonade, but he didn't look her way the rest of dinner. Maybe that was for the best. Because whatever was happening to her around him was not part of her plan.

Elise just needed to keep her head down and get through this summer. Catching feelings would not end well. *Just like last time.*

But she was no longer the insecure and all too trusting girl who'd let herself be used. This time she was a woman who'd learned that it didn't matter how much she gave of herself to a person—in their eyes, she'd always be lacking. So her solution was to stop caring what people thought.

You couldn't hurt someone who didn't care—right?

5

ELISE

lise washed her hands next to Ariel's in the kitchen sink. "Did you have fun today?"

Ariel nodded with a smile.

"I can't believe you have so many animals on the farm but no dog. I thought for sure those two went hand in hand."

Ariel's hands moved in response, flinging little water droplets as she signed. *"Gramma and Gramps had one but he died when I was little. I keep asking Daddy for one but he always says we'll talk about it later."*

A dog might make a great companion for Ariel; they could even get a service pet. "I always wanted one too."

"Did you ever get a dog?"

Elise shook her head, signing as she spoke. "No. My dad didn't want the fur in the house." And they'd said it was pointless because she would be off to college in just a few years and wouldn't be able to take the animal with her.

"If I get a puppy, you can play with it whenever you want."

"That's sweet of you. Now, are you ready to help me make the rest of dinner?"

"Yeah. Is Daddy going to be home to eat with us?"

"I'm not sure. I'll text him and ask." Elise pulled out her phone, swiping the screen to unlock it. A text from her brother popped up.

Ren: *Hey, El, I'm back in town. Maybe we can meet up with Mom and Dad for dinner some night. I know they'd love it.*

A night sitting around a table listening to how much her brother had accomplished and how his life was going great before her parents cast her pitying looks for being the family disappointment—and that was before they knew just how far she'd fallen? No, thanks. She'd rather chew off her own arm than move back home. Visiting for dinner wasn't much better.

Elise ignored her brother's text—she'd put off replying as long as possible. Instead, she pulled up Roman's number that she'd copied from the spreadsheet he'd left for her with every number she'd possibly ever need and then some listed in it.

Elise: *Ariel wanted to know if you'd be home for dinner?*

She pushed the phone back in her pocket. "Okay, let's get supper going."

"Can we make dessert too?"

Sweets to deal with this shit show of an employer? Yes, please. "That sounds like an excellent idea. What were you thinking?"

"Daddy's favorite is brownies. Can we make those?"

"I'll double-check if we have the ingredients, but that sounds good." Elise managed to find her way around the kitchen that was surprisingly well stocked with everything she'd need. Maybe, if she made a nice dinner, it would smooth things over with Roman and break the ice.

She'd found a pork butt in the fridge along with some fresh veggies this morning and figured that was what Roman wanted her to cook. She'd have to ask him tonight about meals and what exactly he wanted in the future.

The smell of the savory roast filled the kitchen after slow cooking for the last several hours. She walked Ariel through prepping the veggies. While they were steaming, she brought out the ingredients for one of her favorite brownie recipes.

"Can I lick the spoon and bowl after?"

"Only if you share." Elise winked, opening the fridge to grab the eggs. She set them on the counter.

"Deal."

By the time the brownies were sliding into the oven, Ariel had flour on her nose and more batter on her chin than was left in the bowl.

"Let's clean you up." Elise grabbed a paper towel and wet it before wiping her down.

She tackled cleaning the kitchen counter next.

"Your phone just beeped. Is it Daddy?" Ariel slid off the stool.

Elise pulled it out of her pocket.

Roman: *I'll be home by sticks.*

Sticks? He must be a voice texter or autocorrect hated him as much as everyone else.

She was tempted to message him back and ask if that was before or after log thirty, but she refrained. She didn't want to give him any reason to fire her. Elise pocketed the phone.

"Looks like he'll be here soon. Why don't we get the salad made? You can cut the lettuce." Elise pulled out the plastic lettuce knife she'd found in the bottom of a drawer and set it on the cutting board.

Ariel pulled her stool up to the counter again.

"Do you know how to do this?"

"Gramma taught me."

"Perfect, so you're already a pro. Go for it." Elise busied herself with the rest of the ingredients and the salad bowl while keeping an eye on Ariel. The timer went off for the dessert. She shut it off and quickly pulled the chocolatey goodness from the oven, placing it on the back of the range to cool down.

A flash of white caught her eye from the window. Roman was home. She quickly surveyed the room. They'd tidied up, and besides the counter where Ariel was working, everything was clean. Dinner was ready. She just needed to make herself indispensable.

Elise walked over to the living room and straightened a few pillows. The door swung open.

"*Look, Daddy! I'm helping make dinner.*" Ariel's chest puffed out in pride.

Roman's eyes flared before panic streaked across his expression. "Put the knife down, sweet pea." He shot towards her while Ariel dropped the utensil. "Where the hell is Elise?"

"I'm right here." She stepped forward into the kitchen.

"You left her alone with a knife!" he snapped.

She flinched before straightening her shoulders. "It's a lettuce knife; it's not sharp at all. We use them in the classroom because they're child safe. And I've been here the whole time with her."

Roman's gaze cut to the item in question, picking it up and running his finger along the dull edge before his shoulders relaxed. "I thought . . ."

"You clearly thought I had no idea how to take care of a child." She kept her voice even and her face blank. He wouldn't get the satisfaction of knowing he'd hit one of her wounds. Not many people seemed to think she was capable. She cleared her throat as Ariel looked back and forth between them.

Bzzzz. A bee buzzed by her ear.

Elise screamed and raised her hands to defend herself, darting towards Roman. She hit a wall of solid muscle. He stiffened. His woodsy masculine scent filled her nose, eliciting a reaction from her traitorous body. Elise looked up at him, taking a quick step backwards at his glare. But she lost her balance. His arms reached out to steady her, his jaw twitching.

"Chill out. It's just a honeybee," he barked before dropping his arms away from her.

He walked towards where the insect had landed on the fridge. He cupped his hands over it and carried the bug outside the door.

"It's one of Daddy's friends that followed him home from work," Ariel explained.

"Oh, well, that's cool, but I'm al—"

"If you're gonna be staying here, you'd better get used to the bees. I'm a beekeeper. They catch a ride home with me on my clothes. Is that going to be too much for you to handle, Elise?" he asked sharply.

"Not at all . . ." Elise croaked, her heart still racing. She didn't want him to think she was any less qualified than he already did. "Don't you wear a bee suit?"

"Not usually, unless they are extra angry." He helped Ariel down from the stool.

"Don't you get stung?"

"Sometimes but only if I piss them off." He placed his hands on his hips. "What smells so good? Did Mom drop off dinner?"

A self-satisfied smile curved her lips. "No, I made the roast you had in the fridge."

Something flashed in his eyes. It might have been regret, but it was gone too fast to read. "You cooked?"

Her smile dropped. "Wasn't I supposed to?"

"We made brownies too! Not the ones from the box either. Elise has a special recipe. But not like Aunt Nova's special recipe. Everyone can eat these—I asked."

Roman chuckled and leaned down to kiss his daughter on

her temple. "I'll shower real quick and then we can eat." He turned to Elise, all humor fading from his expression. "Thanks for cooking."

She forced a tight smile. "You're welcome."

Roman gave her a curt nod and then made his way towards the stairs. She tried her best not to look, but damn, the back view was almost as good as the front. His work pants stretched taut across an ass that put Captain America's to shame.

She forced her attention to the remaining lettuce, finishing up the salad in silence. Maybe she'd skip dinner. Her stomach was in knots anyways. Had she screwed up? Was she not supposed to cook? No, that didn't make sense. So what was his problem? She sighed, weariness weighing heavily on her shoulders.

I can do anything for a couple months. But could she survive Roman Emerson?

6

ROMAN

Roman stuffed a third brownie into his mouth and stifled a groan. These were the best things he'd ever eaten. Elise was not only gorgeous, but she knew how to cook. If he could find a fault in her, it might make things easier. Maybe that was why he'd gone off on her in the kitchen earlier.

The roast had been so tender and it was seasoned to perfection. Ariel even ate her meal with only minimal complaints about the veggies. It seemed helping to make the food had given his daughter an extra incentive to eat it. Of course the promise of dessert was a mighty motivator too.

He'd been relieved when Elise hadn't joined them for the meal—the less he saw of her the better. But he hadn't believed her when she'd said she'd eaten a late lunch and wasn't hungry. God, he felt like a dick. He should apologize.

He leaned against the counter with only the overhead light on the stove illuminating the kitchen. The house was quiet with Ariel sound asleep.

Roman headed upstairs to her room and knocked. Soft

footsteps padded to the door before it opened revealing Elise with her long raven hair spilling down her shoulders. Her sweet jasmine scent danced into the hallway where he stood, stealing his breath. The men's shirt she wore came to the tops of her thighs, showing off her sexy legs. Legs he would like to wrap around his neck while he—

"Roman?"

He jerked his attention back to her face, making sure to mask any emotion from his expression. "Can we talk for a minute?"

She pulled her bottom lip into her mouth before she nodded. Roman spun around and headed back down the stairs to the living room, needing to breathe air not tainted by her tantalizing scent and stop fantasizing about her thick thighs wrapped around him. She followed, taking a seat on the couch so that one whole cushion separated them. She crossed her arms over her chest, her back ramrod straight. It took every bit of his self-control not to look down at her toned legs.

"Ariel told me she had a great day. And she's excited about tomorrow."

Some of the tension left Elise's shoulders as the corners of her mouth turned up into a genuine smile. God, she was beautiful. "I'm glad. I enjoyed our day too."

"About earlier—"

"Look, Roman, I will probably end up doing something you don't normally approve of because I'm still learning the boundaries and your expectations. But I want you to know that I would never put your daughter in a position where she would be in danger. If there is something you prefer we don't do, just let me know and I'll respect that."

He swallowed. That sounded . . . more than reasonable. She was so wise for how young she looked. "Okay . . . How old are you?"

She blinked as if his question had surprised her. "Uh, twenty-seven."

"You seem . . . older."

Her mouth formed a straight line. "Gee, thanks. Just what every woman wants to hear."

"I didn't mean it like that." He ran a hand over his face.

"How did you mean it, then?" She bristled.

"You seem confident and sure of yourself enough to articulate what you need, what's on your mind."

"Yeah, well, comes with the territory of being on your own for your whole life." She clamped her mouth shut as her eyes flashed with regret.

She'd been alone? His heart tugged.

She closed her eyes and swallowed, pain etched on her features before it was gone, hidden behind an unreadable mask. Elise hugged her arms closer to her body as if trying to protect herself from him.

"Is that your wife?" She pointed to the picture frame on the small table beside him.

He didn't even need to look to know which one it was. Tiana was smiling up at the camera while holding a baby Ariel laughing in her arms at the beach. Memories of that day flooded over him. The grief would always be there. Tiana had been his best friend and wife. She had been taken way too soon. "Yeah, that's Tiana."

"She was beautiful."

"She was," he agreed.

"Ariel looks a lot like her," Elise mused.

"Thankfully." He chuckled.

She opened her mouth as if to say something but clamped it shut again.

"What?"

"Uh, what time are you leaving in the morning?" she asked.

He got the feeling that hadn't been what she was originally going to say. "Probably not until six thirty."

"Do you have anything particular you want me to cook for dinners? Maybe you can write out a list of things you and Ariel like to eat so I can keep them in mind?"

"Write you out a list?" Embarrassment itched his skin.

"Yeah, just a few basic favorite meals and such. And if you make a grocery list, I can go shopping too if you want—save you time. I'm sure Ariel would enjoy getting out of the house and the farm for a bit. She can learn a lot from a shopping trip."

A handwritten meal-and-grocery list? He swallowed the ball of nerves clogging his throat. This was one reason he hated getting to know new people. Not everyone understood. Would Elise think less of him if she knew?

A stab of fear raced through him. He hated that what she thought mattered to him, but it did. She didn't realize what she was asking of him.

"Just make whatever and include veggies at every meal. Ariel will tell you what she likes." He kept his voice even, trying not to show the tension radiating in his body.

"Okay. Do you want me to make extras of anything for you to take for lunches?"

Make him lunch? Tiana had used to do that. He hadn't had anyone take care of him in . . . a long time. He was too busy making sure everyone else in the family was okay. After Nash had checked out, that responsibility had all been on his shoulders. But Elise's offer—it loosened something inside him. Fuck, he couldn't have that.

I have to be strong for everyone else. I can't rely on her because she's temporary. As much as he'd like to entertain more long-term ideas with someone like her, Ariel came first. He couldn't risk his daughter being hurt again.

"Roman?"

"No, that's not in your job description. I'm perfectly capable of feeding myself. All I need is for you to keep my daughter safe and happy until I get home. Keep signing with her, and teach her what she needs to know for school in the fall. That's all you're here to do."

She stiffened, her eyes darting to her lap. "Of course. Sorry. I'll try to stay out of your way while I'm here this summer." She stood, those bare legs at his eye level now.

"Elise—"

"Have a good night." She darted away from him, her long limbs carrying her up the stairs and out of his sight within seconds.

He slunk into the couch with a sigh. He'd asked her to talk to clear the air, but now there seemed to be even more tension between them than before. "Two months. I can do this, for Ariel. Just two months."

The summer couldn't go by fast enough.

7
____

ELISE

lise pressed the side of her hand to her forehead, shading the sun from her eyes. Ariel reached through the fence to pet one of the lambs.

"What's this one's name again?" Elise asked.

"*Uncle Ricky calls him Dinner, but I told him that's not nice. I call him Stormy because his wool is grey like a rain cloud.*"

"I like your name for him much better."

A vibration in Elise's pocket had her grabbing her phone.

Sam: *You have this weekend off, right? Come over and stay. We're having a little get-together.*

Yes, technically she had the weekend off. And she definitely didn't want to stay here more than needed, but she also wasn't a fan of big social gatherings.

Elise: *Who's coming?*

Sam: *It'll be Jack, me, Tori, and a couple guys from work. Come on, you need to catch us up on your new job.*

Elise: *I'll think about it.*

Sam: *Jack says you'd better come and make one of your famous charcuterie boards.*

She smiled. She could go and see her friends and have a weekend with food and fun and laughs or stay here cooped up in her room for two days so she didn't have any unnecessary run-ins with Roman.

Elise: *I'll see you Friday night.*

She pocketed her phone, glancing at Ariel who'd moved on towards the chickens.

"Hey, guys. What kind of adventure are you on today?" Nova asked as she walked around the corner of the barn.

"*I was going to check for eggs,*" Ariel signed.

"Oh, well, you can look, but I got them a couple hours ago."

Ariel walked over to the henhouse, peeking into the nests where a couple of chickens roosted.

"How is she adjusting to having you around?" Nova asked quietly.

"Good, I think. She was a little shy at first, understandably. But she's had fun showing me just about every inch of this farm and all the animals. I can't wait to take her into town to the park or go to the beach." Elise tucked a loose strand of hair behind her ear.

"Today's a good day for the ocean. You should go." Nova swiped her brow.

"Roman wanted us to stay on the farm this week."

"Ahh. Well, my brother is a wee bit overprotective with Ariel, but he does have his reasons. Just be patient with him, and don't be afraid to stand up to him. I think you being here is going to help," Nova said.

Elise turned to her, eyebrows raised. "How so?"

"Since Tiana passed, he hasn't left Ariel with anyone but family except for her therapist for an hour. He's kept her in this little bubble. He definitely needs a push now and then. Don't be afraid to say something. My brother is a fair man and open-minded for the most part. He likes to analyze things before he does them, and he's very . . . shall we say risk averse?"

"Why is he so overprotective of her?" Elise asked. Elise would take whatever information she could get on her employer. The better she knew how he worked, the easier it would be to survive this job.

"Well—"

Ariel came bounding up to them. *"Can we go swimming? I'm so hot."*

"Your dad wanted us to stay close to the house this week, but maybe I can find a hose and make a sprinkler for you?" Elise suggested.

"Oh, I can do one better. There's a pond over the hill on the back of the property. I've got the afternoon off anyways. Go change and get some towels, and I'll meet you at Roman's," Nova said before turning and heading back up the hill to her house.

"Alright, then, let's go get ready." Elise took Ariel's hand and made her way back to the house.

Ariel found her bathing suit and changed while Elise quickly did the same. She grabbed a couple towels and scribbled out a note for Roman, letting him know where they would be in case he got home early. Hopefully he could read her chicken scratch.

"Do you have any floats or a life jacket to bring?" Elise asked.

"In the mudroom."

Elise followed Ariel as she led the way. Elise grabbed the puddle jumper and added it to her armload of supplies. "Okay, we got water and snacks and stuff for swimming. Anything else?"

Ariel shook her head.

"Let's go, then."

She and Ariel went outside where Nova was just pulling up in a four-seater ATV that looked more like an off-roading golf cart.

"Ready to cool off?" Nova asked. She'd changed into a bright red two-piece with a black lace cover-up.

"*Yes!*" Ariel climbed into the back, reaching for the buckles.

Elise set her things in the back next to Nova's and sat beside Ariel.

"Okay, everyone set?" Nova asked.

Elise glanced at the little girl beaming beside her. "Yes."

Nova drove them over the yard to the connecting dirt path that led by her house. She kept going as the breeze blew, offering some relief to the stifling heat. The scenery whipped by, tall grasses of a meadow full of wildflowers. A home farther out that Elise assumed was one of the brothers'. The sky was so blue with not a cloud in sight—just the hot sun shining down. A line of trees appeared ahead, the temperature instantly cooling a few degrees once they entered the shaded path.

"*This part is bumpy,*" Ariel pointed out.

Sure enough, Nova slowed as the vehicle jostled Elise from side to side, up and down as it drove over a rocky path.

The trees broke and the blue sky was back. A large expanse of blue water stretched from a sandy shore for what seemed like too far a distance for it to be deemed a pond.

"You have a lake on your property?" Elise asked.

"Technically, it's a pond. It's beautiful, isn't it?"

"Gorgeous," Elise agreed.

"Come on, let's set up on the sandy part." Nova parked the vehicle.

They gathered their things and spread out towels.

Ariel ran to the shore and dipped her toe in before jumping up and down and signing, *"Cold!"*

Elise pulled out some sunscreen from the bag she'd packed and started to cover her body while keeping an eye on Ariel. She'd already covered the little girl before they'd left the house.

Nova stood by her niece before crossing her arms over her chest and shivering. "Fudge, she wasn't kidding. It's like ice."

Ariel splashed her aunt and ran away as Elise put aside the sunscreen.

"Hey! You little traitor, get back here." Nova chased her.

Ariel's smile showed off her newly grown-in front teeth and the few missing on the sides as she darted to Elise and clung to her leg for safety. Elise laughed.

"Help me throw her in." Nova grabbed Ariel's feet.

Elise held onto her hands and they swung her back and forth between them as Ariel's eyes lit up with excitement.

They gently set her feet in the cold water and Ariel splashed them both again.

Elise and Nova laughed.

"That's a quick way to cool off. Is the water always this cold?" Elise asked.

"It'll be better in July and August once it's had proper time to warm up," Nova explained. "Now, who's up for a game of tag?"

Ariel immediately darted down the shore.

"You're it!" Nova tagged Elise and took off after her niece.

Elise laughed and shook her head before she headed out after them.

* * *

Two hours later, Elise was the best kind of tired. Her belly hurt from laughing. Her skin was warm with a light tan. Ariel was stacking rocks in a pile at the shallows in front of her.

"Goddess, I love my life." Nova sighed, cracking open a second spiked seltzer. "You sure you don't want one of these?"

"I'm sure." A lazy day in the sun with a drink sounded like fun, but not while she was responsible for someone else's child.

"We should definitely do this again." Nova took a drink.

Elise ruffled through the bag for a bottle of water and took a few sips before putting it back.

Ariel turned towards them, holding a rock in one palm and a handful of sand in the other. She dropped both, her face lighting up as she signed, *"Daddy!"*

Elise turned around, getting to her feet as Roman drove towards them on a four-wheeler. He shut it off and stalked towards her with a glare. Ariel ran into his arms. He caught her, picking her up, his expression softening when he looked at her. He even cracked a smile as he spoke quietly in her ear. She nodded, and as soon as she was on her feet again, Ariel ran back to them.

Roman followed, his lips in a straight line. If looks could kill, she'd be toast right now. *What is it this time?* Elise steeled her spine, offering him a tight smile. "Hello."

"Nova, can you take Ariel for a walk down the beach?" Roman's voice was cold and even.

His sister got to her feet, dusting off sand with one hand from her butt while holding up her drink with the other. She cut Elise a questioning look. "Sure. But why are you freaking out right now?"

"Just give me five minutes with my nanny, please," he gritted out.

Nova held up her hands. "Okay, fine. Take a chill pill."

She took Ariel's hand and led her past Roman down the other side of the pond, turning around to sign to Elise, *"Stand your ground. You did nothing wrong."*

Roman glanced over his shoulder at his sister as she whipped around, leading Ariel farther down the water line.

"You seem upset," Elise pointed out.

"You think? I told you to stay close to the house. I called you five times and you didn't pick up. And then when I finally found you, my daughter was in the pond by herself without a floaty and you were drinking with my sister on the shore," he snapped, his chest heaving. His gaze dipped before his expression twisted into what she could only assume was disgust and darted back to her eyes.

Elise took a breath. *Do not scratch his face off. Don't do it. You're better than this, Elise.* "Ariel was hot and wanted to go swimming. Nova suggested we come here. The water was too cold for us to go deeper, so Ariel stuck to the shoreline. I brought her puddle jumper just in case." She pointed to it on the ground by a towel. "But Nova assured me there wasn't a drop-off and she stayed in the five inches of water only a few feet from us. My eyes were on her the whole time and I drank nothing but water today. You can ask your sister if you don't believe me."

"And your excuse for ignoring my calls?"

She bristled and stalked over to their things, bending over to ruffle through the bag and pull out her phone. She turned around. Roman's eyes jumped from her ass to her face. The nerve of this guy! Pulling up the home screen, she looked and sure enough, there were the missed calls he mentioned.

"Look, I'm sorry, but my phone didn't ring. The signal here is spotty. But I left you a note on the counter, telling you where we were. Next time I'll be sure to check it periodically even if I don't hear it."

"You're so sure it didn't ring, or you didn't hear it? I'm not trying to be an asshole, but what if there was an emergency?"

Her stomach clenched and her blood turned to ice. She leveled her glare on him. "I would have heard it if it rang, but it didn't. Are you implying I'm unfit to do this job because I'm hearing impaired?"

He sighed and squeezed the back of his neck. "This isn't about you. It's about keeping my daughter safe."

"Is she not safe?"

"She is, *this time*," he admitted.

"Look, I get that you find it hard to trust someone with your daughter, but I'm doing my best here. Maybe if you gave me some clearer guidelines instead of expecting me to read your mind, that would help."

"The next time you leave the house with my daughter, text me where you'll be."

"The note wasn't sufficient?"

He glared at her again, his shoulders tensing to his ears. "No. It wasn't."

What the fuck was the difference between a note and a text? God, this man was rigid. "Fine."

"Just do what I ask; that's what I hired you for."

"Yes, sir," she ground out.

Roman glared at her. She was pretty sure that if he didn't have so much melanin, he'd be red from the anger emanating off him in waves.

"I'd better go. Ariel will be hungry for dinner and preparing it is part of my job description, last I checked." She spun around, grabbed their things and packed them back up quickly. She straightened and headed towards the ATV as Ariel and Nova approached.

"Oh, and, Roman?" she asked just loud enough for only him to hear.

"What?"

She gave him her best ice queen glare back. "As my employer, checking out my ass is highly inappropriate."

8

ELISE

Friday could not come fast enough. Days spent with Ariel were fun, crafting and playing outside in the sun. Elise now knew the names of all the animals in the barn, and her way around most of the property near the houses. As soon as Roman got home and showered, she'd disappear into her room and work on her curriculum. Tweaking it here and there, or adding to her Pinterest board of ideas for themes throughout the school year and ideas on how she'd decorate the classroom. *I can't wait.*

Elise stuffed a couple days' worth of clothing and necessities into a bag and slipped on a summery pale-blue dress that flowed to mid-thigh. She slid on her flip-flops and hiked the bag over her shoulder before taking a quick scan of her room to make sure it was in order.

The full-size bed was made with fresh sheets. Her laundry, folded and put away in the simple white dresser in the room. Satisfied it was tidy enough, she slipped outside the door to the hall. Roman shut Ariel's bedroom door, his hands wrapped around a yellow copy of *Good Night Stories For Rebel Girls*.

His gaze dropped to the bag on her arm. "Leaving for the weekend?"

"Yeah, I'll get out of your hair and be back Sunday evening."

He nodded and passed her, heading into the room at the end of the hall where he closed the door.

"Why thank you, I will drive safe," she whispered sarcastically under her breath on her way down the stairs. She ground her teeth, practically running out to her car. The sooner she could get away from Roman Emerson, the better. Too bad it was only for forty-eight hours.

* * *

Three hours later, Elise had a drink in her hand and her head was warm and fuzzy with a nice buzz. Her best friend Sam sat on one side of her on the couch, and his boyfriend, Jack, was on the other. The men she'd met earlier, Casey and Marcus, were in the small kitchen, talking over the charcuterie board she'd whipped together as requested while her friend Tori argued over something good-naturedly with them.

"Casey's cute." Sam wrapped his arm around her to massage the back of his boyfriend's neck. At the same time, he signed with his free hand. Jack was Deaf and didn't have a CI.

"Yeah, and he knows it." She laughed.

Jack snorted, his chest rumbling with humor. *"Well, he's been taking peeks at you all night."*

Elise looked back to the kitchen, catching Casey in the act. She offered him a friendly smile and then focused back on Jack before signing, *"The last thing I need right now is another man to let me down. I'm done. It's time to focus on me for a little while."*

"*Ron was an asshole. There are good men out there,*" Sam chimed in.

Elise sighed and snuggled into their warmth. "*Why can't we just form a triad? I would be the best girlfriend ever, I promise.*"

Both men laughed so loud, they drew the attention of the three others in the kitchen.

"What's so funny?" Tori asked, refilling her wineglass.

"Just my hopes and dreams," Elise joked before taking another sip of her drink.

"*Even if I was bi, I wouldn't share my man.*" Jack smirked, giving Sam a wink.

"*I love you.*" Sam blew his boyfriend a kiss.

Elise groaned. "*Ugh, can you guys get any more perfect? Seriously. I hope you know how good you have it.*"

"I've heard the best way to get over someone is to get under someone else. Maybe you just need a night to remember you're a fucking badass woman who raised herself. The same one who convinced the entire football team at college to dance in nothing but their jock straps at your fundraiser, like it was *Magic Mike*, college edition," Sam said with an amused smile.

She bit back a grin. "I did do that, didn't I? But it was for a good cause."

"*Paid tuition for the kids who couldn't afford to go to that fancy Deaf school. You helped change their life,*" Jack added.

"Well, I know what it's like to need someplace to belong." She sighed.

Tori came over and took a seat across from them, Marcus and Casey following suit.

"So, tell me how you're liking your new job." Tori turned to glance at the men beside her. "Elise is nannying for the summer until school starts in the fall."

"Oh, what grades do you teach?" asked Marcus, a Black

man in a periwinkle-blue button-up and khakis. His circular wire-rimmed glasses glinted in the overhead light. He was handsome in a nerdy professor type of way. But the stretch of his ironed shirt over his muscular arms made it clear he worked out. Sexy nerdy types were right up her friend Tori's alley. And if the way the man kept glancing at her friend was any indication, it seemed Tori might be his type as well.

"I teach first grade—or I will be," Elise answered.

"That's a fun age group," Casey commented. He was completely the opposite of Marcus. Casey was tall with wide shoulders and built like a linebacker. A man like him made Elise feel small despite her six-foot height, and that seemed rare these days. A lot of men didn't give her a chance because of her height, like it was some reflection on their lack of masculinity to have a girlfriend that was taller.

"It is."

"But I want to know how your nannying is going. It's a little girl you're watching, right?" Tori asked.

"Yeah. She's adorable and sweet. She's a little shy, but once she warms up to you, she's funny and quite the character. We have a lot of fun together." Elise drained the rest of her wine.

"And how's the parents?"

Elise licked her lips, straining to keep her smile intact. "It's just her dad and her. The mom passed."

"Oh, that's got to be so hard for a little one," Tori said.

Elise nodded.

Marcus asked Tori a question, drawing Tori's attention away.

"What aren't you saying?" Jack asked.

"What do you mean?"

"Your mouth gets tight when you hold something back." Jack pointed to the corner of her lips.

"It does not!"

He chuckled. *"Tell her, Sam."*

"He's right."

She sighed, looking into her empty glass. "I need more wine if we're going there."

Sam got to his feet, reaching out to take her hand. She followed him, Jack right behind her, until they made it into the kitchen. Sam pulled out another bottle of chilled moscato and poured it in her glass before topping off Jack's and grabbing another beer for himself.

"Spill it," Sam said.

Elise took a fortifying gulp of her wine before licking her lips and diving in. "It's really not all that interesting. It's just that . . ."

"You're killing me here with the suspense," Jack teased.

"He's really attractive, and I just . . ." She sighed. "I don't know why, but the man lights me up like a fucking Christmas tree. Okay? Happy now that I've confessed my deep, dark secret?"

"Wait, so what's the problem?" Sam asked.

"She just broke up with that other asshole. She's scared, right, babe?" Jack answered for her.

"I mean, I guess that's part of it. But he's made it clear I'm not entirely wanted there."

"Wait, what do you mean, not wanted? He hired you, for Christ's sake," Sam said.

"More like his mom picked me, and he's just going along with it."

"Has he been unkind to you?" Jack asked.

She hesitated. She might not have blood family who had her back, but these two were like two overprotective big brothers.

"What did that bastard do?" Sam's voice had an edge to it.

"Nothing. He didn't do anything. He's just made it clear to me that I'm there to take care of his kid for the summer and not a moment longer."

Jack placed his hand on Sam's shoulder, massaging the muscles there. Sam released a breath and relaxed into his boyfriend's hold.

"We just worry about you. You can stay here, you know," Jack offered.

"No, you guys. Look, I don't need your pity. I dug myself into this hole and I can get myself out."

"Why are you always so stubborn?" Sam crossed his arms over his chest.

Elise matched his stance. "I'm not stubborn. I'm also not going to be the type of friend who takes advantage of you both. You let me stay for three weeks, and that helped me immensely. But I don't want to be a burden. And it's not so bad at Roman's. I meant what I said about Ariel. Things are just a little uncomfortable around Roman, but when he gets home, I disappear into my room and that solves that. It's working out just fine. Besides, no one else wants to hire me for the summer with a pay that's decent enough."

"Just because you need help, it doesn't make you a burden," Jack signed.

"You know that's what friends are for. We're here for you. If you need a place to crash, money to hold you over 'til your next paycheck, someone to help hide a body, whatever it is— we got your back," Sam agreed.

Tears welled in her eyes. These two were the only ones who were always there for her. And she wouldn't ever do anything to screw their relationship up—like be too needy. "You two are the best boyfriends a girl could have," she teased, wrapping them both in a hug.

They laughed together and squeezed her back.

"Don't push your luck," Sam joked.

"So, what's the plan? You gonna tell this guy to go fuck himself? Or stick through the summer?" Jack asked.

"If he does anything to make me feel too uncomfortable, I'll leave. And I can ignore how unfairly hot he is—for the most part. But right now, it's really just about taking care of his kid. And I'd hate to leave them in the lurch. Ariel reminds me a lot of myself when I was younger. She had something traumatic happen and she's pulled away, but I can see her desire to rejoin the rest of the world outside her family's farm."

"I hope you know what you're doing," Sam said, pulling away.

"Me too," Elise agreed.

"Hey, guys, let's play a game," Tori called from the living room.

"I'm in." Elise took another sip of her wine, making her way to the couch. This time, she sat next to Casey. Some eye candy from the boy next door couldn't hurt. Besides, what harm ever came from a little flirtation? And maybe her friend was right, and the key to moving on from the pain of being dumped was to have a one-night stand or a no-strings fling. She eyed Casey, his handsome face lighting up as his gaze met hers.

"Want to be on my team?" he asked.

"Sure. But I have to warn you, I can get competitive."

He smirked. "That makes two of us, then."

This weekend away might be just the thing Elise needed after all.

9

ROMAN

Roman twisted the last of Ariel's hair before wiping his hands free of product. "Where's your bonnet?"

His daughter climbed off the stool by the bathroom counter. *"In my room."*

He followed her as she climbed in bed, grabbing the silk cap. She tugged it on her head. He swept up her twists and pushed them into the cap, safe for the night while she slept. He'd have to show Elise how to take them out in the morning. He checked his phone. Eight thirty and still no sign of her.

"Ready to read your bedtime story?" he asked, picking up a book from her bedside table. He sat against the headboard as rain drizzled outside the window.

"Tell me the story about Mommy." Ariel snuggled up beside him.

Roman's chest squeezed. Ariel would never know what an amazing woman her mother was except for in stories told by him and his mother-in-law.

"Your mama was a special woman. She was beautiful inside and out—just like you. That's where you get it from."

Ariel smiled, her little white teeth showing.

He traced the shape of her oval face as he spoke. "She had your eyes. And they always shined with happiness. You've got my nose, but these lips are the same ones she used to smile with."

"Did she love me?"

Roman's throat grew thick, his voice coming out hoarse with emotion. "More than everything else. You were her most favorite thing in the whole world."

"More than you?" Ariel's sleepy eyes grew big.

"Even more than me." He closed his eyes, memories of their time together crashing over him. The good, the bad, and everything in between. "When she told me she was pregnant with you, she was so happy. We celebrated with ice cream, all her favorite flavors. And after you were born, she picked out your name. She said since she was named after a princess, you should be too." That wasn't completely true, but this little embellishment always brought a smile to his daughter's face. Tiana had picked out their daughter's name.

Roman glanced at his daughter's closed eyes and ran a finger down her soft forehead, then over her button nose before he leaned down and kissed her cheek.

"I love you, sweet pea. More than everything," he whispered.

Roman got up, put the book back, and slipped out of the room. He made his way through the quiet house to the kitchen. He loaded the few dishes into the dishwasher and put the rest of dinner away. Elise had prepped more than enough food than needed. She didn't have to, but it enabled him to spend more time with Ariel which was precious at this time of year. He'd have to thank her. Although what he really wanted to do was lay her over his lap and spank her.

Fuck! He didn't need this right now.

Roman sighed. This situation was awkward as hell, but every time he tried to clear the air, he ended up making things worse. It didn't help when she called him "Sir." She had no idea she was playing with fire.

The sound of a car door shutting drew his attention. He peeked through the curtains, through the blur of the rain.

Elise's arm was wrapped around a man's as they scurried under an umbrella towards the front porch. Was that her boyfriend? Was that who she'd been with all weekend? His gut burned, as the sensation traveled up to his chest. He pressed his hand against his heart. *Must be heartburn.*

Elise's hands rose under the protection of the porch, the light casting her in a yellow glow. She smiled up at the man. Damn, she was gorgeous. Limp hair stuck to her face as her eyes lit up with affection. The burning in his chest intensified.

Elise signed, "I love you," to the man in front of her. He wrapped her in his arms and kissed her cheek before jogging back to his car. Roman's blood heated, a sour feeling twisting his guts. He had no right to be jealous, but fuck, he was.

She opened the door and closed it behind her before clicking the lock and turning towards him.

"Next time you're gonna be out past eight, text me so I don't lock you out."

She jumped and finished spinning around, her hand over her heart. "You scared me."

"And I don't appreciate you bringing strange men to my house where my daughter is." He moved past her.

A light tap of his shoulder had a buzz of electricity shooting through his arm. He jerked back, facing her.

She ripped her hand away. "I'm sorry, but I can't read your lips when you aren't facing me."

His gaze dropped to her shiny pink lips, and that damned

cupid's bow. An onslaught of images of those lips wrapped around his cock flashed in his mind. His dick jerked.

"My implant isn't waterproof, so it's not on. What did you say?" She touched the side of her head showing the missing CI.

He ground his teeth together until they ached, forcing the inappropriate fantasies from his mind. *"I said, next time you're gonna be out past eight, text me so I don't lock you out. And I don't appreciate you bringing strange men to my house where my daughter is."*

Her lips pressed together as she shook her head. "My tire was flat and I screwed something up changing it, so it needed to be towed to the mechanic. I got a ride here rather than calling in tomorrow and leaving you in the lurch. I'll need Jack to pick me up tomorrow and get my car from the shop if that's okay with you?" Her voice was like ice.

"I'll take you when I get home."

"You don't have to. I'll call a friend. I wouldn't want to put you out any more than I have." She gripped her bag tighter, turning towards the stairs.

Bracing himself for the live connection this time, he grabbed her arm. *"I said, I'll take you."*

"Fine." She pulled away from him and headed up the stairs without another word.

The urge to go after her and turn her ass red had him gritting his teeth. Roman scrubbed his hand over his face and sighed in frustration. "You were supposed to thank her, idiot, not start another fight." He wasn't sure what had come over him. The sight of her in another man's arms had awakened something visceral inside him. Something he hadn't felt in years.

And that was what scared him the most.

10

ELISE

Elise swiped the paintbrush across the page, leaving an arch of purple, completing her rainbow.

"Oh, I love it!." Ariel stuck her tongue out of the side of her mouth in concentration as she focused back on her canvas. The sun shone through the trees above, sending golden shapes dancing on their work against the art easel. It was too gorgeous to stay inside, and a good day for some art.

"Now add a unicorn," Ariel signed.

"A unicorn? Oh, dear. You're lucky I could do a rainbow. Art is not my strong suit." Elise laughed, picking up a smaller brush with black paint. She attempted the outline of a horse, adding a horn at the top before she stepped back and tipped her head sideways. "Well, what do you think? Does it have potential?"

Ariel paused her work on a gorgeous assortment of flowers of all shapes and colors, leaning in to get a better look at Elise's attempt.

"It looks like a cow." Ariel smiled and shook her head. *"Aren't*

you supposed to be teaching me? I can do better than that with my eyes closed."

"You little stinker. I gave my best shot." Elise acted affronted, holding up the brush with blue paint. "How dare you mock my art!" She swiped her brush over Ariel's nose leaving a swath of blue paint.

Ariel's eyes got big before a giant smile overtook her and she used her own brush against Elise. Elise laughed as Ariel attacked her, covering her in yellow paint.

"Oh, no you don't!" Elise dipped her brush in the red, but before she could turn back towards Ariel, the little girl tackled her. Cold paint slicked up the side of her face. She squealed.

"Okay! I give up. You win." Elise laughed, her chest heaving as she caught her breath. She sat up, caught off guard by the man standing only a few yards from them.

Roman stood there like a sentry, observing them quietly. How long had he been there?

She scrambled to her feet, straightening her shirt and dusting off her shorts. "You're back early."

"Daddy!" Ariel threw herself at him.

His expression morphed so suddenly to joy you'd have never thought the man scowled a day in his life. Ariel pulled this softer side from him. And as far as she could tell, he reserved his sharp edges for Elise.

"Why don't you two shower, then I'll have one and we can go get your car?" He took Ariel's hand and led her inside.

Elise took a deep breath and exhaled. *Just got to get through these next seven weeks.* And survive this car ride.

* * *

Thirty minutes later, she followed Ariel and Roman down his gravel driveway towards what he'd called the honey shop. The buzzing got louder the closer they got. She clutched her purse tightly, searching around her for any stray bees.

Roman rounded his truck, opening the door to get Ariel buckled in the back before stepping aside to let Elise in. She scanned the cab, looking for any sign of his six-legged friends.

"Is there a reason you're not getting in?" Roman asked briskly from behind her.

She gritted her teeth, using the handlebar to climb in. "Just making sure there aren't any bees."

"You'd better get used to them because the season is just starting. I'll be bringing in honey starting next month, and that means a lot more honeybees."

She swallowed, nerves twisting in her stomach as he shut her door and walked around to the driver's side.

He climbed in and started the engine, casting her a quick glance. "Buckle up."

Elise did as he said. She didn't like that she was vulnerable like this, especially around him. This might give him one more reason to doubt her capability, but she didn't have a choice in the matter—it could be life or death for her.

She pulled out her EpiPen as he shifted into drive. He paused, his gaze flicking from the medicine to her, his brows pulled together in question.

"I'm allergic to bees. So if I get stung and can't get to this myself, I may need help. Do you know how to use it?"

The tightness in his jaw slackened. "Why didn't you say anything that day in the kitchen?"

"I tried, but you made it clear I just needed to suck it up. And I can—I just need you to know what to do in case I can't get to it in time. And I'll show Ariel too. It shouldn't be a problem when we're together, but by your honey house and in your truck it seems more likely to happen."

"I'm sorry."

She blinked, surprised.

Roman pointed towards her EpiPen. "I know how it works. My cousin is allergic to shellfish."

She put it back in the purse and set it by her feet. Roman scanned the truck interior before turning to her once more. "I usually check for any bees before I get Ariel in, but I'll make sure to double-check when I know you'll be joining us."

That was kind. "Thank you. I appreciate that."

His dark brown gaze pulled her in like a magnet. When Roman's attention was fully focused on her, it was hard to look away.

He broke their stare and cleared his throat. "We going to Shattered Cove Garage?"

"Yeah." *Stupid, Elise. He's off-limits. I'm just the nanny.*

The rest of the drive was quiet except for the soundtrack to *Encanto* playing on repeat. Elise stared out the window at the passing scenery. Soft rolling green hills and lush green forest turned into suburban homes with manicured lawns, and then they entered town with rows of small businesses stretching out before them. The garage came into view, the bay doors all open. Roman parked beside her car in the lot.

She grabbed her purse off the floor. "Thanks for the ride—"

"Wait there." Roman climbed out. He jogged around her side of the car and opened the door for her and then the back one for Ariel.

She got out. "Thank you. But you guys don't need to come in. I've got it from here."

"Let's make sure you're good to go." Roman headed towards the garage.

A tall Black man covered in tattoos walked towards them with a bright smile as he wiped his hands on a rag. His overalls were tied around his waist, leaving a stained white sleeveless shirt over his chest.

"Hey, little one." The man signed as he crouched down to bump fists with Ariel.

"Hello."

The mechanic pulled a lollipop from his pocket and handed it to Ariel, who thanked him and opened her candy before Roman rested his hand on her shoulder.

"Ro, long time no see. Something you need me to look at with the truck?" the mechanic asked.

"No. I brought Elise here to pick up her Ford." Roman turned to her. "Elise, this is Link; he owns the shop."

"Nice to meet you."

"You too. Come on into the office and I'll get the paperwork pulled up for you." Link headed into the building.

Elise turned to Roman to thank him for the ride but Ariel was signing to him.

"I'm hungry. Can we go to the diner for dinner? Please?"

He glanced at Elise. "Sure, we could do that. Let's get Elise settled here first."

"Oh, I'm fine. You can go. Thanks for the ride."

"You're coming with us."

She blinked. Boy, he was bossy. "What?"

"To dinner . . . Look, I meant to thank you for making those meals for us over the weekend. You didn't have to, but it made my life easier. Let me repay you by taking you to dinner with us."

"You really don't have to," she argued.

"I insist." His brown eyes locked on hers, stealing her breath.

"Please, Elise? We can get ice cream for dessert," Ariel added.

Elise smiled. "I guess if ice cream is involved, I'm all in."

"We'll wait in the truck and follow you over. Not that I

have any doubts about Link's abilities, but just to be safe," Roman said, grabbing Ariel's hand and turned back towards their vehicle.

A burst of surprise tumbled through her. Roman wanted to make sure she was safe? She didn't have many people in her life who cared like that.

She closed her eyes and shook her head. *He's just my employer. He's a good father, and a good man. That's all it is.* This was just sharing a meal with her employer and her charge. Like a business dinner. What could go wrong?

11

ELISE

Elise dipped her last fry into the mix of mayo and ketchup on her plate before eating it.

"Aren't their fries the best?" Roman asked.

She nodded and took a sip of her iced tea.

"You like the macaroni and cheese?" he asked Ariel.

"Almost better than Grandma's."

Roman chuckled. "Don't tell her that."

Ariel smiled and shoveled another bite of her dinner in her mouth. Roman was different tonight, more friendly. Nothing like the man who'd accused her of nefarious activities the night before. What was going on? Was it just because Ariel was with them?

"It looked like you two had fun painting today," Roman said, meeting Elise's eyes once more. Was he actually trying to talk to her? Was this his attempt at an olive branch?

"Yeah, well, Ariel did pretty amazing. Her flowers were very creative."

"I liked painting you the best."

Elise and Roman both laughed at the same time.

"What are you guys going to do tomorrow?" he asked, picking up his soda and taking a sip.

The door chimed. Elise looked over to the entrance. "Oh, I thought maybe we'd—"

Her breath seized. Her heart felt as if it were being stabbed.

"Elise?" Roman sounded concerned as he turned towards the couple with the little boy with Down syndrome that had just walked in.

To anyone else they might seem like a cute family. *Had people thought that when I was by his side?* Fuck, what were they doing here?

Her pulse raced as she lowered her head, trying to shrink away and hide. Part of her wanted to walk over there and punch Ron in the face, and scream and say how horrible him and his girlfriend were, but in the end it would be Malaki who suffered. That pure, sweet, innocent soul didn't deserve such lying scum for parents. But he wasn't her son. And she'd never even gotten to say goodbye.

Elise didn't even want to think about the lies his mother had no doubt fed him about her. He probably felt abandoned.

Tears formed in her eyes. She knew what that felt like, and she never wanted to make another child feel that way.

"Elise, what's wrong?" Roman reached out and grasped her hand in his, bringing an instant hit of calm.

She looked down at the connection. Fresh feelings bubbled up, mixing with old hurt. She needed to get out of there. She stood so abruptly, she hit her knee on the table. It throbbed. Pain was good. It helped ground her.

"Um, I need to go." She dug in her purse, but Roman's hand landed over hers again.

"Dinner's on me, remember?"

"Right. Thanks. Um, I'll see you at home—your home.

Of course it's not mine," she rambled, everything inside her screaming to flee.

"*But what about dessert?*" Ariel asked.

"Uh, next time."

A warm hand clamped gently around her wrist. "Elise, what's going on?"

She forced what she hoped was a convincing smile. "Nothing, I just forgot I have to run some errands before the shops close. I'll see you two back at the house."

She pulled away and headed for the door, having to pass her ex and the little boy who once was her whole world.

"Elise!" Malaki's voice had her freezing with her hand on the door. Everything in her wanted to turn around and scoop him up in her arms.

"Elise!" he repeated.

"Malaki, sit still," Ron scolded.

Elise turned, blinking away the tears blurring her vision so she could see him clearly. Instead of speaking aloud, she signed so his parents wouldn't know what she was saying. "*Hey, buddy.*"

"*Why'd you leave me?*"

Her heart shattered.

"What is she doing here? Stay away from my fiancé, you tramp," Marigold, Malaki's biological mother, spat.

Elise wanted nothing to do with Ron; she didn't even give him a passing glance. He wasn't worth it. But Malaki was.

"*I wish I didn't have to. I'm sorry, little man. I love you.*" She turned and fled, tears streaming down her face as the ache in her chest grew with every breath.

I wasn't enough.

* * *

Elise lay in her bed, eyes swollen and feeling like sandpaper from her crying. She sniffled and stared at the photo of her and Malaki playing at the park on her phone. His big grin was contagious, as was the absolute joy in his eyes.

The door opened. Elise sat up, pulling the covers over her chest as Roman walked in.

"What are you doing in here?"

"*I knocked but you didn't answer,*" he signed.

She hadn't heard him because she'd taken her CI out. "So you just barged in?"

He flinched. Was she yelling? The last thing she wanted to do was wake Ariel.

"*Can we talk?*"

Great, he probably assumed the worst after that little display earlier. Was he going to fire her? She needed this job.

"*Give me a minute and I'll meet you in the kitchen.*"

He left without another word. She got out of bed and pulled on a pair of pajama shorts and her CI. She stopped in the bathroom to splash her face with cold water. She glanced her reflection and winced. Red splotches marred her usually smooth pale skin. She sighed. "Oh well."

Elise made her way to the kitchen where Roman stood with his back to her in a pair of grey sweatpants that accentuated his firm ass, and a loose T-shirt. His muscular arms flexed as he picked something up. Damn it, why did he have to be so good-looking? It was distracting.

He turned, carrying a steaming cup, and set it in front of her. He'd made her tea?

She wrapped her hands around the mug. "Thank you."

Roman leaned against the counter as she took a seat at the bar. "You okay?"

She inhaled the floral tea and nodded. "Of course."

He stared at her long and hard. Elise shifted under the intensity.

"Want to tell me what that was about earlier at the diner?" It seemed more like a demand than a question, which rubbed her the wrong way. She looked down at the tea. Was the gesture simply to give her a false sense of ease, like he actually cared?

"Not particularly." Had Marigold run her mouth after Elise left? What had that horrible woman said about her?

"Who were those people?"

"My personal life is none of your business."

"It's my business if it affects the care of my daughter."

"Well, this doesn't," she snapped.

"Did you nanny for that family?"

Elise scoffed. Family? Marigold was a deadbeat mother who'd abandoned her son to Ron's care because she'd figured sleeping with her dealer would get her free drugs. Ron had seemed like a good guy when she'd met him, a struggling single dad to a sweetheart of a boy. But she'd never worked for him; he'd been her boyfriend. And Elise had believed his lies, even giving up her career to care for his son. She'd thought they'd been a family—that she would marry him. Oh, how wrong she'd been.

"No. But in the end, I guess that's all I was—a glorified babysitter." How many nights when she'd stayed home with Malaki had Ron been screwing his ex?

"Then—"

"My personal life isn't any of your business. If you have a problem with that, I'm sorry. But this doesn't affect my job performance here."

Roman's jaw pulsed.

She stood, setting the cup of tea back down. "Now, if you'll excuse me, I'm going to bed because I've got to be up early for Ariel's therapy appointment, since it was rescheduled from Monday. We have a full day ahead in which I'll devote every single second to the well-being of your daughter. So if that's all?"

Roman hesitated before he gave a curt nod.

"Goodnight." She turned and made her way to her room. Anger replaced her grief. One thing was for sure—she'd never trust a man to do the right thing again when it came to her. Trust only made her vulnerable, and no good ever came from that.

12

ROMAN

R oman made his way through the newly trimmed field towards his buzzing beehives. Sweat dotted his brow, and his head pounded no matter how much water he drank.

"Is this the last yard for today?" Ricky asked, stuffing some dried hay in the hand-held smoker to calm the bees.

Roman nodded and winced. His hand massaged the sticky skin of his neck and the ache that had seemed to come out of nowhere. "Yeah."

Ricky squeezed the bag to the smoker, creating a few puffs around the stack of hives. The buzzing inside increased. He set it down and pulled out his pallet knife, separating the bottom hive from the stack above with a small tilt. Several bees flew out, but dozens more crawled over the top of the frames within.

Roman wiped his brow, fatigue hitting him hard. On sunny days like today, they had no need for covering their bodies. The bees were happy, and a few stings weren't going to be a problem. He was used to it.

"Do we need a super?" Roman asked.

Ricky didn't answer. Instead, he picked his way through the stack, taking a look at the hives, careful not to disrupt the bees too much or accidentally squish a queen. Roman picked up the smoker, keeping the bees as calm as possible while his brother moved their homes and peeked inside.

"Nah, I think we'll actually have to split some of these," Ricky replied.

Roman inspected the stacks around him. "Don't see any signs of bears or skunks."

"I'll grab the split supplies from my truck." Ricky walked off towards where they'd parked as Roman started inspecting the next stack of hives. He made his way around the yard, checking on the state of the boxes and the bees inside.

"Okay, I've got the frames split from this one. We'll set it aside and see if they hatch their own queen or if we need to bring one over." Ricky started a new stack on a pallet.

Roman shivered and looked up. There wasn't a cloud in the sky, so why did he feel cold all of a sudden?

"So, are we not going to talk about the elephant in the room?" Ricky asked.

"What do you mean?"

"Seriously. I gave you like two weeks without even bringing it up. Even you have to admit that makes me brother of the year." Ricky smirked as he picked up the smoker and started on the next row beside Roman.

"Just say what you're gonna say, asshole. I don't have the patience for your games." Roman growled. Fuck, his back ached.

Ricky chuckled, the sound grating on Roman's nerves. "You and Elise . . ."

"It's not like that and you know it. She's good with Ariel. Damn, I still can't believe I hired her."

"From what I heard, Mom did." Ricky chuckled.

"She did. Elise is good with Ariel."

"Doesn't hurt that she's hot as fuck either." Ricky smirked.

A low growl came from Roman's chest. "Don't you even think about it."

His brother held up his hands, trying to placate him. "Sorry, I didn't realize she was spoken for."

"She's an employee and off-limits. Besides, I think she has a boyfriend." That last sentence tasted bitter coming from his lips.

"Boyfriend? Really? From the way you two look at each other I thought maybe . . ."

"Not happening." Roman got back to work.

Ricky followed. "You think you'll start dating again anytime soon?"

Roman's arms seemed so much weaker than yesterday as he tried to lift a hive. Exhaustion slammed into him. He sat in the grass, pinching the bridge of his nose to stave off the headache. "No."

"Because you haven't moved on from Tiana?" Ricky asked, his voice way more careful than usual.

"Tiana is gone. I've accepted that. But Ariel is my priority. She's . . ." *She can't get hurt again.*

Ricky shook his head. "You don't look so good, Ro."

"Well, I feel like shit too. I think I might be coming down with something."

"Why don't you go home and I'll finish the yard. Still have to take a look for swarms and finish these splits."

"Alright. Thanks. There's one in the back that needs a super added to it." Roman turned to his truck without argument, which was a telltale sign of how crappy he felt. He didn't bother picking up his phone to let Elise know he would be home early. As soon as he shut the door, exhaustion bowled over him. He fought to keep his blurry vision on the road as he started the truck and drove home.

Eyes burning, and body shivering, Roman made it back. He opened the door and walked in to be greeted with silence. Elise's car was parked beside his, so she and Ariel had to be around the property somewhere. Roman just wanted to fall into bed, but he needed a shower to wash the filth of the day away and to check for ticks. He really didn't want to risk Lyme disease. He climbed the stairs, passed Ariel's open door, and paused.

Elise sat against his daughter's headboard, rubbing a cool cloth over Ariel's little forehead as soft words of a story fell from Elise's lips. In the fog of his sickness, the image gripped his heart. His little girl being cared for so tenderly by someone who wasn't family. Elise's gaze met his, her eyes widening before she carefully slipped out from under Ariel, laying her on the bed.

She walked towards him quietly and slipped out into the hallway.

"Did you get my messages?" she asked.

"No, I haven't looked at my phone."

Her brows drew together and her mouth thinned like she wanted to say something. And she'd be well within her rights to. Hadn't he done exactly what he'd been pissed about the other day at the pond? But his brain was foggy and his eyes felt like they were on fire, unfocused and blurry. The idea of looking at a screen made his already throbbing head pound even harder.

"You didn't know she was sick? You just came home early?" She scanned his face.

"I think I got whatever she has. I just need to shower and then I'll take over. You can go hide in your room and hope you don't get whatever it is."

"She threw up a few times. She's clean and resting now. I gave her some tea."

"Thank you. I'll try to be quick." He left her and went to his bathroom where he quickly tore off his dirty clothes and stuck them in a reusable grocery bag, tying it tight until he could worry about any ticks he might have carried in. After inspecting his body and removing the bugs that had crawled under his clothes from the bee yard, he got into the hot shower. The warm water felt so good to his cold body. He wanted to stay under the scalding spray, but Ariel needed him.

Carefully, he got out and dried off, then changed into a pair of basketball shorts and a T-shirt before making his way back to Ariel's room.

Elise smoothed her hand over Ariel's cheek before coming to join him in the hall. "She's got a fever of one hundred and three. I didn't give her any fever reducer yet; I called your mom when I couldn't get a hold of you, and she said to wait unless Ariel got to one oh four or was uncomfortable, said that she usually ran high for fevers?"

He nodded and winced, the pain in his neck intensifying. "Yeah, you did great. Thank—" Roman clapped his hand over his mouth. He ran to the closest bathroom and emptied his guts into the toilet.

Chills raced over his skin as he sunk to his knees. Roman was so cold, but he couldn't get the energy to stand back up and clean himself. He slumped to the ground.

"Are you okay?" Elise's soft voice had him shaking his

head and attempting to hold out his hand but it fell to the floor.

"Don't come in here. Stay away so you don't catch this."

The sink ran a moment before a cool cloth pressed against his forehead. Damn, it felt heavenly. It was the only reprieve from the rolling nausea and pain in his guts.

"I've already been exposed with Ariel. Let me help you." Her calm but firm voice settled over him, and he was too weak to protest.

He heaved into the toilet again before slumping back down onto his ass. She flushed the toilet and wiped the cloth over his mouth. She shouldn't be doing this, but he didn't even have the energy to refuse.

"Do you think you're done?" she asked.

"Yeah."

She handed him a cup of mouthwash. He swished his mouth and spat it into the toilet before doing it once more. Elise gave him a dry cloth to wipe his mouth before she looped her arm under his. He used his remaining strength to get to his feet. Even with his sick-addled brain, the soft scent of something sweet wafted over him like jasmine flowers. Her body pressed against his was sending all sorts of sensations rippling through him, and if he wasn't sick as a dog, he might have been able to make sense of them.

"I just need a minute and then I'll check on Ariel," he mumbled as she led him to his bed.

"I'll worry about her. You need to rest." Elise carefully helped him recline in the bed and covered him up.

He caught her hand. "Elise?"

"Yes?"

He swallowed. "Thank you."

Her full lips turned up. "Of course. I'll bring you some tea."

She turned and left, her hand slipping from his. He rolled onto his side, curling up in the fetal position. His stomach cramped until all he could do was close his eyes and hope it passed quickly.

13

ELISE

Elise smoothed the cool cloth over Ariel's forehead one last time before filling a spoon full of tea and offering it to her. "Try another sip."

Ariel obliged, sitting up on the bed enough to drink some of it down. Her stomach gurgled.

"Do you feel like you might throw up again?" Elise reached for the bowl beside the bed.

"*No. I think I'm hungry,*" Ariel signed.

Elise smiled. "That's a good sign. I'll grab you some crackers and make some soup. I'll go check on your dad real quick and be back. If you need me, just ring this bell, okay?"

Ariel traced her finger over the top of the little bell Elise had found in her toy baskets with other musical instruments. "*Okay.*" Ariel snuggled into her pillow, her glassy eyes staring at the iPad next to the bed.

Elise stood, staying still as a wave of nausea swirled in her belly. She swallowed and steadied herself. She couldn't afford to get sick. Not right now. She made her way to Roman's bedroom and walked inside without hesitation.

"Roman?"

He still looked a bit grey but he seemed better than he was when she'd last checked his temperature and brought him a sip of Gatorade. He'd been asleep since yesterday afternoon.

She picked up the cup she'd left by his bedside, noting it was empty, which meant he'd woken at some point to drink the ginger tea. She collected the mug and headed towards the kitchen. She boiled water for more tea and started a stockpot with water and dashi for the one recipe her mother made every time someone in the house was sick—miso soup. Mrs. Emerson had been kind enough to drop off the groceries for her.

Elise's body ached, and exhaustion sunk into every cell. She wrapped her sweater closer around her and stirred the pot before adding more shredded ginger, chopped green onions, and minced garlic—her own embellishments. After adding the rest of the ingredients, she made Ariel and Roman more tea.

She found Ariel asleep, the tablet still playing her show beside her. Elise set her fresh tea by her bed, shut the tablet off, and pulled her covers up. Next, she went back to Roman's room, replacing the tea on the small table beside his bed.

"Is Ariel okay?" he asked, his voice hoarse.

Elise offered him a small smile. "She's sleeping again. But she's ready for some food."

Roman moved his arms as if trying to sit up, but Elise settled her hand over his chest. "You should rest."

"I need to check on her," he argued weakly.

"She's doing great. Her fever broke this morning. She hasn't thrown up since then. There isn't anything you can do for her now that she's sleeping." She set down the mug on the table beside the bed. "Here, I brought you more tea."

A warm hand encircled her wrist. She looked down at their connection and then back to him.

"Thank you," he said.

"Of course." She stood. "I'm going to get some soup ready. When you're up for it, let me know."

Elise went back to the kitchen and turned off the stove. When Ariel woke, she'd have something warm and comforting to eat.

Elise turned away and sneezed twice into her elbow. Pressure built behind her watery eyes. She fought to keep them open. She made her way to Ariel's room as her stomach dropped, and the urge to throw up made her run to the bathroom. She vomited until there was nothing left. Shaking, she brushed her teeth and cleaned out her mouth. *Oh, God, no. They need me. I can't get sick.*

The chime of the bell from Ariel's room called her. She blew her nose quickly and went into the little girl's room.

Ariel sat up, reaching for her. Elise wrapped her arms around her and then Ariel's little body lurched and hot liquid poured down her back. Elise grimaced.

Ariel started crying. She soothed her. "It's okay. I've got you."

Elise stripped her shirt off, dropping it in the bowl before she picked up Ariel and carried her to the bathroom. Elise stripped her down and started the shower, then took out her own CI and set it on the counter. Elise kept her bra and underwear on as she stepped under the hot spray with Ariel still in her arms. It took all her remaining effort to clean them both up, get them toweled off, and into fresh clothes again.

By the time they made it back to the bed, Ariel was asleep once more. Elise put another sweatshirt on and climbed into bed next to her so that if Ariel needed her, she would be right there. She put her CI back on despite the headache, just in case Roman called out for her. *Maybe I'll take a little nap while*

Ariel sleeps and then get her some soup and crackers. Her stomach churned at the idea of food.

Elise closed her eyes and snuggled against the warmth of Ariel, giving in to the exhaustion. Dreams came in vivid flashes. None of them made sense.

A cool hand smoothed against her forehead, sending tingles of relaxation through her throbbing head. She shivered and curled tighter into a ball. The caresses continued, lulling her into a deeper sense of comfort despite the bone-deep aches in her body.

Roman cursed. Her forehead wrinkled. Why was he in her dream?

"You're burning up, honey."

Elise was definitely dreaming, because Roman would never call her something sweet like that. He didn't like her—more like put up with her. But she had to admit, this dream version of him was nice. Images of Roman without a shirt on flashed front and center in her mind.

"You're so hot," he said.

She giggled—fucking giggled in her dream. "Really? That's the best line you can come up with? I'm disappointed."

"Elise?"

"Hmm?"

"You're too fucking cute when you're delusional."

He thought she was cute? And delusional . . . ahh, even in her dreams he was a grumpy asshole.

"You know I really don't mind you being grumpy in my dreams, but in real life, you're a jerk sometimes."

Roman didn't say anything back for a minute. Darkness clouded the edges of her mind. No, she wanted to hold onto this dream just a little longer. If he was a figment of her imagination, she should at least get the right to lick over those defined abs that she couldn't stop thinking about.

"Elise . . ." His voice came out all gravelly.

Yes, that was what she was talking about. "Just one lick."

He let out a strangled sound and then he disappeared. Maybe it was for the best. If she knew what dream Roman tasted like, felt like against her skin, she might have a real issue looking the real Roman in the eyes and dealing with his dislike for her.

Elise snuggled into the pillow. She just needed to sleep a little longer and then she'd get up and check on Ariel and Roman again. Just five more minutes.

14

ROMAN

What exactly did she want to lick? His mind conjured up a whole host of thoughts, none of which were appropriate for an employer to have about his nanny. Christ, she was burning up though. She was covered in sweat, soaking through Ariel's sheets. He couldn't leave Elise like that.

He checked on Ariel who was curled up on the couch watching cartoons, feeling better enough for that at least. Then he carried his T-shirt back into Ariel's room for Elise. It would be too invasive to go through her things—sick or not. She'd taken care of both his child and him with such delicate kindness, even after he'd treated her so callously since she'd been there. He owed her more than an apology—owed her his gratitude. The least he could do was take care of her like she'd done for them.

"Elise?" He gently nudged her shoulder.

She moaned.

"Come on, honey. We got to get you out of these wet clothes."

"Too tired," she answered without opening her eyes.

"I know, but I need you to get up so I can change the sheets too . . . Elise?"

"Mmmm."

She was so out of it but he couldn't let her stay like this.

"Elise, if you don't wake up and help me, I'm going to have to help change you. Can you wake up just for a minute?" he pleaded.

She let out a pitiful whine that broke his heart. He took a deep breath, pulling down her sweat-soaked blanket. She shivered and curled up into a ball, looking so vulnerable. Everything inside him screamed to take care of her, protect her.

"I'm going to take off your shirt first, but I promise I won't look." He pulled the hem of her shirt, averting his eyes to her face as he tugged the fabric up and over her head, plucking her arms through. He grabbed his T-shirt, slipping her hands in one at a time, taking care to be gentle as he lifted her head and tugged it down. The T-shirt came to the top of her thighs. Next, he slipped his arms under her, picking her up and cradling her against his chest. He was still much weaker than usual, but damn, her body felt amazing against his in this way. She fit perfectly. He carried her to her bedroom and laid her on the clean sheets.

Elise clung to his shirt, nuzzling into his chest like she didn't want him to leave her.

"It's okay, honey." He pulled the comforter over her, tucking Elise in and removing her CI, setting it beside the bed on the small table.

He smoothed his hand over her clammy head. She seemed a bit cooler now. Perhaps the fever had broken.

She leaned into his palm, kissing her lips to the calloused side of his hand. Roman froze, afraid if he moved, she'd wake and realize what she'd done—but also not wanting to let go. *She's just delusional with fever.* That was all this was.

"Elise?"

His only answer was the even rise and fall of her chest. She was asleep once more.

Carefully, he slipped his hand out from her hold, giving her one last, lingering glance before he got as far away from that room as possible. His hand trembled as he stared at the spot she'd pressed her mouth to. He brought his palm to his nose and inhaled, searching for any trace of her scent. It was faint, but it was there. His cock twitched. Roman raked his hands down his face.

"What the fuck am I doing?" *And why do I want more?*

* * *

The next afternoon, Roman made his way to the living room where Ariel was curled up on the couch watching cartoons again. He brushed his hand over her forehead. Thankfully, her fever was gone. She nibbled on the cracker in her hand.

"You feeling better?" he asked.

She nodded.

"I'm going to go check on Elise. Be right back." He went into the kitchen and scooped some of the delicious homemade soup he'd found into a bowl. Roman grabbed a spoon before heading towards Elise's room.

She lay still, her skin paler than usual other than her rosy cheeks. He set the soup down beside the bed on a small table. Brushing her limp hair from her face, he then tucked it behind her ear. Elise stirred, leaning into his touch. She was still warm, but her fever hadn't returned.

"Elise, honey?" he asked aloud, even though she wouldn't

hear him without her CI in, and he gently nudged her shoulder.

"Mmm." She stirred again, blinking her glassy eyes open. "Roman?"

"Can you sit up and drink a little soup?" he asked.

Slowly, she sat up, the blankets falling and revealing his T-shirt on her. The sight of her wearing something of his woke the possessive side of him. He pushed it away. *She's not mine.* He sat beside her on the bed and grabbed the soup, filling the spoon with the rich broth.

She reached for her CI and slipped it on. "I can feed myself."

He lifted the spoon to her lips. "Let me take care of you. It's the least I can do after what you did for me—for us."

Her pink lips parted, and he slipped the spoon between them. She drank down the broth, her eyes locked on his. He fed her a few more mouthfuls in silence.

"Did you make this soup?" he asked, trying for small talk.

"Yes. It's something my mother used to make. I added a few extra things to help boost immune systems."

"You learned how to take care of the sick from her?"

She paused, licking her lips. "No. I've never had anyone take care of me like this."

He searched her eyes, his heart breaking for her. "What about when you were a child?" *Or your boyfriend?*

She swallowed and looked down at the spoon rather than at him. "I didn't live with my parents. I went to a boarding school for the Deaf. They had a school nurse, but she didn't have much of a bedside manner."

Elise had been alone? No one to hold her hand, or wipe her forehead, or bring her tea? "Elise . . ."

A forced smile moved her lips. "How is Ariel?"

She didn't like to talk about herself; that much was obvious.

"She's better. Liked your soup."

"Good."

A knock pulled his attention away from her. "I better get that." He stood, setting the bowl by the bed before heading into the living room.

His mother walked in the door. "You're looking better."

His brows furrowed. "What do you mean?"

"I stopped by two days ago and you looked like death run over. How's my baby?" She moved to the couch to give Ariel a hug and kiss.

"We're both better thanks to Elise."

"Yes, I offered to stay and help but she assured me you were both in good hands and wanted to make sure I didn't get sick before our trip. A real sweetheart, that one." His mother gave him a knowing look.

"Oh, there she is. Did I get all the ingredients you needed for that soup?" his mom asked.

Elise walked down the stairs slowly, now in a pair of yoga pants and one of her T-shirts. "Yes. I had everything I needed. Thank you."

"No, thank you, dear."

"I didn't want you to have to cancel your trip." Elise stopped at the bottom of the stairs, her chest heaving as if it had taken all her effort to descend them. Roman reached out to her, placing one hand on her lower back and the other to grip her arm, steadying her as she made her way to the barstool in the kitchen. He wanted to pick her up and carry her, but she probably wouldn't appreciate that.

"Thanks."

"Of course. Do you want some more soup? Crackers? Tea?" he asked.

"Yes, but I can get it myself." She moved to stand, but he held her in place.

"No. You sit right here. I'll get it." Roman walked around to the kitchen, feeling his mother's eyes on him as he filled another bowl of soup and placed it in front of her.

"Thanks." She grabbed the spoon, stirring the steaming bowl. Elise turned to his mom. "When do you leave exactly?"

His mom leaned against the counter. "Next Monday. We'll be gone for five weeks to tour most of Europe."

"That sounds so fun. I hope you enjoy yourselves. You'll have to take lots of pictures."

Roman set a package of crackers in front of Elise. He wanted to know more about her. "Have you ever traveled outside the country?"

She sipped her soup. "I've gone to Japan a few times to visit family."

"Oh, Asia is next on our list. But it took us twenty years to plan this one. I may be too old by then." His mom laughed. "Well, I'll leave you to it. Make sure this one rests." She pointed to Elise. "And call me if you need anything."

After giving Ariel a hug and kiss goodbye, his mom saw herself out.

"Ginger or mint tea?" Roman asked.

"Ginger, but I can get it myself."

"No." His tone was firm, the same one he used when he meant business with Ariel.

Elise blinked at him.

Roman took in her greasy hair, pulled up haphazardly in a messy bun. Her pale skin had regained some of its color but not much. Dark half-moons under her eyes accentuated how much she'd exhausted herself taking care of them while she too was sick. Still, she was breathtaking.

He leaned in, tracing his finger over her forehead to one

of the stubborn threads of hair that kept falling close to her dark brown eyes. He tucked it gently behind her ear. Fuck, her skin was soft. Elise shivered, her dull gaze flashing with heat.

Reluctantly, he pulled his hand back. "It's my turn to take care of you."

15

ELISE

lise tipped her head back as a warm summer breeze blew over her. A strip of fading orange sunlight shone over her toes on the porch. Large maple trees swayed in the wind and birds sang. Goddamn, it was good to feel human again. Her phone vibrated on the papers in her lap. She picked it up.

Sam: *You coming over this weekend?*

Elise: *Not feeling 100 percent yet. I think I'll stay here.*

Sam: *You need anything, let me know. Okay?*

Elise: *Will do.*

The screen door creaked open and footsteps followed.

Sam: *You're a bad liar even over text.*

She chuckled.

Elise: *I don't know what you're talking about.*

A steaming cup of tea was set on the small table beside her.

"Oh, thank you." She looked up as Roman walked to the front of the porch in front of her and leaned against the railing. One hand gripped the guard behind him, his forearm flexing and enhancing a few spiraling veins. Her attention dragged to his wide chest, flicked down to the long athletic shorts hanging low on his hips before darting back to his face.

He gave a quick nod, his gaze traveling from her feet and up her bare legs, lingering a moment before skimming to her face. Her skin flushed hot. Was he checking her out too?

"Are you going to your boyfriend's this weekend?"

"My—who?"

"Your boyfriend. The guy from last weekend."

"Jack?" She burst out laughing. "Oh, he would get a kick out of that. No, Jack's my best friend, and he has a boyfriend, Sam. I did stay with them last weekend, but I figured I'd stick around this time. I'll keep to myself though, make sure I'm out of your way." She sat up straighter, focusing on the curriculum in her lap.

He sighed. "I think we got off on the wrong foot."

She looked up at him warily.

"I was unkind and not as welcoming as I should have been. I might have overreacted a time or two . . ."

"Or more," she said.

The side of his mouth turned up for a fraction of a second. Roman squeezed the back of his neck in a self-conscious gesture. It was endearing. "What do you say to starting over?"

"I think I'd like that."

"Great. So . . . I don't want you feeling like when I'm home you have to become invisible. I—I mean we'd love it if you joined us for dinner. And don't feel like you have to disappear every weekend—unless you want to."

"Okay. Thank you."

His shoulders sagged in what seemed to be relief as a smile curved the corners of his lips, one side higher than the other. And holy fuck, he had dimples. How had she not noticed them before? Dimples were her weakness. She was totally fucked.

"So, why a teacher?" he asked.

"Well, when I was all alone at a new school and didn't know anyone, not to mention struggling with learning a new language, I had one teacher, Mrs. Garvey, who made all the difference. Cliché, I know, but I wanted to be the kind of guide she was for a student someday. I don't know if I would have survived that first year without her—at least not as well as I did."

"Your parents weren't there at all?"

She blinked and picked up the mug, took a sip to buy herself some time. "It's gonna take something a little harder than tea to get me to open up and spill all my guts to you."

Those all too perceptive brown eyes didn't move from hers, as if he stared hard enough, he'd find the answers for himself.

"Why a beekeeper?" she asked him in return.

"I was never one for the corporate world or a nine-to-five. I like being outside, using my hands."

Her attention dropped to his calloused palms. *And I just bet you're good with them too.*

He cleared his throat. Her gaze snapped to his and the corner of his mouth lifted like he knew exactly where her thoughts had gone. Her cheeks burned hot.

"I went to college—which was mandatory, according to my parents, despite me having dyslexia."

Wait, what? Roman was dyslexic? Everything clicked into place. "That's why you didn't want me to leave you a hand-written note that day at the pond?"

He swallowed, his eyes darting to the porch while he nodded. "Anyways, Ricky and I started our own company. Dad and Mom gave us a graduation gift that served as our initial investment. We were able to buy out a local beekeeper and start from there. At first, we worked on the farm, too, in order to pay the bills. But our business grew and soon we were selling queens, honey, beeswax candles, and propolis, and now we have more orders than honey rolling in."

"That's amazing. But how did you get into it?"

He chuckled. "Well now, that is a story."

"I'm all ears." She smiled, setting her tea down and giving him her undivided attention.

"Ricky and I were four-wheeling and went off trail. The neighbors have a field that's in the lower valley and in the spring it turns into a giant mud pit. Well, of course we couldn't resist." His smile grew.

"That actually sounds like fun. I can see where Ariel gets her mischievous side from."

He laughed. "Yeah, we had a blast, covered head to toe in mud. We raced at one point and ended up knocking over a few of the hives at the edge of the field. Bees went crazy— stung us so many times. The farmer heard us hollering and came out."

She giggled, imagining the two men soaked in mud and fleeing a swarm of insects hell-bent on chasing them.

"Laugh all you want but those fuckers hurt when it's a swarm like that."

"I'm sorry." She covered her mouth.

His grin grew wider, showing off those dimples again. "Nah, I can laugh now. So the beekeeper was contacted by the farmer and my parents were called. Dad suggested we work for the beekeeper to pay for the damage. And we ended up finding we liked it. There was a lot of cool things to learn. Like, did you know male honeybees don't have a stinger?"

"No, I didn't."

"You could hold one. And the worker bees are all female.

The males are only around to mate with the queen, and in the process it ends up killing the drones—the male bees."

"Damn, that seems a cold way to end a one-night stand."

He chuckled and shrugged. "That's the world of honey bees."

He was so different like this. Carefree and relaxed. Talking and joking with her like they were friends. He'd taken care of her when she was sick. Brought her tea and made an effort to make up for their rough start. Those actions spoke so much more than any words ever could.

He cleared his throat. "You're doing a great job with Ariel. She told me how much fun you had today when I put her to bed."

"Ariel's a special girl. I think it'll be an easy adjustment when she's going to school this fall. You've raised an amazing little human."

He crossed his arms over his chest, the snug material pulling tighter. "Honestly, I have no idea what I'm doing most of the time."

"I've worked with a lot of parents and none of them did either."

He just stared at her in silence. Had she said something wrong?

"No one but family has ever watched her. I know I must seem like I'm overprotective, but I failed her once and I can't afford to again." His voice came out hoarse and so defeated.

She studied him, the tension in his shoulders and the guilt in his expression. "If you don't mind me asking, what do you mean you failed her?"

A flash of pain streaked through his brown eyes before he hung his head.

"I'm sorry. You don't have to—"

"My wife died of a brain aneurysm. One day everything was great, and the next, she was gone."

Oh, how awful. Elise's heart broke for both Roman and Ariel. To lose someone they loved so suddenly must have been traumatic.

"I'm so sorry, Roman. That you all had to go through that." She stood, unable to stop herself from walking to him.

"It was years ago. I've made my peace with it. But for Ariel to grow up without a mother . . . What if I could have been there and changed what happened?"

"You blame yourself."

He scoffed. "Who else is to blame?"

She gripped his fist in her hand. He sucked in a breath as she softly pried his fingers open and slipped her palm against his. "I may not know what it's like to go through what you and Ariel have. But I do know it's not your fault. Neither Ariel nor your wife would blame you. You came home and dealt with the tragedy the best you could. You've raised a brilliant and creative little girl who knows she's loved and cared for."

His chest heaved as he stared into her eyes, holding her captive. This should have been a moment about providing him comfort, but it was quickly morphing into something else. Something she had no business getting involved in.

She stepped back, pulling her hand away like it was on fire, her gaze darting to the ground before she turned and gathered up her papers.

"Elise—"

"I was going to make homemade pizza for dinner tomorrow. What do you think about that?" There, she just needed to stick to safe topics. Not hold her boss's hand, damn it.

"Uh, we can order out. You don't have to cook every night."

"Oh, it's no problem. I enjoy cooking. Plus, it's part of

what you pay me for." Right, she just needed to remind him that she was his employee. Keep those lines drawn for both their sakes.

"If you really want to."

"Yes, absolutely. Okay, well, right. I'll just, uh, go to bed I think. It's been a long day and I should . . . go." Elise scooped up her things, grabbed the mug of tea, and darted inside the house, not stopping until she was safely in the confines of her room.

With her heart racing, she set her things down and pressed her hand against her chest. *What the fuck was I thinking?*

But that was the problem. She hadn't been thinking. She'd been feeling—a whole lot of emotions that were not going to get her anywhere but another broken heart.

16

ELISE

Elise sipped her lemonade at the kitchen table as Roman dragged his fingers through Ariel's hair, leaving streaks of white product behind. He'd been tending to his daughter's hair with such care, she couldn't look away. Roman loved his daughter with everything in him. That little girl was the center of his universe.

What would it be like to have someone look at me that way? To have those dark eyes lock on her with even half that affection? She blinked, trying to clear the unwanted thoughts, and took another sip of her chilled drink. It was sure going to be a hot day.

"How about braids?" Roman asked, grabbing a rat-tail comb before he began separating her hair into sections.

"Can I have these too?" Ariel picked up a few colorful flower clips from the bin of hair accessories in front of her.

"Sure."

Ariel looked to Elise, setting her iPad on the table. *"How come you don't braid your hair?"*

"Oh, well, my hair texture is a little different than yours.

I'm not sure it would hold the same way. And certain hair-styles are only for people from that culture to wear."

"*Like my box braids?*" Ariel asked.

Elise smiled. "Absolutely."

Ariel reached out, grabbing a strand of Elise's dark hair. "*Your hair is so straight.*"

"And yours is full of beautiful curls."

Ariel grinned, showing off her missing teeth. "*Are you excited to go to the beach?*"

Elise set her drink down, signing as she spoke. "Oh, I'm not going. Today's just you and your dad."

Ariel turned towards her father. "*We can't leave her here, Daddy. She's going to help me find a mermaid.*"

"We don't want to intrude on Elise's time off." He glanced at her.

A sliver of disappointment settled in Elise's gut. But it was probably for the best that she didn't spend any more time with him than she had to.

"But if you wanted to, we'd be more than happy to have you tag along," he added focused on Ariel's hair.

Elise swallowed. "Um, I . . ."

"I could show you where we usually go so sometime you can take her on your own while I'm working."

That was a big step from his wish that they stay on the farm. "Okay, I mean, if you're sure. I wouldn't want to be in the way of your time together."

"*Yay! We can find mermaids and shells.*" Ariel clapped.

"I'm just doing her hair, and then I'll pack the cooler and the car and we can go." Roman weaved his hands together, braiding Ariel's hair much faster than Elise thought possible.

"I'll get ready and come help." Elise got up and headed to her room.

A day in the sun and sand sounded heavenly. And the fact

that she'd get to see that six-pack of abs he had certainly had nothing to do with the pep in her step. Nope. Nothing at all.

* * *

Seagulls flew overhead, casting curved shadows over the hot sand. Several families and beachgoers were set up on the tan coast. Waves crashed, and kids laughed as they bobbed up and down in the blueish-green waters. The sun beat down on them. Sweat trickled down Elise's temple.

Roman led them in a line, Ariel between them, to an open spot where the hot sand met a rock wall. Being tall had some advantages; Elise could make out several kids digging in tide pools, pulling out crabs and shells.

"Here should be good." Roman set down their cooler before pulling the sand-toy bag from his arm and setting it down. He got to work setting up beach chairs and laying out a blanket.

Elise looked at the umbrella in her arms, trying to figure out how exactly to set it up.

Roman stripped off his shirt, his dark umber skin glistening under the sun. Her mouth went as dry as the sand beneath her feet. He wiped his forearm over his brow before reaching for the object in her arms.

"I got it." He took the umbrella and pushed the giant screw-like end into the sand, his muscles flexing as he twisted and buried it. A flash of heat scorched her body that had nothing to do with the hot sun shining on her. If she'd thought it was boiling out here before, she'd been wrong. Her attention was glued to the flex of his back as his muscles contracted. She couldn't look away. So what if she couldn't have him? A girl could admire a beautiful, godlike man, couldn't she?

A small hand grasped hers, pulling her attention away.

"*Will you go in the water with me?*" Ariel asked.

Cooling off was a brilliant idea. "Yes!" she agreed, too enthusiastically. She tugged her shirt over her head and tossed it onto one of the beach chairs before taking off her ripped jean shorts and doing the same. Her skin prickled as she straightened.

Roman's gaze roamed over her skin like a hot caress. His jaw tightened as a frown marred his marble-like features. Was he not happy with her body? Or was he one of those people that didn't think women should wear a bikini unless they were a size zero? Well, too bad. This was her body and she wasn't ashamed of the extra jiggle in her dimpled ass, the dips in her hips, or the thickness of her muscular thighs. She was six feet tall, for Christ's sake. She had curves and a bit of a belly.

She lifted her chin defiantly. "Is something wrong?"

Roman's gaze jumped to hers, his nose flaring. "Nope. Nothing at all. I'm going to stay here for a few minutes—uh, finish setting up. I'll join you guys in the water in a second." He took a seat, grabbing the beach bag and setting it in his lap as he rifled through it.

Ariel handed her puddle jumper over to Elise. Elise helped her slip her arms in and buckle it.

"Hold on one second. I need to put some sunscreen on us." She grabbed the spray bottle and made quick work of Ariel and then herself.

"Um, would you mind getting my back?" She held out the canister to Roman.

He gritted his teeth.

She pulled it back. "It's okay, I can probably just—"

He stood, grabbing it out of her hand before gruffly ordering, "Turn around."

She did as he said, wanting to get this over with and move

away from the situation. The cool sunscreen sprayed over her back.

"Shit," he cursed.

"What?"

"I got it too thick in one spot."

She wanted to ask him to rub it in, but something about the request seemed too intimate. "It's fine—"

His warm hand landed on her lower back, smoothing the slick substance over the back of her rib cage. Tingles raced through her nerve endings, multiplying and spreading into a wave of arousal. She couldn't hold back the shiver that rocked through her at the connection.

His touch grew firmer. She bit her lip as he continued rubbing her back. God, this was torture.

"It's all rubbed in. Let's go." Ariel wiggled impatiently.

But Roman's hand didn't stop. In fact, he moved over the tie to her upper shoulders.

"Let's go!" Ariel pouted.

Roman's hands stopped at once. He cleared his throat, but his voice still came out hoarse. "Right, all done."

Elise risked a peek at him. His hazy brown eyes seemed almost black with lust—but that couldn't be. Maybe she was projecting what she was feeling onto him?

She took Ariel's hand. "Thanks."

She jogged to the beach with Ariel keeping up with her until the frigid waters of the New Hampshire ocean sent daggers of ice shocking her system.

She gasped and jumped out of the water. "Holy sh—oot! That's freezing."

Ariel smiled and walked in farther like the arctic temperatures had no effect on her little body.

"It doesn't bother me. I'm a mermaid." She splashed some water at Elise.

"You little stinker. No splashing me or I might turn into a popsicle, then who will look for mermaids with you?"

"Daddy will." Ariel pointed.

"I see how it is. Traitor," Elise teased.

Roman walked into the receding wave and hissed, "It's freezing."

"That's what I told her."

He didn't stop though. He continued into the icy waters until he was waist-deep and dove in. Ariel followed him. He rose from the ocean, water dripping down his body as he slid his hand over his face and shook his head. Waves rolling in made his hips jerk forward and his abs flex from the force. Her mouth went dry.

Elise took a few steps into the sea, needing to cool off after that vision. Coming with them might have been a bad idea. At least she was at the beach, and if anyone saw the wet spot on her pink bikini bottoms, they'd assume it was because of the ocean, right?

Roman and Ariel played in the water for a little while longer before they made their way back to shore. They searched for sea glass and unique shells for more than an hour, stopping by the tide pools.

Roman pulled a crab from under a rock and held it out to Ariel. "Go ahead and touch it."

"What do I get if I do?" Ariel asked.

Roman shook his head with a smile. "You get the joy of trying something scary and accomplishing it."

Ariel tipped her head to the side and raised an eyebrow.

"How about ice cream after lunch?" Roman chuckled.

The little girl held one finger out, high above the crab, and slowly moved close enough to touch the top of the shell and pull her hand away. Roman laughed and offered it to Elise.

"No, thanks. I don't want to get pinched."

"You won't if you hold it right," he insisted. "Grab it from the back."

"What do I get if I do?" she teased.

His gaze dropped to her mouth. "What?"

"Sorry. I was just teasing." Tentatively, she reached for the back of the crab, then pulled her hand away when it moved.

"It's not going anywhere. Besides, the pincers are so small it would barely hurt," he said.

The shell was cold and rough against her fingers as she gripped the crustacean.

"There you go." He let it go. "You got—"

It moved its legs and Elise screeched, dropping it into the sand and gripping his arm for dear life. Roman's deep laughter barreled out of him, stunning and unexpected.

The crab quickly recovered and crawled into the nearest tide pool, traumatized enough for one afternoon.

"Can you stop laughing?" She swatted his arm playfully.

Roman was laughing so hard now, he bent over at the waist. She rolled her eyes and crossed her arms, feigning annoyance. But that deep rumble coming from his chest had her smiling too. "I almost became crab food and you think it's funny? I see how it is."

Roman stood, wiping the tears from his eyes. He cleared his throat. "Crab food," he mumbled and shook his head. "Okay, for that I guess you do deserve something."

"I mean, I did totally risk my life. I don't remember crab-wrangling in the job description."

"Crab-wrangling?" A bark of laughter escaped him again as he clutched his impossibly perfect abs.

"*Two ice creams!*" Ariel agreed.

"What do you say? What was that worth?" Roman asked her, his eyes lit up with mirth.

Elise tapped her lips, noting the way his eyes tracked her movements. "I think I should get to bury you in sand."

He tipped his head back and sighed. Ariel clapped her hands and jumped up and down signing, *"Yes!"* in agreement.

"Fine." Roman led the way back to their setup, dutifully lying down as Elise and Ariel got to work. Thankfully, Ariel's sand toys included some pretty durable shovels. They covered him from his toes to his neck all while he lay there with a smile on his face.

Elise packed the sand carefully over his neck. "I think that should about do it."

A tinkling sound filled the beach.

"The ice cream truck is here!" Ariel jumped to her feet.

"You've got to unbury me so I can get up and get my wallet," Roman said.

Elise looked at him and smiled smugly. "Or we could leave you here for the crabs you love so much."

His eyes widened. "You wouldn't." He turned to Ariel. "Help me out of here."

Ariel shook her head. *"No way."*

"Betrayed by my own daughter. See if I buy you any more ice cream," he teased.

Elise grabbed Ariel's hand and then her wallet from the beach bag. "Come on, before the sand monster escapes. Let's get the biggest ice cream they have." She laughed as they ran towards the line forming at the ice cream truck.

A few minutes later, Roman grabbed Ariel from behind, pulling her against his soaking-wet body as she playfully pushed him away. He lifted her above his head, tossing her in the air and catching her.

"You thought you could be rid of me, but I will always come for you, little girl." He added an evil laugh at the end of his statement like he truly was a villain before setting her on his shoulders.

"And you." Roman locked eyes with Elise, saltwater dripping from the dark mass of curls on his head. "You deserve a spanking."

Did he just—? Her mouth hung open. Fuck, that was hot—*no*. She couldn't go there. Not with him

She'd just gotten onto better terms with Roman. She couldn't do anything to jeopardize this job—or her heart.

17

ROMAN

She's the nanny. Off-limits. Roman reminded himself as his traitorous eyes strayed for the millionth time to that hot-pink bikini that put all Elise's luscious inked curves on display. There was something about a woman who was confident in her own skin. Elise was all that and more. Her head tipped back as she laughed at something Ariel signed, her eyes glittering with happiness. Her breasts jiggled with the movement. A sheen of sweat covered her skin, speckled with bits of sand. His focus snapped up to her face. *Why is it so hard to keep my damn eyes off her?*

He'd taken no interest in a woman since his wife had passed. He'd shared something special with Tiana—and he'd never envisioned himself finding that again. Roman hadn't called off all chance of a future with a woman. Not like his brother Nash had done. But Ariel had been his sole focus. She didn't need anyone else coming into her life who could potentially leave her—whether by choice or not. He couldn't let her get hurt like that again. And if he started seeing someone, Ariel would be sure to get attached. But Roman hadn't expected someone like Elise. Nor had he expected the way his body reacted to her.

"The eyes are bubble gum," Ariel signed, her lips blue from the candy embedded into her treat. Her chin was covered in melted ice cream.

"Yum," Elise agreed, her pink tongue darting out to lick the frozen treat dripping down her fingers.

Roman couldn't look away as she licked her lips, his own dessert now forgotten. Elise's tongue swirled around the ice cream, twisting before she stuck the end in her mouth, closing her lush lips around the tip. He couldn't stop the fantasy that played through his head. Elise down on her knees, tearing off that flimsy excuse for a bathing suit. Her luscious breasts on display. Those full lips sliding over his cock as she teased her nipple.

Ariel's small hand tapped his arm, yanking him from the forbidden fantasy. He turned to her, forcing his eyes away from Elise.

"Are you okay?" Ariel asked.

He forced what he hoped was an easy smile. "Yeah, I'm great. Why?"

"You won't stop staring at Elise with your growly face."

He met Elise's eyes quickly before focusing on his daughter. "I'm just hot."

"Maybe we should finish our ice creams and race to the water?" Elise suggested.

Ariel's eyes lit up as she nodded and took another bite of her dessert.

"So, are you familiar with the beaches around here?" Roman asked, trying to get into safer topics.

"Yes. I grew up in Dark Cove, so when I was home for summer break, sometimes I'd come down here." Elise finished her treat and used napkins to clean her hands.

"Does your family still live nearby?"

She nodded. "My brother works in the city, and my parents live in the same house. But most of my extended family is in Japan. My parents are first-generation immigrants."

"So you speak the language?" *Maybe she could teach Ariel some?*

Elise's gaze shuttered, the light that was in them moments ago dimming. "A little."

"Did I just put my foot in my mouth?" What had he said? They'd been having such a good day. He didn't want to ruin it.

She shook her head and smiled but it didn't reach her eyes. "No, it's nothing. Really."

"It doesn't seem like nothing," he pressed.

She stared at the ocean to the side before turning back to him. "Tonal languages are not easy to learn for someone with a cochlear implant. We have trouble with pitch and the tone ranges. So it makes it difficult to speak and understand."

"Oh, well, that makes sense. I'm sorry." Maybe she felt like she was missing out on a piece of her culture? "At least sign language can help bridge that gap with your family."

Elise's forced smile flattened as pain flashed in her gaze. *Fuck.* He'd only been trying to make conversation. What was that about? And why did it make his chest tight?

"Last one to the water is a rotten egg!" Elise got up and jogged toward the beach before he could ask more. Her ass jiggled, her hips swaying with each step. Fuck, she was gorgeous.

Ariel, now done with her treat, ran after her. Roman grabbed the leftover napkins and popsicle sticks, then threw them in the trash before he met up with them at the water's edge.

"You're a stinky rotten egg, Daddy!"

He smiled and sighed, taking Ariel's hand. "So I am. Let's go cool off."

He got a few steps in and turned back. Elise was still at the shoreline, dipping her toes in, arms crossed under her breasts.

Roman turned towards Ariel and leaned down. "What do you say we drag Elise in here with us?"

Ariel smiled and nodded emphatically.

"Okay, but we got to be smart about this and work together. Can you do that?"

"Yes!"

He bent lower, whispering the rest of his plan to her. Ariel gave him a conspiratorial smirk before they both waded through the water towards their target. Roman hung back a little bit, giving Ariel time to complete step one. Sure enough, Elise smiled and nodded, taking out her CI and handing it over to his daughter while Ariel pretended to be curious about her device. He wouldn't want to ruin it with what he'd planned next.

Roman stepped beside her. She turned. He couldn't hold back the smug smile as he signed, *"You thought you could leave me buried in sand and I wouldn't retaliate?"*

Her brows drew closer together in question. He wasted no time in scooping her up in his arms. She gasped as her hot skin pressed against his. Taking advantage of her shock, he jogged farther into the water.

"Don't you dare!" She held onto him, her nails digging into his shoulders as she squirmed, trying to get higher away from the freezing water.

Fuck, she felt good against him like this. Soft curves against his hard edges. He laughed. She wouldn't hear him, but she'd definitely feel the vibration humming through his chest.

"Roman!" A big wave crashed over them, but he kept his footing. She screamed as it receded. He glanced at the shore. Ariel was beaming at them and clapping. He let her go, Elise's body sliding down his. Rock-hard nipples skimmed across his chest. Roman's blood heated. Their eyes locked. The shock and outrage in her expression turning to something more wild and needy. In the midst of her warm brown eyes, desire flickered.

His mouth went dry.

Her gaze dropped to his mouth and then back to his eyes. She felt this too.

Like gravity was bearing down on him, he was helpless to stop his head tipping towards hers.

Smack!

A wall of ice-cold water slapped into his back, throwing him against her in a tumble of saltwater and sand. He got his feet under him and stood, searching the water for her. The flash of bright pink under the surface had him reaching down and pulling her up sideways against his chest.

"Fuck! Elise, are you okay?"

She wiped water from her face and then looked at him with an unreadable expression.

Right, she couldn't hear him. He repeated his question this time in sign, still holding her upright.

She looked down. He followed her gaze to his other hand, holding her upright, only it was cupping her breast.

Roman yanked his arm away so fast she stumbled, but Elise quickly righted herself.

Christ, how had this ended with him feeling up his nanny? Fuck, now she was going to quit. This would be so awkward. Why had he thought picking her up and dragging her in here with him was a good idea?

"I'm sorry. I didn't realize . . ."

She blinked at him and then burst into laughter. She held her belly until she laughed so hard no sound came out.

Her joy was contagious. He chuckled too while keeping an eye on Ariel who stayed on the shore, picking up shells and throwing them into the water.

Elise shook her head and wiped her eyes. *"Ariel was in on this, wasn't she?"*

"Of course."

Elise shook her head with a smile, her septum piercing glinting in the sun. *"You better watch your back, Roman. I'll be getting you when you least expect it."*

"Oh, it's on, honey."

They walked back to the beach.

"How about we get some Thai food for dinner?" he suggested.

"Sounds good to me," Elise agreed.

"I'll put the order in." He picked up his phone and pulled open the app.

"I think I need some hot chocolate." She shivered, reaching for her towel. Water dripped from her chin down her breasts. Her nipples poked against the pink fabric of her bikini top. Colorful swirls from her tattoos glinted on her wet skin under the sunlight.

And I might need another dip in the ocean to cool off this persistent hard-on.

Elise accepted the CI that Ariel held out to her and tapped Ariel's nose. "You little traitor. See if I sneak you any more cookies."

Ariel's eyes widened and she shook her head. *"I promise I'll help you get Daddy back."*

Elise's mouth curved up. "Okay, but we have to figure out something really good."

"Okay," Ariel agreed.

"Already plotting against me," he mumbled and shook his head.

Both girls looked at each other and laughed. Ariel slipped her hand into Elise's as they sat side by side in the beach chairs.

Elise was good with his daughter. And Ariel was learning and growing every day. He couldn't afford to mess with that.

He was lucky Elise had laughed off his little slip-up earlier. Roman had come too close to screwing this situation up. He couldn't do that to Ariel. She needed Elise. Roman would just have to keep his hands to himself—starting as soon as he got alone in the shower.

He could swear he wouldn't fantasize about her while he fucked his hand tonight—but he'd be lying.

18

ROMAN

Roman grunted as he lifted the honey-filled hive onto the back of the truck. Damn, it was heavy. The bees were really pulling in a lot thanks to the flower blooms these last couple weeks.

"I was thinking of going out this weekend," Ricky said, setting his work gloves on the truck bed before walking around to adjust the strap holding the boxes of hives down for the drive back to the honey house.

"You go out every weekend." Roman wiped the sweat from his brow.

"Yeah, but I was thinking one of these days I'd see if Elise wanted to come with me."

Anger and a bite of jealousy churned in Roman's gut. "Haven't we been over this?"

"Yeah, you said you thought she had a boyfriend. But I asked her and she said she didn't."

When had Ricky talked to Elise? Something sour twisted in his guts.

"Are you planning on dating her?" Ricky asked.

"No. Of course not," Roman answered too quickly.

"Then I don't see an issue," Ricky argued.

"She's off-limits."

"You sound like Nash did with Bella."

"That's entirely different. She was pregnant with his kid."

Ricky shrugged nonchalantly. "You seem just as territorial."

"I told you why Elise is off—"

"It's a date, Ro."

"And we all know you don't date. You have one-night stands, women you fuck and then leave. You don't even stay the night."

"Maybe she's into that. The women I see know the score. I don't hide from them what I want—or don't want. Besides, she's an adult. I'm sure she understands the idea of a one-night stand or a summer fling. I would be upfront with her just like I am every other—"

"Abso-fucking-lutely not," Roman growled.

"It's not up to you, is it, though?" Ricky smirked.

"You asshole."

"Hell, maybe she'll be the one to make me want to put a ring on it."

"She won't be," Roman snapped.

Ricky snickered. "I don't know, man. Those mile-long legs could just about change anyone's mind."

"You little fucker—" Roman swung his fist.

Ricky, trained fighter that he was, easily blocked him. Roman jumped off the truck, tackling his brother.

A few grunts and well-placed jabs had Ricky groaning. He struck back, hitting Roman in his gut.

Roman coughed. "Asshole."

Ricky did some sort of interlocking with his legs and Roman knew what was coming; this wasn't the first time they'd ended up like this. Roman maneuvered out of the hold, twisting his body enough to pinch the underside of Ricky's arm.

"Ow! You fucker. That's cheating," Ricky argued.

"You know I fight dirty." Roman swung his arm around his brother, confining him in a headlock.

After a few more moments of struggle, Ricky tapped his arm hard. "Uncle!"

Roman released him and sat, drawing his knees up as he caught his breath.

Ricky massaged his neck. "Damn it, why do you always have to pinch me in that spot?"

"Why do you have to be an asshole?"

Ricky smiled. "Because someone needs to keep you on your toes. By the way, I let you win."

Roman rolled his eyes. "Still a sore loser, as usual."

"You think with all my training I couldn't beat your ass if I wanted to? I went easy on you."

"Fuck you."

"I'd rather fuck your nanny." Ricky shot to his feet and out of reach before Roman could hit him.

"Enough about Elise. I mean it, Ricky. She's off-limits." Roman got to his feet, wiping his hands on his stained pants.

"Fine, but you need to come out with me Saturday," Ricky relented.

"And why would I do that?"

"Because I have a date and she has a friend. And you need a wingman and to get back out there before your dick shrivels up and falls off."

"I thought you wanted to take Elise out. Now you all of a sudden have a date?"

Ricky smirked and shrugged. Fucker had played him. "Just seeing how hot you were for the nanny."

"I'm not—" He pinched the bridge of his nose and counted to ten. He was, in fact, hot for the nanny, but he couldn't have Elise. And he didn't want his brother within ten miles of her.

"In all seriousness, it's time you put yourself back out there. A double date is less pressure. I'll be there to break the ice and ease you into the dating field. My date's hot and assures me her friend is too."

Roman shook his head and sighed. Was he ready to get back out there? He hadn't thought so before Elise. But maybe Ricky was right—though he'd never admit it out loud.

"Ariel is my priority."

"You can be a good dad and date. She's doing great; don't you deserve something for yourself, and some adult fun-time? Maybe, if you got laid, you'd relax some and not be such an uptight asshole who attacks his brother," Ricky teased.

Roman mulled over his brother's suggestion. Maybe he should get out. Ariel was with his in-laws this weekend. And he'd be alone in the house with Elise, unless she went to her friends' place. But if she was alone with him—he was afraid of what might happen. He'd almost kissed her in front of Ariel at the beach, for fuck's sake. And Elise had looked like she'd wanted it too. He couldn't go there and ruin this good thing they had going for them. He was her employer.

"Fine."

Ricky blinked as if he hadn't been expecting him to accept. "Really?"

"Saturday. But let's get out of town." He didn't want to run into anyone he knew. Word got around in small towns and the last thing he wanted was his in-laws hearing about his date from someone else. He had a strained enough relationship with them as it was.

"Fuck, yes!" Ricky clapped him on the back. "About time!"

Roman shared none of his brother's excitement. Something felt wrong about accepting. But he needed to get his mind off Elise and to stop himself from crossing that line with her.

Maybe getting laid would solve everything.

19

ELISE

Elise carried the small gift bag into Renita and James Emerson's home. The smell of roasting meat and other delectable scents made her mouth water. Renita always had something cooking whenever Elise visited. Their home was always warm and welcoming. *This is how a parents' home is supposed to feel.*

Ariel darted past her, rushing into the legs of her grandpa.

"Oof!" James smiled down at her. "You might have a future linebacker here." He leaned down and picked Ariel up, holding her in his arms.

Ariel burrowed into her grandpa's shoulder, clinging onto his neck. James's large hand patted her back as if trying to soothe her.

"I think someone is going to miss you," Roman said, bypassing Elise and moving towards the fridge where he pulled out a beer.

"I'll take one of those." Ricky entered the kitchen from the other side.

Roman grabbed another one and handed it to his brother before turning to her. "Would you like one? Or they have lemonade? Iced tea, milk, water?"

"Lemonade is fine, but I can help myself." Elise might not have been on the clock, but it would feel awkward drinking in front of the family she was employed by.

"I got it." Roman grabbed a cup from the cupboard and poured her a glass.

She accepted the drink. "Thanks."

"I hope you all brought your appetite. I made enough for everyone to have leftovers." Renita wiped her hands on a tea towel hanging from the oven door.

Ariel wiggled down from her grandpa and moved to hug her grandma. Renita smiled and squeezed her tight before making her way to take a seat at the dining room table. Ariel climbed into her lap.

"We'll be back before you know it. And I'll bring you some treats and trinkets from everywhere we travel. You'll like that, won't you?" Renita asked Ariel as she swayed back and forth, the creak of the old rocking chair breaking up the quiet.

The little girl gave a reluctant nod.

"And Elise here will take such good care of you. You'll have so much fun." Renita gave her a wink.

"Oh, absolutely," Elise agreed. "We still have to find a mermaid before summer's out."

Ariel clung tighter to her grandmother in response. She hadn't been her usual energetic self all day.

Elise set the small gift bag on the table by Renita. "I brought you both a little something for your travels. Just an emergency kit for flying, nothing special."

"Oh, that was sweet of you. Wasn't it, James?" Renita picked it up.

"Sure was. Thanks, Elise."

Her cheeks heated. "You're welcome."

"Maybe Ariel can help me open it," Renita suggested.

Ariel sat up, reaching for the gift.

"We're here. Sorry we were late." Bella walked in with her little one in her arms, trailed by her son, Nash, and Nova.

"It's Nova's fault we're late," Nash grumbled.

His sister's eyes narrowed. "It was not. You're the one that disappeared for an extended period of time with your fiancée. I was simply entertaining the kids like the good aunty I am."

"Spinning the baby in circles after she ate sound like a good idea to anyone?" Nash questioned.

Nova crossed her arms over her chest. "No one told me she just ate."

"Okay, enough, you two. Good Lord, I am looking forward to a break from all this bickering." Renita shook her head with a sigh.

Nova stuck her tongue out at her brother.

Renita's eyes narrowed on her daughter as she cleared her throat.

Nova feigned innocence with a smile and a shrug. "Just keeping him on his toes."

"I hope you have someone special to introduce me to when we get home." Renita's brow rose.

Nova's gaze darted around the room, landing on her brother. "Why me? You have two other single children."

"I'm well aware," Renita said dryly, cutting glances between Roman and Ricky.

"Let's eat before your mother's and my hard work gets cold," James ordered.

Elise had been to a few family dinners at this point. The kids and the ladies got their meals first while the men hung back unless they were fixing a plate for the former. It was sweet.

They got settled around the long table in the dining room. Ariel opted to sit between her grandparents rather than in her usual spot by Eli and Elise. Dealing with her separation anxiety was going to be the focus of their next few days. Good thing Elise had a few tricks up her sleeve.

The meal was delicious as always. And the banter, just as entertaining.

"You must think we're a crazy bunch," Nova said to Elise, pushing her near empty plate away.

Elise smiled. "Good crazy. Quite entertaining really."

Nova chuckled. "I bet. My brothers like to push my buttons."

"Seems to go both ways."

Nova shrugged. "Got to keep them on their toes."

"How is—"

Ding-dong!

"Who could that be?" Renita asked as James got to his feet.

"We'll find out soon enough."

"Probably someone trying to save our souls." Ricky snickered.

"Just tell them we worship the devil and were about to do a blood sacrifice if they want to join," Nova called after him. She turned back to Bella's wide eyes and shrugged. "What? It works."

Everyone's heads turned to the entrance to the dining room as James walked back in with a tall man in a tan sheriff's uniform behind him.

"Good evening, everyone. Sorry to interrupt your dinner," the sheriff said.

"Not a problem, Bently. Would you like a plate?" Renita asked.

Bently shook his head. "No, that won't be necessary."

"Is this about Anastasia's case?" Bella asked, reaching to take Nash's hand.

"Yes and no. The news I have isn't about her specifically." He rested his hand on the seat back and sighed, resigned. "There's been a second body discovered in Massachusetts. There's enough evidence to link the two, and it crosses state lines, so the FBI are now going to be investigating the, uh . . ." Bently eyed the kids around the table. "Situation."

"Was another note found?" Nash asked.

"I'm not sure. They gave me a courtesy call and wanted all evidence we've gathered sent over." Bently's jaw twitched. "I'll try to keep you in the loop as much as possible, but I'm sure there will be an agent coming to speak with you."

"Was the second . . ." Ricky hesitated, glancing at the kids. "Identified?"

Bently gave a curt nod. "Simone Lancaster."

Nova gasped, her hand over her heart.

"Are you okay?" Elise asked.

Nova shook her head. "I . . . I knew her. At least it might be the same person."

"I have a picture here." Bently pulled out his phone.

Elise stood. "Maybe I should take Ariel home? Let you all speak in private?"

Roman stood. "I'll come with you. Say goodbye, Ariel."

Ariel clung to her grandparents. They each gave her a good squeeze. Her grandmother whispered something in her ear that made the little girl relax enough so that Roman could pick her up.

"Come on, Eli. Let's play a game in the living room." Ricky got up, grabbing his beer.

Elise turned to Mr. and Mrs. Emerson. "Thank you for dinner, and have a safe trip." She turned to Nova. "If you need anything, just let me know."

She followed Roman out of the house. They walked silently back to his place, his body tense, his eyes alert to their surroundings. Elise searched the woods around them and took a step closer to him. His unease was palpable; it rolled off him in waves.

He opened the door for her and walked in behind her, switching the lock. He placed Ariel on her feet. "Why don't you go watch something on your tablet in the living room for a little while. I need to talk to Elise, okay?"

Ariel glanced at her and then nodded.

Roman waited for her to get settled on the couch before he turned his back to her and signed to Elise. "*I need you to stay close to home this week.*"

"*Are we in danger?*" Elise asked, a sliver of panic making her heart race.

"*I don't think so, but I don't want to take any chances. We'll find out the rest of the details later, but the fact that there is a second body, and Nova possibly knew both of them, doesn't sit right with me.*" He ran a hand over the back of his neck and squeezed as if he carried tension there.

"*I understand.*"

"*Can you check in with me more throughout the day? And keep the door locked while you're home. Don't answer the door for anyone you don't know.*"

Elise swallowed. "*I can do that.*"

He reached out and clasped her trembling hand in his, rubbing the rough pad of his thumb gently over her skin. She met his gaze and the knot of worry in her stomach unfurled. His touch granted her a sense of calm, like he grounded her.

"I won't let anything happen to you," he promised.

She cleared her throat, trying to ignore the flames that licked up her arm from his contact. *"The first . . . victim was found here?"*

He nodded. *"Yeah. She went missing six years ago and was found last year. A note showed up one day with the engagement ring she was wearing when she went missing and a map to her body. She was Nash's fiancée."*

She gasped. *"Oh my god. That's terrible. I'm so sorry."*

His shoulders slumped. Exhaustion shone in his eyes. *"It was a really difficult time for Nash—for us all."*

"He seems to have found his happiness now with Bella. I can't imagine what all this is stirring up for him."

Roman gave her hand a reassuring squeeze. *"Bella brought him back to life. As hard as I—we—tried, we couldn't get through to him. He was just existing. The guilt was eating him alive. He didn't have someone to pull him through until she came along."* He glanced over his shoulder at his daughter.

Someone to pull him through. Nash didn't have an Ariel who needed him. If Nash's fiancée had gone missing six years ago and Roman's wife had passed two years after that—Elise's heart hurt just thinking about all that this family had had to go through. So much loss. No wonder Roman was so protective of his daughter.

"I'm glad you had Ariel," she said.

"Me too."

His gaze darted down to her mouth. He was so close that all she could smell was him—the earthy hint of fermented hops on his breath, and the woodsy scent he carried with him. Each lungful teased her senses.

His rich brown skin was peppered with the shadow of a day's growth along his jaw. Her hands itched to run over it, have that contrast of rough and soft. He licked his lips, that pink tongue darting out and making her want to know what he tasted like.

Her body heated. Flames of need sunk deeper, gathering in her center. Did he feel this too?

"Roman?" Her voice was barely audible to her own ears, spoken with nothing but breath.

He leaned in ever so slightly. If she wasn't fully attuned to him, she would have missed it.

"What are you doing to me?" he rasped, leaning in a fraction of an inch more.

He felt this too? She wasn't alone in this?

Loud music blared from the TV, jolting them apart.

Elise spun to find Ariel turning the TV down with the remote. Roman darted away from her like his ass was on fire.

"I think it's time for your bath." He grabbed the remote and shut the television off.

"I don't want a bath. I want to watch Bluey," Ariel argued.

"Well, it's bath time. Let's go."

Ariel huffed and crossed her arms over her chest.

Elise didn't want to make this awkward and get in their way. It was obvious Ariel was having a hard time tonight. "I'll see you in the morning."

Roman didn't even look at her as he crouched to Ariel's level. Elise went to her room, closing the door and pushing her back against it. Her hand still tingled from his touch.

Could she do this again? Risk her heart for a chance at finding love? The chemistry between Roman and her was explosive. *What would sex with him be like?* She squeezed her thighs together at the thought.

Did he want this too? He'd almost kissed her twice now. And he'd opened up to her tonight. He'd pulled away right after, but they'd had his daughter as an audience.

Did she want to do this? She was already half in love with

Ariel, if not more. But Roman didn't seem like the type of man to treat her like Ron had. Roman was protective. *He's promised to keep me safe.* And she understood his daughter was his priority. But he also seemed receptive to something more between them. Maybe she could put herself out there—for him.

But he'd have to make the first move.

20

ELISE

Elise rinsed the last plate and set it in the dishwasher. "Your dad will be here soon, and after he showers, we're going to get dinner at Atlantis."

Ariel's response was to cross her arms and pout.

"Don't you want to go out?"

"I wanted to go to the park. You said we could."

Elise turned and wiped her hands on the towel. "I know, but that was before things changed."

"It's not fair!" Ariel slammed her hand on the counter, knocking over a glass.

It shattered on the floor.

"Don't move!" Elise ordered. Thankfully, she was in flip-flops, and she walked around the broken shards and picked up Ariel, then moved her out of harm's way and set her on a chair. "Stay here until I get this cleaned up, and then we'll get you some shoes, okay?"

Tears welled in Ariel's eyes.

Elise smoothed her hand over Ariel's cheek. "Hey, are you okay? Did you get hurt?"

"I'm sorry. I didn't mean to. Please don't leave." The girl clung to her.

Elise rubbed her back. "I'm not going anywhere. Accidents happen. Next time you're upset, maybe we can find another way for you to express that?"

Ariel nodded.

Elise gave her another squeeze and a kiss on her temple before grabbing the broom to clean the mess up.

Her phone pinged from her pocket. She pulled it out. Roman had texted her every few hours today, checking in, his concern evident. Ariel had been out of sorts since her grandparents left for Europe two days ago.

Ren: *How about next weekend for dinner with Mom and Dad?*

Ugh. Her brother was relentless. Why go to dinner where no one would sign and they'd all speak Japanese. She'd have trouble following along. And everyone would want to know why she wasn't married and having children yet. Like those were the only options for her.

The front door opened and Roman stepped in. His eyes searched the room until he landed on Ariel. His shoulders relaxed and a smile curved his lips. He glanced at her. "Hey, guys. How was your day?"

"A glass broke. I think I got all the pieces, but just to be safe, everyone should wear shoes for a while in the kitchen." Elise tucked her phone away. She'd text her brother back later.

"Elise won't take me to the park." Ariel faced her father.

Roman stepped closer to her, picking her up. "I told her not to go anywhere. So if you want to be mad at anyone, it should be me. But I'll make sure you go to the park and get out, okay? How about when you get home from Mimi and Papa's on Sunday, we go to Green Park together?"

"Okay. But only if I get my own chocolate peanut butter cheesecake at dinner tonight."

Elise bit back her smile.

"Deal, but you can't eat it all right now. You have to save some for tomorrow." Roman tipped his head and eyed her.

Ariel held up her pinky finger. Roman slipped his around it and tugged.

"Okay, I'm going to shower and change, and then we can go." Roman set Ariel down on the couch.

"I want to wear my princess dress." Ariel headed towards the stairs.

"Alright. We'll leave in twenty." Roman turned to Elise. "Already checked the truck for bees, but I'll look once more when we get back to it."

It was sweet that he'd remembered. "Thank you." She waited until he was out of sight before she, too, climbed the stairs, heading for her room. She didn't think ripped shorts and an old T-shirt were quite up to Atlantis's standards.

Elise opened the almost bare closet, her fingers trailing over the soft cotton of the few sundresses she'd packed. The rest of her things were stored in Sam and Jack's guest room. She picked the jade-green one that was soft and flowy and came just a few inches above her knees. It was hard to find dresses that were the right length for her tall and curvy figure. But this was one of her favorites. She slipped it on, adding some fresh deodorant under her arms. Elise lined her eyes with kohl-black liquid liner, and slipped on some pink-tinted gloss. After twisting her hair into a long braid, she stepped into a pair of black flats. Casting a quick look in the mirror hanging from the door, she smoothed her hands over her tummy and hips. Thankfully, the cut of the dress hid her rolls and accentuated her best assets.

Her belly fluttered with a mix of excitement and nerves. She was going to dinner with Roman and Ariel like she was a part of the family. But she wasn't. Did she want to be?

Images of Roman taking care of her when she was sick, of Ariel laughing with her and having a paint fight flicked through her mind. She loved the way Roman was with his daughter—so patient and kind, yet firm. She pictured him spending hours doing her hair every month. The bond those two had . . . only a fool would not want to be included in their little bubble. But did they want her?

There was only one way to find out.

* * *

Elise took Roman's offered hand and climbed out of the truck. Her dress rode up her thigh as she slipped from the seat. His gaze burned her exposed skin. Since he'd come downstairs, his eyes had been glued to her legs. Normally, she'd be self-conscious of her long limbs, but the heated admiration he kept sending her way had the opposite effect on her.

He cleared his throat. "Ready?"

"Yes."

Roman took Ariel's hand and placed his other on the small of her back. She swallowed as arousal buzzed through her veins. He opened the door for them and ushered them in to the hostess.

"Reservation for Emerson," Roman said, turning a few heads in the restaurant.

"Of course. Right this way." The hostess led them through reclaimed wooden tables filled with other patrons, past black-and-white photos on soft grey walls. Elise did a double take, stumbling. Roman caught her arm, steadying her.

"Is that your parents?" She pointed to one of the blown-up photographs featuring Renita and James holding up a wooden basket of apples, smiles on their faces.

He chuckled. "Yeah. And that's Nash." He motioned to one a little farther down.

"Wow. Do you have one?"

"Unfortunately, yes." He wiped his hand over the back of his head in a self-conscious gesture.

"Actually, the table I have for you is right near it." The hostess smiled.

"Great," Roman grumbled as they continued to follow her around a corner. Sure enough, the image of both Roman and Ricky holding up a frame of honey by a stack of bee boxes hung on the wall. The insects flew around them, and several were clustered on the frame.

"So that's what you do out there in the fields?" Elise asked.

Roman got Ariel situated and then pulled her chair out for her. "Something like that."

The hostess handed them menus. "Your server will be over in a moment, but can I get you drinks to start?"

"An apple juice, and I'll take a glass of the Fates' red if you have it," Roman answered her before turning to Elise. "Would you like a glass?"

"Oh, I'm not sure—"

"You're off the clock," Roman said.

"Well, then, yeah, that would be nice. Red also, please."

"Perfect. Ginny will be over with your drinks momentarily." The hostess spun around, leaving them alone.

"*I want the cheese ravioli,*" Ariel signed.

"Big surprise there." Roman smiled down at her before turning to Elise. "She always orders that."

"Must be good, then." Elise picked up the menu, perusing her seasonal choices. "Is the fish good here?"

Roman snorted. "Supplied by Nash, so it better be."

"Oh. That's why his picture's up on the wall." She turned towards the image of Roman and Ricky hanging beside her, paying more attention to the print on the bottom of the image. *Emerson Apiaries, Shattered Cove, NH.*

"And you provide the restaurant with honey?"

"Yup. They wanted to decorate with pictures of their local suppliers. Mom and Dad provide some fruit from the orchard when it's in season. Along with pork and beef. Nash does the seafood and fish."

"And Nova?" she asked.

"She's the only one not on here—lucky, if you ask me."

"Right, because she can't very well supply weed brownies." Elise laughed.

"That would be entertaining. Bet Atlas and Jasmine would make a killing off desserts." Roman chuckled.

"Are they the owners?"

"Yeah."

"Good evening. I'm Ginny, and I'll be your server tonight. Apple juice must be for you." The woman set the glass of juice in front of Ariel. "And two reds. Oh, and I heard someone at this table might be interested in our coloring contest." She pulled a pack of crayons and a little coloring book from her apron before handing it over to Ariel.

"What do you say, Ariel?" Roman asked.

Ariel hid behind her dad but raised her hand to her chin and then pulled it away in sign for *"Thank you."*

"Thank you," Roman repeated.

"You're welcome." Ginny pulled out her tablet. "Are you ready to order, or do you need a few minutes?"

Elise picked up her menu once more, scanning the items to be sure on her pick.

"I'd love to hear the specials," Roman said. He hadn't even glanced at his menu, and now she understood why.

"Oh, of course. Sorry, tonight has been a little crazy," Ginny apologized. "We have a roast pork tenderloin with sweet corn and collard greens. A lobster risotto. Or a shrimp and scallop alfredo with fresh pasta and broccolini. All local ingredients, all hormone-free, and almost all organic."

"I'll have the pasta. And Ariel here would like cheese ravioli." Roman handed her his menu.

Ginny tucked it under her arm and turned to Elise. "And for you?"

"The burger and homemade fries sound perfect. Medium well, please."

"It will be right out." Ginny turned and left.

"Wow, so you're like town celebrities," Elise teased, pointing up at the image once more.

Roman groaned. "Can we just pretend that isn't there?"

She smiled and shook her head.

"How was your day?" he asked before he glanced at Ariel, who was busy coloring a page with an octopus with her tongue sticking out of the corner of her mouth.

"Better than yesterday," Elise answered.

"Sorry it's been a difficult week. I'm sure I haven't helped, having you stay close to home."

She reached for the glass and took a sip. Flavors burst on her tongue—cherry, and oak, and a hint of orange. "If it makes you more comfortable that we stay close to the house, I can understand that. But how long do you think we'll have to do this?"

He sighed. "I don't know. But it can't be forever. I just wish we could catch this guy."

Elise glanced at Ariel who was still deeply enthralled in her coloring. She signed to Roman, *"Have you ever thought of a service pet for Ariel? One that could also be a guard dog of sorts?"*

Ariel grabbed her apple juice, looking at them like she could sense what they were talking about before going back to her coloring.

"That's something that's come up before, but not an idea I want to discuss in front of Ariel. She's been begging me for a dog for years."

"I understand."

"Have you ever been here before?" Roman asked aloud.

"Once with my family, last year."

"Are you an only child?" He sipped his wine.

"No, I have a brother, Ren. He's eight years older and a doctor."

"A doctor and a teacher. Your parents must be proud." Roman smiled.

"Hardly." She picked up her glass, needing more wine for this conversation.

"What do you mean?"

"Teaching children basic math and early-learning subjects is hardly in the same league as practicing medicine," she argued.

He stared at her without saying a word. Unnerved, she squirmed in her seat.

He tipped his head to the side. "Do you doubt your intelligence?"

"I don't. I just don't delude myself into thinking I'm as smart as someone whose job is to save literal lives."

"You don't think teachers can save lives?" he asked.

"No, they can, but it's not the same thing." She grew more and more flustered. Taking a breath, she exhaled.

Roman leaned in. "I don't think you give yourself enough credit. But I think I can see why."

The problem was, he looked at her like he could see through her. Those perceptive eyes held her captivated.

"Who told you that you weren't good enough?" Roman asked.

Elise's mouth dropped open. *How did he . . .?*

"Here you go." Ginny returned with their meals, setting

everyone's dish in front of them. "Did you need anything else?"

"No, thank you," Roman answered, not breaking his gaze from Elise.

"Alright, I'll be back to check on you soon." Ginny waved.

"Can you cut this for me, Daddy?" Ariel asked.

Roman sliced up the raviolis for his daughter before he turned back to Elise. But she kept her head down, avoiding his eyes.

"I'm sorry if I made you uncomfortable." Roman addressed the tension instead of ignoring it like she'd seemed to do.

"It's fine. My family is a sore subject for me."

"I get that. How about we talk about something else?" Roman suggested before taking a bite of his dinner.

"Like what?"

He finished swallowing. "How about I tell you about the time that Nova almost burned the barn down?"

Elise clapped a hand over her mouth. "Oh my god. Was anyone hurt?"

"No. And it was just a small fire. But to this day, my mom and dad believe Ricky did it."

"Okay, start from the beginning."

And so he did. Story after story of firecrackers and pranks gone wrong. The siblings seemed more than a handful. No wonder Renita had the patience of a saint.

Elise clutched her stomach, wiping the tears from her eyes as she laughed. Ariel joined in at some point, telling her own stories of her uncles and aunt.

"It makes sense now why you worked with your dad to get me in that water. You've been conditioned to be a little trick-ster," Elise teased.

Ariel gave a sly smile. *"But I'm on your side now."*

"Hey, what am I, chopped liver? You're supposed to be on my team, sweet pea." Roman acted offended.

"Us girls have to stick together, right, Ariel?" Elise asked.

"Right."

"I see how it is." Roman chuckled, his eyes lighting up with happiness and something that burned a little hotter as he leveled her with his stare once more.

Without breaking the connection, she reached for her wineglass—but she missed and knocked it instead. The glass wobbled. She steadied it. His hand clamped around hers. Awareness threaded through her at his closeness. Desire pulsed within her as he pinned her with his gaze.

"Careful," he rumbled, his thumb brushing against the top of her hand.

Who knew a hand could be an erogenous zone?

"Roman?" A feminine voice pulled his attention away from her, snuffing out the light in his eyes. The smile slipped from his face and he tore his palm away.

"Nia." He stood, shifting on his feet awkwardly, looking a lot like a kid caught with his hand in the cookie jar.

Who was this woman? Was Roman seeing someone? *Oh my god, not again.*

Nia cast her a suspicious look before she settled on Ariel with a smile. "Hey, sweetheart."

"Hi, Aunt Nia. Is Alexis here?" Ariel asked.

Oh, Nia must be Tiana's sister. Elise wasn't sure how she didn't see the similarities before from the pictures of Ariel's mother.

"No, she's with Mimi and Papa. I had a business meeting. Didn't think I'd run into you guys here." Nia cast Elise another curious glance.

"Sorry, Nia, this is my nanny, Elise. Elise, this is my sister-in-law," Roman introduced them.

The nanny. Of course, she was the nanny. But did you take your childcare employee to dinner? She'd at least hoped they were friends at this point.

Nia's attention darted to the almost empty wineglasses and then back to Roman. "Sorry I interrupted. Have a good night." She nodded stiffly and left.

Roman looked as if he wanted to go after her. His hands fisted at his sides. What was going on?

He sat back down, his face an unreadable mask. Gone was the man who'd been laughing and joking with her moments ago, replaced with this stoic statue.

"Looks like you're about finished. Do you want to look at the dessert menu?" Ginny came over, cleaning their plates.

"I think we'll take the dessert to go," Roman answered.

At the beginning of the night she'd been filled with hope and possibilities, but Roman wouldn't even look at her as they waited for dessert to be brought, nor as he helped her in the car for the silent ride home. The way he'd asked her who told her she wasn't good enough—like he'd cared—had pierced her defenses. Made her believe—it didn't matter. He was so hot and cold, it was confusing.

I must have read into things. Because he'd made it clear where they stood tonight. She was the nanny.

And she should know better than to wish for more.

21

ELISE

Orange light from the setting sun pierced the building clouds as the truck came to park in front of the house.

Elise turned to Roman as she unbuckled herself. Her hand grazed his and he whipped it away.

"Th-thanks for dinner." She tried to keep her face blank. How could they go from him holding her hand to cringing away from her touch so quickly?

He nodded and walked to her side of the vehicle to open her door. Roman's palm pressed against her lower back as if to steady her as she climbed out. But as soon as her feet hit the ground, he backed away with a scowl.

Tears stung her eyes, but she blinked them back. Why was this bothering her so much? She stared at his front door. The idea of going inside made it hard to breathe. She needed air.

"I'm going to go for a little walk, I'll be back."

That got his attention. "Where—"

An ATV rumbled as Ricky pulled in. He grabbed a six-pack from one of the secured milk crates on the back, looking between Roman and Elise. "Thought you might be up for a drink?"

"Have fun." Elise spun around and headed down the path that led towards an overlook to the meadow. She'd been this way with Ariel once and she was pretty sure she knew which turnoff it was. She plucked her CI from her ear and set it in her pocket. She needed a break from everything. Wanted silence.

A chilly wind swept over her. She folded her arms to her chest and walked faster. She approached the first turnoff, a small footpath. She hesitated, looking up the other way. *This must be it.* She kept her head down, watching where she stepped, sure not to trip over the roots and rocks.

Why am I so angry?

Because she'd thought they had something.

There was obvious attraction between them. Roman had made it seem like he was interested—like he could care about her. *Stupid. I should have known better.*

Elise was so caught up in her thoughts, she gasped when the first raindrop plopped on her forehead. She wiped it away as more fell. Fat droplets landed on her even under the thin canopy of trees. She looked up. Gone was almost every trace of orange, replaced with grey rainclouds and an ever-darkening horizon. The ground vibrated before a flash of light lit the sky.

Oh, shit.

A big hand grabbed her shoulder, twisting her around. Elise screamed and swung her fist. Pain lanced her wrist as two wide eyes met hers. Roman lifted a hand to his cheek and winced.

Fuck. She'd punched him *again*.

His mouth moved.

"I'm sorry—"

The ground vibrated again—thunder. The flash of light was only seconds behind.

"Where's your CI?" he asked.

"It won't help. It's not waterproof," she reminded him.

He looked behind him and then to the trail ahead. *"Come with me. We need to get out of the storm before we get struck by lightning."*

He clasped his hand in hers, guiding her quickly through the woods. The rain fell in sheets, soaking her to the bone. Her once flowing dress clung to her like a second skin. Her flats, soggy with water and mud. Branches scratched her legs and arms as she followed him deeper into the woods.

"Where are we going?" she asked.

He didn't stop to answer, just tugged her arm in the direction he wanted to go. She got more frustrated with each step.

Some sort of wooden structure appeared ahead through a copse of trees. Was it a cabin?

Roman led her to the door and pulled her inside, closing the door behind them and eclipsing them in darkness.

He stepped away from her. Panic clawed at her chest. She hated the dark. "Roman?"

A light flickered on. She blinked as her eyes adjusted. It was a large room with some sort of machinery in the middle of it. Stacks of wood were piled off to one side. Except for a few folding chairs and a table directly in front of her, there was no other furniture.

"What is this place?"

"Maple-sugaring shack."

"You make maple syrup here?"

"Is that really what you want to talk about right now?" His chest heaved.

She tipped her head down. "I'm sorry I hit you again. I thought you were trying to attack me."

"You know there's a fucking killer on the loose, and you decided to walk off by yourself in the dark! What the hell were you thinking?" He scowled, anger radiating from him as he moved into her space.

Rainwater dripped from his dark curls down his temple. His skin glistened. The hollow of his throat dipped. His T-shirt clung to his muscles like it was painted on. She shivered, part from the cool, damp air around them and part from the ever-present arousal that swirled inside her at his closeness. His jaw tensed as he tipped her chin up so that she had no choice but to look him in the eyes—darker than she'd ever seen them. Only a hint of the color showed. Like charcoal dipped in honey.

"Well?" Roman asked.

"I needed some air."

"Liar," he said, and she read his lips.

"What do you want to hear? It's the truth. How dare you question—"

"Why were you running away?"

She swallowed, her own breathing coming faster.

Roman stepped closer. Mere inches of earth-scented air separated them. *"Answer me."*

Elise backed up until her shoulders hit the wall behind her. Roman followed her step for step, like a predator stalking prey. "I was upset because I thought . . ."

"What did you think?"

Doubt crept in. "Nothing. It doesn't matter."

A hot hand slipped around the back of her neck, his thumb brushing the edge of her jaw, holding her in place. *"What did you think?"*

Her lips thinned and pressed together in defiance.

Roman's eyes darkened as he leaned in even closer, the pressure of his hand increasing just a fraction—enough to let her know he was in control. "Don't start something you can't handle."

She read his lips. Heated desire spun through her, swirling into a pool gathering in her center. Something instinctual told her to push back.

"Yes, sir."

His chest vibrated against her as if he'd growled.

"Answer. The fucking. Question."

She swallowed and tried to keep her breath even. "You touch me like this, talk to me like this, and then you flinched away from me in the truck. It's confusing."

His throat bobbed as he swallowed. The flash of lightning streaked through the dim space.

"I thought we were at least friends, but you reminded me I'm just the nanny."

His gaze pinned her to the wall like a butterfly on display. *"And that upset you?"*

She nodded as much as his hold would allow.

He leaned in, the smell of fresh rain and forest and man filling her lungs and wrapping around her in a heady embrace. Roman withdrew his hand from her throat and signed, *"I don't need any more friends."*

She flinched, trying to hide the hurt his words inflicted. "You're so confusing."

"And you're infuriating." His hand returned to her neck, adding just a little pressure.

She bristled. "You say I'm the nanny and then you touch me like this. You look at me like . . ."

His hold tightened, firmly locking her in place. Only his thumb trailed down her throat. She shivered. Her nipples were hard and aching as they brushed against his chest with every breath.

"I touch you because it's the only way I can stay sane. It's the only

way to appease the side of me that wants to own, possess, and worship every piece of you."

Her eyes widened, darting from his hand to his mouth. "What's stopping you?"

Another vibration rumbled from his chest, stronger than the thunder outside. His lips crashed against hers. He wasn't gentle but ravenous. His soft mouth melded with hers as his tongue parted the seam of her lips. She opened for him, her body lighting up brighter than the lightning. She clutched his shoulders, wrapping her leg around his hip. His wide palm slid down her back to grab her ass, pulling her against him. His jean-clad thigh came between hers. She rocked her hips as he nipped her bottom lip. She moaned.

Electric awareness skittered over her skin from his touch, tumbling and multiplying as it gathered at her center like a cord cinching tight. The rough brush of his beard against her face as he deepened the kiss sent a fresh rush of desire tumbling through her. A calloused hand collared her neck and squeezed, heightening the heady desire that wound her higher and higher.

She bucked her hips again, needy and desperate. He thrust against her, his cock as hard as granite against her thigh. His other hand gripped her leg, spreading her wider, sliding her dress up around her waist and giving him better access.

She gasped as he hit her clit. He peppered kisses over her jaw, down her neck, his teeth grazing her shoulder.

Pleasure bloomed as he drove his hips against her again and again. His hot mouth latched onto her nipple through her wet dress. She arched her back, her hands pulling him closer. Needing more. His thrusts became more erratic and jerky as his mouth opened, his head falling back, ecstasy glazing his eyes. The blissful look of pleasure shattered his usually stoic expression, exposing a glimpse into his soul.

More. More. More.

The pleas must have fallen from her lips because he pulled away and signed, *"Tell me to stop or I'm going to take you right here and lick your pussy until you scream my name."*

Was that supposed to be a deterrent? "Make me come."

He dropped to his knees, hooking his fingers over her pink panties before sliding them down her thighs. Goose bumps broke out over her flesh. His hot skin was a stark contrast to the chilly air around them.

He slipped two fingers between her slick folds, spreading them before he leaned in and closed his eyes, his nose brushing against her trimmed curls like he was inhaling her scent. *Oh, God.*

"You smell so good. Such a gorgeous pussy. Watch me."

Like she would miss this? No fucking way.

The first swipe of his tongue lashed against her clit like a whip. "Holy fuck!"

His head bobbed between her thighs as she struggled to stay standing.

"Sit on my face."

Her brows drew together. How could she—*oh.*

Roman hooked her legs over his shoulders, still on his knees, her back against the wall as the scruff of his five o'clock shadow brushed against her pussy like he was covering himself in her scent. Fuck, that was hot.

Elise had never been a small woman. She was six feet and more than two hundred and fifty pounds. No one ever picked her up, never mind asked her to sit on their face. But Roman was going at her pussy like a man starving.

"Ohhhh." She moaned as he sucked her clit into his mouth. His tongue flicked and swirled around the swollen bud. A finger slid through her juices before he inserted it inside her, curling it to tap that magic spot. Urgency roared.

Her nails scraped against his scalp, tugging his hair. His fingers dug into her hips as if he couldn't get enough.

She didn't hold back her moans, encouraging him and totally enraptured in the pleasure flowing through her veins as he wound her higher and higher. A second finger joined the first and she burst apart. Her orgasm charged through her.

"Roman!"

He didn't stop. His fingers fucked her harder, his tongue keeping the same rhythm and pace that sent her flying off the edge, wringing every last drop of her orgasm from her. White spots appeared in her vision.

Her body went limp as she surrendered to the onslaught of ecstasy buzzing through her every cell. He held her against him, settling her gently onto her feet. His mouth captured hers, only this time his kiss was slow and sensual. He tasted like her, musky and sweet.

She dropped her hands to the button of his pants, but he gripped her wrist.

"*I already came.*" He gave her a sheepish smile.

When had he . . .

"*It's been a while.*" His gaze darted to the cement floor and then back to her.

That was amazing. And they hadn't even gotten fully naked. She leaned in and kissed him.

He kissed her back for a moment and then pulled away, bending down to pick up her panties from the ground. She plucked them from his grasp and stuffed them into her pocket.

His gaze shuttered before he focused on the wall behind her. "*I think the storm's passed. We should get back.*"

"Right. Okay." That was abrupt.

Roman shut the lights off and took her hand, guiding her onto a different path, this one wide enough for an actual vehicle. He was just as quiet as he had been on the drive home from the restaurant. But maybe that was just him, and he needed to digest things in his own time. Or maybe . . . he'd said it had been a while. Was she the first since his wife had passed? Surely not. But if that was the case, he probably had a lot to process. She could give him that space.

Butterflies tumbled in her belly. Maybe this relationship was the rainbow in the shit storm of her life.

22

ROMAN

Roman might have seemed calm on the outside as he waved goodnight to Ricky. But his heart thundered as if a herd of wild horses were locked inside. He could still taste her on his tongue. One minute he'd been angry at her for walking off alone, and the next—what the hell had he been thinking? Just attacking her like that? He was her employer and he'd crossed a line.

But oh, fuck—how she'd responded. Like she was made for him. Her moans and whimpers were branded in his memories.

He turned around and headed into the quiet house. Ariel had gone to bed hours ago, Elise disappearing after they'd gotten home. Ricky had been a good distraction, but now Roman was alone and able to fully sit with the weight of what he'd done.

An image of Tiana smiled at him from the wall. He stopped in front of it, tracing her face with his index finger. He loved her—a part of him always would. But she was gone.

He'd accepted that—had to. But he hadn't been with another woman since she'd passed. He'd worried it would feel too much like cheating. No one else had tempted him in years—until now.

He sighed and carried the empty beer bottles to the recycling before walking upstairs as quietly as he could. Elise was probably asleep by now or at least had her CI off. But he couldn't face her after what they'd done—not tonight. He had to wrap his head around this first. Every action had consequences. Whatever he did affected Ariel. And she was the most important person to him in the world. He couldn't do anything to hurt her.

Roman walked into his room and shut the door before heading to the en suite. He stripped his clothes and left them in the basket in the corner. His reflection had him pausing. "What do I do now?"

What does Elise want from me? Was this a one-time thing? Or was she seriously interested in me?

What do I want?

He turned the shower spray on and walked in, not waiting for the water to warm up. He hissed at the bite of cold, his hands braced against the wall.

Could he wake up tomorrow and pretend he'd never tasted her? That he didn't know what Elise looked like when she came? Or could he date her? He closed his eyes, picturing what that would look like between them. How would Ariel handle him seeing another woman? Would she be angry? Would Elise resent him for putting his daughter first? Thoughts spiraled through his mind like the dirty water swirling down the drain. Steam rose from the hot water. He scrubbed his body, erasing any trace of her scent.

After his shower, he brushed his teeth and then pulled on a

pair of boxers before sliding in between the cool sheets. Exhaustion had his eyelids growing heavy, but their time in the sugaring shack played over and over in his mind on a loop until even in his dreams, he couldn't escape her.

* * *

The next morning Ariel came into his room and jumped on his bed, pulling him from sleep. He groaned, having slept like shit.

"Go back to sleep. It's not time to get up yet," he grumbled.

Ariel tapped his shoulder. He blinked his blurry eyes open.

"It's past breakfast, but we saved you some. Mimi and Papa will be here soon to pick me up."

Roman flicked a glance at his phone charging by the bed. "Shit—I mean shoot."

Ariel smirked. *"That's a dollar for my puppy fund."*

"Alright. Just give me five minutes. Go grab your bag."

"Elise already helped me pack."

Roman's stomach flipped at the mention of the beauty who'd haunted his dreams all night.

"Well, then I guess I have time to tickle you." He swept his arms out but Ariel ducked and rolled off the bed, then scampered out of the room. Damn, she was getting faster. Or maybe he was getting older.

Roman sat up, wiping a hand over his tired face. He and Elise needed to talk but not with Ariel here. His in-laws would be arriving any minute to pick her up for the night. Fuck. His stomach dipped. What would they think if he started seeing someone?

He stood, grabbed a T-shirt from his drawer, and slid it

over his head before he reached for a pair of black basketball shorts. Anxiety snaked around his rib cage, cinching tight. He took a moment to compose himself before making his way to the kitchen.

Elise had her back to him, wearing a pair of cutoffs with a flowy top that hung off her shoulder, making him want to sink his teeth into it. One bare foot traced the back of her calf, pink toenails on display. Ariel leaned in next to her at the island, showing her something on her tablet. Something about the two of them together felt right. From painting in the yard, to building sandcastles at the beach, to huddling together over a tablet in his kitchen, Elise fit with them.

She turned, her eyes widening as she caught him unabashedly staring. "Oh, good morning. There's some fresh coffee in the pot. And we saved you some pancakes and eggs."

"The panny-cakes are shaped like Micky Mouse!" Ariel beamed.

"Thanks." He made his way to the coffee pot and poured himself a large cup before taking a sip. He leaned against the counter.

Elise glanced at him, her cheeks pink. Questions swirled in her gaze. After Ariel left, they'd talk.

A honk drew his attention to the window overlooking the front porch. "Looks like your grandparents are a little early."

"I'll go get her bag." Elise disappeared upstairs.

Ariel raced to the door and opened it, running to the edge of the porch as his in-laws climbed out of their vehicle.

"Good morning, George, Pat." Roman nodded in greeting.

His father-in-law walked close enough to shake his hand. "Looks like it's gonna be a good day. Not too hot."

This was how conversations with his in-laws went. He'd talk weather and sports with George. Pat would fuss over Ariel before her assessing gaze would land on him. Guilt weighed on his shoulders. The words Pat had screamed at him in the hospital waiting room when he'd gone to tell her that her oldest daughter had left this world still rang in his ears.

How could you let this happen? My baby! You took her away from me. How could you leave her? She was alone—she must have been so scared. This wasn't supposed to happen.

Ariel's hands moved a mile a minute as she signed to her grandmother, telling her about her week with Elise.

"Oh, dear. I'll need you to slow down for me." Pat chuckled.

"Here's Ariel's things. Oh, hello." Elise smiled warmly at his in-laws.

Everything inside Roman locked up. Sweat beaded on his forehead as Pat eyed her curiously before her lips pursed and her gaze narrowed on him.

"Pat, George, this is Elise. She's Ariel's nanny for the summer," he introduced them.

Elise flinched, her smile faltering a moment before she forced it higher. "Nice to meet you. Ariel's been so excited for this weekend. We packed some pictures she painted for you in her things."

"That's nice of you to come so early on a weekend." Pat smiled but there was no warmth in it.

Elise flicked a glance at him.

"Elise is staying with us for the summer. Makes it easier with my early mornings and late evenings," Roman explained.

"I see." Pat's mouth thinned into a disapproving line.

"Well, if that's everything, we should be off. I got a new unicorn floaty for the pool that's probably pretty lonely." George winked at Ariel.

"A unicorn one?" She clapped and then ran to Roman, arms up for a hug.

He picked her up, holding her tight before he kissed her cheek. She pulled away—he'd never be the one to let go first. And then she ran up to Elise and gave her a hug. Elise wrapped his little girl in her arms, holding her with affection sparkling in her eyes. His skin prickled and he looked away to find his mother-in-law watching him.

"You'll bring her back Sunday at five?" he asked.

"Actually, we thought we'd take her out to dinner first if that's okay?" George asked.

"Sure."

Ariel scampered towards their car. George took the bag from Elise, waving goodbye as he did. Pat gave Elise and him one more glance before she followed them.

His heart pounded. Guilt crashed into him. What was he thinking, hooking up with his nanny?

"Do you want some breakfast?" Elise asked.

"What?"

"Uh, I saved some breakfast and kept it warm if you—"

"I'm not hungry."

"Okay."

He turned and went into the house, the urge to flee rising stronger and stronger. What he wanted warred with his duty.

You took her away from me.

Did he deserve another chance at love? Or would it hurt those he'd already done irrevocable damage to?

"The house is so quiet without Ariel," Elise mused, walking beside him.

Sparks ignited from the brush of her arm against his as she passed. He wanted her. To cup her face and bring those full lips to his mouth. To lay her out on the counter here and eat her for breakfast. To know what it felt like to be buried deep inside her.

How could you let this happen?

Elise walked in front of him, oblivious to the war raging within him. Or the fact that he couldn't draw a full breath. Her scent clung to the air around him, suffocating him. The walls seemed to draw in closer. His mind reeled.

"Roman, can we talk about—"

"I forgot I have some errands to run." He grabbed his keys from the wall.

Elise's shoulders slumped. Hurt flashed in her gaze before an unreadable mask took its place.

Fuck, he was an asshole. He sighed and walked up to her. Unable to resist touching her, he cupped the side of her face with his hand. "I'll be back in a couple hours. We'll talk then."

She blinked, hope shining in her brown eyes. "Okay."

Roman pulled away, walking out the door and climbing into his truck. He slipped the keys into the ignition and steered down the driveway. Tears blurred his vision as he pulled onto a familiar road. Pressing a hand to his chest, he tried to ease the ache, but it didn't work. Because his pain wasn't based in the physical.

He had no plan for where he was going, but whenever he was this lost, he always ended up in the same place—Tiana's grave.

Roman wiped his eyes and slipped the truck into park before climbing out. He walked past several headstones until he fell to his knees in front of hers.

"I'm sorry I didn't bring you any flowers this time—I know you love them." He sat on the ground, his back to the cold stone. "I think I made a huge mistake."

Roman drew in a ragged breath. "I met someone. And . . . I think something's there. But I'm scared that—" He swallowed down the sob that wanted to escape. "I'm afraid of fucking it all up like I did with you. I don't know . . . if I can do this again. I don't know if it's right for Ariel. I wish you were here, T. I could really use your advice. You always knew what to say."

He tipped his head back. Birdsong came from the trees. The rustle of leaves joined with a warm breath of the breeze.

He sighed. "What do I do?"

23

ELISE

Elise tried and failed miserably to focus on the paperwork in front of her. Hours had gone by, and Roman hadn't returned. Morning had turned into afternoon, and evening ebbed closer. He was obviously avoiding her, which told her everything she needed to know. *How did I get into this position again?* She could accept that their hookup was a one-time thing, but why couldn't he man up and say that? *But he'd promised to talk when he got back.* So where was he? Anger and humiliation heated her blood.

Her stomach grumbled and she checked her watch. A frustrated scoff left her as pain lanced across her chest. It was dinnertime yet there was no sign of Roman. Would this mean she'd need to find another job? Or was he capable of just pretending none of this had happened? *I should have known better.*

Ding!

She flinched before picking up her phone and closing her binder.

Sam: *You coming out with us tonight? We're gonna go to the club.*

A night out drinking and dancing with her friends to forget this fuckup was mighty tempting.

But what if she was the first one he'd been with since his wife—that was sure to bring up a lot of emotions. Maybe she should give him a little more of a chance? And even if that wasn't the case, she wasn't backing down. They needed to figure this out because her very livelihood was on the line. That kernel of hope inside her had her holding out. She just needed to have a conversation with him and clear this up. That way she could set her expectations and figure things out.

Elise: *Rain check. Got some stuff here to take care of.*

Sam: *If you change your mind, we'll be at The Open Door.*

The rumble of an engine had her slipping her phone in her pocket and her belly tumbling with a mixture of nerves and butterflies. She closed her book as a truck curved around the bend and her heart sank. Oh, not Roman—Ricky. He sure liked to hang out with his brother a lot.

"Hey, Elise." Ricky gave her a warm smile as he climbed out of his truck and shut the door.

"Hey. Roman isn't here. I'm not sure when he'll be back."

He frowned, peeking over his shoulder as he tugged open the collar on his button-up.

"You're all dressed up."

"Yeah, I've got a date, since you keep turning me down. You sure you don't want to reconsider?" He gave her a playful wink.

She laughed. "I'm sure."

He clapped a hand over his heart. "Ouch. So this is what it feels like to be rejected."

She laughed harder. "It's good for your ego."

"You've been spending too much time with Nova. I can see she's rubbing off on you." He sighed. "At least one of us gets to."

Elise's eyes widened before she coughed. "You can't turn that off, can you?"

He smirked. "My charm? No, sorry, that's part of who I am."

"I have a friend just like you."

"I'm one of a kind, baby. I can assure you."

"He was always full of jokes and had a revolving door of *friends*," she added, studying him closer.

"Sounds like the life of the party," Ricky added.

"He was, up until he wasn't." *Until he overdosed and nearly died.*

Ricky's smile faded. "Is he okay now?"

She nodded, her lips curving up once more. "Yeah. He finally found the courage to live his truth. He and his boyfriend are happy together."

Ricky's tan skin blanched, his playful mask slipping only a moment before it was back in full force. "Good for him. More pussy for the rest of us."

She flinched. Ricky had always been flirtatious, but had never gone as far as being so blatantly crude. Was he reacting because she'd hit too close to home?

"Did Roman say where he was going?" Ricky asked.

"No."

"I hope he isn't chickening out," he grumbled.

"Of what?"

"Our double date."

What? Elise's ears rang. If she'd been standing, she would have stumbled back. She tried to keep her voice even. "Oh, was this a last-minute thing?"

He shook his head and turned back towards the driveway. "No. I asked him days ago."

Roman had hooked up with her when he'd already had a date planned? She stood on wobbly knees. Had Roman used her? No. It hadn't felt like that. God, that man needed to get here and clear this shit up. She'd wanted the lines drawn in the sand, needed to know where she stood with Roman, and here they were. It would have been nice if he had been man enough to tell her himself.

A white truck pulled in and parked as her heart raced. Anger and embarrassment raged like an inferno inside her. *Why do I always trust them so easily? All I want is for someone to love me. Someone to at least care enough to be honest with me. To choose me.*

Roman ran up to the porch, warily looking between Elise and Ricky. "What are you doing here?"

"Our double date, remember? We're gonna be late if you don't hurry up," Ricky answered.

Roman's attention shot to Elise. "I totally forgot. Elise, can we talk for a minute?"

She collected her binder in her arms, straightening and forcing a smile she hoped wasn't as tight as it felt. She wouldn't let him know how much he'd hurt her. He wouldn't get any more of her vulnerability. *Stupid me. How could I forget I'm good enough to fuck and watch their kids, but not commit to?*

"Actually, I have plans tonight too. So I guess I better get ready. Have fun." It took everything inside her not to run into the house. She tugged her CI off before the screen door banged closed behind her. She marched up to her room and locked the door, blinking away tears. He didn't deserve them. She plucked her shortest and sexiest dress off the hanger and tossed it on her bed. Taking her phone out, she texted Sam back.

Elise: *Changed my mind. I'll meet you at your house in an hour.*

She grabbed the most uncomfortable bra she owned, because it happened to make her breasts look the best. She slipped on the red sparkly dress, one she typically wore with leggings because it was dangerously short. A quick drag of liquid eyeliner, some dark shadow, and her favorite bloodred lipstick, and her makeup was done. She let her hair loose of the messy bun it had been in all day. Her raven-black hair fell in waves, giving her a mussed look that screamed sex. *Perfect.* She grabbed a pair of heels from the back of the closet. She slipped on the silver heels that made her even taller because fuck insecure men. She gave herself one last cursory glance in the mirror. She looked hot. And now she was going to walk out to her car with her head held high and pretend like fucking her boss, having him give her the best orgasm of her life was no big deal. Like it meant as little to her as it obviously did to him.

She drew in a breath, put her CI back on, and grabbed her purse before heading out to the empty hallway. She walked down the stairs, going straight for the door, hesitating a moment. The house was quiet. Had he already left? *Because I mean that little to him. Like I'm nothing.* She ignored the flare of pain erupting in her chest.

She steeled herself and opened the door, continuing onto the porch. The murmur of voices stopped abruptly. Roman had changed though. She focused on her car and kept walking.

"Holy shit," Ricky commented.

"Elise, wait!" Roman ran up to her, grabbing her arm. "We need to talk."

She tugged it away, not able to even look at him as she dug the keys out of her purse. "I think you've made yourself perfectly clear."

"Where are you going?"

"That's my personal business, and as my employer, that isn't a privilege you get. It's the weekend and I'm off the clock. I'll see you later—I guess Sunday night."

"Don't do this." Roman moved in front of the car door, blocking her from leaving.

"Do what? Tell me exactly what part in this I've played?"

"Relegate me back to the boss. Not after—"

"After we hooked up? Blame it on momentary insanity."

He flinched. "You expect me to pretend like none of that happened?"

She crossed her arms over her chest. "Why not? You've had no problem doing that exact thing since yesterday evening."

He opened his mouth and closed it, guilt flashing in his gaze. She was right and he knew it.

She tipped her chin up. "Admit it. You're just upset you don't get to call the shots and screw the nanny while also having your dating life. You're just like all the rest." Her voice broke. She shook her head, holding it all together when she just wanted to crumble. "You're good too. I actually bought your lines. But I won't be played again."

His shoulders fell as he backed away. "That's not what this was. I made these plans before anything happened with us."

He looked so defeated. She actually started to feel bad for him—man, he was good. She shook her head motioning to his change of clothes. "But you're still going."

"Elise—"

"I'm done with whatever this was. As you've made clear from the beginning, I'm the nanny and nothing else." She opened the car door, tossing her bag inside. She gave him one last look, glaring at him. "Besides, I won't settle for a man who doesn't know what he wants. I won't be someone's convenience again." She snapped her mouth shut. She'd shared too much with her last statement. And he deserved none of it.

Elise got in the car and backed out. Roman stood there, chest heaving, hands fisted at his sides as Ricky approached.

She couldn't hear what he said, but it had obviously been the wrong thing, because Roman's fist shot out and connected with Ricky's jaw.

She gasped and turned the car, leaving the two brothers to sort out their own mess.

She was done dealing with boys who thought they could use her until they had their fill. She wanted a man. And someday—she'd get that. She had to hold on to hope that one of these times, the frog would turn into a Prince Charming who chose her, fought for her, and carried her off into the sunset. Or maybe not. Perhaps Disney had given her an unrealistic expectation of men. Were there any good ones really out there? What if she gave up her search for her someone— and took a note from the men's book and just fucked who she wanted and left before she could be left?

She swallowed the ball of emotion in her throat and pressed a hand to her too tight chest. That wouldn't solve anything. She'd end up just as hollow as Sam had been, lying in that hospital bed after his overdose. She'd seen what chasing something empty to fill a void had done to her friend. She wouldn't do that. So instead, she'd head out to the club with her friends and soak up some of the leftover rays of the warmth of their love for each other. Her best friends would take care of her and get her mind off Roman. They'd know exactly what to do to make her feel better.

She clicked Sam's name on her phone and waited for the call to go through.

"Fuck him and his brother," she cursed.

"Well now, that sounds kinky. But threesomes are not usually as fun as you'd think. Someone always gets more attention than the other." Sam's voice was lit with humor. "But Jack says I just think that because I'm an attention whore."

"Well, he's right. You are." Her chest warmed.

"What's going on? Who do I have to fuck up?" Sam asked, his tone more serious this time.

"No one. I just . . . need you to help me forget the last twenty-four hours."

Sam sighed. "We'll do more than that, Elli; we'll help you remember the badass bitch you are."

Her cheeks hurt from how big of a smile he evoked in her. Tears welled in her eyes, blurring the road in front of her. She swiped her hand over them. "Love you guys."

"We love you too. Now get your ass here safely. We'll have the tequila ready."

"I'm on my way."

24

ROMAN

Roman moved through the writhing bodies. Lights flashed, coating the crowd in a bath of multicolor. The floor vibrated with the bass of the music as the artist sang about a "stupid boy." He scanned the myriad of faces. A couple men grinned together in the darker corner. A group of women laughed at a table near the bar. The line was three deep for a drink. No sign of Elise. Roman pulled his phone out, clicking on her social media. She'd checked in here an hour ago. This wasn't his scene—he hadn't been clubbing in years. No updates on her Instagram.

Did this make him a stalker? No—if she told him she truly didn't want him there, he'd leave. But he was done dancing around the issue. He'd hurt her, and he needed to apologize. The thought of her mad at him, turning to another man, made his gut burn with jealousy. It had been so long since this side of him had come out. This possessive, jealous, obsessive need.

Someone brushed against him as he headed to the other side of the room.

"Hey, handsome. You wanna dance?" the man with rainbow suspenders asked.

Roman smiled. "Thanks, but I'm looking for someone."

"If you change your mind, come find me." He winked.

Roman gave him a nod and sidestepped to the edge of the packed dance floor. He stepped up onto the edge of a platform, looking over the room. A flash of red caught his attention in the middle of the space. Elise's arms were wrapped around one man—the one who had dropped her off that one day—while another had his hands on her hips and her back to his front. Her eyes were glazed, a smile on her face as she danced. Her body, lithe and moving to the beat. Her red lips formed the lyrics.

It didn't matter that these were her friends. Nor that he had no right to Elise. His hands fisted and his teeth ground until his jaw ached. The sight of someone else touching her, grinding against her luscious curves, had everything inside him screaming in protest.

Roman crossed the floor without a second thought. He swerved around writhing bodies, the smell of sweat and cologne melding together. Eyes laser focused on her, he reached for her hand and tugged enough to get her attention.

Elise turned to him, her mouth dropping open as she blinked. The two men she was sandwiched between stepped in front of her as if to protect her.

"Elise," Roman yelled over the thumping music.

She peeked between their shoulders, pushed them apart enough to step through. "What are you doing here, Roman?"

He could barely hear her over the music.

"This is the dad you're nannying for?" one of the men asked, his hands moving in sign.

"Yes," she answered.

"Can we talk?" Roman asked.

"How did you know she would be here?" the other man asked.

Roman focused on Elise. "Your social media. Look—we need to talk about this."

"She's not going anywhere with you," the bigger guy yelled, straightening and puffing out his chest.

"Sam, it's okay." She placed her hand on her friend's arm before facing him. "Look, I'm going to go back to having fun with my friends. You have a good night."

"Please," Roman ground out.

Elise's eyes flared. "Roman—"

"You said you wanted a man who knows what he wants. This is me, coming to get you."

"I don't think—"

"Give me a chance. Don't do this. Don't throw away what happened between us over a stupid mistake on my part. I know I fucked up. Let me make it up to you." He searched her eyes for any chance he hadn't ruined this beyond a hope.

"What do you want to do?" the other man asked her.

Elise turned to her friends. "Roman, these are my friends Sam and Jack. Guys, I'll be right back. We'll be over near the bar."

"You sure?" Sam asked.

"Yeah." She headed off the dance floor towards the section of tables parallel to the bar, farther from the speakers.

She turned around and crossed her arms. The movement made her breasts close to spilling out of the top of her dress. Roman's gaze dipped—he was only human. But he forced his attention back to her eyes.

"I don't know what to tell you. I don't give out second chances easily. Why don't we just pretend this never happened? I'll be back Sunday night and spend the week with Ariel. We'll avoid each other and keep everything professional until the end of summer."

He stepped closer until he was in her space. "Is that what you really want?"

Her eyes darted to his lips and then back. She opened her mouth and closed it.

"Answer me."

"I want . . . I need someone who is open and honest with me. If you wanted a one-time hookup, I would have liked to know so I could set my expectations."

He leaned in, his lips right by her CI, ghosting over her ear. "I don't fuck and run."

She shivered, not as unaffected as she tried to pretend. Her gaze narrowed on him with challenge. "Isn't that what you did?"

His voice lowered as he continued, "I'm not the kind of man that can do casual, Elise. And I don't act on impulse. Not until you."

Her lips parted as her breasts rose and fell with each breath.

"We are not done talking about this. And you will come home tonight. If you want to go back and dance the night away with your friends, go for it. But every minute spent letting another person touch you is one more punishment when you get home."

Her brows drew together. "Who the fuck do you think you are? You don't own me."

He leaned in. "You should have thought about that before you let me taste you. You could have walked away. And I tried, God help me, I tried to keep my distance." He blew out a breath. "You want to know one reason I held back? Because I didn't think you could handle me. This is me—I need control. I need to know you're mine and only mine. You should have walked away when you had the chance."

Her eyes darkened as she licked her lips. Elise wanted this

as badly as he did, from the lust shining in her gaze. She just needed a push.

"But I fucked up, so this is your last chance. If you truly do not want this, then walk away now." He drew in a breath. His body vibrated with adrenaline. It was taking everything in him to give her this choice. "But if you want this—with me—then you're going to say goodbye to your friends. We're going to leave and talk about everything. And then I'm going to fuck you until you can't take anymore—after I spank you over my lap."

"You wouldn't." Her voice was all breath. The only reason he heard it was that the song changed.

"You have no idea what I'm capable of." His lips coasted over the shell of her ear. She shivered. "Do you want more from me? Or do you want to go back to only being my nanny?"

"If that's what I wanted, you'd pretend it never happened?" she asked.

He shook his head. "No. I'll never forget the way you whimpered when my fingers were fucking you. Or how you screamed my name as you came. Your taste is branded in my mind. I won't forget. But if you don't want this, I'll keep my distance and pretend I'm not thinking of fucking you every time I look at you. I'll act like I don't want to make you laugh just for the hell of it, because I love the way your eyes light up when you're happy. I'll pretend I don't hate that I fucked up and hurt you."

She blinked, her brown eyes growing darker. "Is that an apology?"

"No. That comes when we get home."

"An apology and a spanking?" She smirked, and it loosened something in his chest.

He shrugged. "I'll make it memorable."

"Oh, I don't doubt that." She pursed her lips, her gaze roaming over him.

He held his breath, waiting for her consent.

"We'll talk first?" she confirmed.

"Absolutely." His hands gripped her waist, tugging her into him. "Yes or no?"

She swallowed, her delicate throat bobbing with the movement. He wanted to bite her, mark her so everyone here knew she was his. It was taking every last thread of his self-control to hold himself back. It had been so long since he'd let this part of him surface.

"Okay."

Relief cascaded over him. "Go tell your friends goodbye so they don't worry."

"My car is at their house."

"We'll deal with it later."

She nodded and gave him one last look before she headed back to her friends, who hadn't taken their eyes off them from the dance floor.

Was it too good to be true? Elise coming with him after he'd hurt her, after knowing what kind of demands he would have? Or could Elise possibly be the woman who could handle him and accept every part of him—even the greedy, dark side that needed to dominate?

25

___

ELISE

What the hell was she doing? Elise peeked at the man in the driver's seat, shadows dancing over his face as he drove them back to the farm. He had one hand on the wheel and the other gripping her thigh, almost like he wanted to assure himself she wasn't going anywhere.

She'd been so mad at him, but then he'd come after her. He'd demanded they talk it out. He'd said things that she'd only ever fantasized about. Was she stupid for giving him another chance?

"Ask." His voice cracked like a whip in the silent car.

"What?"

"Ask me what you want to know," he clarified.

"Why did you push me away?"

He took a deep breath, squeezing her thigh slightly. "You're the first woman I've been interested in since my wife . . . passed."

Oh my god.

"It scared the shit out of me. There's something here between us—do you feel it too?"

"Yes."

"But I don't just have myself to worry about. Ariel is my number-one priority. She's got to come first in my life. That isn't fair to ask of you . . ."

"I can understand that." She placed her hand over his.

His gaze flicked to her and then back to the road in front of him as he made a turn. "If we do this—start a relationship, I mean—then I need to keep it from my daughter. I don't think she's ready—I don't want to—she's already got so much to deal with."

"Okay. And I need some separation. When I'm on the clock, I'm the nanny. After hours . . . we can explore this," she added.

"I'm not the easiest boyfriend."

Boyfriend? Holy shit—they were really doing this. "What does that mean?"

"I have a need for . . . control. In the bedroom."

Her core clenched. "Well, I don't submit so easily."

He smirked at her. "That will just make it all that much sweeter when you gift it to me after I've earned it. When you trust me enough to give it to me."

Holy fuck, her panties were soaked. This wasn't her. All her partners had been vanilla. The spiciest thing she'd done was using handcuffs she'd gotten as a gag gift from her ex.

"We keep the communication going. Anything you don't like, something you need or want from me, we talk about it when we're alone. That's the only way this will work."

"And you'll be honest with me?"

"Of course." He pulled into his driveway. The truck lights glinted off the windows in the house as he parked.

"And we're exclusive?" she asked.

He turned towards her. "I don't share. And I don't want anyone but you."

Her mouth went dry at the possessive glint in his eyes. The air hummed with some unseen energy. The tension in the cab of the truck was so thick it made it hard to draw in a full breath.

"I'm sorry, Elise. For taking off like that after what we shared without letting you know I needed some time. I'm not used to having someone to share things with. I'll try to do better. And I'm sorry if I made you feel like I used you. That was never my intention."

"I appreciate you saying that." Elise cleared her throat. "So, what now?"

"Now? I make good on my promise." He climbed out of the truck and shut her in alone. Humid air rushed over her as he opened her door, reaching over her lap to unbuckle her before he picked her up and tossed her over his shoulder.

Elise squealed as her dress rose, warm air ghosting across her behind. "Roman! Put me down before you drop me."

His palm slapped against her ass, hard. She gasped.

"I won't let you fall. But if you don't hold still, I'll add another two slaps to your spanking." Roman slid his fingers up her thigh, slipping over her slick folds. "Someone's looking forward to her punishment." His steps didn't falter as he led them to the front door.

"Roman—"

"Trust me, honey." The door swung open and he walked them inside without her bumping into anything. He kicked it shut behind him before he carried her into the dining room.

"Where are you going?"

He set her on the table, her ass on the edge before he collared her throat with his large hand. "Can't wait any longer to apologize properly."

His finger hooked around her panties, yanking. The flimsy lace snapped.

"Roman!"

He kissed her. "If any of this is too much, say 'red.' If you say it, then everything stops. Understand?"

She nodded. His hand tightened on her throat, restricting her movement. "Need words, baby."

"Yes."

His lips crashed against hers, his teeth nipping, his tongue exploring, his mouth claiming. She couldn't think, couldn't breathe—could only take what he gave her.

His hand remained on her throat as he applied enough pressure to urge her onto her back. "Fuck, you're gorgeous, laid out like this for me."

Heat blanketed her as the fire in his eyes blazed, pinning her to the wooden table.

"Keep those legs wide open. Let me see what's mine."

Her brows drew together. "Yours?"

His fingers curled around her thighs. "That's right, baby."

"But—oh!"

His tongue slipped through her folds. "By the end of the night, you'll agree. Now turn over. Get on your knees, ass in the air."

"Roman—"

"That's five."

"Five what?" she asked, rolling over as gracefully as possible, which wasn't very.

The wooden slats of the table cut into her knees. Roman pulled the dress over her head, unsnapping her bra before he pressed her head down and tipped her face to the side. Her cheek met the cool surface. Warm hands trailed up her legs, massaging her thighs before grasping her ass.

Chaste kisses peppered her open thighs, climbing higher

and higher. Teeth grazed her ass cheek and she sucked in a breath.

"Look at you, sitting here so perfect for me. So wet for me already." He moved to her side, leaning in to kiss her lips. "I'm gonna make you feel so good, beautiful. Fly so high. But you have to trust me. Can you do that?"

Could she? She squeezed her inner walls in anticipation, already aching for his touch. "Yes."

Soft lips caressed hers, slow and sensual as he gripped the back of her neck. "Such a good girl."

Oooohhh. Why was that so hot? She wanted more. The urge to please him swarmed out of nowhere and buzzed through her veins. She was like an addict, needing another hit.

His hands never left her, exploring her body, brushing over her back, and arms, and legs. The ache inside her grew. Her anticipation swelled every time he came close to her pussy. She whimpered.

His soft chuckle rumbled in his chest. The smooth fabric of his shirt was a contrast to her bare skin. He was still fully clothed, and she, completely naked. Something about the imbalance made this hotter.

"Have you ever wanted to come so bad you begged for it?" he asked.

"No."

"You will tonight. Gonna beg so pretty for me." He sounded so sure of himself.

He kissed and nipped behind her ear and down her neck, trailing over her spine. Her ass rose higher, an offering just as much as a plea.

He moved behind her, palming her ass and squeezing hard enough to leave bruises. Like he wanted to mark her. She shivered.

"You're so responsive." He groaned before a slap preceded a burning bloomed on her right ass cheek.

"Fuck—"

Smack! Smack!

Pain lit her ass on fire.

"Roman—"

His big hand massaged the space he'd slapped.

"You're doing so good, baby. Just two more."

Two more? That was what he'd meant by five? Could she take it? It fucking hurt.

She squirmed on the table as he squeezed again.

"What happened to the apology?" she asked, buying herself some time.

"This is part of it."

"H-how so?" Was her voice higher?

He patted her ass and she flinched. Another chuckle left his lips. Apparently, he liked teasing her.

"I'm gonna turn the other side just as red as this one. You ran off—left when I told you we needed to talk."

"But—"

"I wanna know you won't do that again. You won't run away when something comes up. I need someone who's ready to face whatever comes head-on. If that's not you, say it now."

She blinked, emotion rising within her. Wasn't that what she'd always wanted? Someone to be there for her through thick and thin? Someone to accept her as she was?

"Need those words, Elise."

"Yes." She nodded. "I won't run. But you can't either."

"Agreed."

Another two slaps rained down on her left ass cheek, harder than the first. She cried out. And then spots filled her vision. Pain melded with pleasure as his tongue sucked her clit into his mouth. Her body tensed, knees cutting into the hard wood.

"Roman—"

His tongue slipped inside her hole, and he was fucking her with his tongue as his thumb swirled her clit. "Such a good girl. You did so perfect."

Her inner walls clenched as her pleasure peaked.

He pulled his hand away. "Don't come. Not until I say."

She whined in protest. "Why—"

"Told you, I'm gonna make you beg for it."

His tongue flattened, stroking between her pussy lips from her clit to her taint. Higher and higher he went with each swipe. Surely, he wasn't going to—

"Fuck!"

His slick, warm tongue licked up the crease of her ass as his hands spread her wide.

"Oh, God!"

The warmth plastered against her body jerked away, leaving her cold as Roman stepped around to her side, leaning so his face came to hers. His hand squeezed the back of her neck.

"Look at me," he commanded.

She opened her eyes, having trouble focusing in her lust-induced haze.

His woodsy cologne wrapped around her as his breath danced over her lips. "No one is in this room but you and me. When you wanna call out a name, you make sure it's mine. There's no deity that's capable of giving you what I'm about to. It's all me." He traced her lips with his thumb. "And when you can't hold back your orgasm anymore, you're gonna beg me—Roman. I'm the only one here who can give you what you want. Give you what you need. You're gonna say, 'Please, Roman, let me come.' Do you understand?"

His dark eyes glinted with a possessive force she hadn't expected. Her breath hitched. His fingers slid around her neck, squeezing the sides. She could still draw air into her lungs, but it made her head floaty, like she was high.

"Answer me. So I can give you what we both need."

"Yes."

He tipped his head to the side expectantly.

"Roman," she confirmed.

His eyelids drooped, his eyes half-lidded, lined in pleasure. "Knew you would be perfect."

He moved behind her once more, his mouth latching onto her clit as he sunk two fingers inside her.

Her eyes opened wide, her legs shaking from the onslaught of pleasure. "Roman, I'm going to come."

"Hold it off." He curled his fingers, hitting her G-spot as if challenging her.

She inhaled deep breaths, trying to not fall over the edge that his unrelenting fingers and tongue were pushing her towards. Liquid gushed from her pussy, soaking the table below her. He groaned.

"Fuck, baby. That's it. Just like that. So wet."

Caught on the razor edge of blinding ecstasy, all pride gone, Elise begged. "Please, Roman. Let me come. Please."

"Come for me." He slapped her clit and she exploded, shattering into a million pieces until nothing was left except warm euphoria, rushing over her and pulling out to the tides of another plane of existence. Her ears rang. Her chest was frozen—she was unable to draw breath. Wave after wave of pleasure roared over her as he continued licking, and sucking, drawing her pleasure out. Oblivion hovered at the edge of her vision. Finally, she sucked in a breath.

Roman lapped down her thighs and back between her pussy lips. "Such a sweet cunt."

Her legs trembled. Ultra-sensitive as his five o'clock shadow scraped against her pussy.

Warm hands wrapped around her. "Lie on your back."

She moved, rolling over. Her knees cried out in protest, but his palms went straight to them, massaging.

He stayed silent, his gaze lazily raking down her body. What did he see when he looked at her?

"You're so sexy, spread out like this. Face flushed. Hair fanned around you. Tits hard. They achin' for me?"

Her back arched. Her nipples were burning, they were so tight. She nodded.

"Play with them for me. Squeeze and pinch them until you can't take it anymore. Make it hurt so good. Now."

She obeyed. With her palms full of soft breasts, she squeezed and let out a moan.

"Good girl."

Another orgasm came out of nowhere. She gasped as the unexpected pleasure splintered through her. "Roman!"

"Mmmmm. You're so fucking responsive. I wanted this to last a whole lot longer, but I need to be inside you. Feel that cunt milk my cock. Promise, the next round I'll see just how many ways I can make you come."

She clenched her pussy, hoping it would help with the building ache, but it only made her feel hollow. She wanted him—needed Roman inside her more than anything else.

"Please? Roman—I need—please?"

He stripped his shirt off one-handed before tossing it on the ground. The sound of his zipper only added to her anticipation. The crinkle of a wrapper had her meeting his gaze. He tore open the condom and slipped it on. She hadn't gotten a chance to see his cock before. He was thick. Veins lined the shaft, pre-cum leaked from the tip, now locked behind a layer of latex. Her mouth watered.

"If you keep looking at me like that, I might lose it before I get inside you."

The image of his cum painting her body had her thighs clenching together.

He grabbed her hips, tugging her to the edge of the table. She wrapped her legs around him as he lined his cock up at her entrance.

"You ready for this? I'm not going to go easy on you," he warned.

"Good. I want you—want it all, Roman—"

His cock surged inside her, root to tip in one thrust.

"Ooohhh!"

His brows drew down as he froze. "Don't move."

Her chest heaved as she waited for his next move. He slipped her heels off one by one, setting them on the floor. After a moment, he slipped out of her with a groan. Oh, did he . . .

"Stand up."

What?

He reached for her hand, helping her up. Her knees were too wobbly to stand on her own, but he was there to steady her.

"Bend your knee and set it on the table."

She turned and did as he said, facing away from him. His hand grazed her spine before the heat of his hard front was against her back. His cock drove into her, slow and purposeful, and so damn deep. Oh, this angle was . . . everything.

She moaned, gripping the table for support. His arms slipped under hers, holding her upright. One hand squeezed the sides of her throat enough to send her higher and higher into hazy, lust-filled bliss as his other pinched her nipple.

His scruff brushed against the sensitive skin of her neck.

"Do you know how many times I've fantasized about having these long legs wrapped around me?"

He drove his hips into her, stealing her breath. Fuck, he was so thick, stretching her walls like she'd never been filled before.

"Every fucking day since I met you." *In. Out. In.* "You should be punished for how much you distract me."

The table groaned as his thrusts grew in power. He kissed her throat before turning her lips towards him. One hand still collared her, holding her up against him as the other spread out over her soft stomach, pressing her muffin top. That would usually have her moving away from his touch due to her insecurities. But the way Roman looked at her, like she was the most beautiful woman he'd ever seen, had her leaning into him. Trusting him as she surrendered to his desires. One finger pressed through her folds, finding her clit.

"Roman—"

"Come for me. Squeeze my cock and take what you need." Roman didn't stop. He pressed against her clit, swirling in a hard rhythm that blended pleasure and pain, sending her soaring.

He fucked her, hard, brutal thrusts driving into her, keeping her locked in a prison of unending ecstasy. She could do nothing but experience the musky scent of sex soaking the air. The taste of his mouth. The sounds of skin slapping against skin, of gasping breaths, and low groans.

He lifted her higher and slammed her down on his cock. Her knee was still supported by the table, keeping her wide open, the angle allowing him to drive into the deepest parts of her core, hitting her cervix.

She could do nothing but scream. Her eyes were wide; color was more vibrant. This man thrusted into her with wild abandon. She'd done this—made him come so undone. A feminine power surged through her, firing her synapses in warm, pride-edged pleasure.

But he'd been wrong about one thing; there was a deity here. His muscular form wrapped around her body like he was carved of granite. His muscles bunched under her touch as she skimmed her hands up to grip the back of his head. The man was the very embodiment of Eros—carnal and primal. Driven by lust, and fueled by desire. She was power-less to him. The more she surrendered, the higher he took her.

"Please, Roman, please," she begged.

"What do you need?"

"Give me everything. Come inside me. Please?" Her inner walls clasped him.

He groaned against the back of her neck before nipping her shoulder and interlocking his mouth with hers once more. His kiss was sensual and soft, a complete contrast to the tight grip he had her in, locking her against his body as he railed her against the dining room table.

"That's it. Take my cock like a good girl. So beautiful when you take your pleasure. So perfect. Gonna come inside this cunt." One finger trailed to her asshole, pushing against the tight hole. *Oh, fuck.*

"This ass will be mine too, one day soon."

Scorching tingles raced down her limbs, gathering in her center. She detonated.

His hips drove forward in frenzied, wild strokes. "Fuck, Elise. So fucking tight. I'm coming, baby. I'm—" His teeth bit down on her lower lip hard enough to leave a mark.

Her nails dug into the back of his neck as he stilled. Panting breaths filled the room as his hands slid down her body, gently massaging her breasts while he slid out of her to dispose of the condom. She winced at the soreness. She would feel him for days. She'd never in her life been so thoroughly fucked before.

She spun around, placing both feet on the ground. She wobbled, but he wrapped his arms around her, picking her up and cradling her against his chest before he kissed her forehead.

"That was . . ." She wasn't sure how to express the magnitude of just how mind-blowing that encounter had been.

"Just the apology. Now we can move on to the main course." His chest vibrated with the rumble of his voice against her side.

"What?"

He chuckled. "Told you, we're gonna see just how many ways I can make you come." Roman kissed her until she was nothing but a boneless puddle in his arms.

"I don't think I can take anymore," she admitted as he walked up the stairs.

He nuzzled her neck. "Trust me."

He hadn't led her astray so far. And she'd be damned if she turned down the best sex of her life. If he wanted round two, well, she was all for it. As long as this time, she got to taste him.

"Under one condition." She sighed as he carried her into his room.

He chuckled. "And what's that?"

"I want you to feed me your cock. Fuck my throat and come all over my breasts."

He tensed, turning towards her with a look that had her heart racing and her thighs clenching.

He kicked the door shut behind them. "What my girl wants, she gets. But be careful what you asked for."

26

ELISE

The dark sky was littered with a million stars. The air was filled with the scent of barbecue and smoke from the grills. Laughter from the dozen or so kids melded with the upbeat music playing in the background.

Elise's belly was full of delicious foods, her face a little sore from how much smiling she'd done throughout the day. Her sundress was still a little wet from the water-balloon fight earlier. When the Emersons celebrated a holiday, they sure didn't cut corners. They'd all met up in the town square, sitting outside Remy's Stardust Café to watch the Fourth of July parade before coming back to the farm for games and food.

"Here you go." Roman handed her an ice-cold water bottle.

"Thanks." She twisted the cap off and took a few sips as he slid into the only free seat beside her at the picnic table.

"Does your family always celebrate the Fourth like this?" she asked.

Roman shook his head. "We don't really celebrate the

Fourth. We just use it as an excuse to get together. The kids enjoy the parade. Juneteenth is the day my people recognize our freedom. The Fourth was only a day of freedom if you were white."

"That makes sense."

"Having fun?" he asked with his mouth by her ear, speaking low enough so only she'd hear. Roman placed his hand over her knee, inching up her dress until he gripped her thigh just below her pussy.

Her eyes skated around the table, afraid someone would know what he was doing, but the table covered them. The battery-powered lamps and tiki torches kept the area pretty well-lit despite the growing darkness. "Yeah, I am. What about you?"

His thumb brushed against her skin. Goose bumps erupted over her limbs. He'd done this to her all day. Small brushes here and there. A few stolen kisses behind the barn. He was careful not to let Ariel or anyone else see, but he hadn't gone long without touching her in some way. Her belly flipped with butterflies. It was amazing to have his attention like this. Like no matter what he was doing, she was in the back of his thoughts, capturing a piece of his attention throughout the festivities.

"It's great. Though I'm looking forward to afterwards, when Ariel's asleep in her bed. Then the real fireworks can start." He brushed his fingers over her sex and she drew in a breath, her cheeks flushing as arousal pooled in her belly.

She took another sip of the cold water, hoping it could calm her down a little bit.

Ricky came bounding up to the table with a big smile on his face. "Who's ready for the final show?"

"Is it time for fireworks?" Anthony, the teenager who worked for Nash, asked. Elise had been surprised to see him show up with Sheriff Bently and his wife, along with a few other teens. The group looked like a United Nations meeting with so many people with different heritages, yet they'd all come together as one big family. *Would they accept me if things progressed further with Roman?*

"Yes, it is. So, get your butts on the blankets," Roman answered.

A series of cheers from the kids broke out before they darted to the area that had been set up with folding chairs and picnic blankets.

"Are you gonna start another fire, Uncle Ricky?" Lyra, Remy and Mikel's oldest child, asked.

He crossed his arms over his chest and gave her an unimpressed look. "That was one time."

Lyra gave a shrug. "It was a big one. The fire department had to come out."

"Listen, kid, don't make me choose another favorite niece," Ricky teased.

"Hey, I thought I was your favorite." Zoey pouted.

Ricky wrapped his arm over her shoulder and tugged her against him. "You are now, Z." He stuck his tongue out at Lyra who just rolled her eyes.

Elise giggled. The dynamic between everyone was full of teasing and laughter. The family seemed to show their love by giving each other a hard time.

"Did he really start a fire?" Elise asked Roman.

He chuckled. "Yup. We used to have a shed at the edge of that field." He pointed to the far end of the meadow beside them.

"Oh my god. Should I be worried?"

"Nah, we got fire extinguishers down there on standby. Ricky's not allowed near the fireworks anymore. Or the smokers. Or the grill. Or the firepit."

"I think I'm starting to get the picture." She laughed.

"Let's go. I've got us the best seat in the house." Roman stood.

Her thigh still tingled where he'd touched her. She got up and followed him.

Ariel ran to him. *"I'm going to sit with my cousins in the front."*

"Okay. Just stay where I can see you," he reminded her before she scampered off to sit near the crowd of kids of all ages.

"Are you related to everyone here?" *Even the sheriff?*

Roman sat on the blanket at the back, patting the space next to him. She joined him, crossing her legs in front of her.

"The Stone family are really close with my parents. More like family that just doesn't happen to be blood. So we were raised as cousins. We call them Aunt T and Uncle Matt. Andre and Remy are their kids. And they grew up with the Evans kids—Mikel, Bently, and Jasmine. So them, their partners, and their kids are all included when we have a get-together."

"It's like one big happy family."

He scanned the crowd in front of them and spoke with his voice a little louder, like he wanted them to hear him. "It is. I don't know what I'd do without these assholes."

"That's a dollar for the swear jar," Remy teased him.

"Come on. The kids didn't even hear me," Roman argued.

Remy shrugged. "And I have college to pay for."

"You should hang around Nash, then. I'm sure you'll get what you need," he joked. "Right, Isabella?"

Isabella adjusted the baby to her breast and shook her head. "Maybe we should start one of those jars at our house. I definitely don't want this pumpkin's first word to be four letters long, beginning with an F."

They laughed.

"You sure you want to marry this guy next month?" Roman asked, motioning to Nash.

Isabella's eyebrows rose. "Why? You think I could do better?"

Ricky snorted. "So much, sweetheart. I tried to give you a chance with me, but you just had to go and get knocked up by my brother first."

Isabella snorted. "Yeah, I hadn't exactly planned that either."

"We know all about surprise babies," Remy added.

"Ahh, but they are the best, aren't they?" Jasmine asked.

"I wouldn't know. And I'd like to keep it that way," Ricky said.

"You just wait. Someday, some unlucky girl is gonna capture your attention for longer than a night and you'll be whipped," Nova teased.

Ricky's smile slipped before he righted it. "Don't hold your breath, sis. The bachelor life suits me." He focused on the starry sky, cupping his hands around his mouth and yelling, "When's this show gonna start?"

In answer, a light shot up from the edge of the meadow into the sky above them with a whine. The kids clapped and cheered. More bangs sounded as colored fireworks exploded and popped in the sky over and over, like blooming flowers erupting in the night and disappearing in a cloud of smoke.

Roman nuzzled her neck and inhaled before kissing her bare shoulder. She scanned the people in front of them, but almost everyone was focused on the firework display in front of them. Ricky's lips turned up as he winked at her before turning back to enjoy the show.

"Do you know how bad I've wanted to cart you off and

have my wicked way with you in that dress today?" Roman asked.

She shivered as he peppered kisses up her neck to her jaw. "You could have."

He peeked at the crowd before them. Everyone was so enthralled with the show. Roman kissed her lips, soft and gentle, but he trembled slightly, like he was holding back. He tipped his forehead to hers. His hot breath coasted over her lips. "We did this kind of backwards. I don't want you to think sex is all I want from you. I need to take you on a date, just you and me."

Her heart stuttered, happiness radiating in her lighter than the fireworks illuminating the sky. "I'd like that."

He rubbed his nose against hers and pulled back.

She glanced at the sky. "It's beautiful, isn't it?"

"Gorgeous."

She turned to him, finding his attention hadn't moved from her. She should make a joke about how cliché that sounded, but she couldn't find it in herself to do so. Because he'd meant it. Roman was a sweetheart. Excited flutters filled her belly once more.

He leaned forward like he was going to kiss her again, but stopped. His attention flicked towards his family. She gave a quick scan of her own, and it was clear they had garnered a bit of an audience as a few heads had turned their way.

He clasped her hand in his and moved so they'd be hidden by darkness, stroking his thumb over her hand.

"What did you do for the Fourth, growing up? Did you and your family get together?" he asked.

"Not really. My parents are first generation; their parents immigrated here from Japan—well, my paternal grandfather is American. That's where I get the height from. He met and married my grandmother during the war. My grandparents were too busy working to put a roof over their heads and food in their kids' bellies to celebrate those kinds of holidays. And I guess my parents adopted those views even though we had the time. They ran their own business, so they used it as a day to catch up on things. My brother usually went to friends' places. So I just curled up with a book at home or hung around the house."

"You didn't go to see friends?" he asked.

"No. I didn't go to school locally, so when I came home for the summer, I didn't really know anyone. Sorry. Didn't mean to bring the mood down." She gave an awkward laugh.

"Don't do that." He squeezed her hand.

"Do what?"

Colorful bursts of light reflected in his eyes as he stared at her so hard, she was afraid he'd see to her very soul. "Don't hide those pieces of you that aren't perfect."

Her breath caught. Her heart squeezing tight.

Roman leaned in and kissed her softly, his lips melding with hers before he nipped her bottom one and pulled away. "I want to know the real you. Complicated family issues and all. I've got my fair share of things in my past that I'm ashamed or just not proud of, but if this is gonna work, we need to be honest with each other."

She nodded, tears welling in her eyes. Roman was asking for so much more than he realized. A part of her was terrified but also hopeful. He wouldn't want to know those things unless he could see a future with her. "I'll try."

"Me too." He kissed her one more time as the bursts and explosions increased in the sky around them, building up for the finale.

Roman tucked her against his chest, his arm around her as

they watched the rest of the show. She was surrounded by friends and so much love; she could feel it in the air. That empty piece inside her didn't feel like it was gaping tonight.

27

ROMAN

Roman's back ached as he jogged down the stairs, fresh from his shower after a long day in the bee yards. The smells coming from the kitchen made his stomach rumble. "I'm starving."

"Good thing we left you a big portion of dinner, then," Elise said, curled up on the couch next to Ariel, braiding his daughter's dark brown hair.

Roman grabbed the plate with baked potato wedges, grilled chicken, and asparagus. "Wow, this looks amazing. Thank you for cooking again."

"You're welcome." She patted Ariel's shoulder. "All done, sweetie."

Roman sat on the other side of Ariel, giving her a kiss on her temple. "How was your day with Elise?"

Ariel snuggled between them while he ate his meal. "*It was good. We painted the shells we brought home from the beach. I made one for Papa and Gramma when they get back from their trip.*"

"I'm sure they'll love them."

"You made one for your dad too, didn't you?" Elise asked.

Ariel's smile brightened as she nodded and jumped off the couch. She disappeared into the dining room before coming back with a bright yellow shell with black lines painted over it.

"It's a bee shell."

He held it in his palm, admiring her work. "Huh! So it is. That's so cool. Thanks, sweet pea."

"I made a rainbow one for Elise."

"It's already put away in my room so I can see it every day when I wake up." Elise bopped Ariel's nose with her finger. Ariel's crooked smile brightened, pride shining in her eyes.

"What else did you do?" he asked.

Ariel sat between them, telling him all about their day. This had become the routine when he got home. Even if it was just for a few moments before Ariel's bedtime, Roman made sure to connect with her. With Elise here, it gave him a sense of fullness, like something he hadn't realized was missing in his life was now there. She just fit.

What if we could have this forever?

They hadn't spoken about the end of summer yet or Elise's plans. This was all so new. It was too soon. But Roman wanted her in his life and Ariel's.

"It's time for bed."

Ariel pouted. *"Can't I stay up a little longer?"*

"No, you've got a beach day planned for tomorrow. You want to be well rested so you don't miss any mermaids," he answered.

"Fine. But can Elise read my story tonight?"

Roman glanced at Elise.

She smiled. "I'd love to."

They got up from the couch, and he rinsed his plate and put it in the dishwasher before following them upstairs. Ariel crawled into bed. Elise picked the book from the bedside table up and opened *The Prince and The Knight.*

"This is one of my favorites."

"Really? Why's that?" Elise asked, snuggling up on one side of Ariel's bed. His daughter leaned against her. Roman took a seat on the opposite side, wrapping an arm around them both. Perhaps Ariel would think it a little strange, and it was a tight squeeze, but he hadn't been this at peace in . . . too long.

"Because everyone thinks the prince needs to find a princess to marry, but he really loves the knight. They save each other. And there's a dragon."

Elise's soft laughter tumbled out of her like a tinkling of bells, warming his chest. "Dragons are pretty cool. Okay, ready?"

Ariel nodded and snuggled between them. Elise began the story, acting out the voices. Ariel looked at her just as much as she did the pictures in the book. Her eyelids drooped closed right before the end of the story. Elise finished it, closing it and setting it beside the bed. She turned back to Ariel, tracing her finger over her profile so lovingly, it made his heart squeeze tight.

"She's a beautiful little girl," Elise whispered, not taking her eyes off his daughter. "She's so smart too. We got some graphic novels from the library today and I found her going through them while I made dinner. She started telling me all about the story. I hadn't even realized she was reading them. They're above her grade level, and she struggled on some of the bigger words, but she was reading them." Pride flickered in her eyes as she met his gaze.

Was there anything more breathtaking than watching someone else love on your child the way their missing parent would have? It socked him right in the chest. Roman's lungs froze before he sucked in a breath. He was falling for Elise. Hell, he might already be half in love with her. It should terrify him, but for the first time in so long, Roman let go of the what-ifs of what could go wrong. Because the way she looked at Ariel, the way Elise responded to him, he'd be a fool not to give everything he had to make this work.

Roman eased his arm out from under his girls—*his girls* was exactly what they were now. He tucked Ariel in as Elise slid off the bed and headed out to the hall. He shut the light off and followed her.

"Thank you." Roman brushed her hair away from her cheek, tucking it behind her ear.

"You don't have to keep thanking me." She blushed.

He took her hand and led her into his room, closing the door behind them. Sitting on the bed near the headboard, he pulled her into his arms. "Yeah, I do. Because I'm so fucking grateful you came into our lives and—" His voice choked with emotion as his eyes grew blurry.

Elise tipped her head, framing his face in her hands as she straddled his lap. "Hey, what's going on?"

He blinked rapidly trying to get a hold of himself and cleared his throat. "Sorry—"

"Don't be sorry for showing your emotions and being human." Her voice was sterner than he'd ever heard. His eyes widened a fraction as he stared at her.

"Sorry, but I don't subscribe to this bullshit toxic masculinity that says a man can't cry."

He blew out a breath and chuckled. "I don't either. In fact, I'm pretty sure I've seen my dad cry more than my mom."

Her shoulders eased. "Good. Now what's this about?"

He swallowed. "To see you, the way you are with Ariel—like how her mother would have been."

"Did I overstep?"

He shook his head. "No, nothing like that. I'm just so grateful for you, for everything you've done for us. How you put up with my grumpy ass."

She giggled, and damn, he loved the sound of it. So light and free. He wished he could bottle it up and store it close to him, carry a piece of her light around with him everywhere he went.

"I mean it," he insisted, tracing the edge of her face with a finger.

Her hands dropped to his chest, one over his heart which was beating so hard.

"I come with a kid and a lot of baggage. My family is dealing with this ongoing murder investigation," he said.

She shrugged. "Well, your kid doesn't belong in those categories. She's definitely a positive."

"See? That's exactly what I'm talking about. You have such a big, beautiful heart."

A soft, shy smile curved the corners of her full lips as her gaze dropped like it usually did when he complimented her.

He cupped the side of her face, forcing her to look at him. "Mean it, honey. So thank you for everything you've done for us, everything you've brought to our life. It means a lot to me."

She nodded and pressed her lips against his. He slid his tongue into her mouth, needing to taste her. But this moment wasn't about lust or sex but something deeper. Something so wholly unexpected, he wasn't quite sure what it was—but it was definitely *more.*

28

ELISE

Elise sipped her now warm tea and turned the page in the binder in front of her. The only light in the kitchen was the pendant above the bar where she sat. The house was quiet; she'd left her CI on just in case Ariel woke in the middle of the night.

The stairs creaked. She turned as a sleepy-looking Roman padded into the room in bare feet with his boxers hung low on his hips.

He rubbed his eyes and then ran a hand through sleep-mussed hair. "What are you doing up?"

She closed her book and spun on the bar seat to face him. "Couldn't sleep."

"Sorry I fell asleep on you." He kissed her cheek, his arms grasping the bar on either side of her, pinning her in place.

She tipped her head and kissed his lips. "No need to be sorry. You have a very manually intensive job. I don't know how you do it all."

Roman nuzzled her neck. His rough stubble scratched her

skin, sending chills down her limbs. "That's why you came—because I can't do it all by myself."

She giggled. "You know what I mean."

"Why don't you come back to bed? I'll put you to sleep." Roman smirked.

"That does sound wonderful, but I didn't want Ariel to wake and find me in your bed. Wasn't sure you were ready to have that conversation with her."

"I appreciate it. And your patience. But I have this thing on my door; it's called a lock—"

She playfully smacked his chest.

"Ow! What was that for?"

"Being a smart-ass." She bit back her smile.

"I like when you get all feisty." He stepped between her thighs, kissing her while his hard cock rubbed against her core, separated only by his boxers and her thin sleep shorts.

"Mmmm, it seems you do," she teased, slipping her hands over his pecs, flicking her tongue over his nipple.

"Fuck, what are you doing to me, woman?"

I hope the same thing you're doing to me.

Roman's lips melded against hers. She parted her mouth and he took it as an invitation, slipping his tongue inside. He tasted so good, like cinnamon and his own unique flavor. He nipped her bottom lip, grinding against her as one hand slipped beneath her shorts, edging past her pussy lips and diving in between her folds.

"Fuck . . . you're so wet already."

"That's what you do to me," she confessed.

Dark brown orbs focused so intently on Elise that her skin prickled with a mix of scorching flames and tingles of ice.

"Tell me to go back to bed, or I'm going to carry you up to my room and make love to you."

Yes, please.

In answer, she hooked her arms around his neck, pulling him in for another kiss. "Take me to bed."

Roman picked her up. She locked her legs around him, holding tight as he kissed her senseless all the while walking out of the kitchen, up the stairs, and towards his bedroom.

She sucked his tongue as he shut the door. The lock clicked. Roman continued to the bed, sliding her down his body, his hard cock rubbing against her the whole way to the mattress.

She hooked her thumbs in the waistband of his boxers, sliding them over his thick, muscular thighs, and toned legs. His erection jutted out towards his stomach, the head dripping with pre-cum. Elise couldn't help herself; she bent down and licked the tip.

Fingers tangled in her hair, tightening at the base of her neck and tugging in that perfect mix of controlled pain that made her thighs clench together as he took control.

"Not yet." His voice was hoarse. "Take your clothes off, slowly."

Roman stepped back just out of reach.

Elise started with her top, pulling the bottom of her sleep shirt over her head, exposing her bare breasts. Roman's gaze raked over her, making her nipples harden into points. Anticipation wound tight as the air thickened, making it harder to draw a breath.

"Now the bottoms, baby."

She sat, tugging her shorts down her hips and tossing them onto the floor with her top.

"Goddamn, you are one beautiful woman."

"Back at you, sexy."

"Scoot back towards the headboard."

She obeyed, climbing higher until her head rested on the pillow that smelled of him, woodsy and clean.

"Now spread those sexy long legs apart. Show me my pussy."

"*Your* pussy?"

He nodded. "That's right, baby. In this bed, I own every piece of you. Thought we'd been over this?"

"Just making sure," she teased.

"Tonight, you're gonna be my fuck toy. How does that sound?"

Heat blanketed her in flames, like a backdraft had sucked the air from her lungs and replaced it with a wildfire of need. She wanted to be his plaything. For him to use her for his pleasure. Elise trusted that he'd give her more than he'd take because that was who Roman was as a lover.

"Need those words, honey."

"Yes. Use me."

He bit his lip, his eyes glazing over with hazy lust. "Play with those tits. Squeeze the tips hard."

She moved her hands to her breasts. Her skin was covered in goose bumps as she pinched and twisted. There was something different about touching herself while he watched. A new level of pleasure swirled through her, knowing it was turning him on to watch her.

"Good girl."

She closed her eyes at his praise, her legs inching closer together.

"Keep your eyes and legs open. I'll be right back." Roman turned and left the room while she opened herself up once again.

He returned a moment later, locking the door once more. He kneeled on the bed below her, setting something behind him.

"Move those feet higher, knees out, and then touch yourself."

A blush burned her cheeks; she was sure they were fire-engine red. She'd never—

"Do it now."

She slipped her fingers down her round belly to her sex, then dipped two fingers into the wet heat.

"Fuuuuuck. You're perfect. That's it, baby. Now swirl them around your clit, but don't come until I tell you. Remember, your orgasms are mine."

Her back arched, one hand still pinching her nipple as the other swirled her clit. She wanted his touch so bad.

"So sexy to see my little fuck toy edging herself," he rasped, moving beside her and lying on his side. "Don't stop." He gently sucked her nipple in his mouth.

Her eyes rolled up. Pleasure wound tighter and tighter in her core.

His lips brushed her ear as he palmed her breast. "Now be a good girl, and come for me."

Roman bit her neck as her orgasm came out of nowhere, slamming through her. She pinched her clit harder as he kneaded her breast and sucked her neck. Her back arched. A tinny sound rang in her ears. Her body locked up with another wave of orgasm. She was powerless to the onslaught of pleasure tumbling through her.

Wetness seeped down her hand, between her legs.

Roman kissed his bite mark gently pulling away. "You did so good. So beautiful."

"I think I got the bed wet." She tried to catch her breath. Holy hell, she'd never come that hard touching herself. She usually had to use toys.

"Wait here." He got off the bed, slipping into the bathroom and coming back out with some sort of material. It almost looked like a mini blanket but thicker.

"It's waterproof." He laid it on the bed, grabbing a pillow

and sliding it underneath. "Come lie on this. Hips on the pillow."

She scooted over. Roman slid between her thighs, gripping one. The distinct buzz of a vibrator filled the air as he held it up with a smirk.

"What . . .?"

"I bought you something to try." He tipped the toy toward her.

"You got me a vibrator?"

"Oh, sweetheart, it's not just a vibrator. The sales lady told me it would make you see God." He smirked. "In this case, I'll use it on you until you experience so much intense pleasure, you know it's me that holds all the power—if you'll only surrender to it."

That sounded promising. "Oh, really?"

"No harm in finding out for yourself. Now, remember not to come unless I tell you. If you do, you'll be punished."

"Maybe I want to be spanked," she teased. Psh, punishment? More like funishment.

He shook his head. "No, baby. My punishment for coming when I didn't give you permission will be that you won't come again the rest of the night. I'll fuck you and use you and get you so close to the edge, but I won't let you come."

Why did that sound so hot to her? Yes, she wanted orgasms, but also to be used so thoroughly and teased to the point of insanity. And she had the choice. It was in her hands —or her self-control capabilities at least.

"Okay. I'll try."

He pressed the toy just above her hole. She tensed as pleasure coursed through her.

"That's it, baby. Gonna take what I have to give you. Gonna make you squirt all over me."

She forced air in and out of her lungs in deep breaths to

try and keep control as he moved the vibrating knob around her clit.

Sweat broke out on her temple as she closed her eyes and accepted what he was giving her.

"You're doing so good."

"Oh, God." She squeezed her eyes shut, his praise bringing her to that razor-sharp edge of coming. *No, not yet.* She wanted to come, but more than that, she wanted to please him.

"What did I tell you about saying that?" He moved the toy over her clit.

She thrashed on the bed. It wasn't strong enough to send her into an orgasm, but it could tease her right to the cliff.

"Sorry!"

"Whose fingers are inside you right now?" He slid two in her, fucking her slowly as the vibrator moved around her clit again.

"Yours!"

"Say my name."

"Roman."

"Good girl . . . you want to come?"

"Yes!"

He clicked a button, and what was once just vibration turned to both that and suction. Motherfucker. Did he want her to fail?

"Come," he commanded, the toy moving its sucking pulses over what felt like a direct nerve on her clit.

Her back bowed off the bed as white spots filled her vision. She moaned. A hand clamped over her mouth.

"Gotta be quiet. Don't make a sound or I stop." He kept that evil toy on her clit as he moved his palm away from her lips and slipped his fingers back inside her, fucking her harder, curling them to hit her G-spot.

Ecstasy fired through her every synapse. Wave after wave of euphoria rocked through her until she was awash in a warm, boneless bath of pleasure.

She had no sense of time or anything else beyond the sensations in her body. The clench of her muscles as he drew more and more carnal satisfaction from her. The burn of her lungs as she held her breath. The black spots that edged her vision until she was limp and had no choice but to surrender to the pleasure.

Roman had complete control, playing her body like he knew it better than she did. The way his dark eyes lit with desire, all aimed at her, only added more fuel to an already raging fire of lust, want, and need. His pink tongue darted out to lick his bottom lip, like he could taste her arousal in the air.

"Such a good fuck toy. Laid out for me to use. For me to drain every last drop of pleasure from."

Pressure built. It was almost like she had to pee. "Please let me come. Please—" She squeezed her eyes shut, trying to stave off the impending climax.

"I love the way you beg." He hit a button, turning the suction higher while fingering her. "Come."

The urge to bear down hit her. She surrendered to it, her ejaculation streaming out of her, sliding between her thighs and soaking the mat below her. Her orgasm splintered through her, stealing her breath, making her dizzy.

"That's it. So perfect. Knew you could do it. Such a good girl. You come so fucking pretty."

She gasped for breath as he leaned in and licked her nipple.

The tip of his dick brushed against her sensitive folds. He hissed, his body tensing before he lowered his forehead to hers. "You feel so good. Hot and wet."

"I would feel even better if you slid inside me."

He stared into her eyes. "I'm clean—I mean I haven't . . . It's been a long time."

"I'm clean too. Got tested recently. And I've got an IUD. I mean, if you wanted to—"

"I want to feel you with nothing between us." He kissed her softly.

"Then fuck me."

He kissed down her jaw, trailing over her neck. Nipping her shoulder, he slid inside her, inch by torturously slow inch. Was he trying to show her he was still in control? Or did he want to savor this? She clenched around him, and he groaned.

His biceps flexed on either side of her as he looked down at her. "You're so fucking tight. Feels so good around my cock."

"Don't hold back." She looped her hand around his neck, meeting his gaze. "Fuck me until you fill me with your cum."

She barely had time to register his growl before he was pounding into her. With her hips on the pillow like this, his cock went so much deeper. His pubic bone hit her clit with each thrust.

"That's it. Take my cock like a good little fuck toy." He moved the vibrator between them, placing it over her clit as he drove his hips into her, sandwiching it between her and his pelvis. With each rock, she was sent over the cliff into dark, carnal bliss. He clamped a hand over her mouth, locking in the sounds until nothing but muted moans, masculine grunts, the buzz of the toy, and the slapping of skin filled the room.

"Keep your eyes on me, baby," he said, holding her gaze.

He thrust into her over and over. His brows drew down in concentration. Sweat glistened on his forehead. Shadows danced over his sharp features. He was wild chaos contained in human form. Flames of desperation and need shone in his eyes, her Eros, draining every last bit of pleasure from her and then some.

"I'm gonna come," he said.

"Fill me up. Give it to me." She hooked her legs around his waist and squeezed him tighter.

He shut the toy off and tossed it on the bed. Roman slammed into her harder and faster before his strokes grew jerky. His cock pulsed inside her pussy as his arms tightened around her.

He kissed her, his lips soft and warm as they both came down. After a peck to the tip of her nose, he slid out of her and moved off the bed, disappearing into the bathroom. Where was he going?

Roman was back a moment later with a warm, wet cloth. He pressed her thighs apart, wiping them first before using two fingers to slip between her swollen pussy. She hissed, so sensitive to his touch. She was still so aroused.

He moved the digits down, scooping up the cum that slipped out of her and pushing it back inside her. "Fuck, there's nothing hotter than my cum dripping out of you."

Her eyes rolled up and she squeezed her thighs together, clamping around his hand as she came again. "Roman!"

"It's okay. I got you." He gripped her leg; his fingers would no doubt leave bruises. That just made it hotter. She would have a mark to remind her of this moment for a few days at least.

Her legs grew limp once more. He pushed them apart and cleaned around her sex.

Leaning down, he kissed the top of her pussy. She trembled. He made quick work of the washcloth and waterproof mat. Roman pulled the covers down and tucked her beside him. Skin to skin, he held her, wrapped in his arms. He removed her CI, setting it carefully on the bedside table. She snuggled into his chest. His heartbeat thudded against her cheek as she closed her eyes, her body intertwined with his, encompassed in safety.

His big hand splayed over her back, caressing her spine and lulling her to sleep. This was exactly where she was supposed to be.

Tears pricked behind her sleepy eyes. She'd never been so seen, so cared for—so loved. Roman was everything she'd ever wanted in a partner and then some. Something clicked inside her, like a piece falling into place. Whatever had held her back from Roman was gone. She wholeheartedly had fallen in love.

29

———

ELISE

Lights flashed as screams of glee melded with the rhythmic notes of the live band playing on a pop-up stage at the entrance to the pier. The carnival ran every summer. There were rides and games. The scent of popcorn and fried dough filled the air from colorful tents with food and local beer. Elise's summer dress billowed against her legs in the warm breeze.

Roman's hand slipped into hers, his rough skin against her soft palm. "Where should we start?"

She glanced at him. He'd chosen an olive-colored short-sleeve shirt that hugged his lean muscles, and a pair of camou-flage shorts with high-top Converse. Her stomach fluttered nervously. They'd had sex multiple times and, as backwards as it was, this was their first date.

"I don't know."

"What's your favorite ride?" Roman asked, holding up the strip of tickets he'd purchased for them.

"I've never ridden any."

He stopped, turning to her with his eyebrows drawn

together in an incredulous look. "You've never been to the carnival?"

She shrugged. "Once, but it wasn't for long and I didn't get to ride anything."

"You said you grew up in Dark Cove. How could you not come for the fun? Not even on dates in high school?"

She swallowed and looked towards the teens throwing darts at balloons at one of the games. "I didn't date in high school."

"We're fixing that. We're riding everything." Roman tugged her hand, leading her towards the line for the closest ride, which happened to be giant teacups.

"We don't have to—"

"Don't worry. I know it's your first time. I'll be gentle." He smirked.

"Am I on a date with Ricky all of a sudden?" she teased.

He barked out a laugh. "It was too easy. Alright, ready to get dizzy?"

"That doesn't sound so fun."

He handed the tickets to the bored-looking pimple-faced teen running the ride. "It's Ariel's favorite."

She followed him into a giant teacup, sitting beside him. He buckled her in and placed his hand around her shoulders.

"If Ariel likes it, I suppose it can't be too bad." She swallowed down her nerves.

"Exactly. You need to know your stuff for when we take her back here together. I mean, if you want to come with us?" he asked.

"I would love that." She smiled.

The cup started moving and she gripped his thigh, her other hand holding onto the circle in the center of the cup. Around and around they spun.

Roman's hard scruff scratched her skin as he leaned in and kissed her cheek. "Having fun yet?"

She laughed. "Yes."

"Then you'll probably like this next part." Roman gripped the center and moved it so the cup spun in a circle too.

"Oh my goodness!"

Lights swirled around them as the ride twirled them around and around. Her vision blurred until the only thing she could focus on was the heat of his body against her side. Elise's hand tightened on his thigh. Her skin prickled with the heavy weight of his gaze on her. Light and free for what seemed like the first time in forever, Elise laughed.

Slowly, the spinning wound down to a stop. Roman unbuckled her and opened the door, holding out a hand to help her out of the ride and steady her.

"Dizzy? Or are you ready for the next adventure?" he asked.

"Mmmm, I think I'll be okay. What's next?"

* * *

Six rides later, Elise was ready for a break. "The teacups are probably my favorite so far."

Roman handed a few bills over in exchange for a basketball. "We haven't tried the Ferris wheel yet."

She turned, eyeing the tall metal contraption closest to the beach. Her stomach dipped. "Maybe we don't need to do every ride."

"That one's my favorite. I promise it will be worth the view alone." Roman threw the ball, hitting the rim before making a basket. The worker handed him a second ball.

She didn't want to make him miss his favorite ride or hold him back. But the idea of being up that high . . . She shivered.

He missed the second shot. Roman went for the third, and it spun around the rim and bounced out.

"You can choose from this wall of prizes," the worker offered, pointing to a lattice full of small stuffed animals on keychains.

"What do we have to get to win the bigger ones?" Elise asked.

The teen motioned to the basketball hoop farthest away. "Get three baskets."

"I'll try again and win you something," Roman insisted.

"How about I try and win you one?" she teased.

Roman shrugged. "You think you got it in you? I want the unicorn." He pointed to the bright pink pony with the rainbow horn.

"Ariel would love that."

"She'll have to fight me for it," he joked.

Elise opened her purse. "I'll do it."

Roman pressed his hand over hers and handed the teen more cash. "A turn for my girl here."

His girl. Flutters erupted in her belly.

She took the first ball.

Roman stepped behind her. "You know what you're doing?"

"Can't be too hard. Just aim and shoot, right?" she asked coyly.

She sunk the first shot, all net, and shrugged as she got the second ball. "Must be beginner's luck."

The second hit the backboard and swished.

"Last one." The teen gave her the final ball.

She lined up her shot, using her left hand as the guide, and scored. She smiled, jumping up and down. "I did it!"

Roman's eyes reflected the colorful lanterns lighting the

pathways through the carnival. "Damn, didn't realize I was going against a professional."

She gave him another coy smile.

"That was fucking hot." He nuzzled her neck.

"I want the pink unicorn, please." She accepted the stuffed animal from the teen.

"Ariel's gonna love having you along when we come next time. My bank account will too. Took me four tries last time to get her a medium-sized stuffy."

"Well, now you can give her this one."

He tucked the unicorn under his arm farthest away from her and shook his head. "No way; this one's mine. My date won it for me."

She laughed. Roman tugged her arm so she stumbled against his chest. With his eyes locked on hers, he cupped her face with one hand and leaned in. His lips softly coasted against hers before he pulled back. "You just keep surprising me. But I guess that's to be expected since we're getting to know each other."

Roman took her hand once more and led her to a line for a food truck. "How'd you learn to shoot like that?"

"Intramural basketball in college."

"Makes sense. You never tried out for the team? I'd figure with an ability to score like that and your height, you'd be a no-brainer."

She shifted on her feet. "No. I hadn't really played organized sports before, but it was nice to exercise. A few friends dragged me along with them."

"Do you trust me?" he asked, stepping up to the counter.

"Um, yes. I guess."

He laughed. "Not a winning endorsement. Don't worry. I'm just talking about food."

"Okay. You're the carnival expert."

Roman turned towards the older woman with a hairnet working in the truck.

"What can I get ya, sweetie?" she asked.

"I'll take an order of fried dough, fried Oreos, cotton candy, and a candy apple. Oh, and two lemonades, please."

He paid and accepted some of the food and drinks, then led them to a picnic table nearby while they waited on the rest of the order.

"Okay, try this first." He handed Elise the blue and pink ball of fluff.

"I've had cotton candy before."

"But not from a carnival. Trust me, it makes a difference," he argued.

She rolled her eyes and plucked a piece, then set it on her tongue and closed her mouth, enjoying the sweet melting sensation.

"Well?" His eyes were glued to her lips.

She smiled and plucked another piece, her tongue darting out to lick it. "It's delicious."

"Try the apple." He moved it towards her.

She gripped the stick, but he didn't let go. Her tongue sliding up the red candy. Roman pulled it away, making her have to lean closer for a second lick.

"My turn." He leaned in and captured her mouth. She sucked in a breath of surprise. He took advantage and slipped his tongue inside her parted lips. Sugar melded with his taste, sweet and minty with a hint of cinnamon. His kiss winded her higher and higher. She didn't care who was around them. His touch consumed her. All she wanted was more.

He pulled away, his lips shiny, eyes hazy and half-lidded. "I hate to ask, but can you get the order? I need a minute before I can walk."

She hadn't even noticed the woman at the food truck

calling out their order. Elise's gaze flicked to Roman's lap where his hard cock pressed against his shorts.

"Oh, yeah. No problem." She slid out from the table and grabbed their fried goodies, thanking the woman before returning.

"Thanks," Roman said, sheepishly.

"No problem. It's nice to know a kiss with me has that effect." She sipped her lemonade. It was the perfect mix of tart and sweet.

"It was that evil tongue of yours enjoying those sweets. Gives me all kinds of fun ideas." He waggled his eyebrows up and down playfully.

"Oh, tell me more." She leaned against his shoulder.

"You'll have to wait until we're somewhere more private. Now, you're gonna try these classic carnival snacks and then we're gonna ride the Ferris wheel."

"Alright." She plucked a fried Oreo and bit into it before licking the powdered sugar from her lips. "Mmmm. It's like a fresh-baked Oreo."

"It's my favorite."

"You've got great taste."

He kissed the corner of her mouth and grabbed one for himself. "I still can't believe you've never been here to really enjoy the carnival when your family lives so close."

"My family and I aren't close. My brother is eight years older than me, and I was kind of unplanned—an accident is more the truth. Then when they found out I was Deaf . . ." She swallowed. The sting of her tears was surprising. She never got emotional talking about this. It was just how things were. There was nothing she could do to change it, though she'd tried so hard for so long.

"What happened?" Roman asked, turning to face her.

She blinked a few times to clear the emotion from her

eyes. "They didn't know what to do with me I suppose. That's why they sent me to a boarding school for the hearing impaired until high school. Then I was mainstreamed."

"How old were you?"

"Six."

"That must have been terrifying."

She nodded, her throat tightening. "I was alone. I didn't know anyone. But it turned out to be one of the best things to happen to me. The school was wonderful. I made friends. Learned sign language. I was finally given the tools to communicate."

"Did you get to see your family often?"

"On breaks. Holidays and summer. But my brother was in sports and programs, and my parents were running their business, so they were gone a lot. And they didn't really . . . we're nothing like your family." She took another drink.

"What do you mean?" he asked.

"I mean, everyone learned sign for Ariel. Not like the basics—they can all carry on conversations in sign."

He tensed. "Your family didn't learn sign?"

She shook her head. "They figured I'd be fine with my CI, I guess. My mom can sign a little. I don't remember my dad ever using it. My brother took a class in college, so he can, but mostly we just speak or text. But the rest of my family, they don't speak English very much. And our language doesn't even have the letter L. So my name is another thing that sets me apart."

"And their language is tonal, which is harder for you to understand with your CI, right?" he asked.

He'd remembered? She was touched. "Sometimes it feels impossible."

Roman was quiet for a few moments. His hand landed on hers, and he rubbed his thumb over the expanse of skin between her thumb and index finger. "That sounds really isolating. I'm sorry."

She melted inside. He got it. And it wasn't pity she felt from him but empathy.

"It's just how it is. So when I saw how your family came together and all learned sign for Ariel, and how your mom fixes her family meal special for Eli and his texture aversions, it showed me exactly the kind of people you are—kind and wonderful. You all really care about others."

Roman pulled his hand away to wrap his arm around her and kiss her temple. "You deserve that too."

She snuggled into him for a few moments. "Did Ariel stop speaking after she found out your wife passed?"

Roman's chest filled with air and then he exhaled, his breath dancing over her hair.

"You don't have to answer." She pulled back to look at him.

"No, it's okay. It's just been a while since I've talked about it." He moved the fried bread dough towards her.

She picked off a piece and took a bite.

"Ariel was home alone there when Tiana died of a brain aneurysm. She was alone with her for hours. Screaming and crying for her mom and me—" His voice broke.

Holy shit. Ariel had been there? Elise pressed her hand to his chest. "I'm so sorry."

Roman shook his head. "I feel so guilty because I should have been there. She didn't text me back and I should have known something was wrong. I'd just thought maybe she'd fallen asleep with Ariel or they were busy having fun."

"Of course you would."

"I should have known something was wrong. Came home sooner. I know I wouldn't have been able to save Tiana. But Ariel went through that alone. The doctor who checked her over said her throat was red and irritated, like she'd been screaming for hours. We thought maybe it hurt too much to talk. But my little girl never said another word after that day. Like she'd given up believing I would hear her and come help her." Roman's shoulders slumped as if the confession carried an invisible weight.

Elise's heart ached for him and Ariel. That was such an awful, traumatic experience. "You blame yourself?"

"Who else is there to blame?"

"Look at me." She cupped his cheek. "You are an amazing father to Ariel. She knows you love her. That little girl worships the ground you walk on. You're her favorite person, maybe except for her gramma, and that's just because she sneaks her cookies."

One corner of Roman's mouth quirked up momentarily.

"No one could have seen something like that coming or known. You could have reacted in so many other ways. But it's evident in your relationship with your daughter and how well adjusted she is that you were there for her."

"I didn't have a choice but to work through my grief for Tiana. I saw what holding onto it did to my brother, Nash. I couldn't afford to check out—I had Ariel."

"Don't you see? That's exactly what makes you such an amazing father. You put her first—always—even when it takes everything inside you."

Roman was silent a moment, searching her eyes. Had she said the wrong thing?

"Thank you." He took a breath. "For saying that. But also for being here for her the way you have. For being there for me."

She smiled. "I wouldn't want to be anywhere else."

He kissed her, soft and slow, his hand gripping the back of her neck. Her palms dropped to his chest, fisting his shirt.

"Get a room, man," someone yelled.

Elise jerked back.

Roman smirked. "Come on. Let's go ride that Ferris wheel."

He stood, quickly cleaning up what was left of their food and tossing it in a bin before leading her to the last ride.

She gulped, staring up at it. The wheel looked so much higher the closer she got. *I don't know if I can do this.* But Roman made her want to push her boundaries and try things she'd never done before.

He gave the last of his tickets to the girl running the ride and led her into the seat. She tried to breathe, but her body tensed up. The bar lowered over their lap as the seat moved back and forth. She closed her eyes instinctively, gripping the metal across her legs as if her life depended on it—because it probably did.

"What's wrong?" Roman asked as they started moving up. Her stomach dropped, coiling into a knot.

"Shit, baby, look at me." Roman's arm wrapped around her, tugging her closer to him, giving her a semblance of safety.

"I'm scared to look."

"You're safe. I won't let anything happen to you. Promise." His assurance melted her from the inside out. "Elise?"

"Yes?"

His palm slid up her bare thigh, past her dress.

Her eyes snapped open. "What are you doing?"

"Distracting you."

"What if someone sees?"

His finger slid her panties to the side and stroked over her sex. "No one can see."

The dark sky above them glittered with stars, but the moon was nowhere to be seen. White lights flashed on the side of the ride, casting half his face in shadows. The sounds of the carnival phased in and out as they rotated higher and then lower on the ride.

"Do you want me to stop?" he asked, kissing her neck. His fingers slid over the part of her pussy lips.

She gasped. "No. Don't stop."

One finger slipped inside her. "Fuck, you're already so wet. This turns you on, doesn't it?"

"Yes."

"Think I can make you come by the time we get back to the top?"

"I hope so," she breathed, giving herself over to his ministrations. He kissed down the column of her neck in between whispering dirty words.

His finger swirled around her clit, over and over in a steady rhythm, winding her higher and higher. Warm sea air brushed against her oversensitive skin. His hot mouth sucked her pulse point before he gently raked his teeth over the same spot. "Look at you, soaking my fingers with all these people around us. Anyone who sees you has no idea you're riding my hand."

"Roman!" She gasped and arched her back, grinding her hips against his hand.

"Shhh, no one gets to hear you but me. You better be quiet like a good girl while I fuck you with my fingers."

"Mmm." She bit her lip, trying to contain the little moans of pleasure that wanted to escape.

His lips coasted over her ear. "Now, baby. Look at the view and come." He pinched her clit with two fingers and slid another inside her as he bit down on her ear.

It started with a tiny explosion, then like a domino effect, the pressure built and built until an avalanche of pleasure shot through her. Her eyes shot wide open. Lights and stars swam in her vision. Summer heat and ocean salt stuck to her skin. She came, flying higher than ever before. The view made her dizzy, but she trusted she was safe with Roman. The intoxicating aftershocks melded together into the blinding peak of another orgasm.

"That's it. You did so good." He stroked her clit as she came down.

He slid her panties back into place, licking his fingers clean as he kept eye contact with her. The seat moved to the bottom of the wheel and stopped. The worker opened the door for them and raised the bar. Roman thanked her and helped Elise out. Otherwise, she might not have been able to walk.

He led her over to the stage, wrapping his arms around her waist, steadying her as they swayed to the song the band was playing.

"That was . . ." She took a deep breath and let it out.

"That was just the beginning of what I'm gonna do to you tonight," he said, nuzzling her nose with his before he tucked her closer and moved to the music.

Holy shit, that was the most adventurous thing she'd ever done. Her body thrummed with adrenaline and excitement. Her knees were still weak from the orgasm. But the rush. Holy shit, that had been incredible.

"What are you thinking about?" Roman asked.

"I had no idea you were such a risk taker." She giggled, still high on oxytocin.

"Only when it comes to you. Somehow you make me want to put it all on the table," he confessed.

She held him tighter. From this point forward, she was all in.

30

ELISE

Elise pulled the fleece blanket a little higher on her lap, adjusting it so it covered Ariel too. The little girl snuggled against her stomach, her eyes focused on the side of the barn where the movie of the month was projected.

The entire Emerson family, minus Mr. and Mrs. Emerson, was camped out in folding chairs or truck beds, or on picnic blankets, cozy and ready for the entertainment to begin as the sun finally set. Elise had never seen a family so involved with one another. Every weekend, they did something together, and everyone attended almost every time. Even when their parents were gone, Nova arranged for the rest of them to get together. Elise loved it. Never wanted to leave.

Roman walked up to them, his arms full of a bowl of popcorn. He sat on the other side of Ariel, his shoulder pressing against Elise's. "I got the snacks. Nova added mini Reese's cups this time."

"Mmmm. Sweet and salty. Sounds good." Elise turned

towards Nova as she brought a giant container over. "Thanks for the popcorn."

Nova waved her off. "Just enjoy the add-ins while Dad's away. He's a purist who believes popcorn should only have butter and salt."

"Nova makes the best popcorn," Eli piped up.

"You haven't even tried mine yet," Ricky said.

"And hopefully, he never will," Nash commented.

"Fudge you." Ricky tossed a piece of popcorn at his brother's head.

Nash chuckled. "Nice improvising."

"Did he burn the popcorn too?" Isabella asked.

"Ricky burns everything. Even water." Nova laughed.

Ricky huffed. "That's because I'm so hot, I cause things to catch fire. What can I say? It's a curse." He shrugged with his signature smirk.

"You wish," Nash teased.

"Is this kind of teasing what I have to look forward to when Alba gets a little bigger?" Isabella asked.

"If you're lucky." Ricky walked up and plucked the baby from the blanket in front of her parents. "Come to Uncle Ricky." He patted her back and held her close. "It's okay. I know you have the meanest, ugliest daddy. But your handsome uncle Ricky will be here whenever you need. Good thing you got all your looks from your hot mama."

Nash grumbled. "You sock-sucking fudge-head, give me my daughter back and stop talking about how hot my fiancée is."

Ricky darted towards the other side of their setup on the grass and shook his head. "Nope. Me and Alba are gonna have some uncle-niece time."

Nash kept his gaze on his brother as he wrapped his arm

around his fiancée. She cupped his cheek, and he tilted his face towards her, leaning in and kissing her.

Elise peeked at Ricky, whose lips quirked up into a smile as he swayed back and forth with the baby. He may have seemed like the annoying little brother most of the time, but it seemed Ricky had a purpose for the things he did from what Elise could tell—at least sometimes.

"Oh, I got the order for the flowers into Lily at the floral shop. And the wine ordered from the Fates' up the road," Nova said to Isabella.

"Thank you. I don't know what I would do without your help." Isabella smiled.

"It's no joke, throwing a wedding together in a couple months," Nash agreed.

"I can't believe it's next week," Isabella added.

"Mom and Dad will be back Monday. I'm picking them up from the airport in Boston," Roman said.

Had it already been a month? The summer was almost over. And so was her time living with Roman. They hadn't had a chance to talk about the next steps yet. But Elise wasn't going to start worrying over it now. They were enjoying each other, learning so much. Was it too soon to expect him to ask her to live there permanently? They hadn't even told Ariel they were dating yet.

"Are you sure you want to settle for this ogre? It's not too late to run away with me," Ricky teased Isabella.

"Bella isn't going anywhere. She's stuck with me, 'cause I'm never letting her go." Nash's arm hooked around the back of Isabella's neck as he pulled her into another kiss.

"Ugh, do you have to do that in front of me?" Eli groaned.

Nash reached out and turned Eli's head away, not breaking the kiss to his mother.

"Ready to start the movie? Ariel's almost asleep already," Roman said.

Elise looked down. Ariel's blinks were getting slower and slower. Elise rubbed her palm over her forehead over and over, taking time now and then to gently trace her profile down her little button nose and around her round face.

Roman's arm wrapped around her, his warm hand resting on the other side of her hip.

"Hold your horses. I had something I wanted to tell you guys," Nova said.

"Are you pregnant?" Ricky asked.

Nova's eyes narrowed. "Absolutely the fudge not."

"Whew! Good, 'cause I didn't want to have to ruin movie night to go kick someone's aaa—ample backside."

Elise couldn't hold back her chuckle at Ricky's effort to not curse in front of the kids.

"Anyways, before I was so rudely interrupted, I was saying the FBI came to see me."

"What?"

"When?"

"What happened?" Nova's brothers all asked simultaneously. The apprehension in the meadow had Elise tensing. The baby fussed like she could feel it too. Ricky adjusted Alba onto his shoulder and patted her back while jiggling back and forth to quiet her.

"I didn't want to do this in front of the kids, but we're never all together. They came to talk to me because I knew the second . . . uh woman. I think it's just some crazy coincidence. But I know it will be all over town tomorrow because they approached me at the café. I wanted you all to hear it from me." Nova sighed.

"What did they say?" Nash asked.

"Nothing much. Just wanted to know how I knew Simone

and Anastasia. How long it had been since I'd had contact with Simone. They said they'd be in touch," Nova answered.

"You okay?" Roman asked her.

She nodded overenthusiastically. "Yeah, I'm totally fine. I just feel bad I wasn't able to help them more."

"Did they say how the other woman, Simone, how she . . . uh . . . was it the same as . . ." Nash struggled.

"They didn't mention that, and I didn't ask. Maybe I should have. Sorry," Nova apologized.

"No, it's fine." Nash shook his head.

"I hope they find who's doing this." Isabella spoke Elise's thoughts aloud.

Nova shivered. "Alright. Movie time." She pressed play and the image on the barn changed.

"I hope you know this conversation isn't over," Nash told her.

"I know, but not with the little ears around." Nova waved him off. "And that really was it."

Music started. Captions appeared at the bottom of the movie.

Roman's lips coasted over the shell of her ear. "This way, if it is more comfortable for you to take off your CI, you can."

Her mouth parted in surprise. Such a small accommodation, but it meant the world to her. That he'd make adjustments to make her feel more at ease, not always expecting her to mold herself to fit into his world. "Thank you."

"Of course." His thumb rubbed up and down her hip bone, dipping just under the fabric of her shirt until he touched bare skin. He stayed like that, running soothing swipes over her flesh like he needed to share that intimate connection with her even while surrounded by others.

She loved the little things he did like bringing her a drink when hers was almost empty, having his family turn on the captions, and secretly touching her so their intimate moments remained largely private. The way Roman offered her tea rather than coffee, knowing her preference and how she took it. How he'd include her in his time with Ariel like she was already part of their family but also not expect her to give up her free time. He'd surprise her with a bouquet of wildflowers from the bee yards he'd worked in every few days. The fact that he'd had her in mind while he worked throughout the day, and that he'd stopped and put in the effort to pick them himself, made them so much more special than a store-bought gift.

That was Roman—his behavior spoke so much louder than his words. And this man's actions told Elise that he wanted her. That he cared about her. That maybe she wasn't the only one falling in love.

31

ROMAN

Roman pushed open Ricky's door without knocking as the last of the sun faded away.

"Well, look who finally graced us with his presence." Andre, his cousin, clapped him on the back with a drink in his other hand.

"Yeah, I figured I'd wait and make an entrance. Can't let all the attention go to Nash. It's not good for his ego," Roman joked. The truth was he hadn't wanted to leave Elise all sexmussed and perfect in his bed.

Andre barked out laughter and stepped aside for Roman to make his way into his brother's house. Where Roman's was homey and lived in, Ricky's was a typical bachelor pad with scarce decoration, but it was always clean.

"Alright, the last of the party is here, so we can really turn up now." Andre handed him a cold beer.

Roman scanned the room. Ricky was fiddling with something in the kitchen with his cousin Mikel's help. Sebastian Wright sat on the couch, talking to Andre and Nash.

"This is it? Just us six? The girls had several cars parked in

Nash's driveway. Where's all your friends, Nash?" Roman teased.

Nash scowled. "Don't start."

"You know our dear brother is an acquired taste." Ricky snickered. "But that's okay because I have all the entertainment organized. So though this may be a small bachelor party, it will be fun." He sighed. "It would be way more fun with strippers though."

"I told you that isn't going to happen," Nash grumbled.

Ricky held up his hands in surrender. "I know. And I would have ignored you, but your future wife promised to cut off my balls and feed them to me if I thought about it, so as much as I love pushing your buttons . . ." He cupped his junk. "I love my cock more."

Nash took a sip of his beer and shook his head, his eyes lighting with mirth. "Damn, I love that woman."

"I would hope so, since you're committing to live the rest of your life with her." Ricky rolled his eyes.

"You'll understand one day, when the right woman comes along and knocks the breath from your lungs. When she causes you to question everything and make a complete jackass out of yourself all because she wasn't a part of your plans," Andre added.

"Speaking from experience?" Roman asked.

Andre smiled. "You know it."

"Well, you don't have to worry about that happening to me." Ricky's voice had an odd tightness to it.

Roman studied his brother. There was a haunted look in his eyes that hadn't been there before. Was something going on with Ricky? His brother blinked and shook his head as if ridding himself of a bad memory before a forced smile split his face.

"Enough about sappy love. We're here to party and live up

Nash's last night as a free man." Ricky clapped his hands. "Now, would everyone make their way to the kitchen and enjoy some of the samples of whiskey I have painstakingly poured for all of you—of course except you, Mikel. I got five different kinds of soda so you wouldn't feel left out."

"Thanks, Ricky. That was thoughtful," Mikel said.

Ricky waved him off. "Go ahead and try each kind. When the glass is empty, you can look under the napkin and get the letters to the clue for our next activity."

"Boy, he really went all in on this," Sebastian said, standing.

The group of men made their way to the bar top while Ricky handed them their flights of drinks.

Nash hung back, crossing his arms as he stood near Roman. "Thanks for being here."

"Did you think I wouldn't? It's not every day my big brother gets married."

Nash shook his head. "No, I mean, yeah, thanks for coming tonight, but I meant . . ." He sighed, stuffing his hands into his pockets as if he felt awkward and out of place. Talking had never been Nash's strong suit.

"You were there for me and for the rest of the family when I checked out. I wasn't there for you like I should have been when you lost Tiana. If anyone knew that pain, it was me. I'm sorry I wasn't the brother you needed," Nash finished, his eyes glued to the dark wood floors.

Roman swallowed the ball of emotion that rose in his throat and playfully punched his brother's shoulder. "You did the best you could. I knew you'd come back to us someday."

Nash's expression softened as one corner of his lips turned up in an almost smile. "Isabella brought me back to life, but you held everyone together even while you were grieving and had a daughter to raise. That's something I'll always look up to you for."

Roman cleared his throat. "Thanks, bro."

Nash nodded as the guys laughed together around the drinks.

"Are you and Elise serious?" Nash asked.

Roman glanced at his brother.

Nash shrugged. "I may be an asshole, but I'm not blind. Plus, I came over one night to get your ATV and heard . . . noises."

Roman winced. "Fuck."

Nash's chest rumbled with a laugh. "Yeah, don't want a repeat of that experience."

"We weren't gonna say anything yet. Not until I'm ready to tell Ariel."

"When do you think you'll be ready?" Nash asked.

Roman sipped his beer. "I was thinking of asking Elise not to move out at the end of summer."

"Damn, really?"

Roman nodded.

"Happy for you, bro."

Roman smiled. "I didn't expect to fall for someone again after T."

"Sneaks up on you, doesn't it?"

"Yeah." Roman wiped a hand over his face and sighed. "Have you heard anything more about the other murdered woman?"

"Just that they have evidence linking her to Anastasia's killer. They wouldn't tell Bently what it was."

"Do you find it odd that Nova knew both of these women?"

Nash leveled his brother with a concerned look. "Do you think Nova's in danger?"

Roman shrugged. "I don't know. I'm just saying, it's quite the coincidence."

"I'll talk to her and tell her to be more alert. Maybe revamp security around the farm."

"Can't hurt," Roman agreed.

"Come on, you two slackers. This whiskey isn't gonna drink itself," Ricky called them over.

"I can't get smashed. I don't want to be hungover for one of the most special days of my life," Nash argued, stepping forward to take the first drink.

Roman joined him, eyeing the napkins with letters written in blue marker. So far, they'd spelled out *"Time to eat so."* Roman and Nash made their way through the amber liquid in their drinks before turning over the rest of the napkins.

"Time to eat some pussy" was spelled out in front of them.

"What the fuck are you up to now?" Nash grumbled at Ricky.

Ricky smirked and opened the fridge. He pulled out a giant cake in the shape of a cat. "So, I asked Remy to make me a pussy cake, and she must not have understood the instructions. It's the best I could do."

Mikel burst out laughing at his wife's creation.

"I assume this has happened before?" Ricky asked.

Mikel nodded. "Once or twice. You have to specify and not use euphemisms."

Ricky shook his head. "After all these years and she's still that innocent? Cuz, you are clearly not doing your job with that woman. Send her my way and I'll show her everything she needs to know."

Mikel swung his arm, narrowly missing Ricky who darted out of the way, laughing.

"Fucker better not go near my wife," Mikel said.

"Yeah, I'm with Mikel here. Leave my sister alone," Andre added.

"Am I the only one that isn't related to anyone here?" Sebastian asked.

"Yeah, because Nash doesn't have any friends. You're his wife's doctor, for Christ's sake. We were really scraping the bottom of the barrel to fill the seats tonight." Ricky shook his head.

"None of you have to be here. I told you I didn't want a party," Nash argued.

"No brother of ours is missing out on a bachelor party," Ricky shot back.

Roman stepped in, always the peacemaker, putting his hand over Ricky's shoulder. "What our dear little brother—"

"By two months!" Ricky interrupted him.

"What this asshole means is he couldn't pass up a chance to throw a party," Roman finished.

Ricky shrugged. "That too."

"Well, I guess we better eat some pussy and finish this fine whiskey so we can all go home to bed." Nash reached for the bottle, pouring a finger of whiskey into his cup.

"You can't go home. It's bad luck to fuck the bride the night before the wedding," Ricky said.

Nash scowled.

"He's right. You gotta stay here tonight," Andre agreed.

"What if—"

"She already dropped you off an overnight bag." Ricky cut Nash off.

Nash sighed. "She might need help with the baby."

"Just admit you're pussy-whipped," Ricky teased.

Nash set his glass down and rushed his brother, grasping Ricky's throat with his huge hand. Roman rolled his eyes. Those two never stopped irritating each other.

"Don't talk about my future wife's pussy," Nash said.

Ricky chuckled and held his hands up. "See what I mean?" He looked towards the other men and swung his arm getting Nash in a headlock before Roman could blink.

Nash swung his arm down, punching Ricky in the leg. "Let me go."

"Not until you say uncle," Ricky teased as Nash's eyes bulged.

"Enough, Ricky. Don't make him pass out at his bachelor party," Roman said.

Ricky rolled his eyes and loosened his arms, ducking out of Nash's way and skirting behind Mikel. "You're no fun."

Nash coughed. "You're gonna pay for that, fucker."

"I love you too, big bro." Ricky motioned to the cake, his smirk growing. "Alright, enough sappy stuff. Let's eat the pussy. It's Mexican hot chocolate flavored."

"You—" Nash moved towards their brother with violent intent in his eyes.

Roman jumped between them, doing his best to hold his mountain of a brother apart from the little shit-stirrer.

"Damn, how has he survived this long?" Andre asked.

"I know how to defend myself and kick ass," Ricky answered.

"You also start ninety-nine percent of the shit you get yourself into," Mikel added.

"Come on, I have a whole list of pussy jokes for tonight. At least let me have them if we can't get real pussy," Ricky whined.

"So now you're a comedian?" Roman asked.

Ricky shrugged. "Maybe."

Nash sighed and stopped resisting Roman's hold. He let go of his brother.

"Can we just get this party over with so I can go to bed and wake up and get married?" Nash asked.

Ding-dong.

"Who else is coming?" Roman asked.

Ricky's brows drew together before he moved towards the front door. "No one. I swear, if your future wife tries to spoil our last night by bringing bad luck—"

Roman followed his brother, keeping his body between Nash and Ricky. Ricky opened the door. A man in a police uniform stood there.

Shit. Was this about the case? Had there been another murder?

The brothers stood in silence, staring at the uniformed officer, one Roman didn't recognize. Was he new on the force?

"Good evening. I'm stopping by because of a noise complaint," the officer said.

Roman opened his mouth to ask him if that was some kind of joke. They lived on a giant spread of land. The closest neighbor was a mile away.

"Noise complaint?" Ricky asked skeptically.

"Yes, a Miss Isabella Noveas called it in. Said there was not enough noise for a bachelor party." The officer lifted something black in his hand before music blared from the speaker.

Some upbeat techno crap thudded through the entryway as the "officer" pushed past the three stunned brothers. He walked into the kitchen, setting the speaker on the counter before he started unbuttoning his shirt.

"Oh, fuck no." Ricky shook his head, and if Roman wasn't mistaken, fear flashed in his younger brother's eyes.

"Which one of you is Ricky?" the "officer" asked.

Sebastian, Mikel, and Andre were falling over each other, laughing.

Nash grabbed a rigid Ricky and thrust their little brother in front of the stripper. "Here he is."

Ricky shook his head vehemently. "Nash is the bachelor."

The man in uniform bucked his hips, clenching his ab muscles as he shimmied the shirt the rest of the way off. "I'm supposed to tell you Isabella said 'you're welcome' for the entertainment."

Ricky's jaw was so tense it was a wonder he didn't break a tooth. The stripper bucked his hips and did a snake-like move with his body, reaching for the button on his slacks. He spun around and ripped off his pants before dancing closer to Ricky.

Ricky fought against Nash's hold, easily slipping out of his brother's grip as his skin reddened.

"Enough!" Ricky yelled.

Nash laughed at him. Roman was enjoying the entertainment, but Ricky was genuinely upset. Roman's brow furrowed as Ricky clicked a button on the portable speaker, ending the horrible music.

"Here, take this and go. Isabella's had her laugh." Ricky reached into his wallet, pulling out a wad of cash and thrusting it at the stripper.

"You sure, man? I haven't even gotten to the lap-dance part of the show," the dancer said.

"Yeah, Ricky. I'd like to see that part." Sebastian eyed the man up and down.

"Take him home with you, then." Ricky motioned towards the door.

After a few more minutes, the "officer" had his uniform back on and a pocket full of cash as he left the house.

"I'll be right back. There's takeout keeping warm in the oven and more beer in the fridge." Ricky left the room, sprinting up the stairs like his ass was on fire.

"What was that all about?" Nash asked Roman.

"The hell if I know."

What was going on with his little brother? Why had a male stripper evoked such a strong reaction in him? It had just been a joke. The man had had some decent moves too.

"Let's get the rest of this night over with. I got somewhere else to be," Roman said.

"Somewhere, or with someone?" Nash teased.

"Hey, I'm not the one getting married tomorrow. I can fuck tonight without any repercussions to my luck." Roman laughed.

Nash chuckled. "Lucky son of a bitch."

"Yeah. I am. But so are you. Tomorrow's the first day of the rest of your life with Isabella and your kids."

Nash swallowed, his eyes growing misty before he cleared his throat and blinked rapidly. "I can't wait. You hungry?"

"I'll eat in a minute," Roman replied.

Nash walked to the bar where the other guys had set up the pizza and wings Ricky had kept warm in the oven for them.

Roman picked up his beer and sipped it. He was so happy for Nash, but he couldn't help remembering his own bachelor party years ago. So much had happened since then. He'd had Ariel. Tiana had passed when they'd thought they'd have forever. And now, Elise had come into his life when he'd least expected. It was too soon to think about forever—he'd only known her a couple months. But he wanted her to be a part of his and Ariel's life, and then he'd see where things led.

They'll lead down the aisle if things keep going the way they have been . . .

Roman blinked, his breath catching. It was too soon to think about marriage . . . wasn't it?

32

ELISE

On Saturday, wedding festivities were in full swing. Elise had planned on staying out of the way, but Nova had handed her a bag full of makeup and insisted she follow her. They were in a beautiful guest cottage tucked away at the back of the property overlooking the pond. Sunlight streamed into giant bay windows as Isabella sat in the living room getting her hair and makeup done. Renita put the finishing touches on Ariel's hair. Nova twirled in front of a floor-length mirror, swiping at a piece of lint on her chest.

Elise sipped her glass of champagne slowly, listening as the ladies spoke about the plan for the day, and Isabella explained her not-so-traditional meeting with her soon-to-be husband to the makeup artist.

"You're a beautiful bride," Elise told Isabella when she finished.

The woman smiled. "Thank you."

Renita stood and walked over to her future daughter-in-law. "I want you to know that James and I welcome you into the family wholeheartedly. I'm so happy to have another daughter, and because of you, two more grandchildren. My husband and I got you a little something." She handed over a small red box.

Isabella held it reverently in her palms. "Thank you so much." She opened the gift and lifted out a long, scarf-like piece of material decorated with colorful shapes and patterns.

"This is a kente. Something my ancestors in Ghana, the Asante tribe, are known for. Each color and pattern has a special meaning. Blue for love, green for growth and energy, yellow for wealth, white for victory," Renita explained.

Isabella's eyes grew watery. "This is so special. I will cherish it forever." She set the box down and hugged Renita.

"You're so welcome, sweetheart."

"Can I wear it with my dress?" Isabella asked.

"You can if you want, but don't feel like you have to." Renita picked up the box.

"Oh, I would love to. Can you help me?"

Renita handed the empty box to Nova and helped Isabella wrap the scarf around her neck, letting it fall down her front.

Renita wiped her eyes. "We're all going to ruin our makeup. Okay, I'm going to check on my son. You ladies finish up here and I'll see you at the end of the aisle in forty minutes. Come on, Ariel. You can come check on Uncle Nash and your dad with me."

Ariel hopped off her padded seat and scampered off with her grandmother out of the room.

"I know we're trying not to cry, but now that my mom has said her piece, I feel like I need to get this off my chest," Nova said as the hairdresser and makeup artist put their things away.

"I can always do a fast touch-up if needed, but I did use waterproof makeup," the artist said.

Nova smiled at her and then turned to Isabella. "I just

want to thank you for becoming such a good friend to me and for pulling my brother out of the hole we'd never thought he'd willingly leave. You've sparked life back in him, and that's the most amazing thing anyone could have done."

Isabella waved her off. "You're giving me too much credit. That was all your brother's doing. He had to do the work himself."

"Yeah, but you gave him a reason to want to try." Nova hugged her before turning to Elise. "And you."

Elise straightened nervously. "What did I do?"

"Don't think I don't see what's going on with you and Roman. You two aren't as inconspicuous as you think."

"Oh, we're not—I mean, we're just—"

Nova pressed her hand on Elise's knee. "I'm glad. Whatever you're doing or not doing, it's making my brother smile more and not take life so seriously. So thank you. Maybe we'll be having another one of these shindigs sooner than later, huh?"

"Dios, leave poor Elise alone. You'll scare her away," Isabella teased.

"No, I think she's made of strong stuff. If Roman's control-freak, helicopter parenting didn't scare her off, she can take a few teases." Nova winked.

"You're not a part of the family until someone gives you a hard time." Isabella laughed.

"So, if you didn't like me, you'd be polite?" Elise joked.

"Exactly." Nova nodded. "Now all we have to do is find a woman for Ricky."

"And what about you?" Isabella asked.

Nova shook her head and reached for her glass of champagne. "Nope. I'm good. I've got my vibrating friends, and I hook up when the opportunity presents itself. I also have good weed, and the remote all to myself, thank you very much. I like it that way."

"Yeah, but can that vibrator snuggle you after?" Isabella asked.

"I can always come find my niece if I need snuggles," Nova argued.

"It's not the same and you know it. Aren't I right, Elise?" Isabella moved the veil from the side of her face.

Elise smiled as memories of last night came flooding over her. A slightly drunk Roman had climbed into bed with her, smelling faintly of whiskey and the woods. She'd snuggled in his arms before he'd slipped under the covers and put his face between her thighs until she'd begged him to get inside her.

"See? That's something your battery-powered friend can't provide." Isabella giggled, pointing at Elise.

Nova rolled her eyes. "Yuck, that's my brother you're talking about."

If Roman didn't want anyone to know they were in a relationship yet, they were doing a terrible job at hiding it apparently.

"Okay, we're all done here, so we'll be off unless you need something else?" the hairstylist asked.

"No, I think we're good. My maid of honor is on her way here, but she said she was able to get her hair done. Thank you so much," Isabella answered.

"Oh, you're welcome. You have a wonderful day and congratulations again," she answered before leading the other woman out.

"Oh my god. You look beautiful!" An excited voice came from the doorway as a beautiful Black woman walked in. A heavily tattooed, blue-haired man followed, grinning.

"Ja'sus, you are a stunner, lass." His Irish lilt was a surprise.

"Is this the bride's room?" another man asked entering the room.

"Oh my god, you all made it! I wasn't sure you would with the flight cancelation." Isabella clapped her hands and rushed to hug her friends.

"I would have walked the whole way from Colorado rather than miss my best friend getting married." The woman squeezed Isabella tight.

"Nova and Elise, these are my friends, Tessa and her boyfriend, Roy, and Phillip. They came all the way from Colorado," Isabella introduced them.

Roy whispered something in Tessa's ear but she shook her head.

"Hello," Phillip greeted them.

"What's going on with you two?" Isabella asked Tessa.

"Nothing. It's your day," Tessa argued.

"It will make her right deliria to know," Roy argued.

Tessa cut him a look and then rolled her eyes and held out her left hand. The giant black ring sparkling from it had more people than Isabella gasping.

"Oh my god, it's gorgeous. Congratulations." Isabella hugged her friend again.

"Thank you, but today is about you. Are you ready to marry Nash? If not, Roy can grab the limo and we can escape in style. No offense." She said the last part to Nova.

"I'm more than sure. I'm just ready to make it official," Isabella assured her.

"Good."

There was a knock at the door before Isabella's mother slipped in with baby Alba in her arms. Isabella's eyes locked on her daughter and she immediately teared up. "Oh, mija. You are exquisite."

"Mama." Isabella held her arms open and hugged her daughter and mother.

Alba wiggled, her little baby feet sticking out from the pretty lilac-colored dress she had on that matched Ariel's flower-girl dress.

Isabella's mother, Catherine, pulled away, framing her daughter's face in her hands. "I know I wasn't very receptive to your choice in the beginning—"

Nova snorted. "Sorry. Champagne went down the wrong hole." She coughed to cover her laughter as Catherine, Isabella's mother, narrowed her eyes.

"It's alright," Isabella intervened. "I've been through quite a bit in life. My first marriage taught me a lot." Isabella looked sympathetically towards Phillip, who tucked his hands into his pockets with a partly sad smile.

Nova signed to Elise. *"I'm not sure if Roman's filled you in, but Isabella's first husband was gay and Phillip was his boyfriend before he passed. Isabella stayed with him after his diagnosis and took care of him until he died."*

Well, that was . . . a unique situation. Could Elise stay friends with a man who'd been her husband's lover? She looked at Isabella with new understanding as the woman finished what she was saying.

"You've all surrounded me with so much love and acceptance, and now having you here during this next phase of my life means the world to me. So thank you."

"Okay, save some emotion for the speeches," Nova teased, dabbing a napkin at her eyes.

"I guess we'll find our seats and see you lovely ladies in a few minutes." Phillip motioned to the door.

Roy kissed Tessa before joining the other man and disappearing out the door.

"I'll go too so we can get started. Your father was just finishing up in the groom's suite. He should be here any moment to drive you to the barn." Catherine kissed her daughter's cheeks and squeezed her in one last hug with baby Alba between them.

Nova held out her hands. "I'll take the little *princessa*."

Catherine gave one more snuggle to Alba before she passed her granddaughter to Nova and opened the door. She turned back to them. "Looks like our ride is here."

Elise stood to help carry Isabella's dress off the ground so it wouldn't get dirty as they walked. Tessa grabbed her bouquet.

"Thank you," Isabella said as she got settled in the limo.

"Of course."

The ride to the barn was quick, although a little bumpy. Nova pulled out her phone, staring at the screen. "Looks like everyone's ready."

Elise climbed out last, carrying the train and spreading it behind Isabella as the bride reached out for her father.

"Papi."

Isabella's father embraced her and Elise's chest tightened. There was so much love shared between them. Of course Elise was happy for the woman, but she couldn't help being a little envious. Her father had never been one for emotions or gentle comfort. She had one memory of running to him with a skinned knee, in tears, reaching up for him, and he'd pressed his hand out and pointed to her mother.

"I'll go find a seat. Good luck." Elise excused herself and walked into the barn, which had been transformed in the last two days. Gorgeous white and purple flowers decorated the space like it was a fairy garden. Hanging lights and flickering candles against the wall were mixed with greenery, and had turned a rustic but modern barn into an otherworldly space. She found a spot in the middle of the crowd, but a warm hand caught her arm. Her skin prickled. Only one person gave her that reaction.

Roman ran a finger along the collar of his tux. A similar kente scarf to the one Renita had gifted to Isabella was tucked around his neck, lying against his suit. He was so handsome in his tux.

"Not here. We saved you a seat up front." Roman motioned towards the area reserved for family.

"Oh, I couldn't."

"Of course you can." His palm settled on her lower back, ushering her towards an empty seat in the front.

"You look absolutely stunning, by the way." His lips brushed her ear.

She shivered, looking down at the simple jade-green dress she'd pulled on last minute. "Thank you. I would have gone shopping if I'd known I would be attending."

"You're perfect." He let her go.

"So are you." She straightened his bowtie and met his gaze. She wanted to lean in and kiss him so badly, but that would be highly inappropriate as Ariel was here somewhere. They were exploring things, as they'd agreed on. And the last thing she wanted to do was take away from Isabella and Nash on their wedding day and possibly hurt Ariel in the process. She leaned on her heels, fighting the magnetic pull, and gave him a swift nod before taking her seat next to Mrs. Stone.

He walked towards the front, lining up next to his brothers, but his eyes remained fixed on her.

Not even when the music started did he look away until Ariel walked down the aisle, tossing flowers out of the basket that Eli held for her. Roman's pride for his daughter shone from him like warm rays of sunshine. Elise's stomach flipped. She let her fantasy play out in her mind. Instead of Isabella walking down that aisle, it was her wearing the white dress.

And instead of a tearful Nash at the front, it was an awed Roman. She shook her head and focused back on the events actually happening.

Roman's gaze slid to her once more, and she couldn't look away. Those brown eyes were filled with hope and intention. Was it too much to believe he was considering the same thing? Could they have a future together? *I fucking hope so.* It was much too soon to think about marriage; they hadn't even gone public with their relationship yet. But here at the wedding it was impossible not to imagine that this may be the last man she ever dated. Because Roman Emerson might just be the man for her.

33

ELISE

Elise shifted in the giant bed against Roman's headboard, pushing her blue-light glasses up to the bridge of her nose. She clicked open her calendar. How was it possible she only had a couple weeks left at the Emerson farm? The summer had gone by in the blink of an eye.

Roman laid his head on her thigh, facing the ceiling. She absently ran her fingers over his forehead and hair.

"What are you thinking about?" he asked.

She wasn't sure how she should bring up her living situation. She'd been hoping he would ask her to stay, but that hadn't happened yet.

"I'm just looking at my schedule for the next couple weeks. School starts soon." She cleared her throat, giving him an opening.

"Don't remind me. Ugh, I know you'll be there, but I'm worried about Ariel."

"She'll do great. I met her aide and she's a wonderful person. A mom of two herself," Elise assured him.

"You'll keep an eye on her at school?" he asked.

"Of course. And I'll make sure she knows where my room is so if she ever needs me, she can find me."

He turned on his side, looking up at her as he trailed circles over her thigh where his borrowed T-shirt met her bare skin. "I wish you were going to be her teacher."

"Me too. But it will be good for her to meet new people and learn to navigate the world one classroom at a time. Besides, she might get sick of seeing me so often, at home and then school . . ." *Please ask me to stay.*

He huffed. "Like anyone could get sick of you." His mouth pressed against her leg, his scruff scratching against her, creating goose bumps down her limbs.

"I, um, have some meetings next week at the school." She set her phone down on the bed.

"Yeah? Just put them on the calendar in the kitchen, and I'll make plans with Mom or Nova to watch Ariel if I'm not able to be home."

"Okay . . . I can't believe there's only two more weeks of break." She tried again. She wasn't going to ask him. If he wanted her to stay, he would ask her—he wouldn't need to be pressured into it.

"Mmmmm."

Disappointment settled in her gut, but she shook it off. "I was thinking of taking Ariel for a picnic on Wednesday up to the pond. I've arranged a special surprise with a local mermaid."

"Sounds fun. Make sure to send me lots of pictures and video."

"Have you thought more about getting her a dog? For emotional support, and as a protector."

"Her therapist recommended it but . . ."

"But?" she asked.

"Dogs don't live very long compared to humans. If I got her one now, even a puppy, she'd fall in love with him or her just to lose them down the road. I feel like I'd be setting her up for pain," he explained.

"But what a great decade she'd have with a loving companion. Don't you think the pros outweigh that? That's the price of love, isn't it? Being willing to endure the pain of loss for the moments we get to spend with the ones we care so much about? What's life without the joy of affection, shared experiences, and hope for tomorrow?" She sighed and twisted one of his curls in her finger gently. "Everything has a flip side. You can't have light without darkness. The same goes for love without pain, because loving someone is letting yourself be vulnerable enough to let them in close enough to cause pain when they leave—by choice or otherwise."

"The ugly side to love," he mused.

She nodded.

"Maybe you're right."

"I'm always right. The sooner you learn that, the better off you'll be." She laughed.

"Oh, I see how it is." He rolled off the bed with nothing but his basketball shorts on as he headed for the door.

"Where are you going?"

"Be right back." He winked at her and left.

She slipped her glasses off and set them on the bedside table, along with her phone. Roman walked back in, a container and spoon in his hands.

"What's that?"

"This is honeycomb." He sat beside her, opening the bin. Sure enough, honeycomb filled the container to the brim with some sort of mostly translucent wax coating it and hiding the golden honey within.

"You can eat it?"

He scooped a small amount out with the spoon and lifted it to her lips. "Yup. You can spit or swallow the wax."

She gave him a sly smile. "You like it when I swallow."

His eyes turned molten as he pressed the spoon in her mouth. She opened, taking what he gave her. The sweet honey flavor melded with the light taste of beeswax. She chewed. "This is good."

"Of course it is. My bees made it."

She laughed and then swallowed the tiny bit of leftover wax. "How could I presume differently? But why does it taste so different from store-bought honey?"

Roman scoffed. "Because that shit is usually watered down with corn syrup or boiled to death and burned. I try not to heat my honey more than absolutely needed and keep it raw."

"Like raw milk? Isn't that dangerous to consume?"

He shook his head with a smile. "No. Honey actually kills bacteria. They've found some in Egyptian pyramids and tombs still perfectly good after all those years. It doesn't go bad unless water gets into it."

"That's pretty cool. You'll have to come talk to my class about your job sometime. Maybe bring some of the bees that don't sting?" she suggested.

"That can be arranged. But right now, I'd like to do a little different show-and-tell—an adult version." He wiggled his eyebrows up and down.

"Oh, yeah?"

"Mm-hmm. I love seeing you in my clothes, baby, but right now, I want to see every inch of you naked."

"Hmmm." She tipped her head to the side.

He swiped honey from the spoon on her lip and then licked it off before nipping her mouth with his teeth. Her thighs clenched together as a tiny moan escaped.

"Now be a good girl and take the clothes off," he said.

She reached for the hem and lifted the shirt over her head, then tossed it onto the floor.

His dark eyes glittered with lust and confidence. Anticipation coiled tight in her stomach. Her breathing increased, her bare breasts rising and falling with each inhale as the cool air teased her hardened nipples.

"Roman—"

"Shhh, just lie back. I got you."

She did as he said, getting comfortable in the bed. Roman dipped the spoon in the bowl before scooping some out and drizzling it over her breasts. She gasped at the sticky sensation. His warm tongue lapped the honey up, circling her nipple, sucking her breast. He left love bites across her pale flesh.

Elise cupped his head as he raked his teeth over her nipple. Her back arched.

"So sweet," he mumbled.

More golden honey drizzled down her belly, over the inside of her thighs. His hot tongue went to work, licking and lapping, all while the spark inside her turned to a raging wildfire of need. The dual sensations of the cool air hitting her wet, sticky flesh and the heat of his body only added to the pleasure.

"Roman, please."

He licked her slit and she gasped. Two strong hands pressed her thighs apart, pinning them to the bed. "Shhh, let me enjoy this honey. Want to taste your pussy, make you come on my tongue. Can you do that for me, baby?"

She nodded.

"Need words."

"Yes." Her voice was all breath.

"Nobody's here but us, so make sure you give me all those sweet little noises. Let me hear how much you love when I eat you out, okay, baby?"

"Whatever you want." She was so turned on, she'd agree to pretty much anything.

He groaned. "Don't say that unless you mean it."

She angled her head to look him in the eyes. She sucked in a breath, the air tainted with her arousal. This was it—the moment when she'd lay it all out for him. Her choice to be vulnerable, to risk everything for whatever time she could have with him. "I meant it. Whatever you want, whatever you need, you can have from me."

A moment of heavy silence passed as something changed in his dark eyes. A kaleidoscope of emotions flittered through his dark orbs before he crawled up her body and smashed his mouth to hers. Hungry lips slid between her parted mouth. His greedy tongue plundered her mouth in desperate, frenzied strokes. Demanding teeth scraped against the sensitive flesh of her lips, then her jaw and throat before he sucked, leaving another mark.

"You're mine. In every way. Gonna make sure you know it too. I'm not the nice guy, Lis. A better man would let you go. But I can't do that. I want every piece of you. And I'm gonna take it." He stripped off his shorts, palming his erect cock. "Get on your knees."

She rolled off the bed and knelt before him, her eyes locked on the engorged head of his cock, leaking pre-cum.

"Open your mouth for me."

Her lips parted, her tongue moving over her bottom row of teeth. He slid the tip of his cock across her lips, spreading his pre-cum over them.

"Do you know how fucking hot it is to see my cum on you? Marking you as mine."

She squeezed her legs together as her sex pulsed with want.

"Look at me."

Her eyes darted past the ridges of his toned stomach, up the thick column of his neck to his hazy expression full of the heady combination of lust and desire, need and barely contained urgency. Elise's body flamed with the urge to make him wild. To break the last frayed thread of control. She licked her lips, her tongue dragging over the tip of his cock as she moaned.

Roman's hand went to her hair. He tangled his fingers in her locks before gripping tight—seizing control. "You're playing with fire."

She licked him again and smirked up at him. "What are you going to do about it?"

A growl reverberated through him as he pulled her hair tighter in his hand, forcing her farther down on his cock. "I warned you."

She opened her jaw so she could take him farther. He drove into her mouth with firm strokes.

"Put your hands behind your back and don't move them until I say, or you'll be punished."

She was half tempted to play with his balls just to push him over the edge.

Pain melded with pleasure as he twisted her hair tighter in his fist. "Make no mistake, your punishment is that you won't get to come. I'll fuck your throat and come all over your face."

Holy fuck, that sounded hot. She whimpered.

"Oh, you are a very bad girl, aren't you, Elise? You'd like that, wouldn't you?"

She nodded as he fucked her mouth slow, getting deeper each time.

"Do as I said, and you'll be rewarded."

She gripped her wrist behind her back. As much as she wanted him to come all over her, she also wanted an orgasm or two. Plus, obeying his commands woke a different part of her that she hadn't known existed. Her head grew fuzzy. Awareness lit every cell. She was so in tune with her body, so present. She swirled her tongue along the thick vein running under his cock as he hit the back of her throat.

"I'm gonna fuck your mouth, and you're gonna take every inch for me, aren't you?"

She nodded and hummed her approval.

"If it's too much, hold up your hands and I'll stop."

The tip of his cock hit the back of her throat, and she resisted the urge to gag. Instead, she relaxed her throat as he drove deeper and harder.

"Fuck yes, Elise. Look how beautiful you are, taking me so deep. Your lips were made for my cock."

Intense pleasure swirled in her center as he used her mouth. In and out. Over and over, his hips bucked, his cock slamming into her throat until her eyes watered.

"You can take a little more, can't you, baby?"

She nodded, opening her mouth as far as it went.

He tipped his head back and thrust into her with a groan of pleasure, blocking off her air supply.

He tilted his face to look down at her with a worshipful expression. "How does it feel to know I control your body? To know you can't even breathe unless I let you?"

Her lungs burned and her eyes watered, but still, she didn't raise her hands to tap out. Because the overwhelming need to please him overrode her primal instinct to draw in oxygen. More than that, she trusted him. He would give her what she needed when she needed it. She was safe with Roman.

"Good fucking girl."

And that was all it took. Three words and she detonated. From the lack of oxygen, the fuzzy, heady feeling of being solely at his mercy, the raw power of his dominance, and the verbal confirmation that she was pleasing him, an orgasm crashed over her. Every muscle clenched. It took everything in her to keep her hands behind her back. He pulled out enough for her to take a breath. Sweet oxygen tainted with his woodsy, clean scent filled her lungs. Roman's cock slid in and out of her mouth. His groans of pleasure intensified.

He pulled out, bending down to take her mouth with his. His teeth raked against her lips, his grip never relaxing from her hair.

"You came from me fucking your throat."

She blinked up at him and nodded, stunned. She'd never come hands-free like that. *Holy shit.*

"I should punish you for coming without my permission."

She opened her mouth to protest.

"But that was the hottest thing I've ever experienced."

She smiled. Roman lifted her up and set her on the bed, sliding his cock inside her with one quick thrust, stealing her breath once more. His calloused hands gripped her hips in an iron grasp before he drove into her with hard thrusts.

"You're mine. Say it," he ordered.

"Yours. I'm all yours."

"Fuck. So perfect. So willing. I could come just watching you take my cock like you were made to ride it."

She moaned, her eyes rolling back with his dirty words, the way he manhandled her, his fingers digging into her flesh. His hard cock pounded into her again and again. His pubic bone hit her clit with each thrust. He had her thighs splayed out as wide as they could go. A slight burn from the stretch only added to the onslaught of pleasure that rolled through her like warm liquid honey, filling her limbs and gathering in her center.

"Touch yourself and come on my cock."

Her hand went instinctively to her breast, pinching and

teasing. He clamped one hand over her wrist and tugged her finger to her clit. "Play with your pretty pussy and squeeze my cock with your cunt."

She swirled the swollen bud, the heat of his gaze sending her over the edge. Her orgasm rocketed through her, wave after wave. His finger took over for hers, swirling her clit.

"That's it. Good girl. Fuck, you're so sexy."

Another wave crashed through her as wetness seeped between her thighs, coating him and dripping to the comforter.

"I'm—"

"You're squirting all over me and it's the sexiest fucking thing," he finished for her, fucking her slow and hard. He groaned. "I'm so close, but I'm not done with you." He pulled out, slapping her thigh. She hissed, her inner walls clenching.

"Keep those legs spread for me, beautiful." Roman reached into the bedside table, pulling out a bottle of lube.

Her brows drew together in question. She was more than wet enough; the soaking bedspread was proof of that. So what was he—

"Gonna take your ass tonight, sweetheart."

Oh, fuck. Nerves mixed with excitement, tumbling in her belly as her heart raced.

Gentle lips pressed against hers. "Relax."

She leaned into him as he palmed her breast, plucking her nipple and massaging it.

"Look at me."

She did. He hovered above her, his umber skin shiny with a sheen of sweat. His intense focus was all aimed at her and filled with a dark promise.

"You said anything. This is what I want, baby. I want everything you're willing to give. Do you trust me?" he asked.

She inhaled. *Do I trust him with this? Is this what I want?* "Yes. I trust you." *I love you.* "I'm all yours."

Roman's lips melded against hers. Despite the gentleness of Roman's kiss, the power and control he wielded hummed through their connection. She would give him everything, freely submitting to his desires, wanting to bring him pleasure. A wave of feminine power flowed through her. She was the reason for each grunt and groan of pleasure. The one who'd made him this hard. And to have captured his complete focus.

Something cold and wet slicked over her asshole. She gasped, squeezing instinctively.

"Relax and trust me. I promise I'll make you feel so good."

She breathed out, focusing on him as he leaned down, taking her nipple into his mouth, sucking and teasing as his finger entered her tight hole. He pushed in a little more until she whimpered from the burn. He removed his finger only to come back with more lube. In and out, he fucked her ass with his finger until she ached for more.

"Such a good girl. Taking everything I have to give you."

He added more lube, but this time another finger stretched her wider. She forced herself to relax and take what he had to give her, trusting in him to bring them both plea-sure. He slid his cock inside her pussy, keeping rhythm with his fingers fucking her ass.

"Hold your knees as high as they can go. Show me what's mine," he said.

She pulled her knees up, locking her hands under her thighs, spread and at his mercy.

Her eyes rolled to the back of her head as he fucked both holes.

"I'm gonna come," she hissed, her muscles tightening as she coasted the edge.

"Wait. Not yet. Don't come until I tell you to."

Oh, God. Her body trembled with the need for release, and she forced herself to take deep breaths. Filled with warm euphoria, she rode out the high, edging the cliff, but not jumping off.

"Roman!" she moaned.

"You need to come?"

"Yes."

"Beg me."

"Please. Please let me come."

"No—" He slipped his fingers out and his cock in a moment later.

He added more cold lube, but this time it wasn't his finger against her ass; it was his cock. He eased it in the first couple inches and she gasped, her nails digging into her thighs.

"That's it. You're doing such a good job. You got this, beautiful. Show me how you can take my cock. Breathe and relax." He pulled out a little and ground his hips deeper into her. It burned less and less as he eased in. Just when she wasn't sure she could take anymore, the hum of a toy buzzed. He clicked a few buttons and slid it directly onto her clit.

"Come for me."

She jolted forward, clinging to his shoulders, her eyes wide, her mouth open in a scream as he fucked her ass, the toy pressed between them.

"Fuck! Roman. Fuuuuck!" Her ears rang. The onslaught of pleasure was stealing her breath and sucking her under. She could do nothing but surrender to the dark ecstasy. He drove his hips, one hand holding the toy, the other bracing himself against the bed. Roman's lips captured hers, and he thrusted his tongue in her mouth as he filled her body in ways she'd never thought possible.

"You're so perfect. So beautiful. I'm gonna come and fill your ass. Are you ready for that, baby?"

"Please," she begged, needing more from the man whom she gave everything to. "It's too much."

"You can take it."

She thrashed on the bed, the pleasure too intense.

A slap seared over her thigh, taking the edge off and soaring her into a new plane of ecstasy, higher than she'd ever been taken before.

"Hold on. I'm coming with you." He jerked, his cock swelling and pulsing inside her. Roman's thrusts slowed as he eased out of her. His cum leaked out of her ass. She shivered as the cool air danced over her sensitive flesh. Roman lay beside her, kissing her neck as he shut off the toy and tossed it onto the bottom of the bed. His fingers skimmed up her thighs and dipped into her pussy. She hissed, her skin so sensitive as her back bowed.

"Come for me one more time."

Her body was already ahead of him. She couldn't have stopped the orgasm if she'd tried. Ecstasy exploded in every nerve ending until she wasn't aware of anything but the heat of his body pressed against hers as his arms slid under her. The room swayed around her as he lifted her against his chest and carried her into the bathroom.

She tried to sit up and look around, but he held her tighter.

"Shhh, I got you, honey. Just relax and let me take care of you."

She closed her eyes, easing against him. She'd never felt more cared for, more loved than in this moment. Elise had never been happier. Everything was exactly how it should be. And for once, she had a place where she was accepted as she was.

Nothing would ever compare to the feelings she had for Roman. Finally, she'd found where she belonged—right here in Roman's arms, in his bed, and in his life. Now she just needed to tell him how she felt. She had no doubt he loved her too. He showed her with his every action. His thoughtfulness. His care. What they had was real and true. He may not have realized it yet, but Elise had just given him the very last piece of herself, and he'd accepted it. Nothing could come between them now.

34

ROMAN

Roman trailed kisses over Elise's shoulder as she tugged the strap of her shirt up. He wrapped his arms around her, tugging her so her back was to his front, and inhaled the floral scent of jasmine flowers and the sweet smell that was all Elise.

She surrendered to him, relaxing in his arms, and it brought him a surge of gratitude mixed with love. The way she'd trusted him last night was humbling.

"I don't want to let you go," he admitted.

Her laugh was as warm as the sunshine rays peeking through the windows in his bedroom.

"I'm not opposed to staying here longer, but Ariel will be home soon, and you still need to get dressed." Elise turned her face to kiss his jaw.

He tilted his head, brushing his lips over her brow before tangling his hand in her hair at the base of her neck. He pulled just enough to lock her head in place before gently kissing her mouth.

The sound of a car door shutting had him pulling away.

"She's here." Elise spoke his thoughts aloud, slipping from his grasp. "I'll go out there. You get some shorts on."

He smirked. "I thought you liked it when I wasn't wearing anything."

A slight blush pinked her cheeks. It was adorable. After all the dirty things he'd done with her, she still got embarrassed over nakedness.

"Not when we will be around other people," she whispered, like she was chastising a little boy.

His cock jerked as she disappeared out the bedroom door, closing it behind her.

Roman grabbed a pair of shorts off the floor and tugged them on before getting a clean shirt on. He jogged down the stairs to the front porch where his mother-in-law stood next to an animatedly signing Ariel.

"And then Gramma took me to the beach and we found sand dollars."

"That's so cool," Elise answered her.

"Hey, sweet pea. Did you have fun at Gramma's?"

His daughter beamed up at him. *"Yes. I have a bucket full of seashells to paint."*

"Maybe your nanny can help you set up your paints," his mother-in-law said.

Elise's shoulders stiffened as Patrice glanced at her and then Roman before Elise held her hand out for Ariel. "Absolutely. That sounds like fun."

"Bye, Gramma." Ariel hugged Patrice and then took Elise's hand.

Elise turned and the red mark at the base of her neck caught Roman's eye. He froze, holding his breath as she passed, his focus averting to Patrice's. Judging by the hard set of her eyes and straight line of her lips, she'd seen it too. *Fuck.*

Any joy and easiness evaporated from his body, replaced with a thick layer of guilt and stiffness.

"Thanks for bringing her back." He gave a curt nod.

"Of course." Patrice opened her mouth, eyeing the door, and then closed it with a slight shake of her head. Pain was reflected in her eyes. "Make sure to send me pictures of what she paints."

"I will."

She hesitated another moment, studying him through a tortured gaze. "Have a good rest of your day."

He waited until she was driving down the road before he turned and went inside. Ariel was set up at a newspaper-covered table with paints, busily working on her shells.

Elise looked up, and he motioned towards the kitchen.

"I'll go get you some extra paper towels." Elise tapped Ariel's shoulder and followed him.

Roman braced himself against the edge of the counter.

"Is something wrong?" she asked carefully.

No. Yes. Fuck! He wanted to go back in time to when it was the two of them lying in bed together after he'd made her come. They'd been sated and blissed out in their own little bubble.

A wave of guilt crashed over him. He should never wish for less time with his daughter. Everything was so tangled in his head.

"Roman?" Elise's soft hand settled on his forearm.

He spun around, leaning his back against the counter and crossing his arms over his chest. "You've got a mark on your throat."

Her hand instinctively touched the patch of skin he'd bitten. "Oh." Her cheeks flushed.

He reached out and pulled her into his arms, needing her touch to ground himself when pieces of him were spinning out of control. It was not like they could have hidden this forever. And what was he really waiting on? If he wanted to be with Elise, he'd have to tell Tiana's parents anyways.

I just need a little more time before I tell them I'm seeing her and face the blame and pain it will cause Tiana's family.

"I'm sorry. I'm the one who made it. I should have said something," he said.

She relaxed into his arms. "Did it cause problems?"

He breathed in through his nose and let it out. "I have a complicated relationship with my in-laws."

"It seems tense whenever you run into them."

He opened his mouth and then bit his cheek to stop himself from saying more.

She pulled away enough to look him in the eyes. "Do you want to talk about it?"

"No."

Her gaze dropped but not before he recognized the flash of hurt in her eyes. Her arms stiffened around him.

He tugged her waist closer to him, knowing full well his daughter might run into the room and see them. "I think they blame me for Tiana."

"That's ridiculous." Elise stood taller like she was getting ready to defend him. It hit him hard that this amazing woman was ready to go into battle for him.

He held up his hand. "I wasn't there—"

She slid her fingers in between his, interlocking them. "You said before that even if you were, there was nothing you could have done."

"For Tiana, no—but for Ariel." His voice caught with a flood of emotion he thought he'd buried.

Elise's soft touch was more than he deserved. "You're human, Roman. You're not gonna be perfect at anything. If you knew she was alone and in danger, wouldn't you have gone to her as fast as humanly possible?"

"Yes, but—"

"Exactly. And haven't you done everything in your power to help her work through her trauma? You and your whole family learned sign language just so you could continue having conversations with her. You didn't fail her, and I know nothing I say will convince you of that. But when I see that little girl look at you, all she sees is the father who loves her. The man who puts her first and makes sure she is loved and cared for. You've done more for her than most other fathers would." Elise blinked away the sheen that covered her eyes.

He brushed his thumb over her cheek. "Thank you."

"For what?" Her eyebrows drew together, causing a little wrinkle on her nose to appear. He couldn't help himself and leaned in to kiss it.

"For being you. For being so understanding. For accepting me as I am, and my daughter. For so many things."

She swallowed. "I could say the same to you. I know I'm not the easiest person to . . . uh, care about—"

"But you are. And anyone who convinced you that you aren't is an asshole. I more than care for you, Elise. I l—"

A crash from the dining room made them both jump. He rushed into the space to find Ariel picking up the bucket of dropped shells.

"Sorry, Daddy. I was trying to get one from the bottom and it tipped over."

"That's alright, sweet pea."

He bent down to pick up the shells as Elise joined him on her hands and knees, reaching under the table. She didn't stand back like an observer. From day one, she'd been there for Ariel and him even when he'd made an ass of himself.

She'd become a part of their team, and his world had gotten a little bigger with her in it.

Elise dropped her handful of shells into the bucket and gave him a hopeful smile.

I love you.

35

ELISE

Elise waited for the all clear text from her friend. Ariel was going to love this. Elise's phone vibrated, and she pulled it out.

Sunny: *Ready.*

She tucked it back in her pocket, shouldered the backpack with their supplies, and grabbed the picnic blanket. She cast a quick glance at the cloudy skies. Hopefully the rain would hold out long enough for her surprise.

"Ready for our picnic?" Elise asked.

"Yes!" Ariel jumped down from the side-by-side.

"Great. How about we walk to the pond first? Then when we get hungry, we can come back to the meadow here?"

"Can we climb the hay bales?"

"I won't tell if you don't." Elise winked.

Ariel smiled and held up her pinky. Elise looped hers around the little girl's and tugged to seal their promise.

"Okay, I'll just set this up quick and then we can head over." She made short work of laying the picnic blanket out and set the backpack on it. "Alright, let's go."

Ariel ran ahead. Elise had to jog to keep up with her. They passed through a copse of trees before the beautiful blue water came into view. Elise searched the pond, looking for Sunny.

A head peeked out from the water only a few feet from shore. Elise waved and Sunny gave a small wave.

Ariel was too busy collecting rocks to notice the woman in the water. The little girl picked up a stone and faced the water. She froze. Her mouth dropped open and her eyes grew round. Elise pulled her phone out and started recording so Roman could see her reaction to finding a mermaid in her pond.

"*Who's that?*" Ariel signed, not looking away from Sunny, as if she thought the woman would disappear if she turned her focus somewhere else.

"Let's find out." Elise took her hand and stepped up to the shore.

Sunny ducked under the water, her mermaid tail lifting from the water and splashing back down.

Ariel squeezed Elise's hand. She was riveted to the scene playing out in front of her. "*She's a mermaid!*"

She squealed in delight. Elise almost dropped the phone. She hadn't heard Ariel ever make a sound. Ariel let her hand go, jumping up and down while pointing where Sunny surfaced.

Sunny swam a little closer, a big smile on her face as her tail splashed the water again. "*Hello. I'm Sunny. What's your name?*"

Ariel froze before the biggest smile split her face. "*I'm Ariel.*"

"*Nice to meet you, Ariel. I love that name.*"

"*You're a mermaid.*"

Sunny nodded. "*I am.*"

"*And you know sign.*" The way Ariel focused on the woman in the pond was filled with so much awe.

"I do. All mermaids do. It makes it easier to communicate underwater," Sunny answered.

"Do you sing too? I read that mermaids sing beautiful songs." Ariel's eyes lit up.

Sunny's smile dimmed before she corrected it. Her hand reached to the jagged scar over her neck, partially hidden behind the shell necklace she wore. *"No. I can't. But my sisters can."*

"Did the sea witch steal your voice like in the movie?" Ariel asked.

Sunny's gaze dropped to the water, pain reflecting in her eyes before she gave a reluctant nod. *"Something like that."*

"I don't talk either." Ariel signed.

Sunny's expression softened with sympathy. *"Did someone steal your voice?"*

Ariel tipped her head to the side as if thinking. *"I don't think so. It just gets stuck."*

Elise had never directly talked to Ariel about her difficulty with speech. It was interesting to hear her take on it. It sounded like she wanted to talk but something held her back.

"Talking can be scary sometimes," Sunny agreed.

"You used to talk?" Ariel asked.

Elise would have missed the slight wince Sunny made if she hadn't been watching. Sunny was so brave to be sharing with Ariel like this. Elise only knew pieces of her story, but what she did know was ugly and terrifying. But she'd made so much progress in her healing, and as soon as Elise had told her about Ariel, she'd insisted she do this for free.

"I did. A long time ago. And I used to sing. If I had the chance to do it again, I'd sing as loud as I could."

Ariel blinked as if lost in thought. *"My mommy used to sing I think."*

This was the first time Ariel had ever mentioned her mother in conversation.

"I bet she had a beautiful voice," Sunny signed.

Ariel nodded with a far-off look.

"Elise told me you really wanted to meet a mermaid. Any friend of Elise's is a friend of mine," Sunny explained.

Ariel glanced at Elise. *"You know Elise?"*

The sparkle returned to Sunny's expression. *"Oh, yes. She's helped me out a few times. So I try to visit her when I'm in the area. Mermaids travel a lot."*

"Do you swim in the ocean? Or do you live in the pond?" Ariel asked.

"I live in the ocean, but all waterways are connected, so I like to visit lakes and ponds when I can." Sunny splashed her tail again and swam so she was only a couple feet from them, her pink-and-green ombre tail on full display. A matching pink shell-shaped bikini top covered her breasts. Her light brown skin glistened with water.

"You're so beautiful," Ariel signed.

"Thank you. So are you. You'd make a great mermaid. In fact . . ." Sunny reached underwater and pulled up a faux seaweed purse. She dipped her hand inside and pulled out a rainbow mermaid tail the perfect size for Ariel.

The little girl shifted from foot to foot excitedly as she clapped her hands together, taking a sharp breath.

Sunny handed it to her. *"Now you can put this on the next time you go swimming. I'm sure Elise can help you learn how to use it with the built-in flippers. That way, the next time I visit, you can swim with me."*

Ariel hugged the wet gift to her chest. *"Thank you so much! I can't wait! Can I do it now?"*

Elise ended the video and tucked her phone back in her pocket. "I think Sunny has to get going, and we still have to have our picnic."

Sunny nodded. *"I do have to get going. I promised my sisters I would help them prepare for a party for my father. Today's his birthday."*

Ariel's bottom lip puffed out. *"Okay. Thank you for coming. I always wanted to meet a mermaid."*

"Of course. I've always wanted to meet a special little girl like you. Not a lot of people believe in us anymore." Sunny smiled.

"I will always believe in you," Ariel promised.

"And I believe in you too. I know that you can do whatever you set your mind to. And I have a magical gift for you." She reached into the bag once more and pulled out a single shell tied to a leather string. *"This necklace has a special power to help you be brave when you feel really scared. All you have to do is hold it in your hand or wear it as a necklace. And repeat this magic spell every time in your head: 'I am brave. I am strong. I am powerful. I can do this.'"*

Ariel clasped her hand around the necklace and hugged it to her chest, giving a firm nod. *"I will. Thank you."*

"You're welcome. Let's take a picture together. Would you like that?" Sunny asked.

"Yes."

Ariel walked in the water in her flip-flops. Sunny did her best to sit up, putting an arm around Ariel. Elise snapped a few photos and gave them a nod.

"I hope your dad has a good birthday," Ariel signed.

"Oh, he will. I'm sure of it. You have a wonderful day. And good luck." Sunny waved goodbye as she rolled deeper into the water and swam farther out, splashing with her tail.

Ariel watched until Sunny disappeared around the bend where Elise had arranged with Nova for Sunny to be picked up with an ATV.

"Can you put this on for me?" Ariel held up the necklace.

"Absolutely." Elise tied it behind her neck.

Ariel smoothed her hand over it and studied it like it was the most precious treasure in the world, her mermaid tail tucked safely under her arm.

"You ready for some lunch?" Elise asked.

Ariel nodded, and they headed back towards the trees. Elise pulled out her phone and shot off a quick text to Nova, thanking her for driving Sunny down and waiting. She sent another to Sunny, full of gratitude for her taking the time to make a little girl's wish come true.

Her phone beeped with a message as Elise blindly followed Ariel through the trail to the meadow.

Roman: *How did it go?*

Elise: *Amazing.*

She attached the video she'd recorded.

Roman: *Awesome. Can't wait to hear all about it tonight. I'm actually on my last yard. Trying to finish up here before the rain, and I should be home within the next hour or so. Want to order out pizza for dinner tonight?*

Elise: *Sounds good. We're gonna have an afternoon picnic right now.*

Roman: *Have fun.*

Elise put the phone away.

Ariel sat on the blanket, inspecting her gifts. *"Can we use the tail?"*

"Maybe this weekend we can come back to the pond and try it out. I'm sure your dad will be excited to watch you."

Ariel set the tail on the material and looked around.

Elise reached into the backpack and pulled out their water bottles and a container with grapes. "Do you want a snack?"

She shook her head and touched the necklace.

"Did you have fun with Sunny?"

Ariel's expression lit up. *"Oh, yes. She's amazing."*

"I bet the kids at school will be so amazed that you met a real mermaid. We can print a picture for you to keep in your backpack if you want."

"Yes, please."

"Are you nervous about school starting next week?"

"Yes."

"What helps me when I'm nervous about something is learning more about it. That way I know what to expect. And I'm going to be a teacher there too, so we'll see each other every day. Is there anything you want to know?" Elise asked.

Ariel snuggled her head against her as a gust of cool wind rushed over them. The trees creaked as they swayed. The leaves shook, a few of them falling to the ground. The clouds parted enough to let a few rays of sun land on their skin. From the look of things, it wouldn't last long. All but a sliver of the sky was covered in grey clouds.

"No. Daddy said he'd go in with me, and we'd get to meet the teacher before school starts," Ariel answered.

Elise wrapped her arm around the little girl. "Okay. Well, if you change your mind, I'm always here for you. And you can visit me any time of the day. I'll show you where my class-room is."

Ariel stayed quiet for a few moments before she tilted her head to look up at Elise. *"Are you going to stay with us forever?"*

Elise's heart clenched. *I want to.* If she didn't pay the deposit by Monday, she'd lose the apartment she wanted to rent. *Damn, I really need to talk to Roman.* "I'll be here for you whenever you need me for however long you want."

"I want you to stay. I love you."

Elise's breath caught as tears burned the back of her eyes. "I love you too."

Ariel sat up. *"Let's play hide-and-seek."*

Elise surveyed the meadow. There were only about five hay bales for them to hide behind and then the trees at the edge of the field. "Alright, but don't go near the water at all. Let's stick to this area."

Ariel shot to her feet. *"Close your eyes and count to twenty."*

The little girl was off before Elise got to one.

Elise counted to twenty and uncovered her eyes. "Ready

or not, here I come!" She made a show of walking to each hay bale. "Could she be here? No. Hmmm. I bet she's close."

A flash of pink caught her eye at the hay bale farthest from her. She took her time, pretending to be stumped. Finally, she crept quietly to her hiding place, jumping out beside Ariel and grabbing her. "Got you!"

Ariel gasped and shook with laughter. "*Okay, my turn. You hide.*"

Elise glanced at the darkening sky. Any sign of the sun was gone now. "Okay, but then I think we have to pack up before we get rained on."

Ariel pressed a hand over her eyes and held up her hand, signing her count. Elise took off, finding another bale to hide behind. It didn't take long at all for Ariel to find her.

"*Got you!*"

"You sure did." Elise laughed.

"*My turn.*" Ariel turned and ran towards the other end as the first few raindrops fell.

"Hold on! We have to go. We'll play at home, okay?"

Ariel stomped her foot and crossed her arms. "*It's no fun playing hide-and-seek in the house. I want one more turn.*"

Another gust of wind rushed against the meadow, blowing Elise's hair into her face as the rain poured down.

"Oh no! Get to the side-by-side. Quick!" Elise waited for Ariel to head towards the blanket before she rushed over. She slipped her now useless CI into her pocket to avoid getting it any wetter. She stuffed what she could into the backpack and rolled the wet blanket under her arm. She tossed it into the side-by-side and jumped into the front seat as buckets of water poured down.

"Are you buckled?" Elise turned to the passenger seat, but it was empty. "Ariel?" She searched the vehicle and then the space around her. "Ariel? Where are you?" Elise climbed out, scanning her immediate surroundings. She ran towards the hay bales, searching, but Ariel was nowhere to be found.

Her stomach dropped, her blood turning to ice. "Ariel! Come to the sound of my voice!" she screamed over and over, running through the meadow and into the beginning of the woods.

Where is she? Oh my god, did someone take her? Did she scream out for me and I didn't hear? The ground vibrated with thunder.

Elise ran into the side-by-side for enough covering to use her phone. She couldn't call; she couldn't hear. So she texted Roman.

Elise: *911 emergency. Ariel is missing. Meadow by pond.*

Her hands shook so badly she could barely type. She copied and sent the same message as a group text to his family. Panic gripped her throat like a vise.

Her phone vibrated in her hand. It was Roman. She clicked answer and spoke right away. "It's raining and I can't hear you. But I'm in the meadow. We were playing hide-and-seek, and then I told her to come back and get in the side-by-side. I picked up the picnic stuff and she was gone. I've looked all over here and called her name over and over." Her voice was choked. She'd do anything to be able to hear him tell her this was all going to be okay right now.

She pulled the phone away from her ear and ended the call.

Roman: *I'm on my way. Calling my parents and the sheriff.*

More texts from his family members vibrated her phone, letting her know that they would be there in a few minutes.

"Ariel!" Elise yelled as the rain let up and became a drizzle.

She trembled, unable to stop. Adrenaline coursed through her veins as terror buried into the marrow of her bones. *I lost her. What if someone took her? No, she has to be hiding. Or she got lost. She was upset. Maybe she ran from me?*

"Ariel!" she called her name over and over until her voice hurt.

A big hand grabbed her shoulder and she spun around, fist raised, but James moved out of the way. "It's just me." She read his lips.

She gave him the same rundown she'd given Roman as Renita, Nova, and Nash all showed up, fear on their expressions.

James turned his back on her, pointing to the woods. Everyone else looked to him, but Elise couldn't make out what he was saying. Everyone but Renita split up in different directions, heading into the woods.

"Do you think she could have gone to the water?" Renita asked.

Elise shook her head. "I don't think so. I told her to stay away from it. This is my fault. We should have left earlier." How could the best afternoon in the world have gone downhill so fast? *I hope she's safe.*

"We'll find her. She couldn't have gone far," Renita assured her. *"You wait here in case she comes back. If she does, you can text us. And when Roman and Ricky get here, you can point them in the right direction, okay?"*

She wanted Elise to stay here by the side-by-side?

Renita must have sensed her hesitation. *"We need someone to stay in case she comes back. I'm going to check by the pond just in case. But we need you here. Okay?"*

Elise gave a shaky nod. "Okay."

Renita headed towards the pond, leaving Elise all alone. It seemed like an eternity went by as she scanned the space around her. *Come back to us, Ariel.*

Movement from the edge of the meadow caught her

attention. Roman sprinted off a four-wheeler. *"Did they find her?"*

Elise shook her head. "I don't think so." She pulled out her phone. No one had messaged that they'd found her.

"You were supposed to be watching her!"

She flinched. "I know. I'm so sorry."

"Where did you see her last?" he asked.

She pointed towards the hay bales. "She was running with me towards the side-by-side. I turned my back for a second to pick up the blanket and backpack and when I got there, she was gone. She was upset that I wouldn't stay here and play another round of hide-and-seek—" She turned back to face him but Roman was gone. His body disappeared into the tree line across the meadow.

A sob was wrenched from her body as tears mixed with the rain streaming down her face. She needed to stay strong for Ariel and Roman. But this was all her fault. She'd lost his child. *He has every right to hate me.*

A flash of black darted from the trail. Ricky ran up to her. "Did they find her?"

She shook her head, her stomach hard as a stone, her heart racing at a million miles a minute. She couldn't stay here and do nothing.

"Your mom went that way; she should be back soon. I'm going to go look for her." Elise ran off into the woods on the far side. She could make this right. She'd find Ariel. The little girl would be wet and scared, but she'd be okay. Elise had to believe it. Because the alternative was not something she could survive.

36

ROMAN

Each beat of Roman's heart was like a sledgehammer against his rib cage. Terror he'd only felt once in his life bled through his veins. His wet clothing clung to his skin. The rain might have stopped twenty minutes ago, but it was getting darker by the minute, and the temperature had dropped. Ariel was alone in the woods probably freezing and terrified.

Unless someone took her like they took Anastasia.

No. He couldn't think like that. She had to be here. He wouldn't survive losing his daughter.

"Ariel!" he yelled again, his voice hoarse.

Only the chatter of squirrels answered him. Roman pushed through some underbrush and scanned the ground as well as the forest for any sign his little girl had come through here but there was nothing.

His phone chirped in his back pocket. He pulled it out, holding his breath that one of his family members had found her.

Mom: *No trace by the pond. I'm waiting in the meadow in case she comes back this way. Ricky's headed southeast. Bently is here with a few of his team. Mikel and Andre too.*

"Where are you, sweet pea?" Roman's voice was hoarse. His eyes burned. All he wanted to do was rage and scream. *Where is my baby girl?*

He checked the time on his phone before sliding it into his soggy pocket once more. She's been gone almost an hour.

He cupped his hands over his mouth and yelled, "Ariel! Where are you?"

What if she was close to him or someone else but stuck and couldn't yell for help? Roman turned. What if he'd already passed her?

Thunder rumbled in the distance, getting closer. *Fuck!* Roman jogged through the next copse of trees, coming to a little clearing in the forest.

A twig snapped. Roman jerked towards the sound. "Ariel?"

"Daddy?" The sweet little voice answering him had him freezing into place, searching around him frantically for the source.

Had he imagined it?

"Ariel!"

"Daddy!" she yelled.

Roman spun around, tilting his head towards the large tree where Ariel peeked out from one of the branches, holding her other arm against her body.

"Oh, baby girl." He rushed towards her, stepping onto one of the lower branches to climb up high enough to grab her and pull her against his chest.

She hissed, tears rolling down her cheeks. "Ow!"

Roman forced himself to pull away enough to look her over. "Did you hurt your arm, sweet pea?"

She nodded. "I—I got l-lost and fell. It hurts so much, Daddy."

He rubbed her back, picking her up and cradling her in his arms, careful of her injury. "Shhhh, it's okay. Daddy's got you. You're gonna be okay now."

He slid the phone from his pocket and sent a quick text letting everyone know he'd found her before he made his way back towards the meadow.

His phone chimed over and over, but he ignored it and kissed his daughter's mud-streaked forehead.

"I—I'm sorry. I shouldn't have run from Elise. I just wanted to play more." She shivered in his arms, and he wished he had something warmer to wrap her up in. Instead, he hugged her closer, jogging as carefully as he could to not cause her more pain.

"Let's not worry about that right now. I'm just glad you're safe. You scared me to death, girl."

"I tried to use the spell Sunny gave me and it worked. It gave me my voice back," Ariel said.

Fuck, he was still assuring himself his baby was safe. He hadn't even digested the fact that she was speaking to him like she'd never stopped. He had no idea what she was talking about—wasn't Sunny the name of the mermaid? Maybe that was where Ariel had gotten the shell necklace she wore.

He ducked under a big branch, careful not to let it scratch his precious cargo. The walk back to the meadow seemed to take forever, but they burst through the clearing and a dozen people were waiting for them, including the EMS.

Everyone ran towards him, asking questions and speaking at the same time. "She needs to go to the hospital. I think she broke her arm." He pushed past his family and walked her straight to the redheaded woman with a navy-blue EMS uniform.

His mother draped a blanket over Ariel's shoulders.

"Let's get her into the side-by-side. That's probably the quickest way to get to the ambulance," the redhead directed.

Roman didn't hesitate to climb into the passenger seat with Ariel tucked safely in his arms. She was still shivering, but less than she had been before. Her eyes drooped.

"It's okay, sweet pea, Daddy's got you. You're safe." *I got to you in time. But I almost lost you.*

He hadn't been there when she'd needed him again. How long had she hidden freezing in the woods, waiting for her dad to come and save her?

I wasn't there. Instead I was busy picking a bouquet of wildflowers for Elise. He'd texted her and said he was working, but that was so he could surprise her. Tonight was going to be the night he told Ariel about them and asked Elise to stay on once school started. He'd gotten off early just so he could drive into Dark Cove to her favorite restaurant and get takeout.

But I should have been here where my daughter needed me.

He leaned down and kissed her temple as the vehicle jostled them. He closed his eyes, reassuring himself Ariel was safe now. His chest felt as though someone had clawed it, raw, and his shoulders sunk under the weight of the guilt.

He whispered, "I promise you. I'll make this right."

37

ELISE

Elise shivered in the ever-darkening forest. She was pretty sure she was still headed in the same direction she had been when she started, even with all the twists and turns she'd made to get around trees and thickets. Fat raindrops dripped from the canopy of trees, landing on her already soaking-wet skin. Her legs and arms were covered with scrapes from wandering in the forest.

"Ariel!" She forced her voice out even though she couldn't hear it herself. Her throat felt raw, but she wouldn't give up. The ground vibrated for what seemed like the dozenth time before lightning flashed. She couldn't see the sky from there with the trees so thick, but then again, she couldn't see much of anything. Had the sun set? Or was it the storm?

Had anyone found Ariel yet? She pulled out her phone. Twelve unread messages. Her foot caught on something. She fell. Pain shot up her leg. Her phone went flying.

"Fuck!" Hot tears streamed from her eyes as she rolled to her back. She sat up as a flash of lightning lit the woods. Crimson liquid dripped out of a long gash in her calf.

"Oh no." Elise gently touched the side of her leg and hissed as more blood streamed down her calf, dripping onto the ground and soaking into the soil. "Fuck, that's deep."

She tugged her rain-soaked shirt away from her body and brought it to her teeth. She tried ripping it, but that was hard to do when it was wet.

She groaned in frustration, more tears spilling from her eyes. "Goddamnit!" She pulled her shirt off, searching the fabric for a weakness. A small hole on the side gave her a burst of hope. She pushed her finger inside, tearing it wider. Relief hit her as the material finally gave. Soon, she had a strip of cloth and a half-torn shirt back on. Elise tied the strip around her wound, hissing at the pain. But she had to apply enough pressure to stop the bleeding. She couldn't call for help when everyone was out searching for Ariel. *And it's my fault she's missing.*

Her gaze wandered over the forest floor. *Where is my phone?* She turned behind her and screamed. White sun-bleached bones were scattered over the ground. Some had bits of moss growing on them. *Oh my god. Are those human?* She scanned the floor, squinting in the darkness. Damn, she needed her phone's flashlight.

Lightning flashed, illuminating an elongated skull that was clearly not human. She breathed a sigh of relief and gave herself a minute to get her heartbeat back under control.

Elise kneeled onto her good leg, reaching out to a small tree nearby to help her to her feet. She needed to find her phone and then she'd have no choice but to figure out a way back. *What if Ariel is still out here?*

Maybe one of the dozen missed messages would tell her they'd found her.

She limped back the way she'd been headed, holding the

trees around her for balance. Her heart sunk as she approached a stream. *No, no, no. I need my phone!*

Panic gripped her chest as she searched the ground wildly. She reached her fingers into the icy water, moving over slimy rocks until she touched something rectangular. She pulled it out and blinked at her now useless device.

All her remaining energy drained from her. She sat and stared as raindrops pelted her skin. It wasn't safe to just sit there. She was probably as lost as Ariel. She had no idea which way was back, but all waterways were connected, right? So maybe this stream led to the Emersons' pond? But was it flowing to it or from it? She wiped the tears from her eyes and sniffed. She couldn't sit here any longer. She was losing daylight by the second, and from what she knew about storms, she was a sitting duck.

Elise forced herself back to her feet. Everything hurt. She was chilled to the bone and shaking. Blood still dripped from her leg.

"Is anyone out there?" she called as loudly as she could. "I need help!" She limped from tree to tree along the stream, repeating her calls.

She went on for what seemed like forever like that. The longer she fought to keep going, the more scared she got. What if no one came looking for her? What if she was well and truly lost? Were there wild animals out there? Bears? Or what if she got struck by lightning? Her breath came in short, sharp bursts as panic set in. She tried to calm her breathing but it was no use.

A light flickered ahead of her. She froze. Her throat screamed at her, but she shouted anyways. "Hello? Is anyone there? I need help!"

The light drew closer as a woman she didn't recognize came into view on the other side of the stream.

"Oh, thank God. Can you help me?"

The light swept over her leg and back to her, blinding her momentarily.

"I'm sorry. I can't hear you if you're speaking, I'm Deaf." Elise signed with one hand while she spoke.

The light moved to the shallow stream before the woman crossed to her side. "Can you read lips?" she asked, pointing the light towards Elise's face.

"Yes."

"Let's get out of here before we get struck by lightning." Her rescuer pointed over her shoulder. "Home."

Elise nodded. The woman wrapped her arm around Elise's waist on the side of her bad leg.

"Thank you." Elise leaned against her and limped as best as she could across the stream.

Her rescuer pointed away from her and she moved in that direction. *I hope we don't have to go far.*

After what seemed like forever, they broke through the trees and a huge house with lights on came into view. Elise sighed in relief. Her muscles burned, and every part of her ached. The woman led her to the porch, and Elise sat carefully on a wooden chair. The woman pulled out her phone, typing quickly and handing it over. Elise read the message.

I'm Sage, and I'm going to get you a blanket and some water. Do you want to go to the hospital? Is there someone I can call?

She looked up to answer her but Sage was facing the woods, speaking. Elise followed the woman's attention and found Ricky jogging towards them. Relief flashed in his eyes as they landed on Elise.

"Are you okay?" he signed, stepping onto the porch.

"Did they find Ariel?" Elise needed to know that the little girl who was entrusted to her care, the one she loved, wasn't still out there in this thunderstorm, alone and freezing.

"Yes."

Elise closed her eyes as tears of gratitude and relief stung them.

A warm blanket was draped around her shoulders and a water bottle was pressed into her hands. She opened her eyes and thanked the kind woman. Two more women had joined her.

Ricky spoke to them. From the bits and pieces she gleaned, he was catching them up on why the Emersons had been out in the middle of a storm.

"Are you ready to go home?" Ricky asked.

She nodded. *"Can you tell Sage how thankful I am for her help?"*

Ricky spoke to the woman who'd rescued her as the women beside her who looked so much like Sage—perhaps her sisters?—listened intently.

Sage patted Elise's shoulder gently. "Of course. I'm just glad I heard you."

Ricky signed her response before stepping closer. *"I'm going to carry you to Sage's truck, and we're going to go to the hospital for your injury."*

She shook her head. "I just want to go home."

He shook his head. *"Rest your voice. That looks like a lot of blood. You might need stitches."*

She shook her head. *"I need to see Ariel and make sure they're okay."*

"They're at the hospital. Ariel has a broken arm, but they should be on their way home soon."

Ariel was hurt? Guilt slammed into her. *It's my fault. I shouldn't have taken my eyes off her.*

"I want to go home."

"Fine," Ricky conceded but he didn't look happy. He slipped his hands under her and lifted her against his chest. One of Sage's sisters appeared with a big umbrella, covering

them until Elise was safely tucked in the front of the truck with Fates' Winery emblazoned on the door.

Sage climbed into the driver's seat and turned the heat on full blast. Ricky rubbed his hand up and down Elise's arm like he was trying to warm her. She just needed to clean her leg and bandage it, and get a hot shower with a hot meal, and she'd be fine. Then she'd have to face Roman. She closed her eyes, trying to hold back her tears. Would he be able to forgive her? Would Ariel? Or was this the end?

Ricky helped her into the house, but she was too exhausted to even wave goodbye to Sage.

"Do you want help changing or getting into the bathroom?" Ricky asked.

"Maybe just help to the bathroom?"

He picked her back up and carried her up the stairs without another word.

"I can walk. You don't have to carry me everywhere," she argued.

He set her on the closed toilet seat. *"You're shivering and bleeding, and almost as stubborn as my brother. Want me to help clean your wound?"*

She shook her head. What she wanted was to rewind time. *"I'll be okay from here."*

"Are you sure?"

"Yes. And thank you, Ricky, for looking for me. I'm sorry I added more stress to an already horrible situation that was my fault too."

He studied her for a moment. *"We're just glad you and Ariel are both safe."*

"Is Roman okay?" she asked, holding her breath as she waited for the answer. *Do you think he'll forgive me?*

Ricky hesitated, his lips parting as if to speak and then closing. He ran a hand over his face, his eyes cloudy. Her heart sunk.

"Just give him some time."

She gave him a curt nod. She forced a smile she didn't feel. "Thank you for helping me."

Ricky pulled out the first-aid kit from under the sink, set it beside her on the counter, and backed out of the room, leaving her alone.

She swallowed down the emotions clogging her throat and got to work, cleaning her wound and stripping naked before climbing into the shower. She sat in the tub as hot water sprayed down on her, chasing the chill from her bones. Her mind raced, trying to come up with what she should say to Roman and Ariel when they returned. Anxiety spun inside her like a whirlwind let loose, wreaking havoc on her nerves.

She hobbled out and dried off. Elise grabbed the bandages for her leg, a few butterfly stitches, ointment, and then a layer of gauze, and applied them to her wound until it stopped bleeding for good. She made it to her room and changed into a pair of leggings and a fresh T-shirt. She grabbed her spare CI and put it on. The sound of voices drew her attention immediately. Her stomach flipped and twisted into knots. She froze as Roman's voice grew louder as he came up the stairs.

"Let me get Ariel in bed and then we can have this discussion," he said.

A door creaked open and then silence reigned for a few moments before Roman's voice returned.

"I'm just trying to understand how someone can lose a child like that," his mother-in-law said.

Roman sighed.

"I'm not trying to be insensitive, but it doesn't seem like she's very capable of watching my granddaughter."

"Elise is very capable," Roman responded, and Elise let out a small breath of relief.

"Ariel is all I have left of Tiana. She needs someone who will care for her like the precious child she is. I don't want to interfere more than I have to, but do you think your romantic feelings for this woman might be impeding your judgment?"

Elise's brows furrowed. Of course not. He'd hired her despite what seemed like strong dislike for her in the beginning. She pressed her ear to the crack in the door, waiting for Roman to tell the woman that was absurd, but he stayed silent.

"I just want what's best for Ariel and you. I'm concerned that she isn't qualified. If you or I had been in that meadow, we might have been able to hear Ariel before she wandered too far." His mother-in-law's words stabbed at Elise's heart.

She might have been hearing impaired but that did not make her less. Ariel was non-verbal, so how would any of them have heard her?

"My daughter always comes first. And I'll do whatever it takes to make sure she's safe. She's all I have left of my wife too. Elise was her nanny for the summer, and that ends this coming week, so you won't have to worry about it." Roman's voice was void of emotion.

Elise blinked as her chest tightened like a vise. She sucked in a breath as quietly as she could. *I thought we were more. How could he say I was just the nanny for the summer? What happened to "let's see where this goes"? Have I been blind again?*

"I know you are a young man. But Ariel needs—"

"No one could ever replace Tiana," Roman interrupted.

Elise pulled out her CI, not wanting to hear another word. Roman would never have a true relationship because he still held his wife on a pedestal. He'd used Elise, strung her along just like her ex. No wonder he didn't want to talk about what would happen when this ended. He'd planned on washing his hands of the whole thing. They hadn't talked about the future because there wouldn't be one. He'd never expressed that he wanted more. Hadn't called her his girlfriend, or even told anyone about them.

How could I have misread the signs?

Because she'd wanted to give him the benefit of the doubt. That was what love did. It blinded you to the other person's faults, had you ignoring red flags and warning signs. Never again.

Did I really fall in love with another single dad just to get my heart destroyed a second time?

Am I really that unlovable?

38

ROMAN

Roman waved goodbye to his mother-in-law. Exhaustion settled into the marrow of his bones as he closed the front door. A creak had him turning around. Elise stood at the top of the stairs, holding the railing. How long had she been there?

"How is Ariel?" Her voice sounded raw, like she was getting sick.

"She's okay. Broken arm; the doctor set it. She's got a pink cast—didn't you get the text updates?"

She shook her head. "I dropped my phone in the stream. I just got back a little bit ago."

His brows rose in confusion. "We found her hours ago. Where were you?"

"I got a little lost." She stepped down the first stair and winced.

Was she hurt? "You were looking for her all that time? In this weather?"

"Of course."

He ground his teeth. What if some psycho had been out

293

there? He had enough to worry about with Ariel; he didn't need to add another person to his concerns. Maybe Patrice was right and he'd let his feelings for Elise cloud his judgement. Maybe he just needed to take a step back from everything to get his head on straight and figure this out.

Roman climbed the stairs with leaden feet. He needed a hot shower and some sleep.

"I'm so sorry, Roman. I swear I only turned my back for a minute—"

He held up his hand. "I don't want to talk about this tonight."

A mixture of pain and fear were reflected in her eyes. He wanted to tell her he understood. Ariel had admitted she'd run off. But Elise was supposed to have been watching her. If he hadn't found his daughter when he did, Ariel could have been in a lot greater danger. If Ariel hadn't called out for him, he'd have walked right past her. Ariel would have been taken from him too. The fear of losing his only child was still a fresh, open wound with jagged edges.

"Roman?" Elise reached for him but he backed up into the hallway.

"It's been a long day. I need some time . . . ." He ignored the rejection flashing in her gaze and headed for his room. The floor squeaked behind him. He spun around, holding out a hand. "I think it's better if I sleep alone tonight."

Her mouth thinned as she straightened her shoulders. "So it's true?"

"What's true?"

"I heard what you said to your mother-in-law. I can't . . . I won't go through this again."

What was she talking about? Go through what again? He was far too exhausted to have patience for a conversation like this. Anger licked his skin. "Then don't."

She flinched. "So, it's just like that? I made a mistake and you're just giving up on us?"

"A mistake is forgetting your purse in the house or locking your keys in the car. It's not misplacing a whole human child." He wished he could take the words back the moment they left his mouth, but it was too late. The damage was already done.

Elise blinked, her eyes shining with tears and what seemed like resignation.

"Elise—" He reached for her but she flinched away from him this time.

"Did you ever . . . Was this all just . . ." She didn't finish her sentence and he had no idea what she was trying to say.

"Maybe it's better if we take a break." He needed a few hours of solid sleep. Right then, he couldn't think straight, his emotions still raw from the events of the day.

"Right. A break." She laughed but there was no humor in it.

They could work through this in the morning once they'd had time to rest and cool down.

"I love her, you know." Her voice caught.

"I know."

She gave a curt nod. "That's it, then. I leave you alone, and you can go back to . . ."

"We'll talk in the morning."

"I don't think there's any need to draw this out," she said.

"I told you I can't do this right now."

"I heard you. Loud and clear. I just don't see any need to prolong the inevitable." Her voice was cold and devoid of emotion, matching the expression on her face.

"What's inevitable?" He sighed, at the end of his patience.

"Don't pretend you didn't just stand here and admit to still being in love with a ghost. That you never planned on continuing this past the summer." She pointed to him and then to her. "I heard you."

"You have no right to talk about my wife," he snapped.

"I meant no disrespect. I'm just stating facts."

"I'm not sure where you got your facts from, but you're crossing a line," he argued.

"And I wanted honesty, but I guess that was too much to ask."

He ran a hand over his face in frustration. "I don't know what the hell you're talking about. But I'm going to go take a shower and sleep before my daughter wakes up and needs breakfast. We'll continue this later." He turned around and walked into his bedroom, closing the door behind him. He had no clue what she meant by him being untruthful to her—he'd always been honest. But bringing up his wife was a low blow. He hadn't meant it the way she'd taken it when he'd spoken with Patrice. But Roman was in no condition to have a conversation that required patience and an open mind. He barely had enough energy to shower. They'd figure this out tomorrow when they'd both had time to cool down . . . or maybe this was a sign. His daughter had been missing and Elise had picked a fight with him rather than meeting him where he was. Maybe he should do some more thinking before asking her to move in. Perhaps they needed to progress slower than he'd planned.

This was a clusterfuck he had no chance of untangling until he had some proper rest. Tomorrow, everything could be figured out.

39

ELISE

Elise could barely see through the tears as she packed her things into her suitcase. She wiped her face, taking a ragged, deep breath. *Just hold it together until you get out of here.* How had everything gone to shit so fast?

Because I fucked up. In more ways than one.

Roman had wanted to talk about everything in the morning, but what was the use in staying? So he could ask her to leave after breakfast? *At least it's more mature than leaving my things on the porch and changing the locks like my last boyfriend.*

It still put her in the same position though. She closed her eyes and sat on the edge of the mattress. She hated that she'd caused the family pain. Would they all hate her? If the man she loved couldn't even forgive her, then they probably wouldn't either. She'd been so set on proving how capable she was, and now she'd failed. *Maybe I'm trying so hard to prove myself because I know I'm not.*

Elise scanned the room, making sure she'd grabbed everything. The flowers Roman had brought home to her days ago sat by her bed, looking a little worse for wear, much like her

297

heart. The ache in her chest throbbed as she tried to hold it together for a few more minutes.

"He admitted with his own mouth that he'd never planned for this to go past the summer. That I'm just the nanny. That he's still in love with his wife. He used me and lied. I was the stupid one who believed him." Her voice broke. She shook her head and got to her feet. "Never again."

Elise rolled her suitcase and carried the bag with her things in it down the hall. She paused at Ariel's room. The light in Roman's room was off. She pushed open Ariel's door. Colorful unicorn, rainbow, and star lights moved over her ceiling. Ariel's little body was curled into a ball, her neon-pink cast covering her arm.

Elise crept beside the sleeping girl, her heart squeezing. She hadn't had the opportunity to say goodbye to Malaki. But she could now with Ariel, and she'd see her at school in a week.

Elise smoothed her hand over the little girl's forehead. Ariel's nose scrunched before her eyes fluttered open.

Elise smiled despite her heart breaking into a million pieces. *"Hey, sweetheart."*

Ariel blinked sleepily, her hands moving in sign. *"Elise."* Ariel opened her arms and looped them around Elise's neck. Elise hugged the little girl back, squeezing as tight as she dared. Tears burned the back of her eyes, but she swallowed the emotion and pulled back to face the little girl.

"I'm sorry you got lost and hurt your arm."

Ariel placed her hand over the necklace Sunny had given her. *"I'm sorry I ran away."*

"You scared me. I'm just glad you're okay. Go back to bed. I'll see you at school, okay?"

Ariel nodded sleepily and snuggled back in her pillow.

"I love you," Elise said as Ariel's eyes fluttered closed.

She stood, taking one more minute to memorize the face of the little girl who'd stolen her heart. Elise straightened her shoulders and left, grabbing her things, and limped to the kitchen where a landline hung on the wall.

Picking up the phone, she dialed her best friends.

"Helloooo?" Sam answered.

"Hey, it's me, Elise. I'm calling from a landline."

Sam laughed. "Jack is telling me to let him text you because I'm drunk, but I want to hear your pretty voice."

Elise didn't want to bring her friends down when they were so obviously having a good time. "Oh, that's not a problem. Are you guys out?"

"No, Jack's cousins are in town, so everyone's staying here and we're playing Kings," Sam explained.

"Oh, that sounds fun. You have a good night."

"Did you need something?" Sam asked.

"Nope, just checking in. My phone fell into some water, so I'll text you when I get it fixed." If he wasn't so drunk, he'd probably be able to read her voice and know she was lying.

"I'll call you when these guys leave in a couple days and we can get together. I need to see you before school starts."

"Sounds good to me."

"Byeeeee."

"Bye." She hung up the phone, sitting in silence for a moment. Tori was on vacation, and there was no one else to call. Where could she go?

She headed out the door, careful to lock it behind her before she loaded her car and climbed in. She started the engine and backed it up, heading towards the last place she wanted to go but the only choice she had.

40

ROMAN

Roman woke with a start. He blinked a few times until his eyes adjusted to the brightness. Sunlight streamed into the window, highlighting the emptiness of the other side of the bed. He sat up and sighed, scrubbing a hand over his face. He'd slept in.

The events of yesterday flashed in his mind. He didn't want to leave Ariel today. She needed an emergency meeting with her therapist, and Ricky could handle working the yards alone this once. Not to mention he and Elise needed to have a conversation.

Guilt squeezed his chest at the things he'd said to her last night.

"Daddy, I'm hungry." Ariel pushed open his door.

Roman did a double take. Damn, he was still getting used to the fact that she could talk to him. "What do you say to going out for breakfast?"

"Yes!" She clapped her hands.

"Go get Elise and ask if she wants to come."

Ariel tipped her head to the side. "But Elise is gone."

Roman's brows pulled together in confusion. "Is her car here?"

Ariel shook her head. "She said she'd see me at school. Can I have pancakes?"

"When did she tell you that?" He stood.

"Last night when I woke up."

Roman's feet were moving before she'd finished speaking. He went straight to Elise's room.

He pushed the door open and sucked in a breath. It was empty of her things. The mattress had been stripped. There was nothing there but a square of paper folded with his name on it. Roman picked it up and opened it.

Roman,

I saved you the time in asking me to leave. You can keep the last check as I didn't fulfill my obligation of keeping Ariel safe as promised. I want you to know that is something I'll always regret. I truly am sorry for any pain I've caused her or your family.

Elise

He read it again and flipped it over, his anger bristling and confusion spiraling. "That's it? Where the fuck did she go?" he asked under his breath.

The doorbell rang.

"I'll get it!" Ariel's footsteps bounded down the stairs.

"Wait for me." Roman jogged after her.

He got there in time for her to open the door. Ricky gave her a bright smile, picking her up and spinning her around. "Hey, princess. How's your arm today?"

"It needs pancakes," she said seriously.

Ricky blinked at her, his mouth dropping open. "What did you say?"

"I need pancakes," Ariel repeated.

Ricky flicked an awed glance at Roman. "She's T-A-L-K-I-N-G."

Ariel scrunched her nose, as if trying to figure out what her uncle was spelling as he set her on her feet.

"It's how I found her," Roman answered.

"Holy ship," Ricky said.

Ariel giggled.

"What are you doing over here?" Roman asked.

"I wanted to check on you guys before I headed into the yards. I figured you'd want to stick close to home today. And I wanted to see how Elise's injury was."

"What injury?" Roman asked.

Ricky looked past him. "You didn't see her limping? Where is she?"

"She's gone."

"Gone where?" Ricky stepped into the house as the rev of another engine drew closer. Nova parked the four-wheeler and jogged up to them.

"How's my mermaid girl?" She picked up Ariel and kissed her cheeks.

"Hungry," Ariel answered.

Nova's eyes widened as a squeal of disbelief left her. "You just talked."

"Feed the kid and tell me where Elise went." Ricky walked towards the kitchen. He pulled the sugar-filled cereal reserved for weekends off the fridge and poured some in a bowl.

"We were going to get pancakes," Ariel protested.

"Wouldn't you rather have this special cereal?"

"Hmmm . . . okay." Ariel climbed onto a seat at the table. Ricky finished preparing her breakfast and set it in front of her.

Nova pointed to his daughter. "Are we just ignoring the fact that she's using her voice?"

"Let's not draw attention," Roman said.

Ricky motioned to the living room. "Let's talk in here."

Roman followed him, trailed by Nova.

Ricky spun around, crossing his arms over his chest. "What the fuck happened last night?"

"What do you mean?" Nova asked.

"When I left, Elise was bleeding, half-frozen to death, and covered in scrapes and mud, barely able to walk because she got lost in the woods looking for Ariel and fell. Sage found her at the edge of their property by the stream," Ricky explained.

Shock hit Roman, stealing his breath. "She looked fine when I saw her." Although, he'd wondered if she was hurt. Was it really that bad? Why hadn't she told him?

Because I was too busy trying to distance myself from her.

"She needed stitches, but she's as stubborn as you. She wanted to wait and make sure Ariel was okay," Ricky finished.

"So where is she?" Nova asked.

Roman handed her the note Elise had left him. She read it and looked up. "What does this mean? Why would you have asked her to leave? Did she think you blamed her for Ariel going missing?"

"Yeah."

"Why?" she asked.

"Because I said some things last night that I shouldn't have," he admitted. "But I told her we'd talk in the morning. That we needed a break, but—"

"A break? You said those exact words?" Nova asked.

"Yes. I meant for the night."

"Then this is probably a misunderstanding." She sighed in relief.

Roman shook his head, regret festering. "I don't think that's it."

"What do you mean?" Ricky asked.

"Patrice was here when I brought Ariel home. She made some comments about Elise not being capable of watching her, and not letting my feelings cloud my judgment. She brought up Tiana." Roman ran a hand over the back of his neck and squeezed.

"Oh, Roman, tell me you didn't." Nova shook her head.

"Didn't what?"

"Tell me exactly what was said," Ricky pushed.

"Why does it matter? She left. Instead of talking this out like mature adults, Elise took off after the first rough night we had. When I needed someone to support me and my kid, she left." His anger rose.

"I don't think searching the forest in the middle of a thunderstorm counts as running away. She was scared to death out there, not able to hear anything. She lost her phone in the stream and hurt herself. That woman was eaten alive by guilt when I left. Now I find out you came home and blamed her on top of that. It was a mistake—one you've made before, or did you forget about the aquarium when Ariel walked off while you searched the diaper bag for a snack?" Ricky narrowed his eyes.

Roman sighed. His brother was right. "I know it was an asshole thing to say. But she left."

"Why did she think you were going to ask her to leave in the morning anyways?" Nova asked.

He groaned in frustration. "I don't know. She said something about how I'm not over Tiana and how I'd never planned for this to go past the summer."

"This, meaning you two having a secret relationship behind everyone's backs?" Ricky clarified.

Roman slapped his brother's shoulder. "Yes, that, fuckhead."

"Why would she think that you'd only meant this to be a fling? I see the way you are around her. I haven't seen you so starry-eyed since Tiana," Nova said.

Roman swallowed, his eyes darting to the wood floor.

"What did you do?" Ricky asked.

"I really don't like you two teaming up on me."

Ricky shrugged. "I guess you know how Nash felt when he fucked things up with Isabella."

"Answer the question," Nova pressed.

"In my conversation with Patrice, I mentioned she was the nanny for the summer, and that's it," Roman admitted.

Ricky tipped his head up, closing his eyes. "Bruh."

"Tell me you didn't. Tell me my big brother, the one who always has his shit together, the one who is arguably the smartest out of all my siblings, wasn't that stupid," Nova snapped.

"Maybe I'm not as strong as you all think. I'm just barely holding it together most days. I didn't get the luxury of falling apart because I'm a single parent," he argued.

"You don't get it." Nova shook her head, her voice quieter. "Did Elise ever tell you about her ex?"

"Not really."

"She dated a single dad. She quit her job to stay home with his special needs son. They talked about getting engaged. She'd thought she was going to marry the guy. She came home one day and found her stuff in garbage bags on the front porch and the locks changed. He'd been cheating on her with his baby mama, who had a drug problem. They decided to get back together. And that's how Elise found out," Nova filled him in.

That must have been the family he'd seen in the diner. *But in the end, I guess that's all I was—a glorified babysitter.* Was that how she thought he viewed her?

He saw his words to Patrice through a different filter. Elise thought he'd played her? "So she thinks when I said it was ending at the end of summer, I meant us too?"

"That's something you should ask your girl," Ricky said.

He staggered back a step. "She left thinking I used her. That I faulted her for yesterday."

"Can you blame her?" Nova asked.

"She should have waited and talked to me."

"Sometimes when you've been hurt by the sting of rejection, it can leave an open wound. So you do whatever you can to not feel that way again, even if it means leaving before you can be left," Ricky said.

Nova and Roman both turned to look at him.

"What?" Ricky asked, tracing a pillow tassel with his finger on the couch.

"Speaking from experience?" Nova asked.

Ricky threw the pillow at her playfully. "Shut the fuck up. I'm more than my good looks, you know."

Nova caught it and chuckled. "Who knew there was such a softie under that hard exterior?"

"It's hard because it's all muscle." Ricky flexed.

"Okay, you just ruined it," Nova teased, throwing the pillow at his face.

"What the fuck do I do now?" Roman asked.

"Now you find her and apologize for being an asshole, and ask to talk it out with her," Nova supplied.

"I still don't like that she just took off. I need someone mature enough to work through shit, not run away."

"I don't think she sees it that way. It sounds like you were having two very different conversations. She took it one way— like you were ending things. She just left before you could actually do the official rejecting. She probably saw it as protecting herself," Nova replied.

"Fuck. You said she doesn't have a working phone anymore. I have no way to get a hold of her until she gets it fixed." Roman stood there feeling helpless.

"What about her emergency contact info?" Nova asked.

"Yeah, Mom should have all that shit," Ricky agreed.

"Can you watch Ariel for me?" Roman asked Nova.

"I suppose. I'm baking today, so she can help me."

Roman cut her a hard look. "You can't make edibles with my kid."

She waved her hand. "Of course I won't. What kind of aunty do you take me for?"

"The stoner you are." Ricky snickered.

"I'm not ashamed. Besides, a bit of pot calling the kettle black, eh?" Nova poked his stomach.

"Whatever. Just don't corrupt my niece," Ricky said.

"I'll be back. And don't let her out of your sight, okay?" Roman asked.

"Of course."

Roman headed towards the kitchen to say goodbye to Ariel.

"Hey, bro?" Ricky called after him.

Roman turned, one hand on the wall separating the living room from the rest of the house. "What?"

The pillow flew at his face, smacking him before it tumbled to the floor. "Tell Elise if she's looking to trade up, I'm available."

Roman flipped his brother off as Ariel came around the corner. "Shut the fudge up."

41

———

ELISE

Elise pushed the food around on her plate. She wasn't hungry—she hadn't been since she walked out of Roman's house four days ago. Her mother's watchful eyes didn't stray from her as her father picked up his noodles with chopsticks and slid his food into his mouth, giving her brother his undivided attention while Ren talked about a case from work.

Her new phone vibrated against her thigh. She pulled it out.

Jack: *Roman called here again. He said he just wants to talk.*

"Elise, you know there are no phones at the table," her mother reminded her.

Ren turned to her. "I'm surprised to see you with it at all, since you never seem to reply to my texts."

Right. Just one more way I'm a failure to this family.

She slipped it back into her pocket and gathered up her barely touched plate. "I'm going to go lie down. I'm not feeling well."

"Don't be like that, Elise," Ren said.

"I haven't heard about what's going on with you this summer," her mother added.

"Seems like Ren's got enough going on for the both of us as usual." Elise didn't wait for a reply before she took her plate to the kitchen and scraped its contents into a plastic container, then stuck it in the fridge.

She made her way to her childhood room. Everything was just as she'd left it after high school. Her mother hadn't touched a thing other than keeping away the dust, it seemed. Her brother's room was across the hall, now turned into a guest room with no trace of him. Like they'd never expected him to return but had known she'd be back here.

She lay on her bed, facing the door of the room. What was the use of talking? Why couldn't Roman just let her get over him in peace? Did he want a few more rounds with her? She hadn't thought that was what he was like, but then again, she'd thought they were building something, not knowing all along she was his dirty little secret. That he was still in love with his wife.

Her door creaked open. Her mother knocked after entering—as usual.

"What do you need?" Elise sat up, her back against the white headboard.

"Are you okay?" her mother asked.

"Fine."

Her mom studied her with a knowing look. "You haven't eaten much since you've been home."

She shrugged. "Not that hungry."

"You showed up in the middle of the night last week. I tried to give you space, but—"

"I'm sorry. I'll be out of your hair as soon as the apartment I'm renting is available. Should be another week. They had to change the carpets after the last tenant left. Something to do with cats," Elise said.

Her mother sighed, looking more tired than she had in a long time. "May I sit?" She motioned to the bed.

Elise nodded and tucked her feet under her. She filled her lungs with a deep breath, trying to fortify herself for whatever her mother wanted to say.

Her mom reached for her knee and then pulled her hand back as if unsure. "You could stay here, you know. You don't have to rent a place if you need some time to get on your feet."

Elise swallowed the lump of emotion rising in her throat and shook her head. "I wouldn't want to be a bother."

"Is that what you think?" Her mother sounded hurt.

Elise stayed silent.

"Look at me."

Elise met her mother's gaze, shiny with unshed tears. Surprise hit her square in the chest.

"You were always so independent. Never needing my help. Even when you started walking. You preferred to grab the furniture than my hand. Always on the go, moving forward." She chuckled. "You have never needed me."

Elise rolled her eyes.

"What?" her mother asked.

"Nothing."

"Tell me."

Years of heartbreak, of never feeling like enough, of being the child with the perceived defect, bubbled over. "I always needed you. But you weren't there."

Her mother flinched, pain in her expression. Her eyes wrinkled at the corners when she frowned. "I made so many mistakes with you."

Elise took a fortifying breath. "What makes me so unlovable? Is it the fact that I'm Deaf?"

Her mother's eyes widened. "Why would you think that?"

"Because you sent me away. And when I came home, I felt more like a stranger than a daughter," she confessed the long-held wound.

"Oh, no. We sent you away so that you would get everything we couldn't give you. So that you would have the best chance at the life you deserved. I'm so sorry if you thought it was because we thought something was wrong with you. I knew I didn't have the capability to help you how you needed."

"But when I was home, you never were. And Ren had this whole life with you and Dad. Dad didn't even learn sign."

Her mother placed her hand on Elise's knee. "We worked to pay for your expensive school. Your father took out a loan to afford your first year. And when we were home, I tried to talk to you, to spend time with you, but you preferred to be in your room. I should have pushed, but I was afraid it would make you shut me out completely." Her mother shook her head and continued, "You've always been so private. Holding in your pain, but also your joy—at least with me. I really thought you wanted your space. I figured you'd come to me when you needed me."

"And you knew I'd need to come back. That's why my bedroom here hasn't been changed, but Ren's has?"

Her mother shook her head. "No, that's not it at all. I had eighteen years with Ren at home. But only pieces with you. I couldn't bring myself to let this go. When you were gone to school, I'd come and sit in here just to feel a little closer to you. I suppose I should let go, but it's hard for me. You're my little girl who's had to overcome so much in a short amount of time. I just wanted to protect you."

"I thought there was something wrong with me," Elise confessed.

Her mother wrapped her arms around Elise, and she relaxed into her embrace. The scent of lemongrass wrapped around her with the familiarity of home.

"I love you. And you're perfect as you are. I'm sorry I ever made you doubt that," her mother apologized in sign.

Something loosened in Elise. Tears slid down her cheeks.

Her mother sniffled and pulled back. "We should have had this talk years ago. But I'd love to start now. Do you think we could build on this, and try to have a better relationship? Whatever you're ready for."

"I would like that." Elise nodded.

"Why don't you start by telling me what's got you so upset you don't want to eat your favorite noodles?"

Elise snorted and shook her head. Her voice caught in her throat, but still she forced the words out. "I fell in love."

Her mother's expression softened. The few wrinkles around her eyes crinkled. "And that's a bad thing?"

"It is when the man you fell for doesn't feel the same," Elise answered.

"Oh, honey, you deserve a man who adores you. Don't settle for any less."

"I think I need to forget about men for a while. Just focus on my job. But . . ."

"But?"

"His daughter goes to my school. She's not my student, but I'll see her. And I want to. I love her too, but it's gonna hurt." Elise's voice cracked.

Her mother rubbed soothing circles over her back. "I wish I could take this pain from you. How do you know he doesn't love you?"

Elise told her mother about what she'd overheard and her

conversation with Roman, all while her mother sat thoughtfully, listening without interruption.

"And he wants to talk to you?" she asked.

"Yes. He keeps calling my friend's number, asking him to get a message to me. And I changed my number when I got my new phone."

"Why didn't you want your old number transferred? Were you trying to avoid contact with him?" her mom asked.

Elise nodded. "I can't trust what he says. Because I love him and I gave every piece of myself to him just to have him lie to my face."

"I hear what you're saying. I'm just wondering, if he planned to walk away, why is he still trying to get a hold of you?"

"I don't know."

Her mother stared at her.

"What?"

"Do you think maybe you should have stayed and had a conversation when you were both rested and calm? I can't tell you how many fights I get into with your father because one or both of us is exhausted and emotional."

"You're taking his side?" Elsie asked, stunned.

"No. Never. I'm just saying if you're serious about this man, you must have thought he was worth it. Maybe he lied and used you. But maybe he didn't. I don't think my daughter is easily fooled."

Elise sighed. "Yeah, well, it wouldn't be the first time my asshole meter was wrong."

Her mother patted her knee. "Hear him out or don't. Whatever you decide, I'll be here to support your decision."

"I appreciate it, Mom."

Her mother lifted her hand to sign, *"I love you. Always. No matter what."*

"I love you too."

"Now, your father is renovating the garage tomorrow, so you might want to take your CI out because of the noise. If you need anything else, I'll be in my room reading." Her mom stood and left.

Elise lay down and pulled out her phone. Thankfully, everything had been backed up to the cloud. She swiped through the pictures she hadn't deleted yet. Roman and her smiling. Him kissing her cheek at the carnival. The three of them with Ariel at the beach, smiling like a family.

Was he really that good a liar or had she overreacted? *But I heard him.* And he'd made it clear he blamed her for Ariel going missing.

No, it was better to keep her distance—her heart was safer this way.

42

ELISE

Elise had forgotten just how wonderful the first day of school could be. There was nothing like it. She'd slipped on a simple royal-blue midi skirt with stars and planets splattered across the fabric, and tucked in her white blouse. She rubbed her hands over the button-up pink sweater as she stood outside her classroom, greeting the kids and their mostly anxious and frazzled parents.

"So happy to have you in my class this year, Sean. Go ahead and find the cubby with your name on it, and get your things situated." Elise smiled at the little boy wearing a dinosaur hoodie.

"I know we spoke over email about Sean's gluten allergy. I just wanted to make sure you knew play-dough also has gluten in there. I've gone ahead and printed off a list of alternatives as well as things you might not realize have wheat in them." Sean's mother handed over a stapled sheaf of papers.

"I will absolutely be careful and make sure to double-check with you ahead of time for anything I have questions about," Elise assured her.

"Thank you." The woman entered the classroom. Kids and parents bustled by, going into one colleague or another's classroom. Elise shifted in her pink heels that matched her sweater. They pinched her feet but looked fabulous with her outfit. She needed a little bit of armor today of all days.

She scanned the hallway towards the entrance for what seemed like the millionth time since she'd come out of her classroom to wait. Still no sign of Roman or Ariel. Her stomach flipped with nerves. She'd been both excited for and dreading this day. Maybe it was like ripping off a Band-Aid. She just needed to get the first run-in over with.

She greeted another two students, pointing out the cubbies and welcoming them to the class while answering a few questions from other parents.

A small hand tugged her arm, drawing her attention. Elise turned, her polite smile freezing momentarily before a rush of emotions curved her lips even higher. "Ariel." She glanced around. *Where is Roman?*

The little girl wrapped her arms around Elise's waist and squeezed. Elise bent down, pulling her into her arms, and fought to keep her emotions in check.

Ariel pulled back to look at her as bodies passed them in the hallway. "Are you coming home today?"

Elise's mouth dropped open. Ariel was talking! "What did you say?"

"When are you coming home? I miss you. And Daddy misses you too. He's been really sad lately," Ariel said.

Elise blinked, still stunned. "I . . . I was just staying with you for the summer, sweetie. But I'll always be here for you if you want to talk. Or whatever you need."

Ariel shook her head angrily and stuck her lip out. "Is it because I ran away? Is that why you left?"

"Oh, sweetheart, no." She pulled her back into her arms

for a hug. "It's not your fault . . . It was just time for me to go." Elise nearly choked on the words. She hadn't wanted to go at all.

"I love you," Ariel said.

"I love you too."

The girl pulled away again and held out her pinky finger. "Promise you'll still be my friend?"

Elise hooked her smallest finger around the girl's. "Promise. Oh, here. I printed the picture of you and our mermaid friend for you to have." Elise dug it out of her pocket and handed it over to Ariel.

Ariel's eyes grew round as she focused on the photo, taking it gently in her hands as if it were a precious artifact. "Thank you."

"Ariel?" a frantic Nova called from down the hall.

Elise waved to her. "Over here."

Nova's whole demeanor relaxed as she walked closer and laughed. "I swear. She's a lot quicker than she looks."

Elise's smile dimmed. Was that a dig at her?

Nova's humor vanished as if she realized how Elise must have taken it. "Oh, shoot, that's not what I—Jesus, I'm not high enough for this shit. Too many kids running around. Too much stimulation is turning my brain to mush," Nova rambled.

Elise reached out and touched her arm. "Don't worry about it."

Nova nodded and slammed her mouth closed, eyeing Ariel before returning her attention to Elise. "So . . . have you had a chance to talk to . . ."

Elise shook her head. "No. I don't think there's anything else we need to discuss. I've got to get back to work. You have a good day."

She waved and walked into her classroom, now bustling

with students. Hopefully they couldn't tell her heart was racing at a million miles a minute, and she could barely take an adequate breath because of the anxiety constricting her chest. She smiled brighter, hopefully channeling first-grade-teacher vibes rather than evil-villain-verging-on-insanity ones. Fake it 'til you make it, right?

* * *

The first day went much as she'd expected. A few homesick kiddos, and a lot of fighting over the limited supplies. One pair of peed pants, and a false alarm of a missing gerbil hidden in one student's backpack later, she gathered her things and made her way out to the employee parking lot to the farthest spot on the end. A warm breeze blew over her, ruffling her hair. She tucked a few strands behind her ear and dug through her purse for her keys as she walked in those ridiculous shoes. *Ow*. Her leg still ached a little from her injury. She flicked a glance up and—

What?

She did a double take. Roman leaned against her car, arms crossed, baseball cap pulled down. She risked a glance back to the school, instinct telling her to avoid him.

Fuck that. She had nothing to be ashamed of. He wouldn't waste any more of her time.

She stepped forward as his head rose. Dark shadows created half-moons below his eyes like he hadn't been sleeping well. That made two of them.

She rolled her shoulders back and tipped her chin up, steeling herself for the inevitable encounter.

"Mr. Emerson." She'd keep it professional like they should have from the beginning.

He straightened, his arms falling to his sides. "Elise."

"If you'll excuse me, I need to get home." She stepped forward on wobbly legs. Butterflies of anxiety were doing aerial stunts in her belly.

"Are you hurt?"

Like he cared. "I'm fine."

He didn't budge. "Can we talk?"

She cleared her throat, blinking away the emotion that rose in her. Anger, yes, but below that was a truckload of hurt and broken promises. Love unrequited was a bitch. "Ariel isn't my student, and I am no longer your employee, so I don't think there is anything else for us to discuss. Please step aside."

Roman hesitated and then shifted out of the way—but just barely. She walked by him, her shoulder pressing against his chest because he wouldn't move. She unlocked the car and pulled open the door, tossing her stuff into the passenger seat and trying to get her bearings. She inhaled a lungful of air tainted by his intoxicating scent. Her head swirled with dizziness.

She turned, staring at his chest. "Y-you should know though that Ariel spoke to me today. Like with her voice, not in sign."

He rubbed his hand over the back of his neck. "Yeah, she's been doing that since I found her in the woods. It's how I located her actually."

"Right." *Ouch.* "Well—"

"Can we talk? Just five minutes is all I ask," Roman pressed.

"I have dinner plans that I need to get to." She slid into the driver's seat. Elise pulled the handle to close the door, but Roman grabbed the corner at the top and stopped it. She risked a glance at him.

"With who?" His voice was gruff.

She narrowed her eyes at him.

He sighed. "I'm sorry."

She slammed her eyes closed, forcing a breath into her lungs despite the tightness in her chest. *Don't do it, Elise. Stay strong.* She opened her eyes. "For what?"

His chest rose and fell several times as she waited for his answer. "I never meant to hurt you."

"Then why lead me into thinking we had something when you planned to end it when school started?"

"That's not—I never planned to do that."

But in the end, that was what he'd done. After she'd made a horrible mistake, he'd decided she wasn't worth it anymore. Was that any better? Only marginally, because it meant he wasn't a calculating asshole—just a scared one.

"I really have to go. And please stop texting and calling my friends."

Roman let go of the door, his shoulders sagging. He looked so pitiful. Guilt settled over her. Why should she be the one feeling bad? He was the one who'd said he wanted a break. That this was going to be over at the end of summer. Her anger boiled to the surface. She huffed and climbed out of the car, jabbing her finger towards him. "You don't get to do this."

"Do what? Apologize?"

"Act like the poor kicked puppy. You broke up with me. You hid me like your dirty little secret—and I let you. I gave you everything, and after I made a horrible and scary mistake —trust me, I know how bad I fucked up—you didn't even give me the benefit of a conversation or the doubt." Her heart thudded, and her hands shook with adrenaline.

Roman's jaw tensed, but he stayed silent, so she continued, "I would have never put Ariel in a position where she could be hurt on purpose. I love that little girl like she was my own—"

She blinked away the traitorous tears. Why did she have to be such a crybaby when her emotions rose?

"I know that. I shouldn't have blamed you. I was exhausted and afraid."

She blinked. "I appreciate you saying that. And I am genuinely, from the bottom of my heart, sorry for losing Ariel. Storm or not, I should have never taken my eyes off her."

"I know. And believe it or not, it wasn't the first time she got lost. I made the same mistake at an aquarium years ago," Roman confessed.

Elise blinked, too stunned to speak. "But you said—"

"I know I blamed you. That was cruel of me. I was terrified. Ariel's lost the person who should have been here to raise her with me—her mother who she loved so much. I got scared and made a rash statement because I don't want to see her lose someone else she loves. That would devastate her. I just want to protect my baby from the hurt." Roman's voice wavered with emotion.

"Why would she lose me?"

"Because anything can happen. Tiana's death taught me that nothing in this world is promised. Not tomorrow, and definitely not forever," Roman answered.

Elise shifted, staring down at him. "Is it Ariel that you're afraid for, or is it you who doesn't want to get too close and risk losing someone you care about?"

Roman's brow furrowed. "Of course it's for her."

Elise shook her head. "You like to pretend you have it all together. You try to control as much as possible in your day-to-day life. But you're still stuck in your grief because you're not ready to fully let go—risk it all for another chance at love."

"You have no idea what you're talking about," he rasped.

"Don't I?"

He stepped forward. "You have no clue what it's like to

come home to find out the entire world as you know it just disappeared. To find out the person you planned on spending forever with is dead."

Elise flinched.

Roman continued, "To know you now have a traumatized toddler to take care of all on your own. To not be able to fall apart because that little girl is counting on you. Your brother is already at rock bottom, and your family needs you to step up. To have the weight of the world on your shoulders when all you want to do is fall apart. But you have to protect them. Love them. And hope to whatever higher power is listening that nothing else bad happens to them." Roman shook his head, his stony expression showing no emotion but anger. "You have no idea what it's like for me. So you sit there with your judgment and assumptions based on your perceptions. But they are not in fact reality."

"You're right. I don't know everything about you. I tried to ask, and you shared some. But I can't force you. Admit the truth—you didn't want to tell me. You didn't want to let me in all the way."

He jerked back as if she'd struck him. "You're the first woman since my wife passed that I've been with. You lived in my fucking house, took care of my kid, and I let you into my bed, into my—"

"What? Into your where?" She pushed, her voice rising. *Say it.*

"I let you into my life more than anyone else in a long time."

"You let me in as far as you were comfortable. But I wasn't in it for just enough. I wanted more—I wanted everything." She inhaled steeling herself as she laid it all bare.

"Then why did you run away?" he snapped.

She swallowed, her chest heaving.

"You called me out for it and yet you did the same thing. I'm not the one who walked away from this—you are."

"That's not fair. You said—"

"I told you I needed the night to get some sleep and process."

"I gave you my fucking heart and the things you said, the things you let your mother-in-law say about me." She shook her head. "I fell in love with you." Her voice broke and she clapped a hand over her mouth as if it would somehow lock the confession back inside. She forced herself to meet his eyes as her hand dropped to her hip and fisted. She stood there, vulnerable before him, waiting with her last shred of hope.

Roman's Adam's apple bobbed as a wash of emotions flashed in his dark gaze. "How did we get here? I thought things were good the way they were. I was going to suggest we tell everyone we were dating. To see if you wanted to stay with us instead of moving out. How did it all go to hell?"

The last of her hope died in a puff of smoke, an ember snuffed out. Her heart sank. She'd just told this man she'd loved him, that she'd pictured a future where they were together, and all he had to say was that?

She nodded, resignation settling into her bones. "Good-bye, Roman. I hope you have a nice life and you find what you're looking for someday." She climbed into her car and pulled the door shut. She started the engine and backed up, not even willing to risk a glance in the rearview mirror. In the end, she'd put it all out there, on the line, and he'd shown his true feelings, or lack thereof. He may have liked her, but he certainly didn't love her. He might not be ready to face the fact that he wasn't ready to move on. He knew the ugly side to love—loss. And apparently, Elise wasn't worth the risk.

43

ROMAN

Roman clutched the bouquet of flowers like they were the lifeline he needed as he approached the headstone. He kneeled in front of the grave, tracing his fingers through the engraved lettering.

Tiana Emerson

Beloved wife, mother, daughter, and friend

May 3, 1989–September 6, 2017

He dropped his arm to his side and tipped his face towards the clear blue sky. Birds chirped from the trees. A lawnmower hummed somewhere in the distance. Cool wind drifted over Roman's skin, bringing the crispness of fall with it. He sighed and turned to sit with his back against the gravestone.

"Hey, T. Today's the anniversary of your . . . passing." His stomach hardened and flipped. Talking to her like she was here when she wasn't never got easier. That was the part of grief that most people didn't want to talk about— the fact that it stuck with you forever. There would always be a hole where the person you loved used to take up space. Learning to live with their absence when there was a piece of your heart missing was the most painful thing. It wasn't that grief got easier with time; you just learned to live with the pain, the loss, the quiet, the empty side of the bed. You found a way to get through this day and then the next until one day, you found yourself living again. But never without the shadow of what could have been. Of the moments missed.

"You know I don't like to bring Ariel on this anniversary. I'd rather her celebrate your life than that awful day." He sniffed, emotion welling in his eyes as flashes of that traumatic afternoon played through his mind.

"She's talking again." He smiled. "She's so amazing, T. So much like you. She's got your sass, your kindness, and your horrible sense of direction." He chuckled before he grew serious. "I almost lost her too."

Roman wiped his eyes before his tears could fall. "I promised I'd keep her safe and I almost failed you. I—" He took a deep breath. "I don't know what the hell I'm doing, T. I know you're gone. There's a part of me that will always be yours. But . . . I have feelings for someone else. And part of that feels like a betrayal to you. I know you'd want me to move on because that's the selfless person you are." The corners of his mouth turned up. "Remember that night we got back from The Shipwreck, and you were so drunk you started taking off your clothes in the car? Someone you worked with had lost their husband and you turned to me, so serious, and told me that if anything ever happened to you, that I should find someone to make me smile again. Someone to love our baby almost as much as you could." Roman shook his head, not bothering to stop the emotion dripping from his eyes this time. "It's like you knew."

The graveyard blurred with his tears as he set the flowers by his side on the grass. "Well, I found her. Elise—that's the woman I told you about before. I messed it up, just like I said I would."

He tipped his head back until the back of his skull connected with the cold marble. "She told me she loved me, and I fucked it up because I panicked. I blamed her for losing Ariel when I knew it wasn't her fault."

Birds chirped as rays of sun warmed his face. "The problem is, what if I lose her too?"

"Sounds to me like you've already lost her."

Roman's eyes flew open as he sat up straighter.

His mother-in-law looked at him with sympathy, a bouquet of flowers in her hands.

Roman scrambled to his feet, wiping his eyes. "I didn't know you were here."

"I usually come in the morning on this date. But something came up and . . . well, here I am." Patrice gave him a sad smile. She walked over to the gravestone and arranged her flowers next to his.

"I was just . . ."

"I talk to her too. She always was a great listener." Patrice's smile turned watery.

"I'm sorry if I upset you."

She shook her head and carefully sat on the grass, facing the marble stone. She patted the spot next to her. Roman joined her.

Patrice inhaled a shaky breath and then turned to him. "I know my daughter is gone. That's a pain I wouldn't wish on anyone. To lose a child, no matter what age, is something I never thought I'd be able to live through."

Roman nodded, his stomach flipping with anxiety. *I can't imagine losing Ariel.*

"But she was your wife. And you loved her with everything in you. George and I could see that from the very beginning.

You two were just kids when you got married, but we weren't worried because of how you treated her," Patrice said.

"I did—I still do love her."

"But it's time you moved on."

"What?" Roman's brows drew together as he blinked in confusion. This was not the way he'd seen this conversation going.

"You're young. You've got a lifetime ahead of you, and you deserve to find someone to share it with."

"I'm not sure what to say," he admitted.

"I heard what you said about Elise. I realize that I might have overstepped and judged her too quickly. Ariel has always had great things to say about her. And since she's come into your lives, that spark is back in you. The same one you had with my daughter." Patrice swiped her eyes and cleared her throat.

"I don't . . . I'm sorry. I didn't mean to rub that in your face—"

"Don't be a fool. I may be old, but I'm not blind. I may be the mother of your deceased wife, but I still care about you and want the best for you. I still consider you my son-in-law."

"I'm sorry I couldn't save her—and that I wasn't there when everything happened." He spoke his regret, owning up to how he'd let Patrice down.

"You have nothing to apologize for. There was nothing you could have done. It was Tiana's time to go." Patrice's words wrapped around his chest and gripped, squeezing the air from his lungs. He looked at her, stunned. The weight of the guilt he'd carried for years slipped from his shoulders.

"You don't blame me? I—I would understand if you did," he said.

She shook her head. "Not at all. There was nothing that could have been done. The doctors said it; the autopsy report stated it. Honestly, I blamed myself for a while. Did she mention something to me that I dismissed? Even a headache? Should I have seen signs? I know it isn't logical, but letting go of that guilt is not easy. I want you to know, I harbor no blame for you. It was no one's fault." Her voice shook.

"I appreciate you saying that. I thought . . ."

"I know. That day is still a blur, but I know I said things in the heat of the moment I didn't mean. I deeply regret any hurt I've caused you. I should have told you sooner."

"I'm glad you're telling me now," Roman said.

"She'd want you to be happy, you know."

He nodded. "I know."

"And Elise makes you happy?"

He blew out a breath and nodded again. "But that's over."

"As I heard." She motioned to the grave. "I hope it wasn't because of Ariel getting lost, of what I said?"

"It's on me."

"Well, from what I heard, you're afraid of fixing things because you might lose her like you lost Tiana," Patrice said.

Wasn't that what Elise had said? "That might be part of it."

"Lose her now and be alone, living in a way that doesn't let anyone else in seems like the safer bet. Can't be hurt more that way, right?" Patrice studied him.

What she was describing sounded a lot like what Nash had done before Isabella, not Roman. "It's not like that."

"Oh? So you're not afraid of opening yourself up to love, risking the chance that someday you might lose this person?"

He sighed. Why did these women all think he was scared? "I mean, that's—it isn't the same thing."

"Isn't it? You're a smart man, Roman. I think you know you're lying to yourself. If you truly love this woman and think there's a future to be had with her, then she would be worth the pain of the unknown. And if you don't . . ." She shrugged. "Then I guess it isn't really love."

His chest rose and fell as his shoulders stiffened. *But I do love her.*

"All I know is, I would trade a lifetime of pain for another day with Tiana. That's love. Take it from me—love is messy. Life is full of ups and downs, but love is steady. In the end, isn't love what life is about? Human connection. Sharing experiences. Having that one person you can always rely on." She swiped a piece of grass from her pants leg. "Love is brave. It's damn terrifying, because of the risk of losing that person. But I never thought you to be a coward, Roman. It's one of the things I always admired about you. The way you stepped up for Ariel when Tiana passed. You're a great father. Tiana would be proud. But it's time you do something for you now. If Elise is that woman, if she loves you and Ariel, I'll find a way to love her too. And if she's not . . . well, I'll be here when you find the woman that does."

Roman didn't want anyone else. Elise was . . . gone. He'd fucked it up and he wasn't sure she'd ever forgive him for how he'd hurt her. But did he even want to be forgiven? Or had he self-sabotaged things because it was safer?

Were Patrice and Elise both right? Had Roman been a coward?

She patted his knee. "Just think about it."

Roman nodded and got to his feet. "Thanks for . . . talking with me. I'll leave you for some privacy."

She smiled up at him. "Think about what I said."

"I will," he promised.

Roman turned and walked through the rows of gravestones and neatly trimmed grass. A whole acre of loved ones lost over the years. Was he stuck in the past? Hadn't he worked through his grief?

Or am I doing the exact same thing Nash did and keeping people at a distance to protect myself?

It was time Roman took a good long look in the mirror. Elise had made it clear she wanted distance, and that he'd hurt her. Maybe it was too late to fix what he'd broken. His heart ached at the thought. But since when did Roman give up on things he cared about?

Never.

44

ROMAN

Roman blew out of his mouth as he lowered the stack of beehives into the back of his truck. Insects buzzed around him in an angry frenzy. He'd opted to wear a veil today seeing as it was overcast and they were already in a grumpy mood before he took their honey-filled hives. He grunted under the weight as he slid the boxes into place and jumped out of the truck bed and onto the ground.

"That about does it." Ricky picked up the smoker and stuffed it into the side by the back window of the cab.

Ricky pulled out his phone, studying it before tapping a reply and sticking it back in his pocket. "So you still haven't heard from Elise?"

Roman shook his head, opening the door to the vehicle to grab two waters from the cooler for him and Ricky. His brother took a drink and wiped his mouth with the back of his hand. "But you saw her at the school?"

Roman sighed. "Yeah. She thinks I haven't moved on from Tiana."

"Well, have you?" Ricky asked.

Roman rubbed a hand over his sweat-slicked skin as the warm end-of-summer breeze blew over his sticky skin. "I thought I was. I am—Fuck, I don't even know anymore. Tiana will always have a piece of my heart. She was my wife, the mother of my child."

"But she isn't here anymore."

Roman's stomach churned. "Don't you think I know that?"

Ricky held up his hands in a placating gesture. "So I don't see the problem. Tell her what you told me."

Roman released a heavy sigh. "You don't understand. It's more complicated than that."

"I think you're making it more complicated than it needs to be. You love her, then tell her. You can figure out all the details together."

"Oh, now you're the expert in love? Mr. Playboy, who has a different woman in his bed every week."

Ricky smirked with a shrug. "Sometimes two. That's exactly what makes me an expert. I know women. And I know my brother. You're so busy holding everything so tightly together, wanting to make it all okay, that you forget to let people in."

"So you think I'm holding back?" Roman asked as images of their time together filled his mind. How many opportunities had he had to tell someone Elise meant more to him? How many times had she insinuated she was ready for more and he'd changed the subject because he hadn't quite been ready to make that kind of commitment? Fuck. She was right. He'd been holding back.

"I'm scared." The confession slipped out in a whisper.

Ricky slapped his shoulder. "Well, buck the fuck up, big

brother. Love is about taking chances. Risking everything in the hopes of one more day with that special person."

"So I keep hearing . . . You're kind of a romantic in a rough-around-the-edges sort of way," Roman teased.

Ricky laughed. "For other people maybe."

"You're trying to tell me you've never been in love? After a speech like that?"

Ricky's smile slipped, his eyes clouding over like he was stuck in some far-off memory. Pain flashed in his dark brown gaze before he shook his head. "Love isn't for me."

"Or maybe you haven't found someone worth risking forever for."

Ricky rolled his eyes. "And I won't. Now, what's your plan for getting Elise back in your good graces?"

"She told me she loved me," Roman confessed.

"Dude, you didn't tell me that. Seems like an easy fix to me. Just go over and talk to her."

Roman shook his head. "I didn't say it back."

Ricky's mouth dropped open, his eyebrows tipping down. "Tell me you are not that fucking stupid."

"I panicked."

Ricky sighed this time, turning to glance around them to the meadow. "Sounds like you need an opportunity to unfuck this mess you made."

"I don't know her number. Or where she's living. She asked me to stop calling her friends to leave messages for her. And I think if I wait outside the school for her again, it might be too much."

"Unless she's into the whole stalker fantasy, to say you're going about this the wrong way is an understatement. Christ, am I actually the one who knows better? Are we really at this point of desperation?" Ricky chuckled.

"What do I do, oh wise one?" Roman teased.

His brother pulled out his phone, typing something. Roman's phone dinged with a new message. He pulled it out, checking to see if it was something about Ariel, but Ricky's name flashed with an address.

"What's this?"

"That is the address of someone who has a wasp problem and needs a nest removed, pronto. I'll drive these back to the honey shop and you can take my truck." Ricky moved past him, climbing into the driver's seat.

"How the hell is that supposed to help me get my girl back?"

Ricky shrugged. "It's not. You're gonna have to do that on your own. Find a way to show her how you feel, and let her know that you're not going anywhere. Oh, and also that you're not hiding her away like a dirty secret because you're still in love with your wife."

"So glad we had this talk. That's very clear. I couldn't have figured that out without you," Roman deadpanned as his brother started Roman's truck, resting his arm on the base of the window.

"Happy to help. Oh, my truck needs gas." Ricky took off, driving through the field and back onto the road in a small cloud of dust.

"Asshole."

Roman made his way to his brother's truck. Climbing inside, he clicked the address in the text and put the navigation on. He'd take care of the wasps and then figure out a way to make this right with Elise.

* * *

Thirty minutes later, he pulled into the driveway of a beautiful family home in Dark Cove. The garage bay was open, the tick of a few angry wasps hitting the ceiling as they flew in and out of a large hole. The thing about wasps was, unlike honeybees that died after a sting, wasps could keep stinging. And they hurt like a bitch, more than honeybees.

"You the bee man?" A woman peeked through the screen door dividing the garage and the house.

"Yes, ma'am."

"Good. My husband thought it was a good idea to install bike racks in the ceiling of the garage but forgot to look for the studs," she explained.

Roman pushed the broken drywall around with his steel-toe boot on the ground. Bits of pink insulation and grey papery wasp nest was stuck to it.

"I see."

"My daughter is allergic and, let me get her—she said she knew your brother."

Roman rolled his eyes. So that was why Ricky hadn't wanted to take this call. The daughter was someone he'd probably spent a night with and Ricky's commitment-phobe reaction had been to mistake a call for help as a marriage proposal and stay as far away as he could. Damn, maybe he and his siblings had a lot more in common than Roman realized. He studied the remaining nest of wasps. It was a big one. But he'd handled similar before. He just had to figure out how to get them out without getting stung too much. He'd definitely put the suit on for this.

"Thanks for coming, Ricky. I didn't know who to call—oh." Elise stood on the other side of the door, her eyes wide next to the other woman.

Ricky, you slick motherfucker. "Elise."

"I'm sorry. I didn't know who else could help." She bit her lip nervously.

"It's not a problem."

"I'll, uh, let you get to it, then." She backed away.

His mind spun, trying to think of any way to get her to stay. "You were right."

She stopped. "About what?"

"All of it. I did keep you at a distance. But it's not because I can't let Tiana go."

Her delicate throat bobbed, but she made no move to reply.

"I was scared. Loving you is the riskiest thing I've ever done in my life. And I thought if I didn't face it, then if something happened to you, I wouldn't hurt as much. It was selfish."

Her chest rose and fell, a sheen of tears glittering in her eyes.

"But then I lost you, and it hurt so fucking bad. Like my soul was torn from my body. And I realized I'd trade a lifetime of feeling like this for one more day of being with you." He stepped up to the screen door, wishing there was nothing to separate them. "I lo—"

"Oh, for Pete's sake, let the man inside so he can properly apologize," Elise's mom called from somewhere in the house.

Elise's cheeks pinked up. Roman didn't miss his chance. He grabbed the screen door, doing a quick scan to make sure none of the insects were nearby. The last thing he wanted was for Elise to get hurt. He dashed inside, closing the door tightly behind him before he spun to look at Elise.

She was beautiful with her raven hair pulled into a messy bun. She wore a pair of cutoffs and a loose T-shirt that hung off one shoulder, showing the tattoos adorning her skin.

"Where was I?" he asked.

"You were about to tell my daughter how much you love her," Elise's mom supplied.

He turned to her, holding out his hand to shake hers. "Mrs. Aki, I'm Roman Emerson. It's nice to meet you."

She narrowed her eyes at him. "Are you the fool who hurt my daughter?"

"Yes, ma'am, I am. But I deeply regret that. And I'm hoping she'll be able to forgive me enough to give me a second chance." He turned to Elise, his hands itching to reach out and hold her. But he hadn't earned that right yet.

"I think I fell in love with you the moment you knocked me on my ass when I thought you had broken into my home."

The corner of Elise's mouth quirked up, giving him hope.

"I think you left a few details out of your story," her mother mused.

"Can you give us some privacy, Mom?" Elise glared at her mother.

Mrs. Aki blew out of her mouth. "Fine, fine."

She left the entryway, disappearing around the corner, but Roman had a feeling she hadn't gone far.

"Sorry about that," Elise apologized.

"She cares about you."

Elise nodded. "Yeah, she does."

"So do I."

She closed her eyes. "Why didn't you say anything the other day? I told you I loved you and you just . . ."

"I know, baby. And I won't stand here and say you don't deserve better than me because you do. But I swear to you that if you give me another chance, I'll probably screw it up at some point—but I won't stop trying to make you never doubt my love for you again. I never want you to think you aren't worth it because you are. You're an amazing, kind, brilliant woman. And I'm just a beekeeper who's wholeheartedly and totally in love with you. I know I fucked up—"

"Language!" Mrs. Aki yelled from the other room.

Elise rolled her eyes and stifled a laugh.

Roman reached for her hand, getting onto his knees. "I know I messed everything up, but I'm here to ask you if you'll—"

"Is he proposing?" Mrs. Aki asked, peeking around the corner.

"No, Mom. Please leave us alone!" Elise shook her head, then turned back to Roman. "You're not, are you?"

Soon. "No, honey. When I ask you to marry me, it won't be in your parents' foyer."

"When?" Elise's eyebrow rose.

"Yes, *when.* You said you wanted everything, and I do too. But right now, I'm on my knees to beg for your forgiveness. To ask you to give me another chance. And to ask you on a proper date. And I'm proposing you be my girlfriend."

"That's quite the list of requests," she teased.

He smiled, studying her unreadable expression. "Do I stand a chance?"

She tugged on his hand. "Get up."

He did immediately, clasping both her hands in his, holding his breath.

She looked down to where they were joined and then to his face. "I won't hide anymore."

"I won't ask you to."

"And I won't be perfect either. I might mess up something with Ariel—"

"I'm so sorry I blamed you. I know you'd never do anything to put her in danger. I trust you with her—with the most precious person to me on this earth besides you."

"That means a lot." Elise breathed out as if relieved. "I

don't want to be the nanny anymore. I don't mind watching Ariel when you need help. I love her, and want to spend time with her, but I also need to know that I'm more than that to you."

"Absolutely. You already are," he quickly agreed.

"Okay."

"Okay? You'll forgive me? You'll give me a second chance?" he clarified as his heart thumped wildly. Hope expanded and grew in his chest like warm rays of sunshine.

She smiled, her warm brown eyes glittering with so much affection it made his knees buckle. He caught himself, wrapping his arms around her. Roman gripped the back of her neck, nuzzling his nose over hers as he softly commanded, "Use your words. Tell me."

"Yes. I love you."

"Say it again." He kissed her jaw.

"I love you."

"I love you too." He captured her mouth with his. Slow, hungry sweeps of his lips between hers became fervent promises and carnal kisses.

A throat clearing pulled him out of his lust-induced haze. "Glad you got that cleared up. But there's still a wasp problem. Maybe you fix that and then come inside to . . . continue working things out with my daughter, yeah?"

Roman gave what he had a feeling was a lovesick smile as he nodded, not taking his eyes off a flushed Elise.

"I'm sorry," she whispered.

"Don't be. She's right. I have a job to do, and keeping you safe is at the top of that list." Roman leaned in to give her one more kiss before he reluctantly released her.

"I'll finish this up, but you won't want to leave for a couple hours at least. How about I pick you up tomorrow at ten? We'll spend the day together, just the two of us, before I go pick up Ariel from her grandparents'. Then, if you want, you could stay for dinner? I know Ariel would love to see you again."

"That sounds fun."

"It's a date." He winked.

Now he just had to prove to her he'd meant every word he said and convince her to never leave.

45

ELISE

Elise checked the mirror in her childhood bedroom quickly making sure she looked presentable. Her stomach twisted and flipped with nervous butterflies. She smoothed her hand down her vintage Pink Floyd T-shirt and double-checked her skinny jeans for any grass stains. Thankfully, there were none.

"Coming." Her mother's voice drifted through the house.

Shit, Roman's here already. She glanced at the clock. He was a full twenty minutes early. She grabbed her Converse and slipped them on before racing downstairs.

Her mother had Roman seated at the kitchen table already and she was handing him a glass of tea. They both turned towards her as she entered the room.

"Hey, Mom. I told you we were going right out." She spoke to her mother but couldn't look away from Roman. *He's actually here.*

"It's just a cup of tea," she argued.

He smiled, his eyes lazily roaming over her as he stood and

lifted a bouquet of pink dahlias and a mix of other flowers. "Good morning."

Elise accepted the gift, inhaling. He'd often brought her wildflowers before. "Thank you." She flicked a glance towards her mother and then looked back to him. "We should get going."

"Roman, you should come for dinner some night this week," her mother said.

"I would lo—"

"You don't have to."

Roman looked between her and her mother as if trying to read the situation. "I would love to."

"And bring that little girl of yours," her mom added.

"Yes, ma'am."

Elise set the flowers in a vase by the sink already filled with a bouquet that hadn't been there this morning. Had Roman bought her mother flowers too? She grabbed her purse from the kitchen counter and hooked it over her shoulder. "Okay, well, I'll see you later, Mom."

She walked towards the entrance, hoping Roman would follow her lead. She reached for the door, but Roman's hand pressed against hers, stopping her from opening it.

His front pressed against her back as he leaned near her ear. "Let me make sure there's no lingering wasps."

"Oh, okay." She dropped her hand and moved to the side.

Roman scanned the garage through the screen door and then opened it, giving another cursory glance around before he opened the door the rest of the way for her. "All good."

She walked to his truck. He opened the door and helped her in before going around to his side and starting the engine.

Elise set her purse on the seat. "Where are we going?"

He turned and winked at her. "It's a surprise."

* * *

Twenty minutes later, they pulled down a familiar road.

"Are we going to your house?"

"Nope."

That was good. Being alone with Roman in a space with a bed would make it mighty tempting to just fall back into the routine they used to have. But she needed more. Needed to know he really could be the man she wanted—the one she deserved.

Roman turned up the road that led to Sage's, the woman who'd rescued her.

"I heard you met one of the Fate sisters." Roman pointed towards the wooden sign on the side of the gravel road as they drove past rows and rows of grapes.

Fates' Winery

"Fates' . . . Oh, Sage and her sisters own Fates' Winery?" Elise asked, putting two and two together.

"Yup."

Oh, are we going to a tasting?

Roman pulled the truck next to a big red barn and parked. He got out and came around to open her door. Roman's hand coasted the small of her back as he led her towards a corral enclosing a chestnut-brown horse and a matching foal except for the white star on its forehead.

"Aww, it's so cute."

"Glad to see you're doing better."

Elise turned towards the voice. Sage stood by the now open doorway to the barn, wiping her hands on her jeans.

"Sage, I hear you've met my girlfriend, Elise." Roman wrapped his arm around Elise's waist and tugged her against his hard body.

Girlfriend? So he was just announcing it now like it was no big deal?

Sage nodded. "I have."

Elise smiled. "Thank you so much for helping me that night."

Sage waved her hand dismissively. "Don't mention it. You ready to ride?"

Elise turned to Roman.

He smiled. "Absolutely."

"Okay, well, they're all tacked up. And everything else is ready to go." Sage gave Roman a meaningful look, like she was saying something without words.

"Perfect. I appreciate it," he said, taking Elise's hand and pulling her towards the barn.

"Have fun." Sage waved with a smile.

Elise followed him into the well-lit barn that smelled like hay and a distinct musk that she guessed belonged to the horses. The other side had a sliding door that was wide open, letting sunlight in. Two big horses stood side by side, blocking the way out.

"Have you ever ridden before?" Roman asked.

"No." Her stomach clenched. "They're so big."

He chuckled. "They're gentle giants. Ariel comes to ride sometimes and she always picks Sprout, the spotted mare there." He motioned to the beautiful horse on the right. "And I usually take old Bear out." He lifted his hand and petted the black horse's nose.

She giggled. "The horse's name is Bear? Don't you think that it might give him a complex?"

He chuckled. "He's a grump sometimes, but he's sweet on Sprout here. Which one do you want to ride?"

"I think I'll stick with Ariel's choice."

"Come on over and meet her. Just keep your hands away

from her mouth or she'll think you've got a treat for her, and you don't want your fingers mistaken for carrots."

Elise clenched her hands into fists. "Okay, sure, that makes me feel better."

Roman moved behind her, taking her hand in his. His chest brushed against her back, the other hand spreading out over her stomach. "Here, like this." He moved their joined hands over the horse's head, gently petting down to the nose.

"She's so soft."

The horse snorted. Elise flinched back.

"It's okay." His deep voice rumbled in her ear. "She won't hurt you, but she can sense your fear."

Elise swallowed and tried again.

"That's it. See? She likes you."

Bear made an impatient noise. Roman laughed, backing away from Elise to pet him. "Don't worry. I haven't forgotten about you."

Elise took a moment to admire him as his long fingers dragged down the horse's snout. The red hoodie he wore contrasted with his dark skin. His strong jaw was highlighted in the shadows of the barn. His jeans hugged his firm ass like a glove. Instead of his usual work boots, he'd worn black boots with a small heel.

"Done lookin' your fill?" Roman asked with a smirk.

She blinked her attention back to his face, her cheeks growing hot.

"It's okay. I took my turn earlier." He winked. "Ready to ride?"

"Oh, um, I guess."

He led her to the side of Sprout. "Just put your right leg in the stirrup, and I'll help lift you. Make sure to swing your leg around and find the stirrup on the other side, okay?"

"Okay." She swallowed her nerves. She'd always wondered

what it would be like to ride a horse. "I might need some help. My leg still hurts."

"I'm sorry about that. Which one is it?"

She motioned to her right side. Roman's hands on her hips had her chest tightening. Her pulse thumped, and the familiar buzz of attraction hummed through her body.

"One, two, three, go."

She gasped as he lifted her onto the horse, and then she held on to the horn-shaped thing on the saddle like her life depended on it. "It's so high."

He kept his hand splayed on her thigh. "Yeah, it takes a little getting used to, but you'll be fine. Promise. Sprout wouldn't hurt a fly, and she doesn't spook easily. She'll do most of the work following Bear anyways."

He adjusted the stirrups and showed Elise how to keep her foot positioned before going over how to use the reins. He led her out of the barn, turning back to mount his own horse.

She held the reins like he showed her, but also held onto the horn for good measure as the animal walked. Her body swayed with the motion.

"Let's go." Roman led Bear through the pasture. Sprout automatically followed.

Elise's muscles ached from tensing. She wasn't completely sure about the large animal.

"Look at that view." Roman pointed off towards the vine-yard with rows upon rows of grapes. "That there is where they make the wine." He changed direction, motioning to the large building to their left.

"Cool."

"Look at you. You're doing great," Roman encouraged her. "Think you're ready to try a trot?"

"If that means go faster, then probably not."

His easy chuckle tumbled out. "We'll work up to it."

They rode like that, side by side through the meadow. Sprout stopped to take a bite of grass every now and then. They moved to the edge of the pasture before Roman got off Bear and opened a gate for them to walk through. He mounted his horse again and led her towards what looked to be a walking trail. The grass was worn away so that a narrow dirt path led into the woods.

Roman led the way down the winding path. The longer they rode, the more at ease Elise became with her horse. Roman took a left at the fork, and after a few minutes of riding, the trees opened up to a sparkling lake.

"Is this the same pond that connects to your family's property?" she asked.

"Yeah. Let's head over to that patch of grass by the tree, and we can tie up the horses and take a break for a bit," Roman instructed.

She didn't need to give Sprout any directions; her horse followed Bear.

Roman slid off his animal first. He tied him up on a low-hanging branch before he took the reins from her and did the same. Elise grabbed his shoulders and slid down, her body dragging against his until her feet hit the ground, her knees knocking. His masculine, woodsy scent mixing with the smell of horses and crisp fresh air made her head spin.

"How was that?" he asked without stepping away.

"Exciting."

"Good." He slid his fingers between hers and clasped her hand in his. "Now come on. I've got something else planned while we're here."

What could he—oh. Right over the hill was a sandy shore with a checkered blanket laid out with a picnic basket.

Roman led her down to it wordlessly, motioning for her to take a seat. She did and he joined her, opening the basket and pulling out a dozen sample-size bottles of wine, two glasses, and the most beautiful and creative charcuterie board Elise had ever seen.

"There are some sandwiches in here too. And some chocolate if you want it." Roman motioned to the contents.

"This is a good start." She plucked a grape from the board and plopped it into her mouth, the warm juices exploding as she chewed.

"Red or white?" he asked, picking up two mini bottles.

"Let's try red first."

He emptied the bottle between the two glasses and handed her one. She took a sip and licked her lips. Dry, earthy notes mixed with a hint of something smoky and a dash of fruit.

"Mmm. This is good," Elise said.

"That one's my favorite of their reds." Roman's gaze flicked from her lips to her eyes.

"You've got good taste."

They shared a few of the bottles, tasting and snacking until Elise had a nice buzz.

"Do you want some more cheese?" he asked.

She patted her stomach. "No, thanks, I'm full."

Roman packed up the items and set them aside before he scooted closer and wrapped his arm around her. She shivered.

Roman tugged his hoodie off, revealing a long-sleeve thermal that hugged his muscular arms and chest to perfec-tion. "Here, put this on."

She didn't argue. Instead, she slipped her arms in the hoodie until she was enveloped in his warmth and scent. "Thank you. I should have remembered to bring a sweater. I got distracted by my mother."

"I know you said you have a strained relationship with your parents. She seemed very concerned for you."

Elise sighed and looked out towards the greenish-blue

water. A few of the trees had started to change colors, fading from bright green to yellow, red, and orange. It was beautiful.

"We had a talk after I went home. I think we're moving towards a better place. She kind of went from keeping her distance to being over-involved overnight, but I think we'll find our way to a happy medium."

He linked his fingers in hers and squeezed. "That's great news."

"You don't have to come for dinner."

Roman was quiet a minute before he asked, "Do you not want me to?"

She turned to him. "That's not what I meant. I just . . . I'm still trying to figure out where we go from here."

His other hand brushed her cheek before he tucked a loose strand of hair behind her ear. "I hope we can go forward. I want . . ."

"What do you want?"

"You. I want you any way I can have you. I get that I fucked things up and that I have a lot of trust to earn back. All I'm asking for is a chance to do that."

Elise swallowed. Lines appeared on his forehead as he waited for her reply, his brown eyes filled with cautious hope.

"You told Sage I was your girlfriend," she said.

"Yeah. I don't plan on keeping that a secret anymore. I'm ready to go all in. It was unfair of me to ask you to hide like a dirty secret."

"I understand why you wanted to keep it from Ariel for a while. This wasn't all on you. I agreed to this, and I should have communicated what I needed better."

His thumb coasted over a patch of skin on her hand in soothing strokes. "I appreciate you being so understanding—it's one of the things I love about you. But I took it too far. I was a grown man sneaking you around like some teenager, and I hate that I made you question yourself and us—that I doubted what we have." His shoulders slumped before he cupped her cheek in his hand, locking her in his attentive gaze. "I told Ariel that I wanted to date you."

"You did?"

He nodded. "She asked if that meant you'd come back home to us."

"What did you say?"

"I told her that I had to ask you, but that I hoped so."

"Was she okay with it?" Elise asked. She didn't know what she'd do if Ariel wasn't on board.

"She grabbed my keys and stuffed them in my hands and said to go get you and make sure to say I was sorry."

Elise burst into laughter. "Why does she think you need to say sorry?"

"Because I was honest with her, and told her I did something wrong that hurt your feelings."

Elise's smile dropped. Emotion was clogging her throat. She swallowed. "I want to believe you. I want to tell you I am one hundred percent ready to go back to living with you, but I'm not there. I need . . . time."

He blinked, but the disappointment that flashed in those big brown eyes was unmistakable. Roman's hand dropped to the blanket. "I understand."

"No, I don't think you do." She placed her hand on his chest and snuggled against him, his arm wrapping her tightly. "I'm moving into my own apartment next week. It's in Shattered Cove, only a mile from the school. I want to date you, to keep getting to know you and Ariel better. I'm not opposed to overnight visits, but I think moving slow is the best thing for me right now." *I need that security until I can trust you again.*

He blew out a long breath like he'd been holding it, confidence lighting his voice. "I'll do whatever it takes to keep you in my life. You want to slow down, we can do that."

"Thank you."

Gripping the back of her neck, he tipped his mouth towards hers. "You don't have to thank me for doing the bare minimum and respecting your boundaries. I've been an asshole, held back by my fears and guilt I carried for too long. But never again. And I'll prove it to you, honey. One day at a time."

Roman's lips coasted over hers, soft and sweet, before his tongue slid in her parted mouth. This kiss was filled with promise. Like he was infusing everything he felt into his fingers as they glided over her thigh while his other hand pulled her closer by her nape. Their tongues danced and their teeth nipped as their mouths slid together in a whirlwind of a kiss. The scrape of his beard against her soft skin made her break out in goose bumps. Arousal spun through Elise, lighting her synapses on fire with need.

She pulled back, breathless. His chest was heaving against hers. His eyes were half-lidded, glazed with lust. His lips were shiny and smooth, contrasting against his dark, rough stubble.

"I choose you," he rasped. "Today, tomorrow—they're all yours. My heart, my soul, my body—you fucking own them. Elise, honey, you're worth risking forever for."

46

ELISE

"R oman?" she asked, the fall wind blowing as she pressed her lips to his right there on the picnic blanket.

"Yeah, baby?"

"Make love to me." She climbed over him to straddle his lap.

His big hands gripped her hips as she ground against his hard cock. "Fuck, I didn't plan for this. Don't want you to think this is the only thing I want from you."

"I don't." She kissed him again, her nails digging into the taut fabric on his shoulders.

"But—"

She let out a frustrated sigh and pulled back. "I really want to connect with you physically right now, but if you're not ready, I can wait."

Roman groaned and rested his forehead against hers. He took her hand and pressed it against his hard cock, which was close to bursting out of his jeans. "Does this feel like I don't want you?"

She shook her head, meeting his gaze.

"You said you wanted to go slow, and I want to respect that."

Shit. She did. "I meant slow like not moving in together right now, not no sex."

"Glad you clarified that." Roman smiled, his dimples on full display.

She leaned in and kissed each one on his cheeks. "Have I told you how much I love your dimples?"

"Hmm, I don't think so."

"Well, I do."

"Have I told you how much I love everything about you?"

She tapped her lips as if thinking. "I can't remember. Maybe you should remind me."

He gripped her hips once again, only this time, he lifted her and rolled so that now he was on top and she was below him. Elise gasped.

"Then let me remind you." He pulled out her hair tie and slid it on his wrist before running his fingers through her long raven strands. Firm yet gentle, he tugged on her locks so that her head tipped to the side. He leaned in and inhaled at her neck, dragging his nose from her shoulder to the shell of her ear. His hot breath tickled her skin. "I love the way you smell, like jasmine flowers."

Roman nipped the sensitive spot behind her ear. She shivered.

"I love how responsive you are." He kissed over her jaw, and then the tip of her nose. "This is so cute, and that little septum ring is sexy as fuck."

"You like my piercing?" she asked.

"And your tattoos." His hand slipped under her shirt and hoodie, touching bare skin as his calloused palm slid up to cup her breast under her lace bra. She arched into him.

"I missed you so much." He kissed her while his fingers plucked her nipple.

She surrendered to his ministrations, grinding against his thigh as pleasure rained over her, pooling in her center.

"So needy. Look at you, riding my leg."

"Please."

"I love the way you beg. So breathless. So greedy. You want my cock, baby?"

She nodded, reaching for the button to her jeans. His hand pressed against hers, halting her movements. She let out a whine.

He chuckled. "Patience, honey. I'm gonna worship this body the way it deserves, and only then will I slide my cock into you. Only when you're so wet you're soaking this blanket. When you beg because this cunt feels so empty without me." He cupped her sex through the material separating them.

"Oh, fuck, please. I need to come."

He unbuttoned her pants, tugging them down her legs along with her panties until she was bare from the waist down. The chill in the air was no match for the fire of lust spreading through her veins.

Roman lay on his back beside her. "Sit on my face."

Elise didn't hesitate. She straddled him, knees over his shoulders, feet resting on his chest.

"Told you to fucking sit so I can eat this pussy properly." He smacked her ass hard and pulled her hips with bruising force until she was properly seated over his lips.

She gasped as his tongue swirled around her clit. "Ohhh."

He groaned, the vibrations shooting straight to the bundle of nerves.

"Roman!"

"That's it, baby. Scream all you want. There's no one out here to hear you."

Scream she did. Roman sucked and licked her clit, sliding a finger over her asshole. She tensed through the onslaught of pleasure. She ground her hips, riding his face, and then hesitated.

Smack!

Needles of stinging pain melded with pleasure. Fuck that stung.

He lifted his hand to sign while his mouth continued to devour her pussy. *"Ride me. Take what you need."*

She thrust her hips, chasing her orgasm. Pleasure cinched, coiling tighter and tighter. Her head tipped back, her eyes rolling up as he pulled the rest of her clothes off, tossing them onto the blanket. Roman's palm skidded over her soft stomach to cup her breast, pinching the nipple.

"Oh, God. I'm so close." Her voice was all breathy with need.

He sucked her clit and hummed while his other hand applied the barest hint of pressure to her hole, and she detonated. An explosion of ecstasy crashed over her as she shattered into a million pieces. Her arousal dripped over him. Dark spots covered her vision as she clenched around him like a vise. He released her clit and lapped her pussy like she was his favorite ice cream treat as she came down.

Elise rolled off him, lying on the picnic blanket with an arm over her eyes to block out the sunlight. Crisp air blew against her burning skin.

He rolled to his side and kissed her soft and slow. Her essence on his tongue made it that much more illicit.

He palmed her breast, kneading gently. She arched her back, her skin ultra-sensitive.

"I love the way you come. It's one of the most beautiful things ever when you surrender to your pleasure like that."

"Roman?"

"Yeah, baby?"

"Make love to me."

"You sure? This is enough for me."

She moved her arm to look at him, cupping the back of his neck and pulling him towards her. "I need you."

He tugged his jeans off, adding them to the growing pile of clothes before he stripped his shirt off, baring his naked body to hers. He was lean with solid muscle wrapped around his muscular frame—not the kind of body that comes from the gym, but from hours and hours of physical labor. Calloused, working man's hands coasted over her body, like he was trying to memorize each dip and curve in reverent worship.

He parted her thighs, then straddled one and lifted her other leg over his shoulder as he slowly slid in a few inches. He thrust in and out, never giving her the whole thing.

She let out a needy plea. "Please, Roman, fuck me."

"Trust me, honey. I'll give you what you need."

He slid out and then back in a little more this time. She squeezed her inner muscles around him, making him groan.

"Fuck, you're so tight."

"Still empty."

"Can't have that." He grabbed her ankle, kissing the jagged line of her injury before carefully bending her leg at the knee, pressing it towards her belly. She gripped it and swiveled her hips so she was sideways at an angle. After a few teasing strokes, he plunged into her deeper than she'd thought possible. She squeezed tight and he didn't move. His cock hit a sensitive spot near her cervix. Her nails dug into his shoulders as he looked down at her.

"I'm gonna fuck you hard and deep, but slow. And when you come, you're gonna scream my name. Understand?"

"Yes!" Fuck, the pressure was so intense.

"Good girl."

He pulled out and pushed back in over and over. Her eyes rolled back, the mix of a dull ache spreading into throbbing pleasure. She pulled her other leg up, curling into as tight of a ball as she could while he fucked her hard and deep just like he'd promised.

His balls slapped against her ass as his hands cupped her flesh, kneading and smacking every now and then. She climbed higher and higher.

Roman pinched her clit and slammed into her, sending her shooting over the edge of the cliff and free-falling into the strongest orgasm she'd ever had.

"Roman!"

"Elise! Fuuuuuuuck."

She was left panting and boneless, shuddering from after-shocks while he pulsed inside her.

"Wow." Her chest heaved against his.

"We're pretty incredible together." He slid out of her and grabbed a few wipes from the picnic basket, cleaning her and then himself up before pulling her against him.

"That was . . ."

"Perfect. That was perfect. Just like you." He kissed her shoulder.

She snuggled into his warm chest, the pounding of his heartbeat lulling her to sleep under the sunshine.

"I love you." His voice was the last thing she heard before she drifted off to sleep.

47

ROMAN

Roman kissed the corner of Elise's mouth and slipped his hand around her waist as she stopped to peek at the boutique's window display on Main Street. There was a bite of chill in the air, but the hot coffee they'd grabbed from the café across the street took the edge off. He loved the sight of her in his clothes, especially with her hair still rumpled from him running his hands through it.

"Want to go in and look?" He checked his phone and then slid it back to his pocket. "We still have an hour before I need to get home for Ariel. Patrice is going to drop her off."

She smiled up at him, her eyes sparkling. "Nah, I'm good. Though I still have a little room for dessert."

"I told you to get the cookie from Stardust." He chuckled.

"I was still full from the picnic."

"Fifteen minutes really makes a difference," he deadpanned.

She swatted his chest playfully. "It's been thirty, thank you very much."

Sweeping his hand lower to her ass, he gave it a light

smack and then squeezed. "Alright. What my girlfriend wants, she gets."

Elise's eyes darted around to the few passersby on the sidewalk. None of them were paying Elise and Roman any attention.

"Does PDA make you uncomfortable?" he asked.

She focused back on him, a slight blush rising to her cheeks. "N-no. I just . . . it's different. You seem different. It's just an adjustment."

Roman intertwined his fingers with hers and led Elise to the crosswalk by the bookstore. "I told you, I'm not hiding this anymore. I want everyone to know I somehow convinced someone as gorgeous and intelligent as you to be my girl."

"Oh, really?" Her eyebrow lifted as she bit back a smile.

"And I want to show everyone else you're off the market."

She giggled, light and free. Happiness swelled in his chest, spreading out like rays of sunshine.

They stopped at the edge of the crosswalk and looked both ways.

"It's clear." Elise tugged his hand.

They crossed the road and went back into the café. Coffee with hints of cinnamon teased their senses. There were many shelves of baked goods all freshly made by Remy and her staff.

"Back again? Do you need refills?" Remy asked behind the counter.

"I told her to get the cookies last time," he teased.

Remy laughed. "Take it from me, cuz, just buy the cookies next time."

"Alright. Might as well give me a dozen. Between my girlfriend, Ariel, and me, I'm sure we'll find a way to eat them all." Roman didn't miss the way Elise's eyes lit up every time he referred to her as his girlfriend to other people. He pulled out his wallet, fishing out the cash.

"Mermaid cookies all around?" Remy asked, opening the display case.

"Add a few double-chocolate and some of those lavender ones too," he answered.

Remy got to work bagging their order. He paid and then accepted the treats with a thank-you.

"Have a good day, you two. And give Ariel a kiss for me." Remy waved goodbye.

Elise headed for the door, but Roman caught her hand. "Let's get a table and sit for a little while."

"Okay."

He found one in the center of the café with just enough room for the two of them. Roman pulled the first chair out for Elise, and she sat before he got settled.

"Which kind do you want first?" Roman opened the bag.

When Elise didn't answer, he looked up. "Babe?"

Elise's eyes carried a watery sheen as she blinked. "Sorry, just . . ."

"What is it? Did I do something wrong?" He reached, took her hand in his, and gently squeezed.

"No, not at all." She smiled, easing some of his worries. "I like this version of you."

"This version?"

She nodded. "The more open, affectionate, and easygoing Roman."

He laughed. "I guess I'm a far cry from when we first met, huh?" Shame tumbled in his gut.

She groaned. "Oh, please don't remind me. I still can't believe I punched you."

"Guess we know you have the fight reflex." He laughed. "You might want to talk to Ricky about some MMA lessons. You could be lethal."

She giggled. "Maybe I will."

The image of Ricky and her getting all sweaty together and rolling around on a mat flashed through his mind. His skin heated, jealousy burning his gut. "Actually, maybe that's not a good idea."

She laughed harder. "Why not?"

His teeth ground together.

"Oh my goodness, are you jealous of your brother?"

"Maybe."

Elise leaned in, just out of reach for a kiss with the table between them. "You have nothing to worry about. I'm a one-man-at-a-time kind of girl. And you've got more than enough stamina to keep me satisfied."

"Oh, really?"

"Mm-hmm."

He leaned forward enough to steal a quick kiss and then sat back down. The dreamy smile and sparkle in her eyes made him feel on top of the world.

"Daddy!" Ariel's voice had his attention jerking towards the blur running in from the doorway. She slammed into his arms.

"Hey, sweet pea." His gaze flicked up to meet Patrice's. Her focus volleyed from him to Elise and back before she gave him a small smile. A hint of pain remained in her eyes, but this time he didn't shoulder the blame. Patrice was just missing her daughter.

"Elise!" Ariel left his arms and crawled right into Elise's lap and hugged her. "I missed you."

"I missed you too." Elise hugged her tight.

"Are those cookies? Can I have one?" Ariel asked.

"Just one. Don't want to spoil your dinner," Roman answered, getting to his feet.

Ariel slid down from Elise's lap and grabbed the bag of dessert, picking out a mermaid one before she climbed back on.

"We didn't know you would be here. Just stopped in for a little treat before I brought her home," Patrice said.

Elise's shoulders seemed stiff, her back straight as a board as she kept her focus on Ariel.

"Yeah, we had the same idea," Roman answered.

"Elise?" Patrice asked.

"Yes?" Elise turned to her, a line of cautiousness weaved over her forehead, her posture still rigid.

Patrice's expression softened. "Ariel and I were talking about the best way to welcome you into the family. I would like to extend an invitation to dinner sometime. Maybe we could all go out somewhere fun, my and George's treat."

Elise blinked as if stunned. "Oh, you don't have to do that—"

Patrice waved her hand. "Nonsense. We would love the chance to get to know you. And I owe you an apology for the way I responded to you and some of the things I said. It was unfair of me to judge you."

"I appreciate you saying that. I'd love to join you all for dinner." Elise smiled.

Patrice nodded. "We'll schedule it, then." She turned to Roman. "I'll put Ariel's things in your truck unless you still want me to drive her to the farm in thirty minutes?"

"No, that would be great. Do you want me to grab it?" he asked.

"It's just her backpack. I think my old bones can handle that. You three have a wonderful evening." She kissed Ariel and gave her a hug before waving goodbye.

Ariel got up from Elise's lap, cookie crumbs around her mouth. "I'm gonna get a coloring page from Aunty Remy."

"Okay." Roman waited for her to scamper off before he turned back to Elise. "You okay?"

She nodded jerkily. "Are you?"

He reclaimed his seat, taking peeks at Ariel rifling through the coloring pages Remy kept for kids in the café. "Patrice and I had a talk recently. We both said things we probably should have a long time ago."

"I'm glad. Are you sure I should go to dinner with them though?"

"Absolutely. If you want to, I mean. I won't pressure you, but you should know that they will always be a part of my and Ariel's life."

"Of course." She didn't hesitate.

"And they know you are also a part of our life." He linked his fingers with hers again.

"She's okay with . . ." Elise pointed to him and then to herself.

"Do you need her permission?"

"Me? No. But I feel like you do."

He sighed. "I think subconsciously I thought so too. But we shared our truths and I told her I loved you. She actually encouraged me to go after you and stop acting like a coward."

"She did?" Elise's eyes widened.

He nodded. "Are you okay with this? Or is it moving too fast for you?"

Her chest lifted before she exhaled, a smile lighting her whole face. "This is perfect."

48

ELISE

"No more chocolate. You'll spoil your dinner." Elise picked up the goodie bag of candy that Ariel had brought home from school and slipped it into the cupboard.

Ariel crossed her arms over her chest and stomped her foot with a huff. "I want one more!"

Elise's head was pounding from a long day of classes with kids hyped up on sugar thanks to Halloween. There had also been an unplanned fire drill, and her car hadn't started this morning, which was why she was currently waiting for Roman to get home from making honey deliveries before they could eat.

"Dinner will be ready in one minute. I just need to plate it."

"I don't want that for dinner. I want macaroni and cheese."

"Well, I'm sorry, but this is what your dad had in the Crock-Pot."

"Ugh!" Ariel stomped out of the room and up the stairs.

"Give me patience," Elise whispered aloud to the universe. She quickly plated their dinner and an extra for Roman, then set them on the table.

"Ariel!" Elise called up the stairs. "We need to eat. Your dad will be here any minute to go trick-or-treating. You still need to have dinner before we go." Elise waited at the end of the stairs in silence for a few seconds.

When no answer came, she sighed and trudged up the steps to the little girl's room. The door was open and there was no sign of her.

"Ariel?"

A thump from the bathroom drew her attention. She walked over and knocked. "Ariel? Do you need help with your costume?"

"No."

A crinkly plastic sound came from behind the door. Elise twisted the knob and pushed the door open.

Wrappers littered the floor by Ariel's feet that hung off the closed toilet seat. Chocolate smears decorated her face. Her eyes widened, one hand clasped around a large bag of Halloween candy she'd gotten a hold of.

"I said no more candy until after dinner. You're going to get sick." Elise reached for the bag.

"You can't tell me what to do! You're not my mom! I hate you!"

Elise sucked in a breath as the weight of the little girl's words stabbed through her heart.

Ariel threw the bag at her and moved to get off the toilet, but her foot caught on her mermaid costume and she face-planted before Elise could grab her.

Screaming filled the tiny room. Elise wrapped her arms around Ariel and lifted.

"What the hell is going on in here?" Roman's voice carried an edge of panic.

Elise froze, unable to turn around. He'd chosen the worst possible moment to arrive. Ariel had never acted like this with her before. Sure, they'd had difficulties. Ariel had a lot of big emotions she was dealing with, and it was an adjustment to have her dad date someone. But over the last couple months they'd found a happy rhythm—or so Elise had thought.

Fear streaked through her. Would Roman ask her to leave? Would he break up with her? There was no way he would stay with her if Ariel wasn't okay with things.

"Daddy." Ariel ran into his arms, breaking out in sobs that tore at Elise's heart. She took a deep breath and turned around, chin up, ready to face the fallout.

Roman picked Ariel up, his eyes skating over the mess of wrappers, then Elise, with questions swirling in his dark brown eyes.

"You okay, sweet pea?" he asked.

Ariel sniffed. "My nose hurts."

Roman inspected the affected area. "I'm sorry. We should get you some ice."

Ariel snuggled into his neck, continuing to cry softly.

"What's going on?" Roman asked Elise.

"I . . . I told her no more candy before dinner. She snuck this up here somehow. I don't even know where it came from."

"Ariel Daisy Emerson, did you sneak into my room and get that chocolate out?" Roman asked.

Ariel hesitated and then cried harder.

"I didn't—I mean, I'm sorry. I should have caught her when she fell."

Roman leveled Elise with a serious look and then shook his head. Her stomach dropped. Dread creeped through her veins, winding around her body and squeezing like a boa constrictor.

"Looks like today's been hard for both of you." Roman's voice was softer.

Elise blinked at him, holding her breath as she gave a slight nod.

"Sounds like Ariel might have had too much sugar and needs some rest and ice," he continued.

"I want to go trick"—Ariel hiccupped—"or-treating."

Roman patted her back. "I know. But Elise told you no more candy and then you came in and snuck it."

Ariel hid her face.

"And then when I came up here I heard you say some pretty unkind things to her."

Elise exhaled, all her attention focused on the man before her cradling the little girl. He wasn't mad at Elise?

Roman set Ariel back on her feet and kneeled so he was at her level. He used his finger to tip her chin up to meet his eyes. "I love you, sweet pea. You know that, right?"

Ariel nodded and sniffed.

"And nothing in this world will change that. You know Elise loves you too?"

Ariel flicked a glance at Elise before her shoulders slumped forward.

"Elise is a member of our family now, and when she tells you to not do something, it's for your own good. You gotta listen to her," Roman continued.

Ariel's little body trembled as her hands fisted.

"Are you feeling angry?" Roman asked.

Ariel nodded.

"Why?"

Tears dripped down her face. "Because she's gonna have a baby and then she's going to love it more than me! And you'll forget about me and be too busy with the new baby." Ariel flung herself into Roman's arms and sobbed.

Roman's gaze darted to Elise. "Baby?"

Elise blanched. "I have no idea what she's talking about."

"Ariel, where did you hear that Elise was having a baby?"

"Tommy at school said his daddy married his girlfriend, and he got a new baby sister. But his parents only give the baby attention and they forget him at school sometimes," Ariel explained.

Elise grabbed a few squares of toilet paper and handed them to Roman. He wiped Ariel's eyes and nose.

Elise kneeled next to them. "You're worried that your dad and I will somehow forget you and not love you?"

She nodded.

"Oh, sweetie, that could never happen. You're your daddy's favorite person in the world. And I will always love you, no matter what." Elise rubbed the little girl's back soothingly.

Ariel released her dad and climbed into Elise's arms. Elise had to sit down so she wouldn't fall over.

"I'm not pregnant, and I have no plans of having one anytime soon," she assured her.

"Nothing will change the fact that you're my girl. I would do anything for you, Ariel. And there isn't anything in this world that could make me love you less or forget about you," Roman added.

"Promise?" Ariel asked in a tiny voice.

Roman held up his pinky. Elise joined hers with his and they offered it to Ariel.

"Promise," they both agreed.

Ariel hooked her pinkies around theirs, and her lips tilted up in a small smile.

"Next time you're feeling upset or worried about something, you need to use your words and let us know, okay?" Roman asked.

"Okay."

"Now, when I walked in here, you were shouting some unkind things to Elise. I think you owe her an apology," Roman pressed.

Elise tensed. "Oh, it's okay—"

"No. It's not." Roman focused back on Ariel. "Sweet pea, no one can take your mama's place. And that is the last thing Elise wants to do. But she's a part of our family, and she loves you and deserves to be spoken to with respect."

"I'm sorry, Elise. I didn't mean it. I don't hate you. I love you." Ariel hugged Elise.

She squeezed the little girl back. "I love you too. All is forgiven. We'll find our way through this together, okay?"

"Okay."

"Now, about the chocolate . . ." Roman said.

Ariel reached down and picked up the wrappers, then deposited them in the trash. "I'm sorry."

"Okay, but you're not getting any more candy tonight. You're gonna go eat dinner and get some real food in your belly before you get sick." Roman stood.

"Can I still go trick-or-treating?" Ariel asked.

Elise climbed to her feet.

"Yes, but you're not eating anything sweet until after breakfast tomorrow," Roman answered.

"Okay," Ariel agreed, not quite happy, but not as upset either.

"Now go start your dinner before it gets any colder." Roman stepped out of the bathroom, clearing the way for Ariel to walk by. Once she was out of earshot, he turned to Elise. "You okay?"

"Me?"

"Yeah, you. I'm sorry you had to hear that and deal with that meltdown."

She couldn't help the hysterical laughter that bubbled up inside her as tears blurred her vision.

"Elise?"

She shook her head and pressed her hand to her chest, trying to calm herself down. "I'm sorry, I just . . . I thought that was going to go a completely different way when I saw you in the doorway."

Roman glanced to the side and then back to her. "You thought I'd walk away from you again."

She sobered at the pain in his brown eyes. "I'm sorry—"

"No. Don't apologize. I deserved that." He stepped into her space, swallowing up all the air in the room. Her pulse pounded as he cupped her face in his big warm hands. "Honey, you're it for me. We're gonna have difficult days like this evening. We'll probably fight at some point. And we'll have a lot of adjustments as our life evolves and our family grows—"

"Grows?" Her eyebrows lifted.

"You said you wanted a baby someday."

"Well, yeah, but—"

He took another step forward, stealing any remaining space between them as he kissed her possessively. His palm slid down her back to cup her ass as he ground himself against her and then pulled back.

"If you think for one second I'm letting you go so some other fuckhead can put his baby inside you, you're wrong. Never." His deep voice sent shivers down her spine.

"It's a little early on to be discussing babies, don't you think?"

"Honey, I don't care if it's today, next year, or years ahead. You're mine and I'm not sharing you. Someday, you'll give me another son or daughter, or two." Those irresistible dimples were highlighted by his smirk.

"Two?"

He shrugged. "I'm not picky. We can have five if you want, just as long as it's me who puts them there."

She smiled. "I think one or two would be good."

"I have a serious question."

"Hmm?"

"If I knock you up, does that mean you'll marry me sooner?"

She slapped his chest playfully. "I haven't even decided to move in with you, and you're jumping to marriage."

Butterflies fluttered in her stomach. This wasn't the first time he'd casually brought up marriage, but she was holding out for an official proposal, and she still needed time. She'd only known the man five months, and if he was serious, they had their whole lives ahead of them.

"So you agree, then. You should move in with us."

She smiled and shook her head. "Not yet. I think Ariel needs a little more time. And I just signed a lease."

"I think she needs you staying here full-time."

"You sure that's not just your cock?" She palmed his erection through his jeans.

He groaned, his eyes glazing over with heat. "Oh, my cock definitely wants you in my bed every night." He brushed his thumb over her cheek. "But so does every other part of me."

"Sweet talker." She kissed his jaw as she looped her arms over his neck.

"It's the truth."

"I love you, Roman."

"Is that a yes?" He smiled.

She laughed. "No, but soon."

"I'll hold you to that."

"You better." She kissed him, slowly teasing him with her tongue until the light squeeze on her backside turned into something more carnal and rougher. His touches turned desperate as his chest heaved against hers.

"Daddy, I'm done eating!" Ariel called up.

They pulled apart. His lips were shiny, his eyes burning with want and so much affection it made her knees wobble.

"Coming," he yelled in answer before turning back to Elise. "We'll finish this tonight after she crashes from her sugar high."

"I'll hold you to it, Mr. Emerson."

"I hope you do." He winked.

EPILOGUE - ROMAN

"Pass the rolls, please." Roman's dad reached out his hand towards him.

Roman grabbed the basket of still warm bread and handed it to his father.

"Thanks. Okay, whose turn is it?" his dad asked scanning the long table filled with their family, Isabella's parents, and Elise's mom and dad, along with her brother, Ren.

Roman slipped his hand over Elise's thigh and squeezed as he leaned in to whisper in her ear, "Have I told you how beautiful you look tonight?"

A slight flush decorated her creamy skin as she glanced around the table.

"Don't be shy now. You weren't this morning when you—"

Elise's hand pressed against his lips, the red on her face darkening. "My parents are sitting three seats away. Could you control yourself for one dinner?"

He chuckled and tugged her hand under the table before stealing a chaste kiss on her lips.

"I'll go," his mother announced before lifting her drink, eyeing them over the rim.

Renita straightened in her seat. "I'm grateful that I have almost my whole family here with us and new people to add to that list, despite a rocky start." She nodded towards Isabella's mother, Catherine, who smiled sheepishly.

"And for being able to make new friends who will hopefully become family one day soon." His mom gave Roman a knowing wink before tipping her head towards Elise's parents. "For my family, a roof over our heads, and this wonderful food that everyone's had a hand in."

His mom sipped from her glass, signaling the end of her turn as they went around the table to say how thankful everyone was, their holiday tradition.

"Where is Nova, by the way?" Elise asked.

"She said she was picking up her date and would be a little late coming from the airport," his dad answered.

"Nova has a date?" Ricky asked.

This was the first Roman was hearing about it. He didn't even know she'd been talking to someone.

His mother's smile was filled with satisfaction. "Yup. Two kids down, two to go."

Ricky snorted from across the table.

Everyone turned towards him.

He shrugged and sat a little straighter. "I'm never settling down. You should just be satisfied with your other children and current grandchildren."

"Famous last words," Nash teased in his grumpy baritone voice.

"Fudge you." Ricky pretended to scratch his nose with his middle finger.

"That's enough. We have company. At least try to act civilized for a couple hours," their mother chastised.

Ricky gave her a saccharine-sweet smile. "Aww, Ma, you know it would be a shame to deprive the single ladies—"

All the color drained from his brother's face. His terror-filled eyes locked somewhere behind Roman.

Roman turned to see what the hell had riled his brother so much as Nova walked in beside a man he didn't recognize.

"Hey, guys. This is Everett. Everett, this is my mom and dad, and everyone else." Nova laughed nervously.

His parents got up to greet their new guest. Roman turned back to Ricky, whose skin had taken on an ashen sheen, his gaze glued to the table, shoulders tight. He ground his teeth.

"Thanks for having me. I hope I'm not intruding," Everett said, taking the empty seat to Roman's right.

"Not at all," his dad replied.

"I suppose I should introduce you to everyone, but there's no way you'll remember all their names." Nova laughed as Ricky got up and walked to the other end of the table.

"So, tell me about yourself, Everett. What do you do?" his mother asked.

"Mom, let him eat something. He's been on a plane since early this morning," Nova interjected.

"It's fine." Everett gave Nova a reassuring smile. "I've been working as a vendor in California for cannabis distributors there."

"And how did you two meet?" Nash asked.

"Everett and I met at a convention some years ago and have kept in contact ever since." Nova's voice rose a little higher in pitch, a sign she wasn't telling the whole truth. But why?

"Long-distance relationship, huh?" Roman asked.

Nova rolled her eyes, grabbing a bottle of wine and filling her glass and Everett's. "Mm-hmm. Oh, Elise, I didn't realize your family would be here."

"Yeah. This is my mom, Mai, my father, Itsuki, and my brother, Ren," Elise introduced them.

"Nice to meet you." Nova smiled at them and then guzzled her wine. Something fishy was going on with his sister.

Roman leaned over to Elise's ear once more. "Do you have any idea what's going on with Nova?"

She bit her lip like she was holding back.

"What is it?"

"I'll tell you later."

"Oh, the puppy wasn't enough? You got another secret, huh?" he teased, his hand sliding up her thigh as he flicked a glance to the black ball of fur chasing a rolling tennis ball around the room. Ariel had woken to quite the surprise this morning. She'd melted into peals of excited laughter and named her puppy Pepper.

"Maybe. Now, finish your dinner," Elise said.

He picked up his fork with a dopey smile on his face no doubt. He took another bite as conversation continued around them. A quick peek at Ariel set his mind at ease. She was busy chatting with Eli about boats at the far end of the table. The only reason he knew what they were saying was she still used sign as she spoke most of the time.

"Are you feeling okay, Ricky?" Isabella asked.

All eyes turned towards his brother, still standing at the other end of the table. He looked like he wanted to be anywhere else but here.

Panic streaked across Ricky's face before his expression hardened into an emotionless mask. He walked back to his seat, reached for his vodka soda and chugged the whole thing. "I'm fine. If I knew everyone was bringing a date, I would have brought Sophia."

"Who's Sophia?" their mother asked in a hope-filled voice.

"Just one of Ricky's many 'friends.'" Nova smirked.

Everett cleared his throat. "Ric—"

"Hey, man, nice to meet you. Anyone else need more wine?" Ricky scanned the table looking everywhere but at Nova's date.

"I'll take another scotch." Their dad handed Ricky his glass.

"I'll take a little more of the riesling. Don't forget to save room for dessert, everyone." Isabella motioned to the table brimming with pies, cakes, and cookies.

"I'm trying to watch my figure. Wouldn't want to look like your husband," Ricky teased.

Nash chuckled and shook his head. "You think you're so funny."

Ricky collected his dishes and walked to the kitchen, narrowly avoiding Nash's slap.

"Excuse me, do you mind if I use the restroom?" Everett asked.

Nova swallowed her drink and set the glass down. "Of course. Third door on your left. Oh, I can show you—"

"No need." Everett left the room.

The chatter resumed among everyone except Roman and Elise. His thumb dipped between her bare thighs, swiping back and forth.

"You know what?" Elise asked.

"Hmm?"

"I've never seen your childhood bedroom."

His brows drew together. "Really?"

She shook her head.

"Well, it's not much. My mom converted it into an office." Roman pushed his plate away, done with dinner.

"I'd still like to see it."

He shrugged. "Sure."

Elise leaned towards him this time, her sweet jasmine scent

wrapping around him with something that was purely her. "Roman?"

"Yeah?"

"I'm not wearing any panties."

His mouth dropped open as he turned to her, his cock hard. "You dirty girl. That's why you want to see my old room?"

"Took you long enough to catch on." She smirked, grabbing her near-empty plate and carrying it to the kitchen. He quickly followed her. They dispensed of their dishes and he trailed after her, admiring the way her hips swayed, and those long legs ate up the stairs two at a time. He grabbed her hand and pulled her back to his front, pinning her to the wall. Collaring her neck, he squeezed ever so slightly until she relaxed into him.

"You've been a bad girl, Elise. Not wearing any panties. What if someone saw under your dress? Huh?"

"Then they'd see my wet pussy," she mouthed off, feigning nonchalance.

He growled, his other hand dipping between her thick thighs before sliding between her slick folds. "This pussy is mine. No one gets to see it but me. No one gets to touch it, but me and you—if I give you permission."

She shuddered against him.

"Say it." He swirled his finger around her clit.

"It's yours."

"Good girl." He nipped the back of her neck and withdrew his fingers. Spinning her around, he raised his glistening fingers coated in her arousal and slipped them between her sexy full lips. "Suck."

She opened her mouth, her pink tongue darting out and swirling over his fingers before she sucked them into her mouth, her eyes locked on his.

"Fuck, you're so sexy when you take my orders."

She pulled off him with an audible *pop* and licked her lips. "You're sexy when you give them."

"I can't wait until later. I need to have you right now." He grabbed the doorknob to his old room and twisted, pulling it open and tugging her in behind him.

"Oof!" He grunted, running into a hard body. "Sorry. We didn't know anyone was in here."

Everett opened his mouth, but Ricky beat him to it.

"No, problem. Nova's date here just got lost. I was making sure he understood what we'd do to him if he hurt our baby sister." Ricky cut Everett a threatening glare.

A mix of confusion and what looked like hurt shone in Everett's eyes.

"Better get those drink refills." Ricky pushed past Roman and left.

Everett didn't take his eyes off Ricky's retreating form. *What the hell?*

"You okay?" Roman asked.

Everett shook his head as if trying to rid himself of something. "Yeah, no, I'm fine. I uh, I'll find my way back down." He rushed past them.

"That was weird," Roman said when he'd left the room.

Elise chewed on her lip before a slight smile turned the corner of her mouth up.

"What do you know?" he asked.

"I thought you couldn't wait to fuck me?" she teased.

"I can't, but you promised you'd tell me what was up with Nova and her date. I can multitask." He picked her up, her tiny gasp going straight to his dick. Setting her on the desk, he stepped between her thighs and dragged his knuckle over her slick pussy once again. His fingers threaded through the hair at the base of her neck. He wrapped it around his fist before he tugged just enough to let her know he was the one in control. "Tell me, honey, and I'll make you come."

"Unhh, Roman—"

"Answer the question, baby." He slid one finger inside her, working her clit with his thumb.

She hissed. "Fuck, that feels so good."

He added another finger and fucked her a little harder. "So wet and tight. I love how ready you are for me."

"I'm gonna come." She gripped his shoulders, her nails digging into his back.

He pulled his hands out.

"What are you doing? I was almost there."

"Answer the question and then you can come on my face. Then we'll go back downstairs and eat dessert with everyone before we leave early. Ariel's spending the night with Mom and Dad. Which means I get to fuck you in my bed, and you can be as loud as you want."

Her eyes lit up. "As loud as I want?"

"Yup."

"Deal. But, Roman?"

"Yeah?"

"It's not just your bed. It's ours."

"Not until you move in it's not."

"It's a good thing the movers come tomorrow, then." She smirked.

Roman straightened. "What—are you saying you're moving in, finally?"

She rolled her eyes. "It's not like I have a lot more to move. You've been taking stuff with you every time you leave my apartment. Don't think I don't know what you've been doing."

Busted. "I just wanted to make it easier for when you finally came to your senses and were ready to move in. You don't even need movers. I can get my brothers to help."

She smiled and pressed her hand to his chest. "It's already set up. Called them Monday."

"You've been planning this for a while, haven't you?"

She shrugged. "Consider it an early Christmas gift, like the puppy."

"And Ariel's necklace?" Roman asked.

Elise shrugged, biting back a smirk. "That's a different kind of gift."

"Does this mean you'll marry me too?"

"One step at a time."

"Are you doing this to torture me? Or do you really not feel ready?" he asked.

She giggled. "It's definitely fun to mess with you, but I'm not quite ready to get married. Let's settle into life with the three of us living together first. We've never lived together as a couple, as a family."

"Whatever you need. But, Elise?"

"Hmm?"

"You're it for me. I'll wait as long as you want, but I won't stop asking. Because one of these days, you're gonna say yes."

"I don't want you to stop."

"Good."

"Now, tell me what's going on with my sister so I can get back to eating your pussy."

Warm, bubbly laughter fell from her lips, gripping his cock. Fuck, even her laughter turned him on. Thank fuck she was moving in, because he couldn't take much more of her not being in his bed every night.

"Everett is not really her date," Elise said. "He's her beard."

Roman blinked in confusion. "Her beard? My sister's a lesbian?" She was bisexual but mainly dated men.

"No. But she wanted to get your mom off her back, so he's her fake date. They're just friends."

"So Ricky didn't have to give him the 'hurt my sister and you die' speech?"

Elise's brown eyes sparkled with something mischievous.

"What else are you keeping from me?"

"Nothing. Just a hunch."

"About?"

"Has Ricky ever . . ."

"What?"

"Been with a man?"

Roman snorted. "No, he's been a little too busy neck-deep in pussy ever since I've known him."

"I had a friend like that once."

"Who?"

"Sam."

"Sam, who's now engaged to your other best friend, Jack?" Roman clarified.

Elise nodded.

"You think Ricky is secretly gay?"

"Or bi, but I don't know. It's just a feeling."

"Why would he keep that from us? He knows we'd love and accept whoever he brought home," Roman said.

"I don't know. Like I said, it's just a hunch."

"I think I would know if my brother was into guys."

"Okay."

Roman scanned through his memories out and about with Ricky, ever since Ricky had moved in with them in middle school. He'd never even gotten close to other guys. Didn't hang out with other men outside of his brothers' friends. Roman had always chalked it up to Ricky being so interested in girls. But looking at it now, it was almost like he avoided other guys.

"Roman?" Elise's voice brought him out of his thoughts.

"Yeah?"

"Are you gonna lick my pussy, or should we go back down for pie?"

Roman knelt, sliding his hands up her thighs, taking the dress with him until it was piled around her waist.

"Oh, I'm gonna lick you alright. In fact, I might not stop until you beg me. Your safe word for me to stop is, 'Yes, I'll marry you, Roman.'"

She giggled. "Oh, really?"

"Absolutely."

"It's cute how determined you are."

He nipped her thigh, making her jolt. "What's cute is you trying to resist me when we both know you want this too."

She gave him a knowing smile. "Quit talking and start licking."

He squeezed her thighs hard enough to leave a bruise— just the way she liked it—and pinched her clit.

She gasped, her eyes hazy with lust, all humor gone and replaced with need.

"Don't forget who's in charge. Now watch me eat you out like a good girl. Keep your eyes on me, and don't make a sound."

He spread her thighs as wide as they would go and dragged his tongue through the seam of her center. "Fuck, you're so perfect."

Her fingernails dug into his scalp as she tugged on his hair, his pain mixing with pleasure.

"Wrap those sexy long legs around my neck."

She obeyed, squeezing him closer. He licked and lapped,

swirling around her clit, edging her to an orgasm but backing away each time she'd almost reached the peak.

"Roman?" Her voice was a breathy plea.

"Yeah, baby?"

"Make me come. Please? I need to come."

"You know the magic words."

"Are you seriously—" Whatever argument she had was cut off by a quick inhale of air and a moan.

"Shhhh. Those sounds are for my ears only." He sucked her clit, taking her over the edge into an orgasm that had her thighs clenching around his head like a vise. He couldn't have moved if he'd wanted to—which he didn't. Time between her thighs was paradise.

Despite his teasing, he was content to wait for her to come around in her own time. They had today, and he'd hope for tomorrow. But forever was his goal.

He licked her as she came down, her legs relaxing. He stood, wrapping her in his arms. Her breathing slowed as she snuggled against him.

Roman kissed her temple. "I love you."

"I love you too."

She slid off the table, getting down on her knees.

"Baby, you don't have to—"

"Roman Emerson, will you marry me?"

Roman blinked down at her. Was this a joke?

The silver wedding band glinting in her palm told him that no, it wasn't.

"Are you seriously proposing after I ate you out?"

She shrugged. "What can I say? You have mad oral skills."

He reached down and took her hand, pulling her to her feet. "Don't mess with me, Elise. Is this for real?"

She nodded with a bright smile, joy dancing in her eyes. "Marry me, Roman, and make me the happiest woman on this earth. I promise to be there on your good days and bad days. To be your partner, the one you can lean on as we go through this adventure called life together."

"I . . ." He was utterly speechless.

"Is that a yes?" One eyebrow quirked up in question.

"That's a fuck yes. Absolutely." His lips crashed against hers, picking her up and spinning her around.

He couldn't hold back the megawatt smile on his face. "You just made me the happiest man in the world."

"Do you like the ring?" She lifted it up, offering it to him.

He took the metal in his hand, turning it over. Some writing on the inside caught his attention.

Forever yours.

"It's perfect."

"Ariel helped me pick it out."

"She knows?"

"I couldn't propose without her permission," Elise said.

"That's why you got her the necklace?"

"Of course. You're a package deal." She smiled.

"I feel like I should be the one proposing to you."

"Why? Because I'm a woman?"

"No—okay, partly, yes—but also because I wanted to do something to make you feel special and beautiful."

"You did." She motioned to the desk.

"If that's all it took, I'll be sure to do it every day for the rest of our lives."

"Maybe we should include it in our vows." She tapped her chin thoughtfully.

He laughed and pulled her in for another hug. Her arms slipped around his waist.

His throat squeezed with emotion as happiness he couldn't contain if he'd wanted to tumbled through him. "Thank you."

"For what?" she asked, so much love in her eyes.

"For risking forever with me."

The End.

Haven't read the other books in the Emerson Family of Shattered Cove series? The series is complete and these 3 amazing romances are waiting for you right now.

Stepping Into Tomorrow

(Book 1: Featuring grumpy fisherman, Nash, and plus size single mom, Isabella, who's looking for a fresh start in Shattered Cove.)

Wishing for Yesterday

(Book 3: Featuring grumpy closeted beekeeper, Ricky, and a man from his past, Everett, who's back in New Hampshire after never forgetting the first boy he loved.)

Promising Today

(Book 4: Featuring bratty Nova, and retired Navy SEAL, Jude, both hunting for answers in Shattered Cove, but find much more than they were looking for.)

Now, turn the page for a sneak peek of Book 3 of The Emerson Family Series, ***Wishing for Yesterday***, (Ricky and Everett's story), right away!

Or visit the website below to order Book 3 in The Emerson Family of Shattered Cove Series right now.

WWW.AMKUSI.COM/WISHINGFORYESTERDAY

SNEAK PEEK OF WISHING FOR YESTERDAY

CHAPTER 1

Ricky

Ricky would always be a bachelor. Relationships were scary as fuck. They forced you to open up parts of yourself that should never see the light of day.

He forced a breath in his lungs. Tiny threads of expectation circled his neck, squeezing tighter with every lovesick look his brothers shared with the women they'd been lucky enough to find love with. Alone in a crowded room, with a bright smile to mask Ricky's true loneliness, he did his best to look relaxed at the long table surrounded by family and friends. He sipped his vodka and cranberry as he glanced out the window to his left. Big, fat raindrops plopped against the pane from the skies outside as the wind whipped the bare trees at the side of his adoptive parents' farmland.

It couldn't have been more opposite to the warmth that his parents' home always held. Low jazz music bled through the Bluetooth speakers in the dining room as conversations and laughter bounced off the pale walls. The yip of his niece Ariel's new puppy drew his attention to the end of the table where she and Eli sat, sneaking bits of their dinner to the already spoiled black and white mutt, Pepper.

"So, you work with Roman and the bees too?" Itsuki, Elise's father, asked from his right.

"Yeah. I own an apiary with my brother Roman, and I'm also branching out to take clients at the gym this winter."

"That's interesting. Will you have time to manage all of it? It seems like the bees take a lot of work," Itsuki said.

"Winter's our slow season. Not much to do except bottle and deliver honey until the snow melts, then the real work begins. You'll have to take a few jars home with you when you go," Roman added.

"I would love that. Thank you," Itsuki said.

"Okay, whose turn is it?" His dad's voice rose over the chatter of the rest of the family.

Ricky took another sip of his drink and let his gaze wander around the table. His father sat at the head, his ma beside him as usual. Across from Ricky were Elise and his brother Roman, whispering to each other. Ricky was certain his brother's hand was busy under the table, no doubt responsible for the blush in Elise's cheeks.

Past them was Nash holding the almost one-year-old Alba as she reached for food from her dad's plate and shoved it by the tiny fistful into her mouth. Most of it seemed like it was ending up on his brother's lap. His brand-new sister-in-law, Isabella, leaned on Nash's shoulder, looking up at him like he'd hung the fucking moon. A pulse of jealousy burned Ricky's gut before he shoved it away.

"I'll go," his ma announced, lifting her drink and eyeing Roman with a knowing look. "I'm grateful that I have almost my whole family here with us, and new people to add to that list, despite a rocky start." She eyed Isabella's mother, Catherine, who smiled sheepishly.

Ricky barely held back a snort.

"And for being able to make new friends who will hopefully become family one day soon." His ma winked before tipping her head towards Elise's parents. "For my family, a roof over our heads, and this wonderful food that everyone had a hand in."

Ma sipped from her glass. Everyone took turns going around the table to say what they were most grateful for, as was their family tradition.

"Where is Nova, by the way?" Elise asked.

Good question.

"She said she was picking up her date and would be a little late coming from the airport," his dad answered.

"Nova has a date?" Ricky asked.

His ma's smile was conspiratorial. "Yup. Two kids down, two to go."

Ricky snorted and shook his head. Almost everyone's eyes darted to him, making his skin itch.

He shrugged and sat up a little straighter. "I'm never settling down. You should just be satisfied with your other children and current grandchildren."

"Famous last words," Nash teased in his grumpy baritone voice.

"Fudge you." Ricky lifted his middle finger and pretended to scratch his nose.

"That's enough. We have company. At least try to act civilized for a couple hours," Ma chastised.

Ricky tilted his lips and gave her the magic smile that helped him get away with most things. "Aww, Ma, you know it would be a shame to deprive the single ladies—"

The door swung open.

His lungs froze.

All the blood drained from his face. *No. It can't be.* Ricky's heart raced, sweat breaking out on his forehead. Terror seized him in an iron grip. *Nononono. This isn't happening.*

Nova walked farther into the room with a goofy, flushed smile on her face, but next to her was a man Ricky recognized all too quickly despite the two and a half decades that had passed since they'd last been together. *It can't be him.*

The urge to flee rose stronger than anything he'd ever felt. He squeezed the arms on the chair, forcing himself to stay put and not draw attention to himself.

Voices melded together, becoming background static. The only thing that got through to Ricky was Nova's boyfriend's name. Everett. Everett fucking Popova. The last time Ricky had seen him had been the worst day of Ricky's life.

His parents got up to greet their new guest. Ricky forced his eyes away from the boy he used to know who'd turned into a man. Ricky studied the dent in the wooden table instead. Every muscle in his body was rigid as a corpse—which was what he'd be if anyone found out how he knew Everett.

"Thanks for having me. I hope I'm not intruding." Everett's deep rumble had a bit of a masculine rasp to it. Ricky's body immediately reacted to it, his hands trembling and his blood rushing through his veins, causing his ears to ring. Hyper aware of the man, Ricky kept his face turned away, hoping to God Everett didn't recognize him. Ricky was nothing like the fourteen-year-old string bean he'd once been.

Everett and Nova took the empty seats next to Roman and directly across from Ricky.

"You're not intruding at all. Welcome, Everett," his dad replied.

"I suppose I should introduce you to everyone, but there's no way you'll remember everyone's names." Nova laughed.

Ricky's skin was scalding hot. He needed to move out of their line of sight. He turned as he stood, putting his back to his sister and the man from his past. Instead, Ricky walked to the other end of the table while his sister rattled off names. He bent down and pet the puppy now lazing by his niece's feet.

"So, tell me about yourself, Everett. What do you do?" his ma asked.

Could anyone else hear how hard Ricky's heart was beating? His gaze cut to the exits of the room. Maybe he could make an excuse and leave before he was recognized. But what if Everett figured it out from a photo or something and then told his family how they knew each other? Fuck. This was bad. This was what he'd always feared—that his past would catch up to him and everyone would find out what a scumbag Ricky really was.

You're a good-for-nothing piece of shit. You'll never amount to anything. Little bitch. Not even a real man.

His biological father's words repeated through his head as Nova said something to their ma.

"It's fine." Everett's voice sunk into his skin like an anchor, pulling Ricky's attention to the face that would haunt his nightmares tonight.

Everett ran a hand through his raven-black hair that contrasted with his pale Eastern European skin. The strands were longer on top and shorter on the sides, in a fade. His grey-blue eyes glittered with mirth as his smooth lips turned up into an enigmatic smile. "I've been working as a vender in California for cannabis distributers there."

Fuck, hearing his voice was like taking a hit of a drug. The feeling swirled in his veins, poisoning him slowly from the inside out. His head spun.

"And how did you two meet?" Nash asked.

"Everett and I met at a convention some years ago and have kept in contact ever since." Nova's voice rose a little higher in pitch. She was hiding something.

"Long-distance relationship, huh?" Roman asked.

Nova rolled her eyes, grabbing a bottle of wine and filling her glass and Everett's. "Mm-hmm. Oh, Elise, I didn't realize your family would be here."

"Yeah, this is my mom, Mai, my father, Itsuki, and my brother, Ren," Elise introduced them.

"Nice to meet you." Nova smiled at them and then guzzled her wine as conversation continued around them.

"Are you feeling okay, Ricky?" Isabella asked.

Ricky flinched at his name as once again, all eyes in the room turned towards him. Hell, Alba even gave him a gummy smile. Why couldn't he turn invisible just this once? He quickly steeled his expression, standing to his full height, and made his way back to his setting, ears ringing. He reached for his drink and chugged it. He'd need some liquid courage to get through this dinner. If Everett said anything, his family would never look at him the same way.

"I'm fine. If I'd known everyone was bringing a date, I would have brought Sophia."

"Who's Sophia?" their mother asked in a hope-filled voice.

"Just one of Ricky's many 'friends.'" Nova smirked.

Everett's eyes locked with Ricky's, and for a moment, Ricky was that teenage boy again, so lost and lonely that he'd trusted another boy with his deepest, darkest secrets. And then life as he knew it had ended.

Everett's eyes widened, recognition clearly dawning. He cleared his throat. "Ric—"

Ricky stood abruptly from the table. "Hey, man, nice to meet you. Anyone else need more wine?"

"I'll take another scotch." Their dad handed Ricky his glass.

"I'll take a little more of the riesling. Don't forget to save room for dessert, everyone." Isabella motioned to the table brimming with pies, cakes, and cookies.

Ricky forced a laugh, trying to look as unaffected as possible by the ticking time bomb sitting next to his sister. "I'm trying to watch my figure. Wouldn't want to look like your husband," he teased.

Nash chuckled and shook his head. "You think you're so funny."

Ricky picked up his dishes as an excuse and darted to the kitchen, swerving out of the way of Nash's slap. When all else failed—misdirection, antagonism, and jokes were his failsafes.

He set his dishes on the counter and braced himself against the sink, his chest heaving, faster and faster. Slamming his eyes closed, he forced himself to slow down. Having a panic attack would only draw more attention to himself. Fuck, he didn't want to appear weak.

"Ricardo?" Everett's deep timbre made his knees quake.

Ricky straightened, wiping down his expression until he hoped he looked apathetic.

He turned around.

"It is you. Man, I—"

Ricky clasped his hand over Everett's forearm and dragged him towards the stairs. "We need to talk."

His hand tingled and burned as if Everett was a source of energy. *Must be a panic attack side effect.*

He passed his old room. There was no way he was taking Everett in there. It would make him too vulnerable. Instead, he reached for the doorknob to his parents' office.

Ricky opened the door, tugged Everett in, and pulled it shut before whirling back around on him.

"How the fuck are you here?" Ricky's shoulders rose and fell with heaving breaths as he spoke his thoughts aloud.

Everett blinked as if taken aback. "I—I came with Nova."

Ricky took a step forward, running his gaze from Everett's shiny dress shoes and up the black ironed slacks that perfectly hugged Everett's lean thighs. The cranberry-red dress shirt pulled taut against his chest had the top two buttons undone, showing off a few dark hairs peeking out. Ricky was just taking in the guy he used to know—he definitely wasn't checking him out.

Everett shoved his sleeves up his muscular forearms and then settled his hands on his hips. "Ricardo—"

"Don't call me that!" he snapped. "My name is Ricky."

Pain flashed in Everett's nearly grey eyes before they clouded over with what seemed like guilt. His shoulders hunched. "Sorry. I didn't mean anything by it."

"Did you know she was my sister?"

Lines appeared on Everett's forehead. "No. Last I knew, you didn't have a sister—"

"That's just it." Ricky sneered, pointing his finger at Everett as he stepped forward to get into his face. Everett's clean, soapy scent with a dash of something citrusy assaulted his nose, making his mouth water. He shook his head, anger rising to the surface, drowning out all other sensations until he only saw red. He reached out for the familiar hum of anger coursing through his veins, staving off the panic, the pain, and the dark desire until everything else was suffocated but rage.

"You don't know me. And whatever you think you do know is wrong. So we've never met before today. Got it?"

Everett's expression morphed into one of pain before his gaze dropped and he nodded. "Sure. If that's what you want."

Fuck, Ricky might have been acting like an asshole, but

this was about survival. This man had the power to ruin everything good in his life that he'd fought so hard and so long for. All of it could be taken away in the blink of an eye.

"Glad we have an understanding." Ricky turned and ran straight into a solid mass of body.

"Oof!" Roman grunted. "Sorry. We didn't know anyone was in here."

Ricky's attention vaulted between Elise's guilty and embarrassed expression and his brother, who was focused on Everett. Questions swirled in his gaze.

"No problem. Nova's date here just got lost. I was making sure he understood what we'd do to him if he hurt our baby sister." Ricky cut Everett a threatening glare. *Keep your mouth shut.*

Hurt shone in Everett's eyes and it fucking tore at Ricky's chest, raking across the scarred flesh of old wounds. They'd been so close once upon a time—and then they had almost died because of Ricky's secret. His heart thumped wildly. Ricky was unable to draw in a full breath. Anxiety set in, spinning through his veins like spiderwebs.

"Better get those drink refills." Ricky pushed past Roman and ran away from the room as his panic attack took over. A rushing sound filled his ears. He took the vape pen from his pocket. Turning it on, he slipped the cartridge into his mouth and drew in a deep breath, filling his lungs and holding the breath before letting it out. He did it three more times until the weed kicked in, calm settling into his bones. His chest fluttered, but he breathed through it. His bio father, Donald, had been right; Ricky was weak. And if anyone else found out, life as he knew it would be over, and he'd be back where he'd started—alone in a nightmare.

To continue reading Ricky and Everett's story, visit the website below to get your copy of *Wishing for Yesterday* today.

WWW.AMKUSI.COM/WISHINGFORYESTERDAY

ACKNOWLEDGMENTS

That was no joke on the dedication to this book. We started this story while a lot was going on in our personal lives. Tack that onto the fact that I (Ash) struggle with imposter syndrome like it's nobody's business and a truckload of anxiety, and somehow, through sheer determination and a lot of encouragement, this story was completed.

Thank you to our editor, Lauren. You always, ALWAYS have a kind word for us and this writing process, so thank you. You help keep us sane and on track while also pushing us to be better.

To our sensitivity editors, Renita and Curtis, you've been with us since the beginning and the book that shall not be named, LOL. Thank you so much for your belief in us and your helpful and sometimes comical feedback.

Our beta and sensitivity readers that share your thoughts and opinions, and take the time to truly dissect the story and give us valuable feedback—thank you!

As always, a huge shout-out to our loyal and enthusiastic ARC readers. We just love how much you love these stories, and look forward to our release-week Zooms that go all night.

To our readers, you are the reason we're able to do what we do and provide you with steamy, diverse, and emotional stories that rip your heart out and put it back together just a little different than before. Thank you for your support in buying our books and leaving reviews.

JOIN OUR NEWSLETTER

The best way to get updates about new releases, sneak peeks, pre-orders, giveaways, and more is by joining our newsletter.

You'll also receive a FREE short novel that's not available on any retailer to read.

Visit the website below to join now.

<u>WWW.AMKUSI.COM/NEWSLETTER</u>

THANK YOU

Thank you for reading *Risking Forever*. We hope you are emotionally satisfied with Roman and Elise's love story. If you enjoyed this novel, please consider leaving a review on your favorite retailer and sharing it with your friends and family.

If you haven't read Nash and Isabella's story yet, check out **Stepping Into Tomorrow** (Book 1 in The Emerson Family of Shattered Cove Series).

Lastly, if you haven't read all the books in **The Shattered Cove Series**, make sure you get your copy so you don't miss out any of the eight amazing romances.

Thank you again for reading *Risking Forever!*

Cheers,

Ash & Marcus

ABOUT A. M. KUSI

A. M. Kusi is the pen name of a wife-and-husband team, Ash and Marcus Kusi. We enjoy writing romance novels that are inspired by our experiences as an interracial/multicultural couple.

Our novels are about strong women and the sexy heroes they fall in love with, are emotionally satisfying, and always have a happy ending.

Discover more about us at:

WWW.AMKUSI.COM

To receive updates about new releases, preorders, give-aways, and more, visit the website below to join our newsletter today:

WWW.AMKUSI.COM/NEWSLETTER

After you join the newsletter, we will send you a FREE story to read.

To contact us, use this email address: amkusinovels@gmail.com.

Happy reading!

Ash and Marcus

tiktok.com/@amkusi.romanceauthor

instagram.com/amkusinovels

facebook.com/amkusi

pinterest.com/amkusinovels

ALSO BY A. M. KUSI

Stepping Into Tomorrow

(Book 1 in The Emerson Family of Shattered Cove)

Risking Forever

(Book 2 in The Emerson Family of Shattered Cove)

Wishing for Yesterday

(Book 3 in The Emerson Family of Shattered Cove)

Promising Today

(Book 4 in The Emerson Family of Shattered Cove)

A Fallen Star (eBook FREE on all retailers)

(Book 1 in The Shattered Cove Series)

Glass Secrets

(Book 2 in The Shattered Cove Series)

Defying Gravity

(Book 3 in The Shattered Cove Series)

The Lighthouse Inn

(Book 4 in The Shattered Cove series)

His True North

(Book 5 in The Shattered Cove series)

In The Grey

(Book 6 in The Shattered Cove series)

Brave Love

(Book 7 in The Shattered Cove series)

Hope Between Us

(Book 8 in The Shattered Cove series)

Beautiful Collision

(A Shattered Cove Novel)

One Holiday Kiss (eBook FREE on all retailers)

(A Shattered Cove Short Story)

Under My Skin (eBook FREE on all retailers)

(A Shattered Cove Short Story)

The Orchard Inn Series

(Our first complete steamy romance series.)

Spicy Word Search Puzzles: An Activity Book for Romance Readers

(This activity book is perfect for when you want something fun to do in-between books or take a break from reading.)

Romance Reading Journal: Record, Track, and Organize Your Novels

(This journal is a simple way to track, record, and review 100 of the books you've read.)

For a complete list of all our books, visit:

WWW.AMKUSI.COM/BOOKS

www.ingramcontent.com/pod-product-compliance
Lightning Source LLC
Chambersburg PA
CBHW061613210726
48287CB00001B/110